Praise for
MAX ALLAN COLLINS
· · · · · · · · · · · · · · · · ·

"*Stolen Away,* which I admire for its mastery of *mise en scene,* has the gritty feel of reality . . . [Collins] weaves the whole of this bizarre, convoluted tale in the breezy characteristic fashion we have come to expect of Nate Heller, that charming cop turned private investigator."

—Mark Harris, author of
BANG THE DRUM SLOWLY and **SPEED**

"Max Allan Collins, in his 'memoirs' of Nathan Heller novels, has accomplished an entertaining, informed, literate, artful, third-person-observed history of the fun-house of 20th Century America. . . . We owe respect and gratitude to Max Allan Collins for the concept and audacity of this major work."

—Gregory McDonald, author of **FLETCH**

"The master of true-crime fiction!"

—CHICAGO MAGAZINE

"Mr. Collins has an outwardly artless style that conceals a great deal of art."

—THE NEW YORK TIMES BOOK REVIEW

"A project unique in modern crime fiction . . . Collins' blending of fact and fancy is masterful—there's no better word for it. And his ability to maintain suspense, even when the outcome is known, is the mark of an exceptional storyteller."

—Robert Wade, **SAN DIEGO UNION**

"Probably no one except E. L. Doctorow in *Ragtime* has so successfully blended real characters and events with fictional ones. The versatile Collins is an excellent storyteller."

—Sandy Campbell, **THE TENNESSEAN**

"Collins displays a compelling talent for flowing narrative and concise, believable dialogue."

—LIBRARY JOURNAL

"There's just nobody better than Collins in this period and setting."

—Cryptus, **DETROIT NEWS**

BY MAX ALLAN COLLINS

THE MEMOIRS OF
NATHAN HELLER

True Detective
True Crime
The Million-Dollar Wound
Neon Mirage
Stolen Away

STOLEN

A Novel of

AWAY
the Lindbergh Kidnapping

MAX ALLAN COLLINS

A
BANTAM
TRADE
PAPERBACK

Bantam Books

New York · Toronto · London · Sydney · Auckland

Although the historical events in this novel are portrayed more or less accurately (as much as the passage of time, and contradictory source material will allow), fact, speculation and fiction are freely mixed here: historical personages exist side by side with composite characters and wholly fictional ones—all of whom act and speak at the author's whim.

Stolen Away
A Bantam Book / June 1991

Published simultaneously in hardcover and trade paperback

LIBRARY OF CONGRESS CATALOGING-IN-PUBLICATION DATA

Collins, Max Allan.
Stolen away / by Max Allan Collins.
p.   cm.
ISBN 0-553-07133-5 (hc).—ISBN 0-553-35233-4 (tp)
I. Title.
PS3553.04753S86   1991
813'.54—dc20   90-43566
CIP

Published simultaneously in the United States and Canada

Bantam Books are published by Bantam Books, a division of Bantam Doubleday Dell Publishing Group, Inc. Its trademark, consisting of the words "Bantam Books" and the portrayal of a rooster, is Registered in U.S. Patent and Trademark Office and in other countries, Marca Registrada. Bantam Books, 666 Fifth Avenue, New York, New York 10103.

PRINTED IN THE UNITED STATES OF AMERICA

FFG   0 9 8 7 6 5 4 3 2 1

FOR LYNN MYERS, JR.
A.K.A. SAM—
MY EAST COAST LEGMAN.

"I was so fed up with this hero stuff,
I could have shouted murder."
—CHARLES A. LINDBERGH

"Fame is a kind of death."
—ANNE MORROW LINDBERGH

"There are, indeed, societies
for prevention of cruelty to animals,
but, unfortunately, not for men."
—BRUNO RICHARD HAUPTMANN

PROLOGUE

MARCH 4, 1932

Chapter 1

The buxom blonde stepped down off the little silver metal stairs of the train with a baby bundled in her arms and a worried expression on her pretty, pockmarked face. A porter helped her by the fur-trimmed arm of her tan fur-collared coat, providing a wooden stool where the final step ought to have been, and she gave him a flickering smile of thanks before trundling away from the Twentieth Century Limited, the sleek streamliner that had whisked her here from New York.

Natural for a mother to be protective of her child—particularly right now, with the papers full of what was already touted as the "Crime of the Century": the kidnapping, night before last, of the Lindbergh kid from his sheltered nursery in a country home in the wilds of New Jersey.

Why the hell that should make a mother nervous in Chicago, Illinois, went beyond logic, but not beyond human nature, which of course has not a damn thing to do with logic. What mother wouldn't identify with the unlucky Lindys? What mother wouldn't read those horrible headlines and hear those hysterical radio commentators and not clutch her sweet infant closer to her bosom, which in this case was an enviable place to get clutched.

The catch was: I didn't figure she was the kid's mother.

As a matter of fact, I was ready to lay odds that this was Lindy, Jr., himself, and not her own precious little flesh and blood.

Only not so little: the child was big for a babe in arms—the Lindbergh child was, after all, twenty months old. And this kid was wearing Dr. Denton's—like Little Lindy when he got yanked from his crib—and was wrapped up in blankets, rather than the snowsuit and cap you'd expect for a toddler.

True, I'd spotted dark curly hair on the child, rather than the missing boy's famous blond locks. But, hell—I didn't buy the dame's hair color, either.

I was sitting on one of three chairs at an unenclosed shoeshine stand against the wall facing the tracks in the train shed of LaSalle Street Station. This particular chair was damn near home to me when I pulled duty here; the shoeshine boy, Cletus, a lad of seventy or so, didn't mind—as long as I got up and wandered off and let him make a living, when the station got busy.

Which was what I needed to do anyway, about now, prowl around and keep an eye out for single-o dips, moll whizzers and cannon mobs. Besides, it was winter, and warmer in the train station itself, rather than out here on the noisy, windy platform.

I was a plainclothes detective on the pickpocket detail, under Lt. Louis Sapperstein, and it was my job to hang around train stations and bus depots and the like, just me and the perverts, looking to get lucky.

And maybe I had gotten real lucky, this afternoon—lucky as Lindy when he made it across the Atlantic. I was already the youngest plainclothes dick on the department; maybe I could be its youngest lieutenant.

We'd been handed a circular this morning, sent around by Chief of Detectives Schoemaker to every division in town, showing a brunette, attractive, hard-faced woman named Bernice Rogers, who was an "associate" of one Joseph Bonelli, "reputed New Jersey kidnap-ring chieftain." Schoemaker considered both Bonelli and his moll likely candidates for the Lindbergh snatch. This was not so farfetched: most of the country had either Chicago's

Capone crowd or Detroit's Purple Gang pegged as the culprits.

As if to ward off that suspicion, Capone himself—locked up in Cook County Jail, after his recent tax-evasion conviction—was filling the papers full of indignation, concern and reward offers for the return of the kid. Hell, Big Al was a parent, too, wasn't he?

I wasn't specifically keeping an eye out for Bernice Rogers. But a pickpocket dick's duties include observing good-looking women, and making sure they aren't crooked, as some good-looking women are known on occasion to be; I collared many a beautiful moll whizzer in my time.

Anyway, as I sat peering over my racing form at her as she approached, my gaze fixed upon that harshly pretty mug of hers, I unobtrusively slipped out Schoemaker's circular from my topcoat pocket to compare the brunette on paper to the blonde in the flesh.

But I barely had the sheet out of my pocket when she walked briskly by, seamed silk stockings flashing. Apparently she had no luggage, other than that precious parcel in swaddling.

So there I sat, as the blonde barreled by, charging through the doors into the train station like she was a quarterback carrying the ball. That woke the kid up, finally, and it began to howl; well, it was alive, anyway.

I hopped down, leaving my racing form on the chair, and nodded to Cletus, who nodded back, as he slapped the shoe leather of some real customer; and I strolled, counterfeit casual, out into the big square airy waiting room.

And she was gone.

The stairs down to street level were directly in front of me; had she taken them? Was she already stepping into a cab at the curb? I looked beyond the stairwell, to the sprawling central newsstand, slow-scanning the half-filled waiting-room pews at left and right. No sign of her. The room was filled with filtered light, from a huge circular window so high it reached up and caught some sky above the el tracks that fronted the station; people bustled through the gauzy midday unreality, ghosts hurrying through the dust-mote-speckled streaks of sun, but none of those people was the blonde.

And then I heard the echoing howl of a kid and there she was: heading with her bundle back to the women's rest room.

I weaved through passengers coming and going, found my way to one of the wooden pews facing where she'd gone in, and settled myself down.

I glanced over at the bank of phone booths. Should I call in? No backup from the detail was available anyway; even Sapperstein, the boss, was out in the field, over at Dearborn Station. I looked up at the silver-metal futuristic clock that loomed like a benignly neglectful God over the station's sprawling waiting-room world: four-fifteen. Sapperstein would be heading back to the Detective Bureau soon.

Didn't matter. I wanted this collar for myself, and right now. If it panned out, I didn't want to share the glory. If it was a false alarm, then nobody need know. Should I go in the ladies' room and grab her while she was changing a diaper? But what if it wasn't her? Or worse, what if it was, and a bunch of innocent ladies got shot to shit with their scanties down around their ankles?

A *Trib* had been left on the pew next to me; I picked it up and pretended to read it. Even the inside pages were full of Lindbergh news. Dopes like me who thought they spotted the kid everywhere from Duluth to Timbuktu.

In less than two minutes, she exited the rest room as quickly as she'd entered.

I folded the paper, tossed it on the pew, yawned, and sauntered after her. She was headed for the stairwell.

Despite her armload, she bolted recklessly down the stairs toward street level like she was being pursued; which she was, only I hoped she didn't know it. I followed her at an easy pace, buttoning my topcoat and snugging my fedora as I went. She had taken the stairs at the right. I took the ones at the left. I wanted to ease up behind her and slip on the cuffs.

When I got to the landing where the two stairways met, she was already gone. And when I took three steps at a time down to street level, hand sliding along the curving stainless-steel banister, I found she was still way ahead of me. I pressed through people huddled around the newsstand by the doors, and stepped outside, into an afternoon as gray as the city itself, icy snow flecking my face, Chicago's famous wind earning its reputation. My breath rose before me like a wraith. The el tracks and station looming before me made the world darker and gloomier still. Where *was* she?

Stepping into a waiting taxi, down to my left.

I headed to the right and picked out another cab. I climbed in, just as the Checker Cab, bearing the babe with the babe, glided by like a memory.

"Follow that car," I said.

And the cabbie, a rumpled-faced Hunky with a shabby green cap and a wide space between his front teeth, glanced back and grinned. "Figured some day somebody'd ask that."

"That's peachy," I said. "Here's your fare in advance."

I showed him my badge, and his cheerfulness faded.

"Might be a fin in it," I allowed, "if you don't lose 'em, and they don't make you."

"They won't," he said, relieved there was maybe a buck in this after all, and wheeled his Yellow out onto Van Buren.

This Bernice Rogers was about thirty, with a record that included prostitution and petty theft. A few months back she had adopted a boy from the Cradle, an Evanston agency; she'd been fussy about the age—had to be less than two years, older than one.

Chief of Detectives Schoemaker, a.k.a. "Old Shoes," a canny old copper, figured the adopted kid was a front. In which case, it would have gone something like this. . . .

The adopted child is looked after by a woman member of the Bonelli gang (presumably Bernice Rogers) for a number of months. People seeing Rogers with the kid assume it's hers. In the meantime, the kidnap gang executes a snatch on a specific kid (presumably Charles Lindbergh, Jr.); the woman then substitutes the snatched kid for the adopted one—while the latter is abandoned or otherwise disposed of.

And when Bernice Rogers is seen with the kidnapped child, suspicion is nil because that child is mistaken for the one she's been seen with previously. You seen one baby, you seen 'em all.

But if that had been the plan, why was Bernice Rogers turning back up in Chicago? Schoemaker figured she'd been out east of late, living rather conspicuously as the mother of a small infant. Were things too hot out there? Was somebody in the gang crumbling under the pressure? Was a double cross in the works?

I smiled and sat back in the cab and relished the thought of answering some of those questions by busting Bernice Rogers. Savoring the idea of being the cop who single-handedly cracked the Lindbergh case, half a continent away. Not bad for a kid, which is what I was: twenty-six years old and enjoying a relatively easy life in undoubtedly hard times.

As for making the collar itself, I was eager, not apprehensive. I knew molls like Bernice could be dangerous, but on the pickpocket detail, you get physical with crooks every day. Hardly a week went by, I didn't take a gun off some punk.

And I had a gun of my own under my arm, besides—a nine-millimeter Browning—and was not afraid to use it.

Not that I was trigger-happy. In fact I carried this specific weapon, rather than the usual revolver most cops carry, partly because I preferred automatics, and partly because this was the gun my father shot himself with.

My father, whose bookstore on the West Side had run to radical literature, was an old union guy who hated the idea that I became a cop. He specifically hated it when he found out, or figured out, that some money I'd given him, to renew the lease on his store, was a payoff I got for testifying in the Jake Lingle murder trial.

The cops and Capone had a patsy lined up to take the fall for that killing, and I was the witness that swung it. It was no big deal: the patsy was a willing participant, getting well paid for his prison stay. And my cooperation got me a promotion to plainclothes and an envelope with a grand in it. But my Papa could not understand that I was just trying to get ahead, trying to land a better job, playing by the rules of the Chicago game.

Well, really, he did understand. What he could not do was condone it. He put this very gun to his head and blew his brains out; that had been last year. And I carried the gun with me to make sure I never forgot that. I wouldn't hesitate to use it, but I wouldn't use it carelessly. It was the only conscience I had.

I was still not above taking a little honest graft—you didn't take a job this dirty and this dangerous for the piddling paycheck alone.

But I owed it to Papa not to abuse the policeman's power. That's what he hated about us: billy-club-swinging, trigger-happy bastards is what we were, to that old communist.

Maybe Papa would be up there watching this afternoon, when I did something worthwhile, did the kind of thing a cop is supposed to do. Righted a wrong like Nick Carter or Sherlock Holmes in the books I read as a kid. Restored a missing child to his distraught parents. Papa would like that, up in heaven. Only Papa didn't believe in heaven and neither did I.

"Not so close," I cautioned the cabbie. "Keep two or three cars behind."

He nodded and backed off. We were on Lake Shore Drive, following the Checker Cab up the Gold Coast—aristocratic brownstone mansions hobnobbing with modern high-rise apartments, fronting an unimpressed, choppy white-and-gray Lake Michigan. One of these days I had to look into finding a flat in this neighborhood—hell, they started at a mere three-hundred-fifty a month.

The Checker pulled off at Irving Park and so did we, moving into an area that had once been an exclusive section of town itself, before the money moved north. Which was a boon for criminals—a whole gang, particularly one on the lam, could move into one of these sprawling six-room numbers, and live a life of ease, with the nightlife of Uptown nearby. If I had a crook's money, I might move in here myself.

Now the Checker swung right on Sheridan Road, where the cab soon pulled up in front of a big brick terra–cotta-trimmed six-flat apartment house—one of many such that stood shoulder-to-shoulder on this street—and let the blonde with the baby out.

My cab rolled on by, and when I looked back and saw the blonde disappear into the six-flat, I said, "Right here."

The cabbie pulled over and craned around and showed me his gap-toothed grin again. "How'd I do?"

"Swell," I said, and I took out a sawbuck, tore it in two and handed him half.

His eyes got wide; he wasn't sure whether he should be pissed off or pleased. "What's this?"

I was already getting out. "You get the other half by hanging around. Pull around the corner, there, and wait—but first find a phone and call Lt. Sapperstein at the Detective Bureau. Tell him I trailed Bernice Rogers to 4072 Sheridan, and want some backup."

"Okay. Who's the message from?"

"Heller."

"Okay, Officer Heller."

"Repeat all the names."

"Uh—Lt. Sapperstein at the Detective Bureau. Bernice Rogers. Heller."

"And the address?"

"4072 Sheridan."

Now I gave him a smile. "Good man."

The snow had stopped, but there was enough wind to blow it around some, a fine white mist that felt good on my face. My heart was starting to race and I breathed slow as I walked, calming myself. Across from the six-flat in question was one of the elaborate neighborhood movie palaces Chicago was so rich in. *Arrowsmith* was playing, with Ronald Colman. I hadn't caught that one yet.

Same was true of the blonde, of course; hadn't caught her yet, either. Inside the claustrophobic vestibule were half a dozen mailboxes and as many buzzers. All but one of the buzzers had a name underneath; neither "Bernice" nor "Rogers" was one of them. I pressed them all, except the nameless one—4-B—and waited for somebody to buzz the inner door open.

Somebody did.

The central stairway stopped at each floor for a small landing and a couple of apartment doors, then jogged on up to the next landing. The janitor had a basement apartment, and I could've checked with him, but he might warn his tenant a cop was on the way. Instead, I went up to the first landing, knocked on the door of Apartment 1-A, and waited.

A cutie about twenty with Clara Bow curls peeked around the door at my upheld badge. She frowned.

"You're new," she said. Betty Boop with a bad attitude and a cigarette.

"Pardon?"

"I paid already this month. I'm not made of money."

"Miss, I'm just here for some information. I don't want your money."

"Oh," she said, warming. She opened the door wider. Her slender little shape was wrapped up in a blue-and-pink floral kimono. She looked as easy as ticktacktoe, but her timing was lousy.

"How can I help you, cowboy?"

"Do you know if any new tenants moved into this building recently?"

"Why, no."

"Well, then—any apartments empty right now, that you know of?"

"No. I don't think so." She blew a smoke ring. "Didn't you check with the janitor?"

I gave her my best suave smile. "Maybe I'd rather talk to you."

Ronald Colman had nothing to worry about, but she bought it just the same, a sultry smirk making the cigarette in her lips erect.

"I've been here over a year, cowboy, and nobody's moved in or out in all that time."

I thought about that. Then I took out the circular and folded it so that all she could see was Bernice Rogers's picture.

"Know her?"

"Sure," she said. "That's Bernice Smith. She lives upstairs in 4-B."

The one buzzer without a name.

"She got a kid?"

"Yes."

"Baby?"

She thought I was calling her "baby" for a second. Then she figured it out and said, "Uh, yes—year-and-a-half old or so."

"What color is the baby's hair?"

"Blond, I think."

"And Bernice?"

"Well, like that picture—brunette."

Interesting.

"If you're looking for her," she said, exhaling blue smoke, "I don't think she's around."

"Yeah?"

"She's on vacation. Over a month already. Her brother's staying in her place while she's gone."

"Thank you, miss," I said, tucking the circular away.

"My name's Marie."

"Thanks, Marie."

"Got a name, cowboy?"

"Nate," I said.

Her cupid lips formed a kiss of a smile. "Careful, Nate."

She liked me. On the other hand, I had a feeling all that was required out of me was a pulse. And five dollars.

I nodded and went on up; halfway up the stairs, I heard her close the door. I unbuttoned my topcoat as I climbed. Then I unbuttoned my suit coat and got the automatic out from its shoulder holster. I'd had both my suits tailored on Maxwell Street to hide the Browning. I slipped my right hand with the gun in it in my topcoat pocket.

And now I was on the fourth landing, looking at 4-B.

I stared at the door, at the brass number and letter. I had no backup. I was trembling a little, my body mixing a fear and adrenaline cocktail. Should I wait? Should I kick the door in, or knock?

I knocked.

The door cracked open. The harsh, pockmarked pretty face glared at me suspiciously.

"What do you want?"

I showed her the badge, and said—nothing. She pushed the door shut before I could.

Inside, she was yelling, "Coppers!"

Gun-in-hand still in my topcoat pocket, I lifted my foot and kicked that fucking door. It sprung open first try.

I rushed in to see two boys in shoulder holsters, white shirts, suspenders, loosened bow ties and unshaven faces standing up hastily from a round table where a gin rummy game had been in progress. Both were smoking cigarettes and a blue haze hung in the room like bad weather. One boy was razor thin with a razor-thin mustache and slicked-back Valentino hair. He wore a revolver in a shoulder holster. The other was big and fat and sloppy and a half-eaten sandwich and several bottles of beer were before him at the table, and so was a revolver, which he went for, and I shot him twice. Once in the chest, once in the head. Shot right through my damn coat. Damn!

The woman began to scream. She was standing in a doorway to what appeared to be the kitchen. The child was not in sight.

The razor-thin guy overturned the table and began to fire at me from behind it. I ducked back out in the hall, to put a wall between us, while his slugs flew through the open door and chewed the wood of the door across the way.

"Give it up!" I said, my back to the wall. The smell of gunpowder scorched the air. "Place is surrounded. You want out alive, it's with your hands the hell up!"

The gunfire subsided.

"Slide your rod out in the hall," I said, my gun out from my coat pocket now. "Don't throw it, *slide* it!"

After a moment or two of hesitation, the guy pitched it. It clunked against the baseboard of the floor at my left, harder than I liked but it didn't go off; the barrel was still trailing smoke.

"Playing it smart, finally," I said, stepping back inside, where I saw that he was indeed playing it smart—his version.

He held the small, black-haired, angelic-faced baby around its waist with one hard forearm; the child was asleep, or doped. The blonde was against a wall over at my left; her eyes were round and wet, her hard face distorted with fear, a knuckled hand up against one cheek. She wore a simple blue frock that hugged her curves. Behind her on the wall, crooked, hung a peaceful Maxfield Parrish print.

The razor-thin man had small eyes, but they looked large, the white showing all round. He looked crazed and quite capable of squeezing the trigger of the small automatic pressed to the unconscious child's head.

"Let me pass," he said. His voice was as thin as his mustache.

"No," I said. "Put the kid down."

"You kidding? He's my ticket."

To hell.

"What's your name?"

"What do you care, copper?"

"What's your name?"

The blonde said, breathlessly, "Eddie."

I didn't know whether she was answering my question, or talking to him. And I didn't care.

"Put the kid down, Eddie, and I won't mention you took a hostage. I'll even lay the resisting arrest off on your dead pal, here."

"Don't make me laugh," he said, and laughed. He moved forward a step, holding his tiny hostage tight, keeping the nose of the gun against the kid's temple.

I shot Eddie between the eyes.

Not as impressive a shot as it sounds, close as he was to me; what was more impressive was the dive I made toward him as he dropped the kid. I caught the sleeping baby like a touchdown pass.

I sat on the floor, cradling the slumbering kid in my arms, the smoking gun still in one hand, the corpse of the thin guy at my feet, the other corpse between me and the blonde, who was stuck to the wall like a fly. I had just killed two men, and it would hit me later, but right now I felt good.

"You . . . you shot Eddie," the blonde said. She was shaking her head, disagreeing with reality.

"No kidding," I said. Rocking the child as I eased back onto my feet.

"How could you risk it? He had his finger on the trigger . . ."

"A shot in the head kills all reflex action, lady."

"Am I . . . under arrest?"

"You're under arrest."

"What . . . what charge?"

"Kidnapping."

She sighed. Nodded.

"This *is* the Lindbergh baby, isn't it?"

She cocked her head, like she hadn't understood me. Her Master's Voice.

"Well?" I said. "Isn't it?"

"Mister," she said, "that's Hymie Goldberg's kid."

"Hymie Goldberg?"

"The bootlegger. In Peoria. He's loaded. We were gonna get five grand for the little bastard."

My boss burst in the open door, then. Lou Sapperstein, a sturdy, balding cop of about forty seasoned years. He took off his hat, eyes wide behind wire-framed glasses; snow dusted his topcoat like dandruff. He had a .38 in one hand.

"What the hell are you up to, Nate?"

"I just cracked the Hymie Goldberg kidnapping," I said.

And I handed him the baby.

I

The Lone Eagle

MARCH 5 – APRIL 18, 1932

Chapter 2

"There's somebody I want you to meet," Eliot Ness said.

I sat slumped in a hard wooden chair in Eliot's spartan, orderly office in the Transportation Building on Dearborn.

"And who would that be?" I asked.

"Al Capone," Ness said, with the smile of a mischievous kid.

Eliot was leaning back in his swivel chair, sitting with his back to his rolltop desk. He was a fairly big guy, about my height—six feet—with broad shoulders on an otherwise lithe frame; his upper torso had gotten powerful from a stint dipping radiators at the Pullman plant as a youth.

The biggest surprise about Eliot Ness—for those who'd read newspaper and magazine accounts of his exploits as a gang-busting prohibition agent—was his youth, his boyishness. Eliot was twenty-eight years old, with a ruddy, well-scrubbed appearance and a sprinkling of freckles across his Norwegian nose. That he was an ambitious young exec moving up the ladder of life was evident only in his impeccable three-piece steel-gray suit and black-and-white-and-gray speckled tie.

"Actually," Ness said, reconsidering a bit, or pretending to, "I'd prefer you didn't meet him. I just want you along to listen."

"Listen to what?"

"Snorkey says he can get the Lindbergh kid back."

I sighed, shook my head. "It's just a scam, Eliot. Besides, none of it has anything to do with me."

He put his hands behind his neck, elbows flaring out. "Nate—you're the resident kidnapping expert around this town right now."

I gave him a Bronx cheer. "Why, 'cause I stumbled onto getting some bootlegger's kid back for him? We couldn't even make the charges stick against that Rogers dame!"

He shrugged with his eyebrows. "How were you to know Hymie Goldberg would claim the woman was acting as his intermediary?"

"Yeah, right—his intermediary. That's why her brother Eddie shot it out with a cop."

Eliot shrugged again, shoulders this time. "Why do you think these snatch-racket gangs prey on their own kind, so often? Their victims are primarily borderline characters like themselves—bootleggers and gamblers and the like. Who know their fellow underworld denizens would never seek help from the cops at the outset, and won't rat them out at the finish line."

Eliot was the only guy I knew who might actually use the word "denizens" in a sentence, let alone one that also included the phrase "rat them out."

"But these days," he continued, "most major gamblers and bootleggers and panderers don't go anywhere without bodyguards. So the snatch-racket boys are looking to greener pastures, monetarily speaking."

"Like the Lindberghs."

Eliot nodded. "We're already seeing a pattern of industrialists and bankers and businessmen being hit. Remember the Parker case in California? That little girl was dead and dismembered before the ransom was even collected." He sighed, shook his head. "With prohibition winding down, kidnapping could be the next big racket."

"Well, it's easy money. What are you gonna do?"

It was a rhetorical question, but Eliot answered it literally.

"I've sent a petition to the federal government. Recommending capital punishment for the transportation of a kidnapped person from one state to another."

"You'd like kidnapping to be a federal crime?"

He nodded sharply, smiled the same way. "No offense, Nate, but too many local cops are either incompetent or on the take."

"I'd tip my hat to you," I said, "if my hands weren't so full of apples I took off pushcarts."

"That's not fair, Nate."

"Hey, I've seen J. Edgar's boys operate. Third-rate accountants and lawyers who graduated bottom of the class."

"I'm not talking about Hoover—I'm talking about my own unit . . . and the IRS squad, of course. Speaking of which . . . Elmer Irey and Frank Wilson are going up from Washington, D.C., tomorrow, to Hopewell, New Jersey. To meet with Lindbergh."

"Why? Kidnapping isn't a Treasury matter by any stretch of the imagination."

"Well . . . I don't think Lindbergh has any more confidence in J. Edgar's boys than you do. That's why he called his pal Ogden Mills . . ."

"Who?"

He lifted an eyebrow. "The Secretary of the Treasury? Of the United States? Of America?"

"Oh. That Ogden Mills."

"Lindy wanted Mills to send him the agents who 'got Capone.' "

"Meaning you, Irey and Wilson."

"Yes. But I'm tied up with the mop-up operation here, and besides, Irey and Wilson would rather work without me, I'm sure."

Elmer Irey, Frank Wilson and Eliot Ness were indeed the feds who nailed Capone. Eliot's Justice Department unit squeezed Capone's financial nuts in the vise, and confiscated the records Irey, Wilson and their pencil-pushers turned into evidence. But there was friction between Justice man Ness and the IRS boys; both factions seemed to resent the credit taken by the other.

"I've recommended a Chicago Police Department liaison be assigned to the case," he said. "On site, at Hopewell."

"Why?"

"Early indications are this is a gangland operation, very possibly of midwestern origin. I'll fully brief you, before you leave. . . ."

"Brief me!" I sat up. "What are you . . . ?"

"I've cleared it with your boss."

"Sapperstein?"

"Chief of Detectives Schoemaker. And the Chief himself. And the Mayor. You're going to Hopewell."

I opened my eyes wide as I could and looked at nothing. "Well . . . that's swell. Nice break from hanging around train stations and bus depots. And it could be good for my career, but . . . why me?"

Eliot shrugged. "You made some nice headlines, cracking the Goldberg case."

I snorted. "Right. I killed two guys up there, and what did it amount to? The dame went free, the case was closed, and who knows how many accomplices are still running around loose?"

Eliot waggled a lecturing finger at me; he was barely a year older than me, but he had a bad habit of treating me like a kid. "Nate, you put a baby back in his mother's arms. Doesn't matter that it's the arms of some bootlegger's common-law wife. A kidnap ring getting busted up, and a kid going safely home, is exactly what the public wants to hear about right now."

"Well. It was dumb luck."

"Much good police work is. The case got enough national play that when I spoke to Lindbergh on the phone yesterday, and mentioned you, he was enthusiastic that you come."

My skepticism was fading; excitement was creeping up the back of my neck. "But, Eliot . . . why did you suggest me?"

His face was blank and hard. "I don't trust Irey and Wilson— that is, I don't trust their judgment. They're good investigators, when they're examining ledger books . . . but they don't have your street savvy."

"Well, thanks, but . . ."

"You should know a couple of things. My suggestion that you be sent was met with enthusiasm in various quarters."

"Why in hell?"

He shrugged. "Different people want you out there for different reasons."

"Such as?"

Eliot counted them off on his fingers. "Lindbergh wants you because he thinks you're some kind of police hero, who saved a child. I want you there for my own purposes. But . . . there are people within the department who want you out there because they feel, should it come to that, you can be 'handled.' "

Now I was getting irritated; I shifted in the hard chair. "Just because, once upon a time, I . . ."

He held up a hand. "Nate. I know. The Lingle case put you in plainclothes. But it also taught you a few lessons you did not expect to learn. I assume you're still carrying the Browning your father . . ."

After a beat, I nodded.

He smiled faintly. "I don't have many police contacts, Nate. You're one of a very small handful of men on the Chicago force that I feel I can trust. I'm *right* about you. The men in the shadows, who think you'll sell out for a sawbuck, are wrong."

"Eliot, you are so right," I said. "It would take at least a C-note."

He didn't know whether to smile or not. So he just shook his head.

"Come on," he said, rising. "I want you to hear what Snorkey has to say. . . ."

Cook County Jail was on the West Side, not far from my old stomping grounds, in the midst of a Bohunk neighborhood where Mayor Cermak had relocated both the jail and the county court-house. His Honor did this, he said, to "help real estate" in the area. That was about as straightforward a statement as any Chicago mayor ever made.

The assistant warden, John Dohmann, took us up five flights in a steel-and-wire elevator that opened onto a heavy iron-barred door, labeled Section D. Dohmann turned a heavy double key in the lock and revealed bars that enclosed the vast sunny concrete room that was Alphonse Capone's cell, a cell that might have housed fifteen in this badly overcrowded facility. Outside the bars, facing the cell, sat a United States deputy marshal with a billy club on his belt.

I'd lived in Snorkey's kingdom for many years, and it was unnerving approaching the monarch's throne room, even if it was concrete and steel.

Capone—who wore not a jailhouse-gray uniform, but a blue flannel suit with a tan shirt and no tie—sat playing cards at a table with the only other prisoner in the cell, a small, pretty young man of perhaps nineteen. On the way up in the elevator Dohmann had mentioned that Capone had been allowed the cellmate to help him pass the time with handball and cards. Looking at this kid gave the term "handball" new implications.

"Ness!" Capone said, and stood, walking over with a huge paw thrust forward.

Eliot wore the faintest ironic smile as he accepted the hand through the bars and shook it.

"No hard feelings between us, right?" Capone said, with a disarming grin.

"None," said Eliot.

Capone wasn't as big a man as you might think, and—like his adversary Eliot Ness—was much younger than the public thought of him, perhaps thirty-two or -three. His shoulders were broader than any fullback's, however, and his head was as round as a pumpkin. His full face was deceptive, as he was not fat.

What really struck me, though, were his eyes: greenish-gray, small and round and glittering, half-lidded under black bushy eyebrows that met between them like conspirators.

When he placed his big, veined hands on the bars, it was like a strong man about to bend them for a stunt; but his feet were small, almost dainty, in expensive black leather shoes with pointed toes.

"Is there any news?" Capone asked, earnestly.

"About what, Al?" Ness asked.

"The kid!"

"Nothing."

Capone sighed sadly.

I stood by the seated guard, back a ways. Eliot never made a move to introduce me and Capone hardly gave me a glance; I was just another nameless Ness man, accompanying the chief. Why insinuate myself into this conversation between old friends?

Besides, I kind of savored the irony of having Capone mistake me for an Untouchable.

"Understand this, Mr. Ness—I don't want no favors. If I ain't able to do anything for that baby, lock me the hell back up."

"Looks like you are locked up, Al."

"Look. I know how you feel about me. But if they'll only let me out of here, I'll give 'em any bond they need. *If* they're interested in getting that child back!"

Capone was trying to sound sincere in his concern for Charles Lindbergh, Jr., but what he conveyed was menace.

"You accompany me yourself, Ness. I will spend every hour of the night and day with you at my side, till we get that kid back."

"Just the two of us, huh, Al?"

"And I'll send my younger brother to stay here in the jail and take my place till I get back. You don't think I'd double-cross my own brother and leave him in here, do you? Even if I *could* make my getaway from the great Eliot Ness! Hah?"

Ness said nothing; his faint ironic smile said it all.

Capone's gray complexion began to redden. The lids had lifted off the gray-green eyes. In the jail cell, the pretty gunsel was playing solitaire, paying no attention to any of us. Sunlight through the barred windows made patterns on the floor.

Capone tried to channel his anger into earnestness. "Let me have a chance to show what I can do! I would know in twenty-four hours whether the child's in the possession of any regular mob, or some single-o working his own racket. Anybody that knows anything in the underworld knows he can trust me. There is no mob going that wouldn't count on me to make the payoff, if the family of the kid wants to go the ransom."

"And what do you want from the federal government, Al, if you manage to pull off this trick?"

He cut the air with his hands, like an umpire calling somebody safe. "It's no trick. If I can't do any good for you, then I come back here, and let justice go on with her racket."

"You didn't answer my question, Al. What do you want if you succeed?"

His hands clenched into softball-size fists. A vein in his forehead began to throb; his scar turned white on his fleshy cheek.

His expression was like a very pissed-off bull studying a red cape.

"What the hell do you think, Ness? I want out! I want this goddamn sentence set aside! What in fucking hell do you *think* I want? I was railroaded! I was double-crossed!"

Capone had worked out a plea bargain that would allow him to pay off his tax debt and get a two-and-a-half-year sentence, which with good behavior he could have done in a walk. But Judge Wilkerson had not been party to the deal, and sentenced him to eleven years in federal prison.

"You guys want me to cough up three hundred thirty-six thousand dollars! I don't know where you get these figures, 'less it's the moon! You never proved I ever received *one dollar*—maybe you proved I spent *some* money, but that don't prove I have any income. What I spent might've been given me by admiring friends. And you guys can't tax gifts!"

"Al, like the man says—tell it to the judge."

"The judge! That son of a bitch won't even let me out on bail! Other people convicted on income-tax raps get set free, till the highest court passes on their appeal. Not Capone! They leave me to rot in stir. They make *me* pay expenses of the trial—they don't do that with no others. Fifty fuckin' grand I paid!"

Ness stood with folded arms; his smile was gone. So, I gathered, was his patience.

Snorkey sensed that, too.

"I just don't understand you guys," he said, trying to sound reasonable, but damn near whining. "When I came to Chicago eleven years ago, I had only forty bucks in my pocket. I went in a business that didn't do nobody no harm. They talk about the unemployed. Well, I give work to the unemployed. At least three hundred young men are getting from one hundred fifty dollars to two hundred dollars a week from me, in the harmless beer racket. Put me out of business, and all my men lose their jobs—they have families and little houses. What do you think they'll do? Go on the streets and beg? No. These are men I've taken out of the holdup and bank-robbery business and worse and gave *real* jobs. Where will they go, and what will they do, when you put me out of business?"

"We'll find cells for them, too, Al."

His eyes blazed. "You're so high and fuckin' mighty! Sharing in a bootlegger's profits by way of income tax, you're aiding and abetting after the goddamn fact. It's like the G was demanding its percentage of a bank burglar's haul!"

"Old news, Snorkey. Very old news."

The rage was bubbling in Capone, but he restrained himself.

"Look, look," he said, patting the air in a peacemaking gesture, "never mind that. Never mind any of that. I just want to help, here. There isn't a man in America that wouldn't like to return that child to its folks, whatever it cost him personally."

He pointed to a picture of his young son gilt-framed by his bed in the cell.

"I can imagine," he said, gray-green eyes glistening in the sorrowful mask of his round face, "how Colonel Lindbergh feels. I weep for him and his lovely wife."

"Do you really?"

Capone's lip began to curl in a sneer, but he pulled back, and meekly said, "They'll listen to you, Ness. You tell them."

"Then tell me something you didn't tell anybody else. You've run this vaudeville routine past Captain Stege, and Callahan of the Secret Service . . . but if you want to convince *me,* tell me something new. Tell me why you really think you can get that little boy back."

Silence hung in the air like a noose.

Capone licked his fat lips and, mustering all the earnestness he could, said, "There's a possibility a guy who did some work for me, once, did this awful thing. He is not in my employ now. Understood? But if he did it, and I can find him—and I *can* find him—we can get that kid back."

"Who is it, Al? Give me a name."

"Why in hell should I tell you?"

"Because you care about that kid. Because you cry yourself to sleep at night, over this 'awful thing.' "

Capone lifted his head, looked down at Ness suspiciously. "If I tell you, you'd take it as a show of . . . sincerity?"

"I might."

The glittering eyes narrowed to slits. "Conroy," he said.

"Bob Conroy?"

The big head nodded once.

Eliot thought about that. Then he said, almost to himself, "Conroy lammed it out of Chicago years ago."

Conroy was said to be one of the shooters in the St. Valentine's Day Massacre. Word was he'd gone east, when the heat got turned up after that noisy little affair.

Capone clutched the bars. "I can find Conroy. Get me out of here. Let me help."

Ness smiled blandly at Capone. "I wouldn't let you out of that cell to save a hundred kids."

The round face filled with blood.

"So long, Snorkey."

"Only my friends call me that," the gangster said ominously. "You son of a bitch . . . who the hell do you think you are . . ."

"I'm Eliot Ness," Eliot Ness said pleasantly. "And you—you're right where you belong."

From behind us, as the deputy was unlocking the big steel door for us, Capone called out, "I'm going to the papers with this! Lindbergh's going to hear about my offer!"

Going down in the elevator, Eliot said, "Lindy already has heard, obviously. That's why Irey and Wilson are going up there. To advise him."

"Do you take Capone seriously?"

"Well, this morning, President Hoover and his cabinet discussed his offer."

"Jesus."

"The Attorney General suggested exploring whether Capone's proposal would have to be referred to the Circuit Court of Appeals."

"For Pete's sake, Eliot. Capone's just trying any desperate measure to get out of stir . . ."

"Right. But how desperate *is* he?"

"What do you mean?"

"Desperate enough to engineer this kidnapping himself, so he can 'solve' it, and earn his freedom?"

The elevator clanked to a stop.

"What do you think, Eliot?"

"I think with Capone," he said, "any evil thing is possible."

Chapter 3

The road to the Lindbergh estate was called Featherbed Lane; but the winding, rutted dirt path was hardly rest-inducing. In fact, it woke me out of a sound sleep I'd been enjoying since shortly after leaving Grand Central Station, at ten A.M., where the Twentieth Century Limited had deposited me into the care of a stuffy, well-stuffed Britisher named Oliver Whately.

Tall, rawboned yet fleshy looking, dark hair thinning and slicked back, Whately was Colonel Lindbergh's butler, not a chauffeur, and he seemed to resent the duty. I'd tried to make conversation, and got back a combination of stiff upper lip and cold shoulder, so I buttoned my lip, settled my shoulder against the door of the tan Franklin sedan, and began sawing logs.

I needed the sleep. I'd been up much of the night, moving from the smoking car to the dining car, drinking too heavily for my own good. The Chicago P.D. had predictably seen fit to buy me the cheapest accommodations possible—frankly, I counted myself lucky I wasn't in the baggage compartment—and I had slept only fitfully, in my Pullman upper.

But it wasn't the accommodations, really. It was me. I was nervous. I'd never been east before, and certainly never met anybody as famous as Colonel Charles A. Lindbergh—except maybe Al Capone, and we hadn't really met, had we? Besides which, Lindbergh was one of the few men on this disreputable planet that a Chicago cynic like yours truly couldn't help but admire.

Only a few years older than me, Lindbergh was, of course, one of the most famous and admired men in the world. Five short years ago he'd piloted his tiny, single-engine plane—the *Spirit of St. Louis*—across the Atlantic Ocean; this 3,610-mile jaunt—the first solo nonstop flight from New York to Paris—had made the gangling, unassuming youth (twenty-five years old at the time) an immediate international celebrity. Without meaning to, he won hundreds of awards and medals, including the Distinguished Flying Cross and the Congressional Medal of Honor. Judging by the papers and newsreels, he was a quiet, even shy midwestern boy who'd managed to give Americans a hero in an age of immorality and corruption.

I didn't believe in heroes, yet Lindbergh was a hero to me, too. I felt strangely embarrassed about this, and oddly uncomfortable about going to meet him; and uneasy about encountering him at such a sad, desperate point in his life.

"Sour land," Whately said, suddenly, in a bass voice that rattled the windows of the sedan, and shook me from half-awake to fully.

"What?"

Whately repeated himself, and it turned out to be one word, not two: "Sourland—sometimes known as the 'lost land.' " The butler, dressed in funereal black, sitting back regally from the wheel, nodded his big head toward his window at the tangled thickness of woods through which the long black-mud private lane had been cut.

"They say," he said, "that Hessian soldiers fell prey to the maze of these woods, and, giving up, settled here." He looked at me ominously. "They mixed their blood with Indians'."

He said this as if he were referring to a laboratory experiment, not some good-natured redskin nookie.

"Later, runaway slaves hid in the Sourland Mountains," he added, darkly.

I made a clicking sound in my cheek. "I bet some more blood got mixed, too."

Whately nodded, his expression grave. "The descendants of the Hessians and their interbred rabble live in tar-paper shacks and caves in these hills and mountains."

"Funny neighborhood to stick a fancy house in," I offered.

"The Colonel chose the location from the air," Whately said, shifting gears on the sedan and the conversation. He sounded matter-of-fact, dismissing from consideration the wild bands of mixed-blood hillbillies he'd summoned up. He lifted one large hand off the wheel and painted in the air. "Colonel and Mrs. Lindbergh chose the crest of a knoll, higher than fog could disrupt."

"He has a landing strip, then?"

Whately nodded. "Even this dirt road itself discourages travelers and sightseers. The Colonel likes his privacy. A remote estate is a necessity for the Lindberghs."

"And a liability."

He turned his head slowly and looked at me down his long nose, which was quite a trip. "Pardon?"

"Stuck out in the middle of nowhere, they're an easy target. For cutthroat mix-breed hillbillies, say—or a kidnapper."

Whately snorted and turned his attention back to driving.

Autos and ambulances swarmed the roadsides by the white-washed stone wall with wrought-iron gate. Some of the cars bore the cachet of a particular news service, while the ambulances were an old press trick: they'd been converted to mobile photo labs— retaining their sirens, of course, to insure getting where they needed to as fast as possible. Standing out in the bitter March air, mixing cigar and cigarette smoke with that of their breaths, were hundreds of reporters and photographers and newsreel cameramen, gathered like flies at a dead animal. An abandoned ramshackle farmhouse, well outside the gate but in sight of it, was providing shelter for dozens of newshounds.

Several New Jersey troopers stood on guard at the gate. They looked as crisp as the Sourland weather, light-blue uniform jackets, leather-visored caps, yellow-striped riding britches.

"They look like chorus boys in *The Student Prince,*" I said.

Whately arched an eyebrow in what seemed to be agreement, as they passed us through.

More than a house, less than a mansion, the Lindbergh home, standing alone on a patch of ground cleared out of the dense woods, was a rambling, twin-gabled, two-and-a-half-story structure facing the forests and hills of the Sourland. Featherbed Lane came up behind the whitewashed fieldstone house, like an intruder; then the lane opened into a wide court and swung around its west side, into a smaller paved court cluttered with automobiles. A picket fence half-heartedly surrounded the sprawling, French-manor-style house and gave it a homey, civilized touch, as did the windmill that spun sporadically in the bitter breeze; but none of it quite compensated for the loneliness of the wilderness-surrounded site.

The place looked unfinished. Other than the landing strip beyond what would be the front yard, no landscaping had yet been done—the grounds were a barren patchwork of snow and weeds and dirt. And the windows, most of them, lacked curtains.

"When did the Lindberghs move in?" I asked Whately, as he pulled the sedan to a stop.

"They've only been spending weekends here," he said.

"For how long?" I didn't figure this place had been habitable longer than a month or two.

Whately confirmed that: "Since January."

"Where do they spend the rest of their time?"

Whately frowned, as one might when a child asks repetitious and pointless questions. "Next Day Hill."

"What's that?"

"The Morrow estate. At Englewood. If you'll just come with me."

He got out of the sedan and so did I. The day was gray and cold and I was glad I'd brought my gloves. Whately got my traveling bag out of the back of the sedan and handed it to me. I thought maybe he'd carry it, but then he wasn't my butler, was he?

I followed the tall, fleshy Britisher to the three-car garage, one door of which he swung open to reveal a herd of cops at work in a makeshift command post. It was Sunday afternoon, but nobody

had the day off. A trooper at a switchboard was frantically trans-
ferring calls to a nearby picnic table of plainclothesmen working a
bank of phones, while at two other picnic tables, uniformed troopers
sorted mail into various piles, with the discards going into already
well-filled barrels. A pair of teletype machines chattered, spewing
paper onto a cement floor crawling with snakes of telephone wires
and electrical cords; the smell of cigarette and cigar smoke mingled
with that of steaming hot coffee.

"This, sir," Whately said to me, infusing "sir" with more
disrespect than one syllable ought to be able to convey, "is where
police personnel congregate."

"Hey," I said, "I'm supposed to talk to . . ."

But Whately was outside, pulling the garage door down, shutting me and my question—the final unspoken word of which was
"Lindbergh"—inside.

A potbellied, bullet-headed flatfoot pushing fifty, with hard
tiny eyes behind wire-frame glasses and a face as rumpled as his
brown suit, approached me with something less than enthusiasm.

"Who are you?" he said, in a half-yelled monotone. "What do
you want?"

I thought I better show him my badge. I set down my bag
and did.

"Heller," I said. "Chicago P.D."

He just looked at me. Didn't glance at the badge. Then, slowly,
the gash where his mouth should be turned up at one corner—in
amusement, or disgust, or both.

"I'm here to see the Colonel," I said.

"We have several colonels here, sonny boy."

I let that pass. Put away my shield. "Are you in charge?"

"Colonel Schwarzkopf is in charge."

"Okay. Let me talk to that colonel, then."

"He's in conference with Colonel Lindbergh and Colonel
Breckinridge."

"Well, tell them Colonel Heller's here."

He tapped my chest with a hard forefinger. "You're not funny,
sonny boy. And you're not wanted here, either. You're not needed.
Why don't you go back to Chicago with the rest of the lowlife
crooks?"

"Why don't you kiss my rosy-red ass?" I suggested cheerfully.

The tiny eyes got wide. He started to reach out for me.

"Don't put your hands on me, old man," I said. I lifted one eyebrow and one forefinger, in a gesture of friendly advice.

The eyes of thirty-some state cops were on me as I stood toe to toe with one of their own, probably a fucking inspector or something, getting ready to go a few rounds.

A bad moment that could get worse.

I raised both my hands, palms out, backed up and smiled. "Sorry," I said. "I had a long trip, and I'm a little washed-out. Everybody's under the gun here, everybody's nerves are a little ragged. Let's not have any trouble, or the press boys will make us all look like chumps."

The inspector (if that's what he was) thought that over, and then said, "Just leave the command post," stiffly, loud enough to save some face. "You're not wanted here."

I nodded and picked up my bag and found my way out.

Shaking my head at the inspector's stupidity, and my own, I knocked at the door adjacent to the big garage. I was about to knock a second time when the door cracked open. A pale, pretty female face peeked out; her bobbed hair was as dark as her big brown eyes, which bore a sultriness at odds with her otherwise apple-cheeked wholesome good looks.

"Yes, sir?" she asked, in a lilting Scots burr tinged with apprehension.

I took off my hat and smiled politely. "I'm a police officer, here from Chicago. Colonel Lindbergh requested . . ."

"Mr. Heller?"

"Yes," I said, brightly, enjoying being recognized as a human being, and a specific one at that. "Nathan Heller. I have identification."

She smiled wearily but winningly. "Please come in, Mr. Heller. You're expected."

Taking my topcoat, hat and gloves, she said, "I'm Betty Gow. I work for the Lindberghs."

"You were the boy's nurse."

She nodded and turned her back, before I could ask anything

else, and I followed her through what was apparently a sitting room for servants—though no one was using the magazines, radio, card table or comfy furnishings, at the moment—into a connecting hall. Following her shapely rear end as it twitched under the simple blue-and-white print dress was the most fun I'd had today.

In a kitchen larger than my one-room apartment back home, a horse-faced woman of perhaps fifty, wearing cook's whites, was doing dishes. At a large round oak table, seated with her hands folded as if praying, sat a petite, delicately attractive young woman—perhaps twenty-five—with beautiful haunted blue eyes and a prim, slight, sad smile. A small cup of broth and a smaller cup of tea were before her, apparently untouched.

I swallowed and stopped in my tracks. I recognized her at once as Colonel Lindbergh's wife, Anne.

"Excuse me," I said.

"Mrs. Lindbergh," Betty said, gesturing formally toward me. "This is Mr. Nathan Heller, of the Chicago Police."

Betty Gow exited, while Anne Morrow Lindbergh stood, before I could ask her not to, and extended her hand. I took it—her flesh was cool, her smile was warm.

"Thank you for coming, Mr. Heller. I know my husband is looking forward to meeting you."

She wore a plain navy-blue frock with a white collar; her dark hair was tied back with a blue plaid scarf.

"I'm looking forward to meeting him," I said. "And it's an honor meeting you, ma'am. I wish it were under happier circumstances."

Her smile tightened, bravely but not convincingly. "With the help of men like yourself, perhaps happier circumstances will find us."

"I hope so, ma'am."

There was a sudden sparkle in the sad eyes. "You needn't call me 'ma'am,' Mr. Heller, though I do appreciate the sentiment. Are you tired from your trip? You must be. I'm afraid you missed lunch . . . we'll have to get you something."

That touched me; I felt my eyes go moist, and I fought it, but goddamn it, it touched me. Everything this woman had been through, these past four or five days, and she could still express concern—real concern—about whether my trip had been pleasant, and if I'd missed my lunch.

And then she was up and rummaging in the Frigidaire herself, while the woman who was apparently her cook continued wordlessly to wash dishes. "I hope a sandwich will be all right," Mrs. Lindbergh was saying.

"Please, uh . . . you don't have to . . ."

She looked over her shoulder at me. "Heller's a Jewish name, isn't it?"

"Well, yes. But my mother was Catholic." Why did I sound defensive, for Christ's sake?

"So you eat ham, then?"

So much for the discussion of my religious persuasion.

"Sure," I said.

Soon I was sitting at the table next to a beaming Anne Lindbergh, who was enjoying watching me eat the ham-and-cheddar-cheese sandwich she'd prepared for me. It wasn't a bad sandwich at all, though personally I prefer mustard to mayonnaise.

"I'm sorry you have to wait to see Charles," she said, sipping her tea (she'd provided me with some, as well). "But things are hectic here, as you might imagine."

I nodded.

"Actually, it's settled down, some, the last two days. Those first several days were sheer bedlam. Hundreds of men stamping in and out, sitting everywhere . . . on the stairs, on the sink. People sleeping all over the floors on newspapers and blankets."

"The press is a problem, I suppose."

"Terrible," she admitted. "But the troopers are keeping them at bay . . . and, in their defense, the news people *were* cooperative when I gave them Charlie's diet."

Charlie, of course, was her missing son.

"They published it widely," she said, with satisfaction. "He has a cold, you know." She swallowed, smiled her prim, charming smile and said, "I admire men like you, Mr. Heller."

I almost did a spit take. "Me?"

"Such self-sacrifice and energy. Such selfless devotion."

She sure had me pegged.

"You brought a mother and a child back together," she said, "didn't you?"

"Well . . . yes, but . . ."

"You needn't be modest. You can't know the hope that gives us, Charles and me."

She reached out for my hand and squeezed it.

Had I given her false hope? Maybe. But maybe false hope was better than no hope at all.

"Excuse me," a voice behind us said.

The voice came from the doorway that led to the sitting room and outside; it was a male voice, so my first thought was of Lindbergh himself. Instead it belonged to a square-jawed six-footer about forty with dark blond hair combed straight back and a small, perfectly trimmed and waxed mustache. He was in an officer's variation of that blue uniform with yellow-striped riding britches; all he lacked was a riding crop, a monocle and a saber.

"Colonel Schwarzkopf," Anne Lindbergh said, without rising, "this is Nathan Heller of the Chicago Police Department."

Schwarzkopf nodded, resisting any urge to click his heels. "Mr. Heller—if I might have a moment?"

"Colonel," Anne said, troubled by Schwarzkopf's expression and tone, "I thought you were in conference with Charles."

"Yes, Mrs. Lindbergh. But he and Colonel Breckinridge needed a word in private. Mr. Heller?"

I thanked Anne Lindbergh for her kindness in general and her ham sandwich in particular. Schwarzkopf bowed to her, in his silly formal way, and the two of us stepped into the room beyond the kitchen, a spacious well-stocked pantry.

He looked at me with disdain. "I don't know how you people do things in Chicago. Judging by what I read in the newspapers, you don't do them very damn well. Murder in the street. Corruption in city hall. It took the *federals* to nail Capone."

"This is fascinating, learning all about Chicago like this. But don't I have an appointment with Colonel Lindbergh?"

He trained his hazel eyes on me like the twin barrels of a twelve-gauge. "In New Jersey, I run a force of one hundred and twenty hand-picked, highly motivated and rigidly disciplined men." He thumped my chest with a forefinger—just like that inspector out in the garage had. "You're in my territory, mister. You'll play by my rules, or you won't play at all."

I grabbed his finger in my fist; I didn't squeeze it, I didn't get tough with him. I just grabbed the finger and stopped him thumping me with it. His eyes and nostrils flared.

"Don't put your hands on me," I advised. "You might get your uniform mussed."

I let go of the finger and he drew it back, indignantly.

Through clenched teeth, he said, "You were rude and disrespectful to one of my key people, Inspector Welch, who is no doubt twice the policeman you'll ever be. You used coarse language of a kind that may be acceptable in Chicago circles, but will not, mister, be countenanced here—not in my world."

I smiled pleasantly. "Colonel Schwarzkopf, let me make a couple things clear. First of all, I'm just here to advise and to help, because several people wanted me to come, including Colonel Lindbergh. Second, that asshole Welch called me 'sonny boy,' twice. Do I look like a refugee from a Jolson picture to you?"

That froze him. He did not know what to say to me. He did not know what to make of me. He just knew, whatever I was, he didn't like it or me.

"I don't think you're going to fare very well with Colonel Lindbergh," he said, finally, with an icy smile.

"Well," I said, shrugging. "Why don't you lead the way, and let's see."

Nodding curtly, he did.

Chapter 4

ootsteps echoing on hardwood floors, I trailed Schwarzkopf through the foyer past the second-floor stairs and into a large living room where a dog was barking. I didn't see the animal at first, but its bark was ringing through the open-beamed room, the shrill sound of a small, hysterical pooch. To my left, French doors led to a flat terrace where a New Jersey trooper, in his perfect light-blue uniform jacket with orange piping, stood guard. Despite the bustle of activity elsewhere, this room was empty, but for the barking dog, who revealed himself as a little white-and-brown wirehaired fox terrier on a pillow on a green sofa. Fireplaces stood like brick bookends at either side of the big room, both unlit, emphasizing the coldness of the house.

That coldness wasn't restricted to temperature: the newness of everything—the vague smell of recent paint and plaster, the absence of personal touches (the hearth was bare)—made the house seem charmless, impersonal.

"Wahgoosh!" Schwarzkopf barked back at the dog as we passed.

I didn't understand what he was saying—some Teutonic curse, for all I knew.

"Mutt's been barking constantly since we got here," Schwarzkopf said, with quiet irritation.

"Did he bark the night of the kidnapping?"

Schwarzkopf shook his head no.

"You know what Sherlock Holmes said about the curious incident of the dog in the night."

Schwarzkopf frowned, nodded toward the terrier. "That damn dog didn't do a damn thing in the night."

"That was the curious incident," I said. "Inside job, you think?"

Schwarzkopf shrugged, but his manner said yes.

Just beyond the living room, sitting on a straight-back chair leaned against the wall, was a small, dark man in a three-piece black-and-gray pinstripe with a flourish of white silk handkerchief flaring out of his breast pocket.

"Hiya, Colonel," he said to Schwarzkopf, not getting up. His accent was New York through and through.

Schwarzkopf, who seemed to like this guy even less than he liked me, grunted.

"Ain't ya going to introduce us?" the cocky little guy asked, nodding toward me. He had a tabloid newspaper, *Daily Variety,* in his lap.

"No," Schwarzkopf said, as we moved past.

I jerked a thumb back at the guy and began to speak, but Schwarzkopf cut me off with: "Don't ask."

He came to a halt before a big white door and knocked twice.

"Come in," a voice within said. The voice of a young man—a weary man, but most of all young.

Slender, blond, handsome, haggard, Lindbergh stood behind a big dark oak desk cluttered with notes and phone messages, and smoothed his brown suit coat—he wore no tie, his collar loose—smiling warmly at me, extending a hand, as if we were old friends. Seated across from him was a lanky, distinguished-looking gray-haired, gray-mustached fellow in his fifties in a three-piece gray tailored suit. He also rose as I entered, and just kept rising—he was as tall as Lindbergh, easily, and Lindbergh was probably six-three or -four.

"You'd be Mr. Heller," Lindbergh said. He nodded to the man in gray and said, "And this is my attorney, Colonel Henry Breckinridge, from New York."

I reached across the desk and received the firm handshake I'd expected from Lindbergh; Breckinridge was equally firm with his handshake and smiled in a tight, businesslike but friendly manner. His face was soft, his features bland, but his steel-gray eyes under bold strokes of black eyebrow hinted at something stronger.

Lindbergh gestured to the chair next to Breckinridge and I sat, while Schwarzkopf stood behind us, at parade rest. Lindbergh's smile disappeared. "Sorry about the mix-up—Whately was supposed to bring you directly to me."

"That's no problem, Colonel."

He sat. "Well, I apologize if there's been any inconvenience. God knows we appreciate your presence. I know Anne is thrilled to have you on the case, after your success with those kidnappers in Chicago."

"Well . . . thank you. I'm just here to help, if I can."

Attorney Breckinridge spoke up in a mellow, modulated voice that must have served him well in court. "We're expecting agents Irey and Wilson of the Treasury Department later this afternoon."

"They're good men," I said.

"I received a call from Eliot Ness," Lindbergh said, "recommending you highly, Mr. Heller. We hope you can stay on until—well, until Charlie is home and in his mother's arms."

"I'd like that."

"I've spoken to Mayor Cermak," Lindbergh said, "and he indicated your department would assign you here until I choose to release you."

"Well . . . that's fine." It seemed odd, though, to be assigned directly to the victim's father; why not to Schwarzkopf? Not that I wanted to be.

The phone rang, once, and Lindbergh answered it. His responses were monosyllabic and I couldn't get the gist of the conversation; I let my eyes roam around the dark–wood-paneled study.

Several walls were dominated by books, not the usual unread, leather-bound variety you see in a wealthy home, but novels and books of poetry mingled with scientific and aviation tomes. A fireplace on the wall opposite the door cast a warm glow; above the mantel was a framed aeronautical map. Light filtered in through a sheet that had been hung over the uncurtained window, across the room behind me. This was, I knew from what I'd read, the window directly under the one that the kidnapper had gone in. The nursery would be directly above us.

There were no mementos of fame in this room: no replicas of his silver monoplane, no medals, no trophies. Other than the well-read books and several framed family photos on his desk—among them the curly-haired cherubic Charles, Jr.—this study seemed as unlived-in as the rest of the house.

Lindbergh hung up the phone and smiled tightly. "They've picked up Red Johnson in Hartford."

"Good!" Schwarzkopf said.

It struck me as strange that this call had come directly to Lindbergh; shouldn't the chief investigator, who was obviously Schwarzkopf, receive it? Why did the head of the New Jersey Police seem to be reporting to the victim's father? Curiouser and curiouser.

"Red Johnson," I said, remembering the newspaper accounts. "Isn't he the sailor-boy boyfriend of your nurse, Betty Gow?"

Lindbergh nodded; his face revealed nothing. He had a pale, hollow-eyed look, but no emotion, nothing, could be read there.

"The Hartford boys will hold him and grill him," Schwarzkopf said. "But we'll get our shot."

"Did you meet Betty?" Lindbergh asked me.

"Coming in," I said. "Pretty girl. Seems nice enough."

Lindbergh nodded. "She's innocent in this," he said, with a troubling finality.

Schwarzkopf spoke up. "That doesn't mean *Red Johnson* is innocent. That sailor may have pried some information loose from the girl. She could be the 'inside man' without intending to be, Colonel—let's not lose sight of that."

Reluctantly, Lindbergh nodded.

Breckinridge turned toward me in his chair. "How much do you know about the case?"

"Just what I've read in the *Trib*, back home," I admitted. "But I'm not so convinced it had to be an inside job."

Lindbergh looked up. "Oh?"

I shrugged. "There was a lot in the papers about the construction of your house, here. I remember seeing pictures and articles about the layout of the rooms, who was to occupy them and so on, months ago. And hell, I live in Chicago. Surrounded by these woods, you could be observed easily—a guy posted in a tree, with binoculars, could determine in a matter of weeks what your pattern was."

Schwarzkopf, shaking his head, no, said, "But their pattern was broken. The Lindberghs had been staying here weekends only. But because little Charles caught a cold, Mrs. Lindbergh didn't want to travel, and they stayed over an extra night."

"That does sound like an insider tipped an outsider off," I allowed. "And the dog not barking indicates a friendly, familiar face might be involved."

Schwarzkopf grunted in vindication.

But I continued, directing my comments to Lindbergh: "I'm just saying I wouldn't rule out a gang specializing in the so-called snatch racket keeping your house staked out, 'round the clock, seven days a week. In which case, the change of pattern becomes irrelevant."

Lindbergh was looking at me carefully. "I'd like to show you around myself, Mr. Heller," he said, standing. "I'd like to get your firsthand reaction to some things."

"That's why I'm here, Colonel," I said, with a serious smile.

Schwarzkopf was frowning again.

Lindbergh caught it.

"Colonel," Lindbergh said, addressing the cop, not the lawyer, "I expect you to cooperate fully with Detective Heller. He's come a long way to lend us a hand."

"Yes sir," Schwarzkopf said dutifully, respectfully. The guy really did seem to view Lindbergh as his boss.

Lindbergh was out from behind the desk now; he gestured to the phone. "Henry, if you wouldn't mind . . ."

"Gladly," Breckinridge said, and rose and took Lindbergh's position behind the desk. One of the most expensive lawyers in

New York—in the country—was playing secretary for Lindy.

Schwarzkopf stepped between Lindbergh and me. "Would you like me to accompany you, Colonel?"

"That won't be necessary, Colonel," Lindbergh said.

If one more colonel showed up, I'd jump off the roof.

"I'd best join my men at the command post," Schwarzkopf said, summoning his dignity. His footsteps were echoing across the living room as Lindbergh and I exited the study. That dark, dapper little guy was still sitting in the hall, reading his show-business paper. He stood up, upon seeing Lindbergh.

"Any news, Colonel?" the guy said, eager as a puppy (speaking of which, the dog had begun barking again, at Schwarzkopf).

"Red Johnson is in custody over in Hartford," Lindbergh said.

"Hey, that's swell."

"Nathan Heller, this is Morris Rosner."

"Hiya," he said, grinning, extending his hand.

I took it, shook it.

"*Mickey* Rosner?" I said.

"You heard of me?" he asked. It was damn near "hoid."

"The speakeasy king, right?"

He straightened his tie, hitched his shoulders. "Well, I'm in the sports and entertainment field, yes."

"There's nothing sporting *or* entertaining about kidnapping," I said.

Lindbergh cleared his throat.

"Mr. Rosner has made his services available as a go-between," he said. "Since it's the general consensus that the underworld is involved in this . . ."

"My lawyer is a partner in the Colonel's office," Rosner interrupted.

"In your office?" I said to Lindbergh.

"Not that Colonel," Rosner said.

"Oh," I said. "You mean Breckinridge."

"No," Lindbergh said. "Colonel Donovan."

Which way to the roof?

"Colonel Donovan?" I asked Lindbergh.

He said, "William Donovan."

"Wild Bill Donovan," Rosner said to me, and from the tone of his voice he might as well have added "ya joik."

While I was trying to sort out how you get from Wild Bill Donovan, currently running for governor of New York, to Broadway bootlegger Mickey Rosner, Lindbergh was explaining to the latter just who and what I was. "Mr. Heller is our liaison man with the Chicago Police."

"The Chicago Police," Rosner said, smirking. Then with a straight face, he said to me, "You think Capone's offer is for real?"

"I don't know," I said. "What do you 't'ink,' Mickey?"

He raised his eyebrows. "Capone's a king in his world. What he says generally goes. I think the Colonel should maybe pay attention to the Big Fellow."

Mickey didn't say which colonel he meant.

Lindbergh nodded to Rosner in dismissal, and the little bootlegger sat down and returned to his reading.

The dog had stopped barking, but resumed when he saw me. Lindbergh said, "Shush, Wahgoosh," and the dog fell silent.

"What the hell is 'Wahgoosh'?"

"The pooch's name," Lindbergh said, with that shy midwestern kid's smile of his.

"Oh," I said, as if that made sense.

"You'd have to ask Whately what it means. Wahgoosh was Oliver's dog, but we've kind of adopted the little yapper."

"Colonel," I said, "do you really think it's advisable to have the likes of Rosner around? That no-account bum could be in on the crime . . ."

"I know," Lindbergh said, gently. "That's one of the reasons why he *is* around."

"Oh," I said again.

Lindbergh opened the front door and led me outside into the chilly overcast afternoon; he nodded to the trooper on guard at the door. Lindy hadn't bothered with a topcoat, so I didn't say anything, but it was goddamn cold. I followed him across the yard to the left, back toward where his study would be.

We walked directly outside his study window, below the second-floor corner window, which faced southeast. He pointed up.

"That's where they went in," he said, meaning the kidnappers.

"Why isn't this area roped off?" I said, looking at the ground, hands tucked under my arms. "Was it *ever* roped off?"

"No," he said.

"Weren't there footprints?"

There certainly were now. Hundreds of them. Grass might never grow on this ground.

Lindbergh nodded, breath smoking. "There was one substantial footprint—belonging, apparently, to a man. It seemed to be that of a moccasin, or a shoe with a sock or perhaps burlap around it. There were also the footprints of a woman."

"A woman? So there were two of them, at least."

"So it would seem."

"Have the moulage impressions been sent to Washington?"

Lindbergh narrowed his eyes. "Moulage impressions?"

"Plaster casts of the footprints. Say what you want about J. Edgar's boys, they have a hell of a lab. For one thing, they'll tell you exactly what that man was wearing—moccasin or potato sack or glass slipper."

"Colonel Schwarzkopf's man took photographs, not plaster impressions. Was that a mistake?"

I sighed. "Is Bismarck a herring?"

Lindbergh shook his head wearily. "I know mistakes were made that night. It's possible plaster casts weren't taken simply because the reporters trampled this area before there could be."

That was still the fault of the coppers in charge; but I'd said enough on this subject.

"Look, Colonel. We can't do anything about mistakes past. The early hours of this case were understandably a jumble."

Of course, a good cop knows that the early hours of any major felony investigation are the most important, the time during which you allow *no* mistakes. But I didn't say that, either.

"What we can do," I said, "is not make any more of 'em. Mistakes, I mean."

He nodded gravely. "Would you like to see the nursery?"

"First, I'd like to see the ladder they used. Is it still around?"

It ought to be in an evidence locker in Trenton, but with the command post here, I figured it was worth asking.

He nodded. "It's in the garage. I'll have the troopers bring it around. Excuse me for a few moments."

Lindbergh loped off; he had a gangling gait, and seemed slightly stoop-shouldered—as if he were embarrassed to be so tall, or so famous. Or perhaps it was the weight of it all—from the kidnapping itself, to living out this tragedy in the center ring of a goddamn circus.

Despite the trampled ground, blurring any footprints, there still remained in the moist clay, near the side of the house, the indentations of the feet of the ladder. The indentations were below, but to the right of, the window of the study, which explained why Lindbergh might not have seen anybody going up a ladder outside his curtainless window.

Two troopers returned, Lindbergh leading them; each of the men carried a section of the thing, and "thing" more than "ladder" was the correct word: a ramshackle, makeshift affair that seemed composed of weathered, uneven lumber scraps. The rungs were spaced too widely apart for even a tall man to make easy use of it.

Lindbergh set his section down. "Put it together, would you, men?"

"Good God," I said. "That thing's a mess, isn't it?"

"It's ingenious in its way," Lindbergh said. "Slopped together as it is, inexpert as the carpentry may be, it was designed so that each section fits inside another. One man *could* carry it, though it's been kept separate like this, for examination."

The troopers were inserting wooden dowels to connect the sections. The top rung of the bottom section had broken, apparently under a man's weight.

I walked over and pointed to the broken pieces. "One of the kidnappers did that?"

Lindbergh nodded. "And I may have heard the bastard climbing either up or down. I heard what sounded like the slats of an orange crate breaking, around nine o'clock."

"Were you in the study?"

"No—the living room, with Anne."

"Did you check on the sounds?"

"No," he said glumly. "I just said, 'What was that?' to Anne, and she said, 'What was what?' and we both went back to our reading. Shortly after that, she went upstairs to bed and I went into the study."

So Lindbergh was probably in the study at least part of the time the kidnapping was taking place.

"Place that in the holes, would you?" he said to the troopers.

It took both of them to maneuver the clumsy, towering affair. They placed it carefully in the indentations in the ground and placed it against the side of the house, where it rose several feet above, and to the right of, the nursery window, stretching damn near to the roof.

"Well, it's way off," I said, craning my neck back. "Obviously."

"I just wanted you to see that," he said. "We figure the kidnappers miscalculated on the ladder."

"They sure as hell didn't have a carpenter on their team," I said. "So, what? They must have just used the lower two sections."

Lindbergh nodded. "The ladder was found over there . . ." He pointed about sixty feet to the southeast. ". . . with the two bottom sections connected." Then he directed the troopers to haul the ladder down, remove the dowel and lift off the top section, and put the now two-sectioned ladder back up.

"It's still way off," I said.

Now the ladder was about three feet below the nursery window. And, again, to the right. You could see the places on the whitewashed fieldstone where the ladder had scraped; no doubt about it: only two sections of the ladder were used, and this was where it rested.

"Well, what do you make of it, then?" Lindbergh asked.

"I'm revising my opinion about this not necessarily being an inside job."

Lindbergh's frown was barely discernible, but it was there. "Why, Mr. Heller?"

"Somebody had to have handed your baby out to an accomplice on the ladder. That's about the only way it figures . . . unless two people went up the ladder, one at a time. I doubt that thing would support two people at once."

"Perhaps that's why it broke," he suggested.

"The weight of the child, added to whoever carried him down, probably did that."

"Good God. If Charlie fell . . ."

I lifted a hand. "From that height, there'd have been the impression of whoever fell—and it would've probably been both of 'em, the child and the kidnapper. If . . . excuse me, Colonel . . . if the kidnapper dropped the child, but managed to retain his own footing on the ladder, there still would've been an impression in that wet ground."

Which even the New Jersey cops couldn't have missed.

"Perhaps a woman went up first," Lindbergh said, studying it, hand on his chin. "We know a woman was standing around out here . . ."

"A woman's touch might explain the baby staying quiet. I mean, the baby didn't wake up crying, or someone would've heard him, I would imagine."

"Yes. My wife was in the next room, separated only by a bath." Impulsively, grabbing my arm, he said, "Come. Look the nursery over."

We went up the uncarpeted stairs, and the upstairs was as clean, fresh-smelling and impersonal as below.

Lindbergh hesitated outside the nursery, and I went on in. He stayed in the doorway and watched me look around.

It was the warmest-looking room I'd seen here—and the most lived-in. Evergreen trees, a country church, and a man with a dog were gaily pictured on the light green wallpaper; between the two east windows was a fireplace with a mosaic of a fisherman, windmill, elephant and little boy with a hoop; on the mantel was an ornamental clock around which were gathered a porcelain rooster and two smaller porcelain birds. A kiddie car was parked near the hearth. Against the opposite wall was the child's four-poster–style maple crib; nearby was a pink-and-green screen, on which farmyard animals frolicked.

"That's where he takes his meals," Lindbergh said from the doorway, pointing to a small maple table in the middle of the room. Specks of dried-up food still remained.

I was looking in the crib. "Are these the baby's bedclothes?"

"Yes. Exactly as they were."

The bedclothes—blankets and sheets—were barely disturbed; they were attached to the mattress with a pair of large safety pins. The impression of the child's head was still on the damn pillow.

"Whoever did this lifted the child out without waking him," I said. "Or, if the boy did wake, he wasn't startled. A familiar face, a familiar touch?"

"Or," Lindbergh said, almost defensively, "a woman's touch. Perhaps a woman did go up the ladder first . . ."

"I'd buy that sooner," I said, "if the rungs weren't so damn far apart."

I walked to the southeast window, the kidnappers' window. It was recessed, window-seat deep. Below it, against the wall, was a low cedar chest. It was almost as wide as the wide sill itself. On top of the cedar chest was a black suitcase, on which sat a jointed wooden bunny on a small string.

"That chest houses Charlie's personal fortune," Lindbergh said, trying to sound cheerful. "His toys. He has plenty, I'm afraid."

I smiled over my shoulder at him. "And when you get him back, you're going to buy him another damn chestful, aren't you?"

Lindbergh smiled shyly. "I intend to spoil Charlie rotten."

"Good for you," I said, kneeling at the chest. "Was this chest moved away from the window at all? Disturbed in any way?"

"No."

"How about this suitcase?"

"No."

"Any mud, any scuffs, on the suitcase, or the chest?"

"No."

"Where was this toy rabbit found?"

"Right where you see it. Right where it usually was."

I stood. "The house wall is a foot and a half thick, and the sill is almost as wide. Anybody entering through that window would have to span a distance of almost three feet to actually get in this room proper. Doing that without leaving mud, without moving the chest, without disturbing the suitcase or toy rabbit, and all without making a ruckus . . . very improbable."

Lindbergh said nothing.

I opened the window and felt the rush of cold air. The shutters wouldn't close. "Are the shutters on any of the other windows warped like this?"

"No."

"They must have known about this," I said, trying unsuccessfully to shut them.

"A chisel was found outside," Lindbergh said, "which would indicate they thought they'd have to break in. They just got lucky, picking this window."

"I don't know what the chisel was for, other than maybe to make somebody assume what you just assumed. This window wasn't pried open, was it?"

"No. It wasn't locked; we lock the shutters, not the windows."

"But this window is directly over the curtainless window of your study below. The French windows, on the other side of the room, over a side door, are what a kidnapper who didn't know about the broken shutter would've come in through."

Lindbergh said, "Now you're sounding like Schwarzkopf."

"Good," I said. "Then he's thinking like a cop."

"You've changed your mind, then. You're convinced this *is* an 'inside job.' "

"I haven't changed my mind," I said. "I'm just keeping it open. The worst and most common investigator's error is making a snap decision at the outset about who or what is behind a crime. I noticed some scientific studies and books and such in your library."

"Yes."

"Well, in science, if you start out with an answer you want to prove is correct, it screws your research up, right? Because you're only looking for the evidence that proves your point."

Lindbergh nodded.

I walked over to him. He was still in the doorway.

"You don't want to think your servants could be involved, do you? You trust them. You like them."

"I hired them," he said.

And that, of course, was the nub: if a servant did it, then Lindy was, ultimately, responsible. And he couldn't face that.

"In science," I said, "the truth hurts sometimes. You wouldn't want a doctor to lie to you, would you?"

"Of course not."

"Then I'm not going to lie to you. Nor am I going to kiss your ass. I'm going to level with you, and tell you how I see things."

His face was deadpan for what seemed an eternity. I realized I may have crossed the line with Lindy; tomorrow at this time, I could be getting off the train back in Chicago. Which was fine, if the alternative was standing around making like a horse's-ass yes-man.

But I wouldn't have to, because Lindbergh smiled, big and natural.

"Do you mind if I call you 'Nate'?"

"I'd be honored," I said, and meant it. "Could I call you something besides 'Colonel'? Every time I say that, eight heads turn."

He laughed softly. He extended his hand to me, as if we hadn't shaken before.

"My friends call me 'Slim.' I'd appreciate it if you called me that, at least when we're more or less in private."

We shook hands, loose and casual.

"Okay . . . Slim," I said, trying it out. "I'll be more formal when it seems appropriate."

"Thanks."

We headed back downstairs, where Schwarzkopf—looking like a hotel doorman in that fancy-ass uniform—met us halfway.

"Colonel," he said, "agents Irey and Wilson are waiting to see you."

Chapter 5

Elmer Irey and Frank J. Wilson were waiting in Lindbergh's study; neither had taken a seat. They stood there, hats in hand, both in black, like twin undertakers.

Irey and Wilson were the Ike and Mike of law enforcement—wearing different-color ties wasn't enough to lessen the sameness. Both men were in their mid-forties and wore round-lensed black eyeglasses like Robert Woolsey of the Wheeler and Woolsey comedy team—a couple of solemn, long-faced, round-jawed, dark-haired, jug-eared feds as interchangeable as a pair of socks.

Irey was the boss; he was the chief of the Internal Revenue intelligence unit. Wilson—and if you had to tell them apart, Wilson was the balding one—was his chief agent.

The two men traded blank looks upon seeing me, but in that blankness was a wealth of contempt.

Then Irey stepped forward and, with a smile as thin as the ace of spades, offered his hand to Lindbergh, saying, "It's a great honor meeting you, Colonel. I wish the circumstances were otherwise. This is Agent Wilson."

Wilson stepped forward, shook hands with Lindbergh, saying, "An honor meeting you, Colonel."

Lindbergh offered them chairs and, as Breckinridge had just hung up the phone, took his position behind the desk. Breckinridge stood behind him and to his left, like a field marshal. Schwarzkopf and I took chairs on the sidelines.

Irey, his hat in his lap, glanced around the study at what must have seemed to him an unnecessary crowd of observers.

"I think, Colonel," Irey said, in a voice bread-and-butter bland, "that we might want some privacy."

Lindbergh looked to his left, then to Irey and said, guilelessly, "The door is closed."

Edgily, Wilson said, "Colonel, we really should speak to you confidentially."

Lindbergh's smile was a tad tired. "Gentlemen, I can't tell you how pleased and grateful I am that you've taken your Sunday to make this trip. Your help, your counsel, is something we greatly need. But the men in this room are my closest advisers."

Who, me?

"Colonel Breckinridge is my attorney and one of my closest friends," he continued. "Colonel Schwarzkopf is in charge of the State Police in whose jurisdiction this matter lies."

Irey said, "With all due respect to Colonel Schwarzkopf, there have already been numerous flaws in the methods employed by the state police."

"Really?" Schwarzkopf said, icily. "Such as?"

"Your fingerprint man," Irey said, turning to look at the frowning Schwarzkopf, "failed to find any latents on the ransom letter or envelope, the ladder, the chisel, the window, the crib or the boy's toys."

"It took an outsider," Wilson chimed in, "to come in and take another try . . . and he found all sorts of prints, even after ruling out those of your own troopers. Thirty to forty on the ladder alone."

"Have you sent those prints to Washington?" Irey asked Schwarzkopf. "The Bureau of Investigation has a vast collection of fingerprints of known criminals."

"This is not a federal matter," Schwarzkopf said stiffly.

Egos. A kid's life at stake and they were playing at fucking egos.

"Colonel Schwarzkopf stays, gentlemen," Lindbergh said. "You may disagree with his methods, but he is, after all, the man in charge."

Said the man in charge.

Wilson said, flatly, "And what about Heller?"

These T-men knew me, a little, from Chicago. I'd been on the fringes of their Capone investigation. They'd been on the fringes of the Jake Lingle trial.

Lindbergh nodded at me and smiled tightly. "Detective Heller is our liaison man with the Chicago Police Department."

Irey maintained his poker face; Wilson's cement face cracked a smile.

"Colonel Lindbergh," Wilson said, "the first thing we of the Intelligence Unit learned when we took on the Capone case was not to count on the Chicago police."

Irey gave Wilson a quick, cutting glance. "What Agent Wilson means," Irey said, "is that this case is not a Chicago matter."

That wasn't even close to what Wilson meant.

"It isn't a federal matter, either," Schwarzkopf insisted.

"Colonel Lindbergh," I said, rising, "I'll be glad to step outside."

"No, Nate," Lindbergh said, motioning me to sit back down. "Stay, please."

And Irey and Wilson did double takes, hearing Lindbergh call me by my first name; and at that moment Eddie Cantor had nothing on Schwarzkopf, in the banjo-eyes department.

"Detective Heller," Lindbergh said, "comes highly recommended by a colleague of yours."

"Eliot Ness," Wilson said, with just a hint of a smirk.

"Yes," Lindbergh said.

"I believe Heller is a police contact of Eliot's," Irey said. "Isn't that correct, Heller?"

"That's correct, Elmer."

Irey, who hadn't looked at me when he spoke to me, now turned his head my way. His eyes were blue-steel and hard in his placid face. "Heller, you don't know me well enough to use my first name."

"My apologies, Mr. Irey. You might attach a 'mister' to *my* name, while you're at it."

Lindbergh smiled faintly, briefly.

Irey nodded. "Point well taken, Mr. Heller." He turned his attention back to Lindbergh. "I don't want us to get off on the wrong foot, Colonel. While I don't wish to be critical, I would be less than frank if I didn't say I'm disturbed by the presence of questionable characters such as . . ." And I thought he'd insert my name here, but he didn't. ". . . Morris 'Mickey' Rosner."

"I can well understand that, Mr. Irey," Lindbergh said. "But I hope you can understand, gentlemen, that I'm pursuing every avenue that presents itself, where the safe return of my son is concerned."

Wilson sat forward; he turned his hat in his hand, slowly, like it was a steering wheel. "Colonel, according to newspaper accounts this morning, Rosner has engaged the services of two more underworld types . . ."

"Salvatore Spitale," Irey said, reading from a small notebook, "and Irving Bitz." He looked up from the notebook. "Proprietors of a speakeasy on Forty-First Street in New York."

Lindbergh nodded. "And I've given all three of them expense money. Gentlemen, your disapproval is noted—and I thank you for expressing that disapproval in so restrained a fashion. Rest assured you're not alone in your opinion."

Schwarzkopf cleared his throat. "Colonel Lindbergh feels that by letting the underworld know we've appointed go-betweens from their ranks, we may facilitate negotiations with the kidnappers. Personally, I share your misgivings, Mr. Irey, Mr. Wilson . . . but I will accede to the wishes of the Colonel."

There he went again, treating Lindbergh like his goddamn boss. At least Irey and Wilson knew that the coppers ought to be in charge.

"I've asked you to come up, Mr. Irey," Lindbergh was saying, "because I feel I should talk to somebody in an official capacity about this Capone offer."

Irey nodded somberly. "You'll be hearing even more about it

tomorrow. We understand Capone was interviewed this morning by Arthur Brisbane, who flew to Chicago for the privilege."

The New York *Journal*'s Brisbane was Hearst's most highly paid editor and columnist, a self-important double dome whose purple prose on the Capone offer would further inflame a Lindbergh-inflamed public.

"It'll be in Brisbane's syndicated column tomorrow morning," Wilson said, "all over the country. Everybody and his duck will be telling you to take Scarface up on his proposition."

Lindbergh leaned back in his chair and studied Irey and Wilson as if they were frost forming on his monoplane wings. "What do you gentlemen think?"

"We think it's a bluff," Wilson said confidently, sitting back. "We think you should disregard it."

Irey, measuring his words, said, "I hate to say this, Colonel . . . but Capone doesn't know who has the child. He is a desperate man trying to deal his way out of jail."

"We know he thinks," Wilson said, "or *says* he thinks, a former gang member of his did it."

"Bob Conroy," I said.

All heads turned my way.

"Is Detective Heller right?" Lindbergh asked, eyes tight. "Is this Conroy the one Capone claims took my son?"

Irey nodded, slowly; Wilson nodded, too, but two nods for every one of Irey's.

Irey said, "Our preliminary investigation puts Conroy nearly one hundred and fifty miles from here, the night of the kidnapping."

"Excuse me," I said. "Have you talked to Conroy yet?"

"No," Irey said, not looking at me. "We have agents in New York who are investigating. Two alibi witnesses place Conroy in New Haven, Connecticut."

"Well," I said, "New Haven isn't the moon. In a fast car, a hundred fifty miles is nothing, these days."

"We intend," Irey said, an edge of impatience in his voice, "to find Conroy, of course, and talk to him . . . but he didn't do it."

Lindbergh's expression darkened. Then he said, "Should you make that assumption, going in? I've been told that the biggest mistake a detective can make is to form a snap decision early on about who or what is behind a crime."

Both Irey and Wilson shifted in their seats; it was perfectly coordinated, like a couple of really good chorus girls. It made me smile.

"You're right, Colonel," Irey said to Lindbergh. "We'll keep an open mind about Conroy—we'll find him, and we'll talk to him. We don't see it as a major lead, however . . . because we don't think Capone is sincere."

"Colonel," Wilson said, "Big Al just wants out of jail."

Where you boys helped put him, and you'll be goddamned if you'll let the bastard out even if it is to help save a kid's life.

Lindbergh cast his hollow gaze my way. "What do you think, Nate?"

"About Capone? It could be a hoax. But I don't think we can rule out, at this early stage, the possibility that Capone may have engineered the kidnapping."

"That's absurd," Wilson said.

But Irey said nothing.

I said, "You said it yourself: he's a desperate man. He's also a public figure—like Colonel Lindbergh. What better target could he choose than a man who, in a bizarre way, is one of the few people in this country on his own level? Besides, can you put *anything* past a man who can turn a tender holiday like St. Valentine's Day into something forever grisly in the minds of the masses?"

"You think," Lindbergh said to me, with a gaze so flatly penetrating it was unnerving, "that Capone may truly know where my boy is? Because he wants to 'solve' a crime he committed—or that is, had committed for him?"

"It's possible," I said. "All to buy his cynical way into the public's affections—and out of a jail cell. And it's an opinion held by the federal agent instrumental in putting him away—Eliot Ness."

In other words, screw you, Agents Irey and Wilson.

"Mr. Heller may be right," Irey said, more gracious about it than I figured he'd be. "I think it's a long shot, frankly . . . but I can't in all honesty rule the possibility out."

Even Wilson seemed willing to begrudge me my opinion. "I

think we should find Bob Conroy and *make* him talk." He paused ominously, then added, "But we don't need to let Al Capone out of stir to accomplish that."

"I hope," Lindbergh said quietly, "that you will proceed with caution. It's been my position from the very beginning that there must be no police interference . . ." He raised his hand and cut the air with it. ". . . no police activity of any kind that might interfere with my paying the ransom and reclaiming my boy."

That ultimately wasn't—or anyway shouldn't have been—Lindbergh's decision, of course, but Irey and Wilson let it go. I knew when it got down to brass tacks, Irey would act like a cop. Wilson, too.

"I wonder if we might see the kidnap note," Irey said.

"Certainly," Lindbergh said. He pulled open a desk drawer. The note, which ought to have been in an evidence envelope in Trenton, was handed to Irey. I moved in and looked over his shoulder as he read.

In pencil, in an uneven, shaky, possibly disguised hand, on cheap dimestore bond paper, the letter said the following:

> Dear Sir!
> Have 50.000 $ redy 25 000 $ in
> 20 $ bills   1.5000 $ in 10 $ bills and
> 10000 $ in 5 $ bills. After 2–4 days
> we will inform you were to deliver
> the Mony.
> We warn you for making
> anyding public or for notify the Police
> the chld is in gut care.
> Indication for all letters are
> singnature
> and 3 holds.

The "singnature" was the faint impression of two blue quarter-size circles, their left edges the most distinct, creating the impression of two *c*'s, with a red nickel-size spot to the right of the second *c*; also three holes ("holds") had been punched, one through the red spot, two others at left and right.

Schwarzkopf said, "Obviously, we haven't released the content of the note to the press. Only by that signature can we know for sure that subsequent notes really are from the kidnappers."

Then why was the fucking thing stuck in Lindbergh's desk? Every servant in the house had access to it!

"I would suggest that you put this document under lock and key, immediately," Irey said. He was speaking to Schwarzkopf, not Lindbergh, although he was in the process of returning the note to the latter. "Who have you shared this with?"

"No one," Schwarzkopf said. "The New York Police have requested copies, but we've declined. So has J. Edgar Hoover. I feel this is a matter for the New Jersey State Police, and distributing this document frivolously, even to other law enforcement agencies, might have unfortunate results."

That sounded halfway reasonable, but it boiled down to Schwarzkopf not wanting to share the spotlight, didn't it?

"Of course, we have given a copy of it to Mr. Rosner," Lindbergh said.

Irey and Wilson looked at each other. I rubbed my eyes.

"What?" Irey said.

Lindbergh shrugged. "Mr. Rosner wanted to show it to certain individuals in the underworld—Owney Madden, among others—who might be able to identify the handwriting or that strange 'singnature.' "

Madden was an underworld figure who was to New York, roughly, what Capone was to Chicago.

"Let me get this straight," Wilson said tightly. "The New York Police can't have a copy, J. Edgar Hoover can't have a copy, and we can't have a copy. But Mickey Rosner can."

Irey, obviously disturbed by this news, and rightly so, said, "I'm afraid the legitimacy of any future notes is endangered. You've opened yourselves up to interlopers."

"Gentlemen," Breckinridge said, "a mutual friend of ours, Bob Thayer, a partner in Colonel William Donovan's office, accompanied Mr. Rosner to see Madden and several others of that ilk. Rosner never left Thayer's sight, nor did his copy of the note."

"I believe we'll have no difficulty," Lindbergh said, defensiveness creeping into his tone, "telling communiqués from the real kidnappers apart from those of any pretenders seeking extortion money." He reached into the still-open desk drawer. "In fact, though it's not publicly known . . . we have received a second letter."

The usually unflappable Irey sat up; Wilson was already sitting forward.

Lindbergh handed Irey another white bond sheet, written on both sides in ink. Again, I read over Irey's shoulder:

> Dear Sir. We have warned you note to make
> anyding Public also notify the Polise
> now you have to take consequences. ths
> means we will have to hold the baby untill everyding
> is quiet. We can note make any appointment
> just now. We know very well what it
> means to us. Is it rely necessary to
> make a world affair out off this, or to
> get your baby back as sun as possible.
> To settle those affair in a quick way
> will be better for both seits. Dont be
> afraid about the baby two ladys
> keeping care of it day and night.
> We also will feed him
> according to the diet.

Below this were the words "Singtuere on all letters" and an arrow pointing to a symbol similar to the one on the first note, but in this case the blue circles were distinct. The central, smaller circle was again blood-red; and three holes had again been punched.

Irey turned the letter over and on the other side it said:

> We are interested to send him back in
> gut health. Ouer ransom was made aus
> for 50000 $ but now we have to take
> another person to it and probable have
> to keep the baby for a longer time as we
> expected. So the amount will be 70,000—
> 20.000 in 50 $ bills   25.000 $ in 20 $ bills
> 15000 $ in 10 $ bills and 10.000 in 5$ bills
> don't mark any bills or take them

from one serial noumer. We will
inform you latter were to deliver the
mony. but we will note do so
until the Police is out of ths case
and the pappers are quiet.
The Kidnaping we preparet
for years. so we are preparet
for everything.

"When did you receive this?" Irey asked.

"Yesterday," Lindbergh said.

Irey passed the note to Wilson, who'd already leaned over to read it, but now read it again. "I'm no handwriting expert," Irey said, "but that does look very similar. As does the distinctive symbol."

"It's not exactly the same," I pointed out.

"But close," Irey said. "Can I see the first note again?"

Lindbergh obliged him.

"They contain many of the same misspellings," Irey said, pointing to the first note. "Good is 'g-u-t,' money is 'm-o-n-y.' "

"Signature is misspelled in both notes," I pointed out, "but in two different ways."

Wilson said, to nobody in particular, "A German, you think?"

"Possibly," Irey said. "Probably."

"Or somebody trying to sound German," I said.

Lindbergh's eyes narrowed. "Why would anyone do that?"

I shrugged. "Same reason you'd try to disguise your handwriting. To leave a false trail. The war's not that distant in the American mind—Germans make swell fall guys."

"You might be right, Mr. Heller," Irey admitted. "There's another oddity, here—particularly in the second note. Small, easy words like 'not' and 'soon' and 'hole' are misspelled; but larger, more difficult words, such as 'consequences,' 'appointment,' 'interested,' among others, are spelled correctly."

"So maybe somebody's posing," I said. "Maybe it's somebody literate playing semiliterate German immigrant."

"Or," Wilson offered, "a semiliterate German using an English/German dictionary . . . looking up only the hard words."

"Could be that," I admitted.

Lindbergh seemed to be enjoying listening to some real cops discuss the case; Schwarzkopf, not surprisingly, hadn't contributed a goddamn thing. His face twitched with frustration.

"What interests me more than the way the letter looks," Lindbergh said, "is what it says. It says my son is in good health, and that his abductors saw the diet Anne and I gave to the papers, and they're following it. That's good news."

"They're also hitting you up for another twenty grand," I said.

"That doesn't concern me," Lindbergh said.

I didn't know whether that meant that he was rolling in dough, or that he didn't measure his son in monetary terms.

"It's clear to me," Lindbergh continued, "that police participation in this case has to be minimized."

"What?" Irey said. "Colonel Lindbergh, you can't be serious . . ."

"I'm deadly serious. The biggest mistake I made was waiting two hours for the fingerprint officer to arrive, before I allowed that first note to be opened. I'd already called the police in, and the newspapers were already all over the story, before I knew that that note would warn me against the participation of either group."

"Colonel Lindbergh," I said gently, "there's no way you could've kept either the cops or the reporters out of this case."

"Gentlemen," Lindbergh said, standing, "I appreciate your counsel."

He extended his hand to Irey, who suddenly realized he was being dismissed; awkwardly Irey stood, as did Wilson.

"Colonel," Irey said, as they shook hands, "I have to return to Washington, but Agent Wilson is setting up shop with several other agents, in New York. They'll be working the case from there."

"Discreetly, I hope," Lindbergh said.

Irey didn't seem to know what to say to that.

"We'll, uh, keep Colonel Schwarzkopf informed of our progress," Wilson said. "I hope he'll pay us the same courtesy."

Lindbergh came out from around the desk and put a hand on Irey's shoulder; it was a rare gesture of warmth from this reserved man.

"I know you're disappointed by my desire to deal honestly

with the kidnappers," he said. "You want to capture them, and of course I would like to see that happen, one day, as well . . . but my priority now is to get my son back, safe and sound."

"I'm a father myself," Irey said softly.

"On the other hand," Lindbergh said, walking the men to the door, "as far as Capone is concerned . . . I wouldn't ask for the release of that monster, if it *would* save a life."

Irey nodded solemnly.

Then Wilson asked if they could have a look at the nursery, the kidnap ladder and so on; Lindbergh put Schwarzkopf in charge of that.

Which I thought was a smart move. Even Lindbergh knew that Schwarzkopf and the feds had better get used to each other.

Then I was alone with Lindbergh and Breckinridge.

"Thanks for your insights, Nate," Lindbergh said.

"My pleasure, Slim," I said, trying to get comfortable with this level of familiarity.

"What do you know about psychics?" he asked, suddenly.

"Not a hell of a lot. Most of 'em are bunco artists."

"But some aren't?"

"I don't know. Why?"

"I'd like you to help Colonel Breckinridge check a couple of them out. One of them has quite a reputation. His name is . . . what is it, Henry?"

Breckinridge checked his notes.

"Cayce," he said. "Edgar Cayce."

Chapter 6

Paradise, in the off-season, was a hell of a place. From May to October the hamlet of Virginia Beach, a block wide and six miles long, swelled from around 1,500 inhabitants to 15,000 or more, as the concrete walkway above its endless white beach was jammed with tourists and summer residents. Right now those sidewalks were bare of anything but blowing sand, and most of the cottages that had begun popping up between the dunes were as empty as the rambling, shingled, many-balconied Victorian hotels that gave Virginia Beach the eerie atmosphere of a ghost town.

Colonel Breckinridge was behind the wheel, but I had done my share of the driving, as well. It was an eight-hour trip, even in Breckinridge's fancy Dusenberg sedan—which I'd taken up to one hundred miles per hour, once, while Breckinridge was sleeping, just to see what it would do. It might've gone faster than that, if I'd have pushed it, but I backed off when the thing started to shake. Later I realized it was me, shaking. That Dusenberg was as smooth as sliding down a brass banister, and about as noisy.

When I wasn't driving, I was sleeping; the few hours I might've slept the night before were spent tossing and turning. Colonel Lindbergh was going to line up a hotel room for me, but with the influx of reporters, that would take some doing, even for Lindy. In the meantime, they put me up in the house, on a cot.

Which was fine; but the spare bedrooms were all taken (Breckinridge and his wife Aida had moved in, as had Anne Lindbergh's mother) and the cot provided me was in the nursery.

I sat staring in the half-light—the moon entering through the curtainless glass like another abductor—at the crib, the cedar chest, the windowsill, the festive wallpaper. Turning all of it over in my mind like evidence I was trying to make sense of. Feeling the presence of the child, his innocence haunting the nursery, like a tiny, nagging specter.

Also, my stomach had been churning. The Lindberghs had invited me to supper that night, and their cook—Elsie Whately, butler Oliver's wife—had served rare roast beef with boiled potatoes and carrots and Yorkshire pudding. It looked delicious but the meat was tough and the rest of it flavorless. Only in America would the wealthy be saps enough to hire the English to cook for them. In conversation, at the dinner table, while I was attempting to eat my roast beef, Anne's mother—noting how little her daughter was eating—had reminded her she was eating for two, now.

It seemed that Anne was again pregnant—three months along.

Before dawn, as if we were heading out on a fishing trip (which perhaps we were), Breckinridge collected me from the nursery and we took off in his fancy car, with its leather-and-wood interior and built-in backseat bar, just the two of us.

Now it was early afternoon in Virginia Beach, and Breckinridge turned right on Fourteenth Street, and then off onto a curving road. But for a nearby Catholic church, the house was isolated, a large, dark-green shingled affair on the bank of a small lake. The spacious lawn, with its wide trimmed hedge and shrubs and trees, had begun turning green, as if spring had arrived here early. We parked in front and started up the curving flagstone walk, next to which a small wooden sign bore the neatly wood-burned words: *Association for Research and Enlightenment.*

Which was probably just another way of saying: step right up, suckers, right this way. . . .

"We have every reason to believe this man Cayce is sincere," Breckinridge had said in the car on the way down, "even if he is the crackpot I suspect he is."

"Why do you figure him as sincere?"

"Well, for one thing he comes highly recommended from friends of the Lindbergh family. Tom Lanphier arranged this psychic reading for us."

"Who the hell is Tom Lanphier?"

"Major Lanphier," Breckinridge had said with mild indignation, "is a distinguished aviator, and Vice President with TAT."

Well, at least he wasn't a colonel. TAT, of course, was Transcontinental Air Transport, the so-called Lindbergh Line, for which Lindy was a highly paid technical consultant, having charted their coast-to-coast flight routes.

"The Major believes in Cayce, and feels the man can help us."

"And what do you think, Colonel?"

"I think we're wasting our time, just as you do. But I think it's more likely that Cayce is a self-deluded fool than an outright charlatan."

Breckinridge explained that Cayce, son of a Kentucky farmer, a sixth-grade dropout, was known as a seer and a healer—and was called the "Sleeping Prophet" because all of his readings were given in his sleep.

"Oh, brother," I said.

"It's self-hypnosis of some sort. He goes into a sort of trance; it's claimed that Cayce can give detailed diagnoses of illnesses, assigning home remedies as well as medical ones, using highly technical terms he's supposedly never heard of, when he's not asleep."

"Brother," I repeated, and dropped off to sleep myself, against the window of the Dusenberg; but I didn't give any psychic readings.

The woman who answered our knock gave me a start. Not because she was wrapped in ash-cloth or wearing a turban or anything: quite the contrary. She was a small, slender woman in her fifties, with dark, graying hair and large, luminous brown eyes; she wore a simple blue-and-white print dress with an apron, and looked about as sinister as milk and cookies.

What gave me the start, frankly, was the delicate prettiness of her face: she had the same sort of fragile beauty as Anne Lindbergh.

Breckinridge must have noticed the resemblance, too, because the lawyer damn near stammered, as he removed his hat and said, "We've come as representatives of the Lindbergh family. We have an appointment . . . ?"

She smiled warmly and took the lawyer's hat. "I'm Gertrude Cayce," she said. "You'd be Colonel Breckinridge. And the other gentleman?"

"Nathan Heller," I said.

"Police officer?" she asked pleasantly, gesturing us inside.

"Why, yes."

She laughed; it was the lilting laugh of a much younger woman. "No, I'm not psychic myself, Mr. Heller—your profession just shows on you."

I had to smile at that, as we were ushered into a modest, unpretentious home entirely lacking in occult trappings. It was also lacking in luxury. Faded floral wallpaper and a recently re-covered sofa and easy chair were typical of the lived-in look of the place.

She guided us down a short hallway toward a room that had been added onto the main house; here, I thought, I would encounter the mystic trappings of the soothsayer game: we would pass through a beaded curtain into a room where the signs of the zodiac were painted on a wall around which hung weird masks, across an oriental carpet to a table where a crystal ball was overseen by a stuffed cobra and a swami in a pink turban and caftan holding a black cat in his arms. . . .

But there was no beaded curtain; no curtain at all, or door, either. We entered directly into a cluttered room lit by natural light from windows on two sides that looked out on a dock and the lake. A worn studio couch was against one wall; at one end of the couch was an old straight-back chair with a black cushion, and at the other a schoolchild's wooden desk chair. Over the couch were countless inscribed photos from, apparently, satisfied customers. The other walls were thick with framed family portraits, prints of Robert

E. Lee and Abraham Lincoln, and religious pictures, including a
cow-eyed Christ and an etching of the Good Samaritan. Against
one wall was an old wooden filing cabinet, near a wooden bric-a-
brac rack whose shelves brimmed with seashells, colored rocks,
miniature elephants, and various worthless trinkets. A frayed throw
rug covered most of the wooden floor.

"This is Edgar Cayce," she said, gesturing formally, "my husband."

He was rising from an old, beat-up typewriter at a big, messy
rolltop desk. He was as tall and slender as Lindbergh, but not at
all stoop-shouldered; he had the perfect build for and general look
of a stage magician, but not the demeanor. His hair was thinning
and brown, and his round, small-chinned, genial face was at odds
with his long, slender frame; he wore rimless glasses, and appeared
to be, like his wife, in his mid- to late-fifties. He moved quickly
toward us, extending his hand first to Breckinridge, then to me.

"Colonel Breckinridge," he said; his voice was warm, soothing.
That much fit the charlatan mold. "And you are?"

"Nate Heller," I said. "I'm with the Chicago police."

He smiled; he had the aura of a friendly uncle. His lips were
full, his eyes as gray-blue as the water out the window behind him.

"You take in a lot of territory in your job, Mr. Heller," he
said.

"I don't usually cut this wide a swath. But the Lindbergh
kidnapping isn't your usual case."

He grew sober. "No. It is not. Would you gentlemen sit down,
please?"

He plucked several wooden chairs from against a wall and we
sat in the middle of the room, his wife joining us, like four card
players who forgot their table.

"I pray that I can help you, gentlemen," he said, hands on
his knees, his kindly face solemn. "Like all Americans, I have great
admiration and affection for Colonel Lindbergh. Of course, I can't
promise anything. My gift is not something I can control."

"Your gift?" I asked.

Cayce shrugged. "I don't claim to understand it at all. I
only know I do have some kind of strange gift, or power. I put
myself to sleep, and words come out of me that I don't hear at the

time and don't even understand later, when I read them transcribed. I do know, that in the thirty-odd years I've been at this, thousands of folks have been healed and helped and not one has been harmed."

Spoken like a true con man.

"Now you realize, I rarely deal with criminal matters," he said. "My readings are primarily related to health problems."

"Psychics have been known," Breckinridge said, in a friendly tone, "to help the police, on occasion. There have been recorded instances of success. . . ."

He raised his hand. "I've dealt in such matters, but I don't like to. Once, many years ago, I gave a reading about a murder in Canada." His eyes looked upward, as if he kept his memory on the ceiling. "There were two old maids, both of them wealthy, both of them misers. . . . One of them said the other was shot and killed by a prowler. The police interrogated every suspect and vagrant around the countryside, and got nowhere. I gave a reading in which I stated that there'd been no prowler—one sister killed the other in a rivalry over a suitor. After which, I said, the surviving old maid had thrown the murder gun out of the window, where a heavy rain carried it some distance away. The police found the gun exactly where I said it would be, down a slope in the muddy ground— and then they came around to arrest me. Said only an accomplice could know the details I did."

I smiled. "But you had an alibi."

"An excellent one," he said, returning my smile. "First of all, I was many hundreds of miles away at the time. Second of all, I had never met any of the principals."

"That would do it," I admitted.

"But that," Cayce said reflectively, "was not what put me off detective work. Shortly thereafter, a private investigator contacted me about some stolen bonds he was trying to track. I agreed, reluctantly, to help him. I described the person who'd stolen the bonds, a woman on the 'inside,' who had a red birthmark on her thigh, and a bad scar on her toes from a childhood accident." He shook his head. "It seems my description fit the wife of the owner of the bonds—who thought the little woman was in Chicago visiting her sister. Instead, she was in a Pennsylvania hotel with her boyfriend. It was a hotel I identified in my reading, and they were both brought to justice."

"Why," Breckinridge asked, "did that 'put you off' of the detective game?"

"Because," Cayce said, "I don't like to feel that my power is being used to hound and punish anyone. Even if they are crooks, and deserve to be caught."

"I didn't like it either," his wife said. "Edgar was given his gift for healing the sick. Whenever he has used it for any other purpose, he's been struck with severe headaches and other physical ailments. It makes him ill and unhappy—and it frightens me."

Cayce was nodding. He obviously viewed his wife as his partner in the practice of his gift—or grift, whichever.

"Why are you making an exception, here?" I asked him. Smelling an approaching con.

Cayce lowered his head. His hands were still on his knees, but slack, now. "Some years ago, Gertrude and I lost a son. He was a sick little boy, colicky, crying endlessly. My wife was very worried, but I was busy with readings for patients. And I've always been . . . reluctant to use the gift where my own family is concerned. . . ."

He touched his fingers to his eyes, head still lowered.

Then he continued: "I was stunned, when the doctor told me Milton was dying. Colitis. They had done all they could, but he was a small boy, and frail. Finally, I gave him a reading, wondering why, dear God, I hadn't done it before."

And now tears were rolling down Cayce's cheeks.

I felt very uncomfortable. I was pulled between thinking I was a heel for doubting this guy, and wondering if I was seeing the world's greatest scam artist at work.

His wife rose and stood next to him and put her arm around his shoulder; her eyes were moist, but the tears weren't flowing like Cayce's were.

"I awoke," he said, "and knew the answer without asking. My father, who helped me with my readings, looked pale, looked terrible. My wife was weeping. And in the hour before dawn, my son died . . . just as my reading had said he would."

His wife squeezed his shoulder. They smiled at each other, as she dabbed his tears away with a hanky.

Christ, this was embarrassing! I hated being close to this, whether it was legitimate or ill.

I didn't know whether Breckinridge bought it or not. But he said to Cayce, "And this is why you are willing to get involved in the Lindbergh matter."

Cayce nodded vigorously. "I will do anything I can to reunite that family with its missing boy."

Mrs. Cayce left the room, while Cayce began to take off his coat and necktie. He loosened his collar and cuffs and sat on the studio couch and began to untie his shoes. Then a good-looking blonde in her late twenties, in a trim pink-and-white dress, her sheer hosiery flashing, entered the room with Mrs. Cayce trailing behind.

Now we were getting somewhere.

"This is Gladys Davis," Mrs. Cayce said.

The blonde smiled at me and I smiled right back. She was carrying a steno pad, I noticed. So the clairvoyant had a dishy dame for a secretary. Now I was starting to feel at home.

"Miss Davis has been our secretary since 1923," Mrs. Cayce explained. "Her older sister was in our Christian study group."

Praise Jesus.

"What do we need to do?" Breckinridge asked Mrs. Cayce.

"Nothing, dear," she said, touching the lawyer's hand. "You and Mr. Heller just sit quietly and watch. It would help if you would use our initial moments of meditation to turn your own thoughts inward."

That was me. I was one reflective son of a bitch.

Miss Davis settled her sweet frame into the schoolboy desk chair near the couch, where Cayce had stretched out, his hands on his forehead, palms up; what was he going to do, wiggle his fingers and pretend he was a bunny rabbit?

Gertrude Cayce took the chair near her husband's head. He looked at her lovingly, and she looked at him the same way, and stroked his cheek lightly. It was a moment between them that seemed very real to me—suddenly the dishy secretary seemed just a secretary.

He closed his eyes, slowly moved his hands down from his

forehead until his palms were flat against his stomach. He began breathing deeply, rhythmically.

Then the secretary and the wife bowed their heads and began to pray or meditate or something. This was our cue to turn our own thoughts inward, I supposed. Breckinridge looked at me blankly and I shrugged and he shrugged, and we looked toward the now apparently slumbering Cayce.

He sighed deeply. Then his breathing became light and soft, as if he were taking a quiet nap.

Mrs. Cayce repeated something, which Breckinridge and I could not hear, but took to be the hypnotic suggestion that would trigger the "reading."

I got out my pencil and notebook; what the hell—I was here.

Cayce began to mumble. He seemed to be repeating his wife's incantation.

Then he damn near shouted, and both Breckinridge and I jumped, a little, in our hardwood chairs. Tough on the tailbone.

"Can you give us the exact location of the missing child," Mrs. Cayce asked him gently, "at the present hour—and can you describe the surest way to restore the child unharmed to his parents?"

"There are many channels through which contacting may be done," he said, in a clear, normal voice. "These are the channels that are acquainted best with the nature of racketeering. These individuals are part new, partly *not* new to such rackets—see? That is, one who has been in the employ of such—the others, entirely new."

In that gibberish, it struck me, was what might be a grain of truth: experienced racketeers working with somebody recruited from the inside at the Lindbergh house.

Mrs. Cayce tried again. "What means should be used to communicate with the kidnappers?"

"There are already many in motion. Someone who may make arrangements or agreements, for the release or return without injury to the baby, would be best."

That was brilliant.

"Is it possible to get the names of these people?"

"The leader of authority of the group is Maglio."

Maglio? I knew of a Maglio: Paul Maglio, sometimes known as Paul Ricca, one of Capone's cronies! I wrote the name down. I underlined it three times.

"Excuse me, Mrs. Cayce," I said, softly. Worried I might spoil things by interrupting.

But she only looked back with a gentle, Madonna-like smile. "Yes, Mr. Heller?"

"Would it be possible for me to ask Mr. Cayce a few questions?"

Without hesitation, she said, "Certainly," and rose from the chair and gestured me toward it.

Hating myself for getting sucked into this swami's act, I went to the chair and sat.

"Can you tell me about the kidnapping itself?" I asked. "How did it happen?"

"The baby was removed from the room, about eight-thirty P.M., carried by a man," he said. "Another man was waiting below."

I didn't want to prompt him unduly, so I just said, "Below?"

Cayce nodded; his eyes remained closed. He looked peacefully asleep. "The child was lowered to the ground and taken to a car. Now we find there are changes in the manner of transportation. . . ."

That did make sense, of course; changing cars made sense. But you didn't have to be psychic to figure that one out.

"Another car is used," he said. "They moved northward, toward Jersey City, through a tunnel and across New York City into Connecticut, into the region of Cordova."

I was writing this stuff down; God knew why, but I was.

"On the east side of New Haven," he said, "following a route along Adams Street, they took the child to a two-story shingled house, numbered Seventy-Three. Two tenths of a mile from the end of Adams Street is a brown house, formerly painted green, the third house from the corner. There is red dirt on the pavement. The child is in a house on Scharten Street."

I felt like a fool, writing this prattle down, but part of me was caught up in it. Cayce, like any good faker, had a certain presence.

"Is the baby still at this address?"

"Yes."

Breckinridge was standing next to me, now. He said to Cayce, "Was Red Johnson involved?"

"Involved, as seen."

"Was the nurse, Betty Gow, involved?"

"Not directly."

"Who else?"

"A woman named Belliance."

That name rang no bells with me.

I took over for Breckinridge. "Who guards the baby now?"

"The woman and two men who are now at home."

"Where?"

"Follow my instructions," he said testily, "and you will be led to the child."

"I know New Haven well," Breckinridge said. "I've never heard of Cordova. Can you tell us through what channels Scharten Street might be located?"

"By going to the street! If the name's on it, that's a right good mark!"

Breckinridge looked at me with wide eyes and I shrugged.

"Follow my instructions and you will find the child. We are through."

"Where . . ." Breckinridge began, but Mrs. Cayce gently moved between him and Cayce. She was shaking her head, no, raising a palm to us both, in a stop motion.

She bent forward over her husband and murmured something, to bring him out of it.

A few moments later, Cayce drew a long, deep breath and his eyes popped open. He sat up. He yawned, stretching his arms.

"Did you get everything down?" he asked his secretary.

Miss Davis bobbled her pretty blonde head.

He stood. With utter certainty, he said to Breckinridge, "Follow what you heard—whatever it was I said—and you'll get that child back."

Dazed, Breckinridge said, "Well . . . thank you. We'll follow up on everything we heard here, today."

Cayce beamed, patted Breckinridge on the shoulder. "Splendid. My secretary will send you a carbon of the transcription. Do let me know how it comes out. We like to follow up on these things."

He might have been talking about some kid's cough he prescribed a poultice for.

"What do we owe you, Mr. Cayce?" Breckinridge said.

Here it comes, I thought. Here it finally comes.

"We normally charge twenty dollars for a reading," he said. "I wish it weren't necessary to charge at all."

Twenty bucks? That was chicken feed for a racket like this.

"But in this case," Cayce said somberly, "I will make an exception."

Ah! Now comes the sting—he knows he's dealing with dough—Lindbergh and Breckinridge and Anne Lindbergh's wealthy family, the Morrows. . . .

"Pay me nothing," he said. "And please, as to the press . . ."

That was it, then—he wanted the publicity.

He waggled a finger, like a schoolteacher. "Not a word to them. I don't want the notoriety. I don't want to be involved in criminal cases again. Much too unpleasant."

I felt like I'd been whacked by a psychic two-by-four. With a mystic nail in it.

Mrs. Cayce served us supper in her cozy kitchen, before we left; it was pot roast and potatoes and carrots, much like the meal at the Lindberghs—only the meat was tender and the side dishes delicious, in the best country manner.

"Some day you gentlemen will have to have life readings," Cayce said, helping himself to a heaping portion of mashed potatoes. "Would you be interested in who and what you were in a former life?"

"Reincarnation, Mr. Cayce?" Breckinridge smiled. "I thought you were a Christian."

"There is nothing in the Bible to refute reincarnation," he said. "Although I can do a reading on Mr. Heller without going to sleep."

"Oh, really?" I said, lifting a fork of food. "What was I in my previous life?"

"An idealist," he said, blue-gray eyes sparkling. "All cynics were idealists, once. More pot roast, Mr. Heller?"

In the Dusenberg, I asked Breckinridge what he'd made of all that.

"I'll be damned if I know," he admitted. "And you?"

"I'll be damned if I know, either. I won't say I'm convinced, but I will say I want to track everything he gave us."

"A street map of New Haven would be a start. We might be able to get one of those at a gas station, on the way back."

"Good idea. You know, the first of the two Italian names he mentioned—Maglio—is the name of one of Capone's top lieutenants."

Breckinridge gave me a sharp look. "Interesting. And he indicated Red Johnson was involved."

Betty Gow's sailor.

"Aren't we supposed to get a shot at questioning that guy?" I asked.

Breckinridge nodded. "Tomorrow."

"Do you think he's a good suspect?"

"Colonel Lindbergh doesn't like to think his servants might be involved, even indirectly . . . but after what the Hartford police found in Johnson's car, I'd say he's an excellent suspect."

"What did they find in his car?"

Breckinridge turned his attention from the road to show me a raised eyebrow.

"An empty milk bottle," he said.

Chapter 7

It was almost ten o'clock, the next morning, when I stumbled downstairs. The little fox terrier looked up from its perch on the living room couch and began barking hysterically at me. Next to the mutt was Anne Lindbergh, wearing a prim blue sweater-suit, sitting across from her mother, Mrs. Dwight Morrow; the latter was doing needlepoint, the former reading a small leather-bound book.

They began to get up and I asked them please not to.

Mrs. Morrow was a small woman in her late fifties, with her daughter's delicate features; she wore a blue dress with white lace trim and pearls and a crucifix. Her hair was more brown than gray, though I would imagine it would be getting grayer as the days progressed.

"Wahgoosh!" Anne said sharply. "Be still."

The dog stopped barking, but he continued to growl and give me his best evil eye.

"I understand you and Henry drove down to Virginia yesterday," Anne said, smiling, "and back again." She gestured for me to sit next to her on the couch and I did. Wahgoosh expressed snarling displeasure.

"That sounds like quite an outing for a single day," Mrs. Morrow said.

"We didn't get back till the middle of the night," I admitted. "How worthwhile a trip it was, I couldn't say."

"You spoke to a clairvoyant, I understand," Anne said.

Mrs. Morrow shook her head, barely, as if thinking, *What next?*, and returned her attention to her needlepoint.

"Yes," I said. "A sincere gentleman, I believe."

"Not a faker, like so many of them."

"No. But he gave us some specific information, including street names that we tried to check, on various maps, without any success."

"I see," Anne said, with a patient smile.

"What are you reading?" I asked.

"Ben Jonson."

"Oh."

"The poet."

"Right."

She read aloud: " 'Although it fall and die that night, it was the plant of flower and light. In small proportions we just beauties see; and in short measures, life may perfect be.' " She looked up at me with shimmering blue eyes and a crinkly brave smile. "I like that line . . . 'It was the plant of flower and light.' "

Jesus. Had she written off her kid as dead already?

"That's a nice poem," I said. "Tell me something . . ."

"Certainly."

That fucking dog was still growling at me.

"Why do you think your dog was quiet that night?"

"Wahgoosh? He was in the opposite wing of the house. When he's not on the sofa, here, where we really shouldn't let him be . . . or sleeping on the floor in the nursery near Charlie . . . he has a little bed in the servants' sitting room. Whately first brought him into the house, you know, and we sort of adopted the little fellow. He couldn't have heard anything through the howling wind, all that distance."

"You know . . . and excuse me for raising this, Mrs. Lindbergh . . . but there are those who suspect one of your three servants might be involved."

She shook her head. "No. Betty and the others, we trust implicitly."

"That's not always a good way to trust."

"Pardon?"

"Implicitly." I turned to Anne's mother. "Mrs. Morrow, how big a staff do you have at your estate?"

The older woman looked up from her needlepoint. "Twenty-nine. But I assure you, Mr. Heller, they're all trustworthy."

"I'm sure they are, Mrs. Morrow. But how many of them knew, or could have known, about the change of plans for Anne and her husband and son, to stay over an extra day or two here?"

Mrs. Morrow lifted her shoulders in a tiny shrug, not missing a stitch. "Most of them. Perhaps all of them."

I thought about that.

"You know, Mr. Heller," Anne said, reflectively, "there was something else odd about that evening. The evening that Charlie was stolen away, I mean. . . ."

"What was that, Mrs. Lindbergh?"

Her eyes tightened. "My husband was supposed to give a speech that night, to the alumni at New York University. But he's been so overworked lately, he mixed up the dates. He drove home, instead."

"You mean, he wasn't supposed to be here that evening?"

"No."

I leaned forward. "You realize that only someone within this household—or possibly the Morrow household—could have known that."

"Yes. But that assumes the kidnappers knew. That this wasn't all just a matter of . . . chance. Blind, dumb chance. That's . . . that's what I have so much difficulty accepting."

Behind us a voice said, "Everything in life is chance, dear."

It was Lindbergh. He was wearing a corduroy jacket over a sweater and open-collar shirt; his pants were tucked into leather boots that rose midcalf. He looked like a college boy—a hung over college boy, that is. His face was haggard as hell.

He came up behind his wife, behind the couch, and placed a

hand gently on her shoulder. She reached up and touched the hand, but did not look back at him.

"You can guard against the high percentage of chance," he said, "but not against chance itself."

She nodded wisely. She'd heard him say it before.

I said, "You're right, Colonel. But don't go writing off everything you don't understand as happenstance. In my business we learn to look at coincidence with a jaundiced eye."

He nodded, but I wasn't sure he'd paid any attention. He said, "Have you had any breakfast, Nate?"

"No, sir."

"Let's round you something up. I'd like a word with you."

We excused ourselves to the ladies. He walked briskly and I followed along, till he came to a sudden stop in the foyer, beyond earshot of his wife and mother-in-law.

"This fellow Red Johnson is being brought around today," he said.

"Yes."

"He isn't technically under arrest, you know. The Hartford police have turned him over to the custody of the state police, here. He'll be held in Newark."

"Well, that's good."

He put his hands in his pockets, rocked gently on his feet. "This is going to be hard on Miss Gow, if this beau of hers was using her for information."

I thought, *Yeah, and so fucking what?*

But I said, sympathetically, "Yes, I know."

"You know, she was badly embarrassed when the papers were full of that Scotty Gow nonsense."

The first several days after the kidnapping, the press and the cops of several cities had latched onto the notion that one Scotty Gow, a Purple Gang member in Detroit, was the brother of Betty Gow. Miss Gow had worked in Detroit, and Lindbergh's mother lived in Detroit, so everybody put two and two together and came up with three hundred and five.

"He wasn't her brother," I said.

"Of course not. Understand, I'm in general pleased with Colonel Schwarzkopf's handling of this situation, but this persistent, sometimes boorish questioning of my staff does not please me."

I didn't know what to say, so I didn't say anything.

"I'd appreciate it, Nate, if you would do two things for me."

"Sure."

"Don't pester my servants with questions—don't be part of this inquisition. And let me know if you see Schwarzkopf or his chief bully, Inspector Welch, overstepping the line."

"Sure. But, Slim . . . there *is* reason to suspect an insider was involved. The cops are just doing their job."

"It's silly," he said impatiently. "This thing was obviously the work of seasoned professional criminals. This is the underworld's doing, not my damn household staff!"

"The underworld could have recruited somebody from your . . ."

"Perhaps they recruited Red Johnson. But that's as far as I can see it going. I'm going to keep out of the way of the police when they interrogate him, so be my eyes and ears, if you would."

"Fine," I said, surprised that he'd bow out of the Johnson questioning. "Is something else up?"

Then he headed into the kitchen, talking as he went.

"I'll be tied up most of the afternoon with an in-law of mine," he said. "There's a possibility the kidnappers have tried to make contact with us through an outside party."

"Really?"

"I can't say any more, at this point, and please don't mention what I just said to anyone."

I nodded.

Then we were in the kitchen; Elsie Whately was slicing a cucumber on a wooden counter using a wide, thick knife. She smiled wanly at Lindbergh, who asked her to fix me some eggs and toast.

"How do you like them?" he asked me. He was getting a pitcher of orange juice out of the Frigidaire.

"Scramble the eggs and keep the toast light, if you would," I told her.

Her mouth flinched in surly acknowledgment, and she left the cucumber half-sliced and went to work on my breakfast.

Lindbergh had poured us both full glasses of orange juice. He brought the pitcher to the table.

I sipped my juice, and he gulped his.

"You seem optimistic today," I said.

"I am. It's foolish to be any way at all—better to just take every day and move through it in a straight line. Win out over it."

"I feel the same way," I said. "Only I usually settle for breaking even."

"By the way, I haven't had any luck freeing up a hotel room for you. The reporters have everything locked up at Gebhart's. And that's the only hotel in Hopewell. I may be able to get you something at Princeton. It's only ten miles from here, and I've a secondhand car for you, that the servants had been using for grocery shopping and such, before we went under siege. Now we're having everything brought in."

"Well, a car—that's swell. I hope I prove worth all this trouble."

"What kind of per diem are you on, Nate?"

"Four bucks a day."

"Food?"

"And lodging."

"I thought something like that might be the case." He lowered his voice so the cook couldn't hear. "I hope this won't offend you . . . but I'd like you to accept fifty dollars a week from me, as long as you're here, to help defray the expenses you're going to have."

I grinned. "You got it backwards, Slim. Chicago cops take offense when you *don't* offer 'em money."

He grinned back. "Okay," he said. "Colonel Breckinridge will give you an envelope, each Friday."

"Well, thanks. I hope I won't have to collect many of those from you."

Lindbergh poured himself another glass of orange juice. "Was your trip to see the fortune-teller worth the time?"

"I'm not sure."

"That's what Henry said."

"I want to have a couple things checked out by the feds. Do you have a number where Agent Wilson can be reached in New York?"

"Yes," Lindbergh said, and fished out a small black book; he gave me the number and I wrote it down in my notebook.

Then Lindbergh polished off his orange juice and, with a little wave and a shy smile, left me to my breakfast, served up by the sullen Elsie Whately. The eggs were dry and the toast was dark. Just as I was finishing up, Betty Gow came in to get herself a cup of coffee.

She looked very pretty, as usual, wearing a dark green dress with tiny white polka dots and a white collar; she was neat as a pin—neater. She glanced at me nervously, and, coffee cup in hand, was moving back toward the servants' sitting room when I called out to her.

"Join me for a moment, won't you, Miss Gow?"

She hesitated, and a flinch of a smile crossed her face; then she haltingly approached me and sat down.

"Say, Elsie," I said, friendly as an election-year politician, "could I talk you out of a cup of that stuff?"

"Yes sir," she said, unenthusiastically.

"Cream and sugar, Elsie?" Betty asked.

Elsie nodded curtly.

"How are you bearing up under all this, Miss Gow?" I asked.

"It's a bit of a trial, isn't it, Mr. Heller?"

"I wish you'd call me Nate."

"All right."

But she didn't suggest I call her Betty.

Elsie brought me my coffee, and Betty the cream and sugar. Normally I drank mine black, but I stirred some sugar in, and cream, too. We'd both had Elsie's coffee before.

"I understand your friend Red Johnson is dropping by today," I said.

"I don't think 'dropping by' is exactly how I'd put it."

"He hasn't been arrested."

"No. But he's in custody." She added more sugar, stirred, looked into the muddy liquid.

"I hope you don't mind talking, a little."

Her smile was tight and pretty and sarcastic. "Do I have a choice?"

"Well, sure. You're free, white and twenty-one . . . barely. And Colonel Lindbergh has asked me to help look into this." Of course, he'd have me on the next train out of here if he knew I was ignoring his request to leave the help alone.

"It was my understanding," she said, "that the Colonel only wants to get his son back. That pursuing those responsible is not his inclination, at this point."

"I think that's right. But I'm a cop, Miss Gow. I'd like to try to understand what happened that night."

She sipped her coffee; her eyes looked right past me, cold, unblinking, and a bit bloodshot.

"You talked to Red Johnson on the telephone, didn't you?" I asked. "The night of the kidnapping?"

She nodded. "He called me about eight-thirty. I tried to call Henry on the telephone at Englewood, before I left for Hopewell, but I couldn't reach him—he wasn't at his boardinghouse. So I left word for him to call me, in the evening, at Hopewell."

"And he did."

"Yes. We'd intended seeing each other that evening, but when he called, I told him how it happened that I wasn't at the Morrow house. I told him . . . told him the baby had a cold."

"How long had you known Johnson? When did you meet him?"

"I met him last summer. He had a job as a deckhand on the *Reynard,* the Lamont yacht."

"Lamont yacht?"

"Thomas W. Lamont. He and the late Mr. Morrow were partners in J. P. Morgan and Company. The banking house? Last summer, last August to be exact, the yacht was anchored off North Haven, Maine, where the Morrows have a summer home. I was there with Mrs. Lindbergh and the baby. Henry used to play cards with the Morrow chauffeurs. One of them introduced us and we hit it off. Then, in the off-season, the *Reynard* was moored in the Hudson, near the Palisades. Which allowed us to continue seeing each other."

"Were you two serious, Miss Gow?"

She shrugged; sipped her coffee. "We dated quite often. Boating, movies, dancing—the Palisades Amusement Park was nearby."

"Were you engaged?"

"No. I like Henry, Mr. Heller. He's a good-hearted bloke. I don't think he's capable of being involved in something like this. I know there's speculation that he . . . used me to get information. I just don't believe it."

"Where does your loyalty lie, Miss Gow? With the Lindberghs, or with Henry Johnson?"

Her smile was thin as a razor slash. "Who do you think told the police where Henry could be found? If you'll excuse me."

She went into the servants' sitting room; I followed her.

"Thanks for your time, Miss Gow," I said.

She was sitting absently paging through a film magazine; she didn't look up, didn't respond.

I went outside.

The usual barely controlled chaos was afoot in the command-post garage; troopers were going through the mail, bags of which were piled against one wall. Inspector Welch, the hard-nosed, pot-bellied flatfoot who'd confronted me shortly after my arrival, met me as I was about to step inside.

"Are you still around?" he said.

"I seem to be. Where's Schwarzkopf?"

"That's Colonel Schwarzkopf to you, sonny boy."

"That's Mr. Sonny Boy to you, bud." I brushed by him.

Schwarzkopf was leaning over the telephone switchboard, having a word with the trooper at that post. "Ah," he said, spotting me, "Heller." Almost glad to see me.

"Any news from the front?"

"Henry 'Red' Johnson is due here momentarily. Would you like to sit in on the interrogation?"

"Yes, thanks," I said, realizing he wouldn't have made the offer if Lindbergh hadn't requested it. "Tell me, Colonel . . . is there any reason to think there might be a connection between this case and New Haven, Connecticut?"

That damn near startled him. "Actually, yes."

That damn near startled me. "No kidding," I said.

"Why do you ask, Heller?"

"That psychic in Virginia Beach mentioned New Haven."

That made him less interested, but he said, "A number of the workmen involved in the construction of this house were from New

Haven. They were among the first people we questioned. Detective Heller, I realize you have a low opinion of the New Jersey State Police. But we have been, and continue to be, running a first-class investigation. Within the first forty-eight hours after the crime, we interrogated three hundred and twenty people, in New York, New Jersey, and Connecticut."

"That's a lot of interviews. I didn't know you had the manpower."

"We were, and are, stretched to the limit."

"Who were those people you questioned?"

"The Lindbergh and Morrow household staffs, neighbors, delivery boys, carpenters and various workmen involved in the construction of the house . . . we've been very thorough."

"Yeah, it sounds like it. Say, you think you could arrange an open phone line for me, Colonel?"

"Certainly."

He walked me to one of the tables where troopers were manning phones and cleared a space for me. He stood there for a moment, until he realized I wasn't going to place the call until he left.

I used the number Lindbergh had given me and got Treasury Agent Frank J. Wilson on the first try.

"What's going on out there, Heller?"

"We're about to have a talk with Red Johnson."

"The Norwegian sailor? Found a milk bottle in his rumble seat, I hear."

"Right. You boys checking up on him?"

"Not us, but I understand J. Edgar's crew is checking on his immigration status."

"Not a bad idea. Would you like a lead?"

"Why not? We're not getting any help from Schwarzkopf, that's for damn sure."

"You found Capone's boy, Bob Conroy, yet?"

"No."

"You said witnesses put Conroy in New Haven, Connecticut that night, right?"

"That's right."

"Well, apparently this house was built by workers from New

Haven. Schwarzkopf was suspicious enough to send his state cops in there doing an investigative sweep."

"That is interesting."

"Also—and this is a long shot, and I'd appreciate it if you wouldn't ask me my source . . . but see if you can find an Adams Street and/or a Scharten Street, in New Haven. And maybe a section of town called Cordova."

The line went silent; he was writing it down.

"Okay," he said. "Anything else?"

"If you get anything, call here and leave word for me to call you. If there is an Adams or a Scharten Street, I'll give you more specifics."

"Fair enough. I appreciate your cooperation, Heller."

"That's okay, Agent Wilson."

"Make it Frank."

"Okay, Frank. I can always use a friend in the IRS."

"Just keep an eye on Schwarzkopf. He's a rank amateur. Don't let his military bearing fool you—between graduating West Point and falling into law enforcement, he served a hitch as a department-store floorwalker."

"Impressive credentials."

"He's never patrolled a beat or arrested a criminal in his life. He's in way over his head, Heller."

"Well, if he starts going down for the third time, I'll throw him something nice and heavy."

"That would be my advice," Wilson said.

After I'd hung up, I joined Schwarzkopf, who was conferring with the bullet-headed Welch. "Any sign of our wandering sailor boy?" I asked.

"Yes," Schwarzkopf said. "He's arrived."

"You could've fooled me."

"You noticed the contractor's shack just inside the gates?"

The small shack had been used as a guard outpost for troopers, primarily to keep reporters and sightseers at bay.

"Sure," I said.

"We're going to question him there."

"Away from the house and Colonel Lindbergh, you mean."

"Right." Schwarzkopf gestured to Inspector Welch. "I want

you two men to start fresh. I can't have any animosity among my men."

I was his man, now? Lindbergh must've really lowered the boom.

"No hard feelings," I said, and extended my hand to Welch.

We shook hands, exchanged insincere smiles, and followed Schwarzkopf to a patrol car. A trooper drove us to the weather-beaten shack, the inside of which wasn't much bigger than an outhouse. Two troopers stood guard over a man in a straight-back chair. The troopers looked spiffy; the man did not. It was cold and everybody's breath smoked.

Husky, freckled, his hair a dark reddish brown not unlike my own, Betty Gow's sailor looked tired and frazzled; in his early twenties, ruggedly good-looking, he wore a light-blue work-shirt and dark-blue trousers, clothes obviously slept in.

"The Hartford police have turned you over to us, Johnson," Schwarzkopf said, planting himself before the suspect like a cop directing traffic. "You know why you're here."

"I don't know nothing 'bout Lindbergh kidnap." He had a thick, rather melodious accent—Swedish or Norwegian or something.

"You'll have to prove that," Welch said, poking him in the chest with a hard finger.

"Tell us where you were," Schwarzkopf said, "and what you did on the night of March first of this year."

Johnson sighed, wearily. "Oh kay. On night of kidnap, I meet friend of mine, Johannes Junge, 'bout eight o'clock."

"Who is this Junge?"

"He live in Englewood. Husband of seamstress at Morrow house. We take short drive in my car—sometime 'round quarter of nine, I call here and ask speak to Betty."

"How did you know she was here?"

"I had date with Betty for Tuesday, but I call earlier and learn Betty would not be in Englewood that night. Baby have cold. Lindberghs, they decide best not to make baby make trip between two homes."

"So you called Betty Gow."

"Yes. She ask, what's big idea? I said, oh, I just thought I call you up and tell you I'm sorry not to be seeing you tonight. She say, oh, I see. I say, how is baby? She say, I think he going to be all right. I say, uh, when you think you get back? She say, I don't know; please don't call here anymore—they might not like it. She hang up. I hang up." He shrugged.

"Then what did you do?"

"Junge and me, we go to Plaza Theater in Englewood to see movie. When we come out of show, we go to ice-cream parlor. Had couple those chocolate nut sundaes. Then I went home to my room at boardinghouse."

This guy sounded like a hardened criminal, all right.

"When was this?"

"Sometime 'bout midnight."

Schwarzkopf seemed stumped by the forthrightness of the suspect. He looked at Welch, who said, "Mind if I take over?"

I knew what that would amount to—rubber-hose roulette. So I said, "Excuse me, Colonel. Could I ask Mr. Johnson a few questions?"

Schwarzkopf, rather stiffly, said, "Certainly. Johnson, this is Detective Heller of the Chicago Police."

"Hi, Red," I said.

"Hello."

"You smoke?"

"Yah."

I looked at Welch. "Get this man a smoke, would you?"

Welch dug out his own Camels and reluctantly lit the sailor up. The boy sucked the smoke in eagerly.

I just stood there, letting him smoke and relax.

Then I said, "How much did you spend on that long-distance call, Red?"

"Pardon?"

"You called from a public phone?"

"Yah."

"From Englewood to Hopewell. How much money did you feed the pay phone?"

"Was thirty-five cents."

I looked at Welch, who was standing there like a fireplug, and looking just about as intelligent. I made a writing motion with my finger and he looked at me blankly for a moment, then nodded, and took out his notebook and wrote down what Johnson had just said.

"What movie did you see, Red?"

"Saw two. Don't remember names. Sorry."

"Who was in the first one? What was it about?"

"Uh, funny movie. That fat guy and skinny guy."

"Laurel and Hardy?"

He nodded vigorously.

"What about the second feature?"

"Fighter and little kid. Sad picture."

I looked at Welch. "*The Champ.*"

Welch smirked and scribbled.

"You know where that ice-cream parlor is?"

Johnson nodded and reeled off the address; Welch wrote it down.

"What about this milk bottle they found in your car?"

He shrugged. "What 'bout it?"

"What was it doing there?"

"I guess I forgot to throw it out."

"Where'd you get it?"

"I bought bottle of milk on my way up to Hartford, Wednesday morning."

"Where?"

"Can't remember exactly. Guess it was somewhere along the road, near Englewood."

"What was the idea of buying a bottle of milk? Somehow I picture you drinking something a little stronger, Red."

"No, no. My stomach bad. Doctor told me drink lots of milk."

"What doctor?"

"Morrow family doctor, in Englewood. Forget his name."

Welch stepped in. "Now listen, Johnson—where is that baby?"

"So help me God, I don't know. I don't know a thing about it!"

"You know Betty Gow pretty well?" pressed Welch.

"I guess you could say that."

"Where'd you meet her?"

"Up in Maine, over year ago."

"How?"

"Well, I work for Mr. Lamont, and his estate was near Morrow summer place."

"When d'you see Betty last?"

"Sunday. No—Monday night."

Welch straight-armed him. "Which—Sunday or Monday?"

"Both!" Johnson winced with pain.

"Where did you see her?"

"In Englewood."

Welch grabbed his shirt front, wadding it in a tight fist. "Why did you call her and ask about the baby, the night of the kidnapping?"

"Because it was on account of baby that she broke her date with me! Naturally, I ask about baby."

"Ever been in Lindbergh's home?"

"Yes."

"How many times?"

"Two . . . three times, I think."

"When were you there last?"

"Maybe two weeks ago."

"Know the layout of the place pretty well, do you?"

"I guess I do."

"Ever been in the nursery?"

"No, never."

"Ever been on the second floor?"

"Yah."

"Where on the second floor?"

"In Betty's room. That where she can have visitor after working hours."

"Where's that from the nursery?"

"Next to it, I think."

Johnson was answering the questions as fast as Welch could fire them; the sailor was holding up under it.

Welch let go of the sailor's shirt and turned to Schwarzkopf and said, quietly, "Clear this shack out—leave me alone with him, and I'll get you the truth."

Schwarzkopf nodded; that seemed to sound good to him.

"Colonel," I said, "Inspector . . . let's step outside a second, fellas, what say."

We stood outside the shack; nearby were the stone walls of the front gate, beyond which reporters milled like ants in search of a picnic. They were dying to know what was going on in our glorified outhouse.

"Why beat a confession out of him at this point?" I asked. "First of all, he's a sailor and probably pretty tough—it would be hard to get him to confess to anything, without hurting him to where it would show."

Welch bristled. "Are you telling us how to do our job?"

"God forbid. I'm convinced when it comes to beating worthless confessions out of innocent suspects, you're the guy to call."

"Fuck you, Heller."

"Take a number, Welch. Colonel, why don't you check up on Red's alibi, before your inspector starts wearing out rubber hoses on Johnson's thick Swedish skull."

"He's Norwegian," Schwarzkopf said. But he was thinking. "If those facts check out—the cost of the long-distance call, the movies he says were playing, the ice-cream parlor, the doctor prescribing milk—we may have an innocent man on our hands."

"I know," I said. "And it's a pity—when he talks, he sounds just like those goddamn ransom notes."

Chapter 8

The Old Princeton Inn was on Nassau Street, the main thoroughfare of the college town the ancient four-story brick hotel was named after. Even at nine P.M., well past business hours, the shops screamed their orange-and-black allegiance to the Princeton Tigers. This old village seemed cheerfully dependent on its young benefactors.

But this was a week night, a school night, and the streets were as empty as a phys ed major's mind; it was as if the looming Gothic university buildings were taking names of any collegian not home studying. The deserted street, the orange and black that dominated every storefront, conspired with the bitter March wind and a moonless, starless night to make me as uneasy as a homeowner on Halloween—and a homeowner who didn't spring for candy treats, at that.

I was, after all, on my way to a séance.

"I'm sorry to ask you to do this," Lindbergh had said, earlier that afternoon, sitting behind his desk in his study, "but it seems to be the only way I can get you a hotel room."

"That's okay," I'd said. "But I'm starting to feel like the resident spook chaser around here."

"That's exactly what I've decided to have you do," he said. He pointed at me forcefully. "You're going to be my chief investigator into all things that go bump in the night."

I sat up. "Huh? What?"

He and Breckinridge began to laugh, which was a welcome sound, even if it was at my expense. Slim had a prep-school sense of humor that, I'd been told, manifested itself in practical jokes. He had on at least two occasions hidden the baby from Anne and Betty Gow, just to get 'em both going; the night of the kidnapping, the initial reaction of both Anne and the nurse had been to think it another of Slim's gags.

"Nate," Lindbergh said, "you know very well that you're our resident Chicago underworld expert. Not a spook chaser."

"That's a relief to hear."

"But under the circumstances we have to hear this couple out."

It seemed a self-proclaimed spiritualist named Martin Marinelli and his wife, who called herself Sister Sarah, had been staying at the Old Princeton Inn for days, now. Marinelli had phoned the Lindbergh estate frequently, and sent letters and telegrams, claiming to have "good news" and "important information" about the kidnapping. The troopers monitoring calls and letters in the garage command post had deflected all of this, writing Marinelli and his wife off—rightly, no doubt—as cranks.

Slim apparently spoke to the manager of the Old Princeton Inn, personally, trying to wrangle me a room. The manager had explained that the reporters had everything tied up, except for one suite taken by these two psychic characters, who'd been making it known to all concerned that they had "revelations from the spirit world" about the case.

Some of the reporters had glommed onto the pair, and the spiritualist couple had been holding psychic court for days. But now the fortune-tellers were old news. The manager had offered to talk to them for Lindbergh, to see if they would relinquish their room.

"The only way they'll give up their suite," Lindbergh explained with wry matter-of-factness, "is if we see them."

"You're not going along, too, are you?" I asked him.

"No. Too much going on here. Some promising developments." He didn't elaborate.

"Well," I sighed, "anything to get a roof over my head."

Any roof that wasn't over the kidnapped kid's nursery, that is.

So now Breckinridge, his usual gray, three-piece-suit self, was knocking on the door to 414 in the Old Princeton Inn; we had hung our topcoats in the lobby. The dimly lit hallway fit the Halloween mood.

The door cracked open. A thin, sallow male face peered out; bald, spade-bearded.

"Ah," the cadaverous figure intoned, in a mellow, minister's voice, "you would be Colonel Breckinridge."

"Yes," Breckinridge said. "Are you Martin Marinelli?"

Opening the door wider, the cue-ball bald, devil-bearded fellow nodded. He was wearing a flowing black robe; around his neck was a heavily jeweled gold cross on a gold chain. He turned his gaze on me, arching a plucked-for-effect eyebrow. His eyes were small and dark, but piercing, in deep sockets.

"And who would you be?"

"You're the psychic," I said, nicely. "You tell me."

Breckinridge flashed me a reproving look.

Marinelli's nostrils flared, and he stepped back, and shut the door; it clicked ominously.

I sighed. Without looking at Breckinridge, I said, "Yeah, I know. I got too smart a mouth. But I can't take too much of this carny hokum lyin' down."

"Speaking of lying down," Breckinridge said, "*I* already *have* a place to sleep tonight."

"Good point. Knock again, I'll behave."

Breckinridge's fist was poised to knock when the door swung open.

Marinelli, seeming to float in space in the long flowing robe, was haloed in soft light against darkness.

"Come in, gentlemen," Marinelli said, gesturing theatrically. And this he directed to me: "But I would request you leave your skepticism in the hallway. If we're to have success this evening, we will need open-minded cooperation from all participants."

The sweet, smoky scent of sandalwood beckoned; somewhere in the darkness, incense was burning.

We were in a nicely furnished sitting room—lit, or barely lit, by a large red candle dripping wax in the middle of a wooden card table set up in the middle of the floor, with three chairs. There were several closed doorways, one of which was to a bedroom, presumably. If we could chase these fortune-tellers out, I'd have some pretty fancy digs.

"You still have not given your name," Marinelli said to me, sternly.

I stood twisting my hat in my hand, wondering why the flickery darkness was making me so damn nervous.

"My name is Heller," I said. "I'm a police officer assigned to the Lindbergh matter."

"I sense you are not local," Marinelli said.

He didn't have to be psychic to know that; I have the flat nasal Chicago accent you'd expect. But Breckinridge seemed a little impressed.

"I'm not local," I said, and smiled politely, and didn't tell him a nickel's worth more.

Marinelli gestured grandly to the candle-dripping card table, finding an extra chair for me; one of those already placed at the table seemed to be reserved.

"Gentlemen," Marinelli said, after we'd settled into our wooden folding chairs, "I am the father of the One Hundred Twenty-Seventh Street Spiritualist Church in Harlem. My wife Sister Sarah Sivella is the mother of that church. As you have already surmised, Mr. Heller, I have no great gifts of second sight, myself. But my wife has definite, even staggering, abilities in that realm."

"Abilities," Breckinridge said, "which she is willing to lend to the search for Charles Lindbergh, Jr. Is that correct?"

"She does not use these abilities," he explained patiently. "They use her."

"What do you mean?" Breckinridge asked.

Marinelli sculpted the air with his hands. "She did not seek information, on this matter, directly, consciously. She began speaking of the kidnapping during the course of a séance at the church. The séance was part of our regular church ritual, that happened to have been held one day after the tragic occurrence."

"So you came here," I said, "to be close to Colonel Lindbergh."

"Yes. To try to help. Ours is a Christian church. We believe in the father-motherhood of God. Christ, the son of the father-mother God, is the light that shines through wisdom and love in the human heart."

Great. A guy with a Satan beard in a black robe in a room lit by a blood-red candle is going to tell an agnostic Jew about Jesus. What a guy will go through to get a bed to sleep in.

"Life is governed by five cosmic laws," he was saying. He held up five fingers and ticked them off; maybe I should've taken my notebook out to write these down. "Reincarnation. Cause and effect. Opportunity. Retribution. Spiritual communion . . ."

Wasn't that six?

"I'm afraid I fail to see what relevance this has," Breckinridge said, "to the situation at hand. Specifically, the missing Lindbergh child."

Marinelli raised a hand as if passing a benediction; his nails were long and manicured. "Gentlemen, my wife will join us momentarily. I will begin by inducing an hypnotic trance. Then we will join hands, and I must ask you not to break the circle."

Well, this was a far cry from Edgar Cayce and his down-home soothsaying. Here we had what looked to be a traditional phony séance—and if this snake-oil merchant thought I was going to buy his scam, he was as nutty as he looked.

"Mr. Marinelli," I said, "I mean no offense, but I know the Chicago supply house that sells you people your glow-in-the-dark trumpets and bells. If you have something to say about the kidnapping, fine. But spare us the cheesecloth ghosts, paste-and-newspaper ectoplasm and levitating furniture."

Marinelli's smile was faint and condescending. "You are under a basic misapprehension, Mr. Heller. Sister Sarah is not a physical medium. You'll hear no bell ringing, table rapping, nor experience any table tilting or other unexplained transportation of objects. Sister Sarah is a *trance* medium—she materializes no trumpets and summons no visible spirits. She wanders the landscape of her own mind, listening with an inner ear to spirit voices."

"Joan of Arc got burned at the stake for that," I reminded him.

"Ah yes," he said, raising a forefinger heavenward. "But these are more enlightened times."

Tell that to the Scottsboro boys.

"Sister Sarah," he went on, "is what we call a 'sensitive.' She has a control, a spirit guide, who frequently speaks through her."

"This 'spirit guide,' " Breckinridge said, interested despite himself, "is a specific entity?"

Marinelli nodded momentously. "His name is Yellow Feather."

"Yellow Feather?" I asked. And I looked at Breckinridge and said, again, "Yellow Feather?" How bad did I want this room, anyway?

"Yellow Feather," the bald spiritualist continued, "was a great warrior. An Iroquois chief."

"Dead many moons," I said.

"That is correct," he said, ignoring my sarcasm. "If you have no other questions, Mr. Heller, Mr. Breckinridge . . . I will summon Sister Sarah."

"Yeah, I have one more question," I said.

"Yes, Mr. Heller?"

"Do you shave your head?"

Breckinridge kicked me under the table.

Marinelli only smiled. "No. My hair fell out when I was a youth. It was a psychic sign. It signaled my psychosexual awakening."

"Just wondering," I said.

Marinelli closed his eyes, bowed his head slightly. The incense-scented room was an eerie study in shadows and shapes as the wavery candlelight, and a modicum of street-light from the sheer-curtained windows, turned the mundane hotel furnishings into Caligari-like onlookers. Those windows were rattling as the wind crept in over their sills. Maybe our medium wasn't of the flying horn and floating disembodied head variety, but this was a séance all right.

Our host, hands folded, began to hum monotonously.

A door opened and a figure in black and crimson seemed to glide in. She was standing next to me before I knew it, a small, beautiful woman with large, dark unblinking eyes, a pale cameo of a face and full, sensuous lips made scarlet by dabs of lip rouge. Her dark eyebrows, unlike her husband's, were thick and unplucked and somehow the effect was exotic; she was caught up in a rose-scented cloud that banished the sandalwood. She looked like a whore, and she looked like a Madonna.

And, what the hell, I have to tell you: I liked it. There was no sign that my hair was falling out, but I was having a psycho-sexual awakening myself.

Like her husband, she wore a floor-length flowing black robe; but she also wore a hood, lined with blood-red satin. Unlike her husband's robe, hers was not loose, rather it was contoured to her shape, clinging as if wet to a slender, high-breasted figure. Her nipples were erect and looking right back at me. Maybe she wasn't a physical medium, but if I didn't cool off, this table *was* going to rise.

"Good evening, gentle friends," she said, in a small, musical voice; she looked to be about twenty-two. "Please don't get up."

Thanks for that much.

Her husband pulled out the chair reserved for her, and she primly sat. She drew her hands out of the long sleeves of the gown like a surgeon preparing to wash up; she placed her small, delicate hands, the nails of which were long, razor sharp and as red as a gaping wound, flat on the table. The candle wax that had dripped onto the wood was damn near the same color as her nails. This pair was good. They were worth whatever they charged.

"Thank you for your presence," she said. Her hair, what I could see of it under the hood, was jet-black and pulled away from her face; she wore a single, circular gold earring, the one overtly gypsylike touch. "You are Mr. Breckinbridge."

Breckin*bridge*, she said.

But Colonel Breckinridge did not correct her; it isn't polite to correct a psychic.

"You are a police officer," she said to me, smiling as sweetly as a shy schoolgirl.

"That's right," I said. Breckinbridge, Schmeckinbridge, if this babe said she was psychic, she was psychic by me.

"And your name?"

"Nathan Heller," I said. Christ, she smelled good.

"Mr. Heller, will you take my hand?"

Is the Pope Catholic?

She joined hands with me, and squeezed. Yowsah.

"When my companion has induced my trance state," she said, "please clasp hands with Mr. Breckinbridge. And Mr. Breckin- bridge, please clasp hands with Martin. And Martin will take my hand, and the psychic chain will be established. Please do not break the psychic chain."

"I wouldn't dream of it," I said.

Marinelli slowly, pompously, removed the golden, jeweled cross from around his neck. Holding it by its chain, he began to slowly pass it before the great big beautiful brown peepers of his wife.

Wife, hell. She called him "companion," and he introduced her as Sister Sarah Sivella, not Marinelli. If anything, they were common-law. My conscience was clear, thinking the thoughts I was thinking.

He was mumbling something; an incantation, something—it was barely audible. But she seemed to hear it. Her eyes traced the slow, sensual movement of the cross before her, and when Marinelli with his free hand snapped his fingers, *click!*, her eyes shut as tight as yanked-down window shades.

Then he clicked his fingers again and her eyelids rolled up the same way. Those eyes, deep brown and flecked with gold, were open wide in the stare of the dead. Her face seemed to lengthen; her expression was blankly sour. It spooked me. Breckinridge was similarly transfixed.

We both knew this was a bunch of bullshit; but the act was a good one, thanks to its fetching heroine, and we were caught up. We had all joined hands, now; in my right was the smooth delicate hand of the pretty medium, and in my left was Breckinridge's big lawyer-soft paw.

"Who am I speaking to?" Marinelli asked.

"Ugh," she said.

Ugh?

"Chief Yellow Feather—are you with us?"

She nodded. "Yellow Feather here." Her voice was forced down into a male register. It sounded as ridiculous as you're thinking.

I would've laughed, and on reflection did; but at that moment, I just went along with the ride. She smelled good, and I never heard a twenty-two-year-old dame with her nipples poking out of her shirt talk like an Indian before.

"Mr. Breckinbridge," she continued, in the deep mock-male voice. What do you know? Chief Yellow Feather had the name wrong, too. "Spirits say kidnap note was left on windowsill in nursery."

Breckinridge remained unruffled, when I glanced at him, but we both knew that this piece of information had not been released to the general public.

"Is this correct?" Marinelli asked Breckinridge.

"I'm not at liberty to confirm or deny that, sir," the Colonel said, in a stiffly dignified manner that seemed about as silly, under the circumstances, as the voice of Chief Yellow Feather.

"Mr. Breckinbridge, you got note at your office today."

"Note?" Breckinridge asked.

"Kidnap note."

"No notes have been sent to my office." He seemed relieved to be able to say that; it was, as far as I knew, the truth.

"All right," said the girl huffily, in her big-chief voice. "Be at your office tomorrow. Nine in morning."

"That's pretty early."

"Be at office!" The "chief" was firm.

"All right," Breckinridge said, probably just to placate him. Her. Whoever.

Marinelli said, "Chief Yellow Feather—have you received any other spirit messages?"

"Yes. I see name."

"What name do you see?"

"Jafsie."

I asked Marinelli, "Can I ask her a question?"

But Sarah answered. "You may speak to Yellow Feather," she said, in her own voice.

"Yellow Feather, spell that name, please."

"J-A-F-S-I-E." This was intoned in the deep Indian voice.

"Thank you, Chief. Is the baby well?"

She shook her head slowly; her face lost its blankness and became sad.

"A baby's body," she said in her own voice, "will be found on the heights above Hopewell."

Breckinridge looked at me sharply and I at him.

Marinelli snapped his fingers and she jerked awake.

She withdrew her hand from mine; we all let go of each other's hands, sat back, relaxed. We sat quietly in the flickering candlelight, listening to the wind make like a wolf.

"Why did you bring her out of it?" I asked Marinelli.

"I can sense when the psychic strain is too much," he said gravely. "We can arrange another sitting . . ."

"Not at this juncture," Breckinridge said, shifting his chair. "But I would like the address of your church, in Harlem."

"Certainly. Let me write it down for you."

Marinelli rose, disappeared into the darkness.

Sarah looked tired; she slumped; her hands disappeared into her lap.

"Were we successful?" she asked quietly.

"You gave us information, child," Breckinridge said, gently. "Whether it was helpful, well, that would be premature for me to say."

"Do you remember what you said?" I asked her.

She smiled at me, warmly. "I go into a trance, and I say things. Later Martin tells me what I've said."

"I see," I said.

Her hand, under the table, settled on my thigh.

"You have kind eyes, Mr. Heller," she said.

She began to stroke my thigh. I began to levitate again.

"Your eyes," I said, "are very old, for so young a girl."

She continued to stroke my thigh. "I've lived many times, Mr. Heller."

Now she was stroking something else.

"I can tell you've been around," I managed.

"Here's the address," Marinelli said, returning with a scrap of paper for Breckinridge.

Her hand slipped away.

"You can reach us day and night," he said. "We live on the church premises."

"Thank you," Breckinridge said, rising. I kept my place, for the moment. It wasn't *that* dark in the room.

"We, uh, do appreciate you clearing out of this suite," I said. "I'm the one who's going to be using it."

"We *will* be staying the night, you understand," she said. "Or, actually—I will. Martin is going on ahead, by car, shortly, to prepare for weekend services. I'll be going home by train, tomorrow."

She was giving me what I might best describe as a significant look. I'm a detective. I pick up on these things.

"Do you need any expense money?" Breckinridge said.

"No," Marinelli said. "If what we've said proves helpful, we would not be adverse to having our names in the papers. Like any Christian church, we are missionaries, spreading the word."

I got up. "Well, thank you, both. Sorry if I was rude, earlier, Reverend."

"All true believers begin as doubters," he assured me, gesturing us toward the door.

"Safe journey," she told us, and we were in the hall.

We sat in the Dusenberg at the curb for a while.

"What do you make of that?" Breckinridge asked.

"I'm not sure. Those two aren't in the same class as Edgar Cayce, that's for goddamn sure."

Breckinridge nodded. "Marinelli certainly sends out mixed signals—talk of Christianity coming out of a satanic countenance, theological mumbo-jumbo that sounds more pagan than Judeo-Christian."

"Sounds like a promising new religion to me—life after death, and psychosexuality, too."

"But are they con artists?"

"Marinelli obviously is," I said, shrugging. "I'm not sure about the girl."

He nodded. "She seems to be sincere, like Cayce, believing herself to possess psychic powers. But *does* she?"

"I wonder. It's interesting that when she started saying that the kid was dead, he snapped her out of it."

Breckinridge looked grim. "What are you saying?"

"I don't know. I don't know. She knew one detail the general public doesn't. She predicted a couple things—if they come true, I'm going to be suspicious."

"I already *am* suspicious." His hands settled on the steering wheel. "Are you ready?"

"No," I said. "Let me out at the first all-night drugstore."

"Why?"

"Where else am I going to find a package of Sheiks at this time of night?"

"What?"

"Never mind. Have somebody pick me up here around noon tomorrow—at the café on the corner, over there, will be fine."

"What have you got in mind?"

"I'm going to do some poking around on my own," I said.

Breckinridge, more mystified by me than by the séance we'd just witnessed, let me out at a drugstore. I made my purchase, walked back to the old four-story brick hotel and waited for Marinelli to leave.

Hoping to hell it hadn't been some ghost feeling me up under the table.

Chapter 9

My driver was a ruddy, blond, good-natured man of perhaps thirty named Willis Dixon, one of three patrolmen under the command of Hopewell Police Chief Harry Wolfe. Dixon wore a black leather jacket with a badge pinned on, a matching cap and khakis, with a black tie snugged crisply in place. A neat-looking uniform, for a local cop, but a distant second to the blue and pink costumes of the New Jersey State Police chorus boys.

"We been reduced to chauffeurin' and other shit work," Dixon had told me pleasantly, when he picked me up at precisely noon at the Princeton Café. I bought him lunch before we left, and heard all about how Colonel Schwarzkopf had frozen out Chief Wolfe and his staff—the first cops on the scene, after the kidnapping—from the inner circle of the investigation.

Right now we were rolling along a gravel road, cutting through the ominously lonely Sourland Hills countryside, snarled as it was with underbrush that thickened on either side into heavy, rugged, seemingly impenetrable woods.

"I'm going to pull over for a minute," Dixon said. He had

apple cheeks and a space between his front teeth, a moronic countenance that probably served him well as a cop; his eyes were dark
and shrewd, and that's what counted.

"Why's that, Willis?"

We'd been on a first-name basis ever since I bought him lunch.

"It ain't to take a leak," he said, and grinned in his knowing
dumb-ass way. "I think we'll find something that just might interest
you." He pronounced it "inner rest," which was precisely the kind
of rest I could've used.

As he pulled over, I realized the undergrowth had been cleared
up ahead, to make way for a sloping, landscaped lawn. We'd come
upon the occasional farmhouse or shack, along the way; but nothing
like this. Here, in the middle of this overgrown but desolate landscape, was what at first glance seemed a mansion: a gray three-
story frame building with a white-pillared porch in front of which
evergreens perched like obedient pets. A beautiful structure, really,
of modern vintage, despite its modified Southern plantation motif.

We got out of the unmarked car and walked toward the big
building, which on closer look resembled a hotel more than a private
residence, but there were no signs to identify it as such or to attract
business.

And it was obviously empty—though apparently such had not
been the case for long. Several of its windows had been broken out,
and it wore a general air of disrepair and neglect. Which was
puzzling in itself: why a building of this size and worth would be
abandoned made no sense at all. Had a bank foreclosed here,
there'd have been at least minimal upkeep.

"Come around back," Dixon said; he had dug a chaw of tobacco out of his jacket pocket and took a healthy bite.

Leaves and twigs under the thin frozen layer of snow crunched
under our feet as we climbed the gently sloping ground, and circled
around, to approach the rear of the building.

"Holy shit," I said.

Dixon grinned at me, chewing his tobacco vigorously. "Pretty
sight, ain't it?"

The whole ass-end of the big building was blown out; two large
barnlike double-doors, on the ground floor, had been torn away—
one was missing entirely, another hung by a thread and a prayer.

On the lower, built-up basement level, the wood walls between brick support posts had also been blown out. Lumber and refuse were piled behind the building to form a misshapen hill half as wide as the structure itself and a third as tall.

"Must have been one hell of an explosion," I said.

"Must have been one hell of a still," Dixon said. He spat tobacco juice.

"Is that what this place was? A moonshine distillery?"

"No! That was just a little part of the operation."

I pushed my hat back, scratched my head; the cold air was nipping at me, and seemed as impatient as I was. "Well, it looks like a hotel. What was it, a roadhouse?"

"Kee-rect, Nate." He smiled brownly. "Not your regulation roadhouse that dots the back roads of our beautiful land, from sea to shinin' sea, the kind designed to pull in your tired businessmen or your thirsty pampered college kids. No sir. And it wasn't for the Hopewell clientele, neither."

"Willis—what the hell was this place?"

He beamed at me; a hick taking great pride in educating a city slicker. "A gangster hideaway, Nate. Where all the big shots outa New York and your other major metropolitan areas gathered to enjoy their own company in their own private whoopee parties."

"Jesus. Including Chicago?"

He nodded. "I spotted Cook County plates 'round these parts many a time."

"Why didn't you ever bust this place? Oh. Sorry."

He waved a dismissive hand. "No, no. It ain't that. It's not that I wouldn't taken a taste if it was offered me. But this is not our jurisdiction. It's outside of city limits."

"Whose jurisdiction is it? Oh. Sure—the state police."

He nodded again. "Schwarzkopf's little girls, is right." He put his hands on his hips, spat an elegant brown stream into the pile of rubble. "Think of it, Nate. Some of the biggest wing-dings imaginable, with Broadway entertainers and whores so pretty they qualify as table food. Gamblin' and orgies and it all took place right inside there, for the sole enjoyment of our nation's mob chieftains."

Capone would have been here. More than once. Just a few miles from the Lindbergh estate.

Dixon began to wander, hands on hips. "Can you picture it? How could a night of revelry pass by without those big shots making some passin' reference to the famous Lindy and his family, so close by? I'll lay you twenty to one that many a night they passed the time tossin' around how much easy dough there was that could be had by grabbing that famous kid."

"But they never went through with it," I said, thinking aloud. "It just stayed idle speculation, fun after-dinner talk, because the estate was *too* close. Suspicion would point in their direction."

"Right! But then this big old still blew to hell and back, and a guy was killed in the explosion, one of them that ran it, and the place was closed down."

"So protecting the roadhouse was no longer necessary."

"Right-o," Dixon said. "And since there never was an arrest or raid or anything out here, what sort of trail was there for anybody to follow?"

"Somebody should've tried," I said. The wind sighed, rustling the trees. "Somebody should be trying right now. . . ."

A few minutes later, we were pulling into the Lindbergh estate. As we drove around by the command-post garage, Dixon said, "Well, I'll be damned—look who it is!"

He pointed to a trio of men standing outside the garage, milling about with expressions of impatience. One of the men was older and clearly the leader, albeit an unlikely one: a short, round bald man in a rumpled brown topcoat, a straw fedora in one hand, with which he was slapping his thigh. White-mustached, lumpy-faced, he was smoking a corncob pipe and looked like a gentleman farmer, although not much of one—gentleman *or* farmer. His two associates were taller and younger, and better dressed, but not much; they looked like plainclothes cops, backwoods variety.

Dixon pulled in next to another of several cars parked in the outer cement apron and turned the engine off, but left his hands on the wheel. His expression seemed weirdly glazed.

"That's the Old Fox himself," he said.

"Old Fox?"

"Ellis Parker. Don't tell me you never heard of him."

I'd heard of him, all right. That fat, bald, rumpled, apparent nonentity was Ellis Parker, a.k.a. the Old Fox, a.k.a. the Cornfield Sherlock, a.k.a. the Small-Town Detective with the Worldwide Reputation. Parker was chief of detectives of some county or other in New Jersey—I didn't remember where—but he was widely known as one of the nation's top investigators, and frequently was brought in on cases in East Coast cities larger than his own tiny Mount Holly, wherever the hell that was.

I'd read of many of his cases; he was written up in magazines and in the papers, and there were books about him. How at Fort Dix he discovered who murdered a soldier by investigating the fellow soldier (one of a hundred-plus uniformed suspects) who had the best, most complete alibi; how he discovered that a soaking-wet corpse had been treated at a tannery to fool the medical examiner about time of death; how he tracked a homicidal mulatto with a sweet tooth by alerting every restaurant in his own and neighboring counties to be on the lookout for "a pudding-loving colored boy."

"I suppose it was natural he'd show up around here," I said. "This case could use a mind like his."

"Twenty to one Schwarzkopf won't agree with you," Dixon said, sourly. He shook his head, admiringly. "I've had an application in over at Burlington County for over two years, now. There's a hell of a waiting list, though."

"You ever meet the old boy?"

"Sure! Burlington is the adjacent county."

"Really. Why don't you introduce me, then, Willis?"

A few moments later we'd ambled over to Parker, who nodded at Willis.

"Constable Dixon," Parker said. He seemed to force a smile as he offered a hand, which Willis shook. "How the hell are you, son?" His voice was as rough-hewn as his appearance; his face was stubbled with white, his eyes were sleepy and blue and anything but piercing; his tie was food-stained and floated several inches below the notch of his collar. Sherlock Holmes posing as his own dim-witted Watson.

"Fine, Chief Parker. This is Nate Heller."

Something in the eyes came to life. "The Chicago feller. The Capone theorist."

I grinned and shook the hand he thrust forward. "Well, nobody ever accused me of being any kind of theorist before, Chief. Where did you hear my name?"

He sidled up close to me; he smelled like pipe tobacco—foul pipe tobacco. He slipped a fatherly arm around my shoulder. "I have my confidants in that horse's ass Schwarzkopf's camp."

"Do tell."

"I hear you're the boy who has stood up to that asshole of creation, Welch."

"Well, that's true."

"I hear you suggested that he kiss your behind."

"Words to that effect."

He laughed heartily—he apparently liked subtle humor—and patted me on the back. "Allow me to introduce my deputies."

He did. I don't remember their names.

"Maybe one of these days Constable Dixon here will come work for me," Parker said, finally relinquishing my shoulder.

Dixon lit up like an electric bulb. "I'd like that, sir."

"You wouldn't happen to have any pull with the Colonel, would you, son?"

"Schwarzkopf?" Dixon asked.

"Hell's bells, no! Not that asshole. *Lindbergh!* We've been cooling our heels for two hours, waiting to see Lindy. Schwarzkopf's giving me the goddamn runaround."

I raised a hand. "Let me see what I can do."

Parker's lumpy face broke apart in a smile. "That's goddamn white of you, son."

I went inside, through the servants' sitting room and then the kitchen, where I saw Betty Gow and Elsie and Ollie Whately in passing, as well as Welch and several of Schwarzkopf's upper echelon lounging having coffee and sandwiches. The living room was empty, but for the little dog Wahgoosh, who barked at me as usual, and I growled back at him. Rosner wasn't around, either, his chair outside the study empty but for yesterday's folded-up racing form.

I knocked on the study door. "It's Heller, Slim."

"Come in, Nate," Lindbergh said, and I did.

"I hear you stayed over in Princeton last night," he said, looking up from some mail he'd been reading, material the troopers had culled from the hundreds of letters that had come in today.

"Yeah, I was able to, uh, get into that room a day early."

He nodded noncommittally, only half-listening. "Henry went into the city, to his office, early this morning. He said he felt these spiritualist people were probably charlatans."

"Yeah, probably," I said, and sat down. "Where's Rosner?"

"Pursuing some underworld leads in New York City, today."

Cops and robbers, with the robber playing cop.

"Slim—there's somebody outside you ought to give a few minutes to."

"Who would that be?"

"Ellis Parker."

Lindbergh nodded, blankly. I might have said Santa Claus or Joe Blow.

"Surely you've heard of him," I said.

"Yes. He's very well known." He paused. He sighed. "If you think I should see him, I will."

"Okay. Slim—are you holding up okay?"

"I'm fine."

"You getting any sleep? You look like hell."

He smiled thinly. "It's nice to have somebody around who isn't afraid to tell me the truth. Yes, I am getting some sleep. Some."

"Okay. I'm not your nursemaid or anything. But if you're going to be the guy making the key decisions, you got to be on top of things."

"I know."

"Good. I'll bring Parker around."

Minutes later, I was ushering Parker in, and Lindbergh rose and the men exchanged greetings and admiration. Then everybody settled into their chairs, Parker leaning forward. He had the foul-smelling corncob pipe going, held in one hand.

"Colonel Lindbergh, I've been a detective for over forty years. I've investigated twenty thousand cases, including over three hundred homicides. All but twelve of those homicide cases wound up in convictions."

Lindbergh's face was impassive; but his eyes tensed, just barely, at the mention of the word "homicide."

Parker inserted the pipe in his tight mouth; he looked a little

like Popeye the Sailor. "I've offered my services to Colonel Schwarzkopf, but have been rudely rebuffed—and as you may know I'm
on the outs with Governor Moore. So coming aboard in an official
capacity hasn't been open to me. But I couldn't sit idly by, just
one county away, and not offer you my services. I'd like to be of
help to you, sir."

Lindbergh smiled politely. "That's kind of you, Chief Parker.
But I have to say I'm satisfied with the way Colonel Schwarzkopf
is handling the matter."

Parker grimaced. "No offense meant to you, Colonel, but that
jackass has done every damn thing wrong, in this case, from A to
Z. His failure to make a thorough search of the entire community
within a wide radius of your estate is frankly, sir, shameful, inex-
cusable."

Lindbergh said nothing.

"Ideally, I would like to head up the team of detectives in
charge of the case—a mixture of my own boys and state troopers.
But I'm available strictly as a consultant, if that's your pleasure."

Lindbergh said nothing. His eyes were like stones.

Parker shifted uncomfortably in his seat.

Then Lindbergh spoke. His voice was as expressionless and
unemotional as a telephone operator's. "I have great respect for
your achievements, Chief Parker. But I've already read and heard
some of your opinions about this case, in the papers and on the
radio. And I will have no truck with cheap shots, second-guessing
and theorizing."

"Colonel Lindbergh, my only concern is to offer my help in
your time of . . ."

Lindbergh raised a hand in a stop motion. "I won't have police
officers from every which where tripping over themselves, seeking
their own glory at the possible expense of my son's life. Colonel
Schwarzkopf and I have the situation in hand. Good day to you,
sir."

"Colonel Lindbergh . . ."

"Thank you for coming."

Parker rose; his neck was red with anger, but he merely nodded
to Lindbergh and went out.

I stayed behind.

"That guy is one of the most brilliant detectives alive," I said. "And your boy Schwarzkopf is a goddamn department-store floor-walker!"

"Nate," Lindbergh said tersely, his hands flat on his desk, "Ellis Parker is accustomed to getting the lion's share of the lime-light—he's done remarkable work in the past, but he's dazzled by his own publicity."

"I'm sure he is jealous of Schwarzkopf," I said with a shrug. "But a guy like that, who is a great detective by anybody's yardstick, ought to be turned loose on a major crime like this—particularly when it's in his own backyard, for Christ's sake. It only makes sense!"

"No," Lindbergh said.

I looked at him.

"Okay," I said.

I went out. Lindy wanted to hear the truth from me, it seemed, but didn't necessarily want to pay it any heed.

I caught up with Parker outside, just as he was about to climb into a Burlington County police car.

"I'm sorry I couldn't be more help," I said. "I'd like to have had you involved."

"Who says I'm not going to be?" he said, one foot on the running board. And he winked at me.

The dust of Parker's Ford on the dirt lane hadn't settled when Breckinridge's familiar Dusenberg pulled in. The lawyer looked grayer than usual as he climbed down from his fancy car and came straight over to me. He took me by the arm, took me aside.

"Heller," he said. "What did you do last night?"

"It wouldn't be gentlemanly to say."

"You spent the night with that medium, didn't you?"

I shrugged. "Slim said I was the resident spook chaser. Who else are you going to get to lay a ghost?"

He grabbed me by one arm. Almost shook me. The unflappable Breckinridge was definitely flapped. "What did she have to say?"

Actually, she hadn't said much at all. She'd moaned a good deal and even screamed a couple times. But I wasn't about to share my memorable evening with Sister Sarah with Breckinridge. I'm just not that kind of guy.

Besides, what would a stuffed shirt like Breckinridge know about a night of wild passion with a woman whose pale flesh glowed in the half-light of a flickering candle, who let me ride her and who rode me, till I was raw and sweating and dead from exhaustion. Sister Sarah could make a ghost out of any man.

But we hadn't talked. I knew no more about her from spending the night with her than I did after that séance. Including going through her purse and her suitcases and other personal belongings, after she went to sleep.

"Hey, pal," I said indignantly, "I don't kiss and tell, okay?"

"She said a letter would come today. To my office."

"Yeah, so?"

"This came by mail, to my office," he said grimly, "this morning."

He took an envelope out of his pocket, hastily opened it and held the letter up for me to see.

Specifically, he showed me the signature: blue and red interlocking circles with three holes.

Chapter 10

The letter Breckinridge received included a brief note telling the attorney to "handle inclosed letter to Col. Lindbergh." The letter itself said the following:

> Dear Sir: Did you recieve ouer letter from
> March 4. We sent the mail in one off the letter
> pox near Burro Hall—Brooklyn. We know
> Police interfere with your privatmail; how can
> we come to any arrangements this way.
> In the future we will send ouer letters to
> Mr. Breckenbridge at 25 Broadway. We belive
> Polise captured our letter and dit note
> forwarded to you. We will note accept
> any go-between from your seid. We will
> arrange this latter. There is no worry
> about the Boy. He is very well and will be
> feed according to the diet. Best dank for
> Information about it. We are interested to send
> your Boy back in gud Health.

Below this, again labeled "singnature," were the distinctive blue and red circles with trio of small holes. On the reverse the letter continued:

> Is it nessisery to make a world's affair out off
> it, or to get your Boy back as soon as possible.
> Why did you ingnore ouer letter which we
> left in the room? The baby would be back
> long ago. You would note get any result
> from Police, becauce this Kidnaping was
> planed for a year allredy. But we was afraid,
> the boy would not be strong enough.
> Ouer ransom was made out for 50.000 $
> but now we have to put another lady to it and
> propperly have to hold the baby longer as we
> expectet so it will be 70.000 $.
> 20000 in 50 $ bills 25000 in 24 $ bills 15000
> in 10 $ bills 10000 in 5 $ bill. We warn you again
> not to mark any bills or take them from one serial
> No. We will inform you latter how to deliver
> the mony, but not befor
> the Police is out of this cace and the
> pappers are quiet.
> Please get a short notice aboud this letter in the
> New-York American.

Frank J. Wilson squinted behind his round black-framed glasses as he read the note, and read it again.

We were in Lindbergh's study, Lindy, Breckinridge, Schwarzkopf, Wilson and myself. Lindbergh had rejected my suggestions to make the New York cops and J. Edgar's boys aware of this new communiqué; but he did agree to call in Treasury Agent Wilson.

"I think the letter is encouraging," Lindbergh said to Wilson, "don't you?"

"Encouraging?" Wilson asked. He was seated across from Lindbergh. I was seated next to Wilson; Breckinridge and Schwarzkopf were standing on either side of Lindy like mismatched bookends.

"My son is in good health," Lindbergh said brightly, "and they want to keep him that way. They're following the diet . . ."

"You take these people at their *word*?"

"I have no reason not to," Lindbergh said. "I'm reluctant to have you involved in this at all, Agent Wilson. They make clear that if I hadn't called the police in, at the start, I might well have Charlie back in his mother's arms, this very minute."

Wilson didn't bother discussing that. He knew there was no point.

"They apparently think the police intercepted the previous letter," Schwarzkopf pointed out, needlessly.

Breckinridge nodded. "Maybe we've clamped down the lid on the press *too* tight. If we'd let it be known the second note had been received . . ."

"You're trying to second-guess lunatics," I said. "They warn you not to let anything out to the press, then wonder why you haven't let 'em know you got their second letter!"

Wilson was still looking at the note. "As before, the easy words are misspelled, and the more difficult words are frequently correctly spelled."

"It's obviously a genuine communication from the kidnappers," Lindbergh said.

"The unique signature symbol is present," Wilson agreed. "It makes reference to the letter left in the nursery, as well."

Breckinridge came around the desk and pointed to a specific line as Wilson studied the letter.

"That sentence bothers me," Breckinridge said. " 'We will not accept any go-between from your side.' "

"It's straightforward enough," I offered. "It's a rejection of Rosner and his cronies Spitale and Bitz."

"Perhaps we should publish a message in the press," the attorney said, "stating that we're open to following any other methods that the kidnappers might suggest. Anything that will insure a safe return of the boy."

"That sounds reasonable," Lindbergh said.

Wilson seemed to be ignoring all this. He gently returned the letter to the desktop, and removed a small notebook and stubby pencil from his suit coat pocket.

He said, "This psychic who predicted that Colonel Breckin-ridge would receive a letter today . . . her name is Sivella?"

"Sister Sarah Sivella," I said. "Her husband's name is Martin Marinelli."

He wrote that down; from my notebook, I gave him the address of the church in Harlem, and he wrote that down, too.

"They knew about the note on the windowsill, as well," Wilson said.

"Yes," I said.

"On the other hand," Wilson continued, "they've been hang-ing out with reporters for days. They may have gathered some information that way."

"None of the reporters, to our knowledge," Lindbergh said, "knew that windowsill detail."

"There's one other thing," I said. "One damning little item."

All eyes were on me.

"Sarah Sivella consistently referred to Colonel Breckinridge as 'Mr. Breckin*bridge*,' at the séance last night. And that is exactly how he is referred to in that letter."

It was like I'd struck everybody in the room with a board.

Wilson broke the stunned silence: "What else did she say?"

"Some of it was gibberish," I said, shrugging. We hadn't men-tioned to Lindbergh the prediction that the baby's body would be found.

Then, suddenly, Lindbergh stood. "Thank you for coming by, Agent Wilson."

Wilson, disconcerted by this quick dismissal, stood and said, "Thank you for sharing this new information with me, Colonel."

"I want you to stay away from those spiritualists," Lindbergh told him. It sounded like an order.

"Pardon me?" Wilson asked, hollowly.

"Those spiritualists. If they're legitimate, and they may well be—extrasensory perception is very real, you know, Agent Wil-son—I don't want them harassed. If they in fact are a part of the kidnap gang, I don't want my son's welfare put at risk by police action. These notes make it clear that I'm to keep the police out of this, if I hope to get my boy back alive and well. And Agent Wilson—I intend to do just that."

Lindbergh nodded curtly, and Wilson knew the meeting was over.

I walked him out to his car. Breckinridge and Schwarzkopf stayed behind with Lindy—which was fine with me. I wanted Wilson's ear privately.

We stood in the cold and chatted sotto voce, just briefly. I told him about the gangland roadhouse Dixon had shown me and he found that of great interest.

"You know Pat O'Rourke, from Chicago, don't you, Heller?" Wilson asked.

"Of course," I said. "Damn good man."

"He's working with me in New York, now," Wilson said. "I'm going to assign him to infiltrate that spiritualist church in Harlem. We'll find out why these 'spirits' know so much about this damn kidnapping."

"O'Rourke's an excellent choice," I said.

O'Rourke had gone undercover for three months in the Capone organization when Eliot, Irey and Wilson were putting their case together. He was a good bet to pick up on any Capone connection between Marinelli and his congregation.

"How's the search for Bob Conroy coming?" I asked.

"That son of a bitch has dropped off the face of the earth," Wilson said glumly.

"Start dragging the lakes," I said.

He nodded, sighed, said, "Heller—whatever differences we may have had, let me say this: I appreciate what you're doing. That is, keeping me informed, when otherwise I'd be frozen out."

"Swell. How about angling me a break on my taxes this year?"

"Screw you," Wilson said, good-naturedly, and got in his black Ford and headed back to New York.

Schwarzkopf approached me, as I stood watching Wilson's dust.

He said, "There's an interrogation you should sit in on."

"Really," I said. "I'm beginning to enjoy this new spirit of cooperation."

Several snazzy troopers and rumpled, potbellied Inspector Welch were standing in the servants' sitting room. Seated in a chair that had been dragged out into the middle of the braided-rug-covered floor was a pretty, pleasantly plump girl in her twenties, wearing her maid's black uniform with white lace apron. Her hair was short and brownish blonde, her eyes brown and flitting, her face round, her front teeth protruding slightly, chipmunk-cute. She had her hands in her lap, playing with a white hanky.

Seated just behind her was a male police stenographer, plainclothes, fingers poised over keys.

"Miss Sharpe," Schwarzkopf said, "we need to take a statement from you."

"I've given you a statement," she said, imperiously. Or maybe it was just her English accent.

"We'd just like to clear up a few details."

She pursed her lips, raised her chin and replied in a snippy schoolgirl fashion. "Why are you so interested in my personal life? Why don't you mind your own business and get on with the job of finding these kidnappers?"

Her manner was cold and defiant, but it seemed at least partly a mask: her eyes and her hands moved ceaselessly. She was as nervous as a wife with one lover in the closet, another under the bed and hubby in the hall.

Inspector Welch took over. "Look, sister. We're just doing our job. Don't make it tough on yourself. Surely a cute kid like you don't have anything to hide?"

Welch was trying to be nice, but it came off like a threat.

"Don't you bully me," she said.

Welch rolled his eyes at Schwarzkopf, who said, "All of the other servants at the Morrow home have been cooperative. Why are you so difficult, Miss Sharpe?"

"I resent being questioned, and I am cooperating—but only because I have no choice!"

Her defiance was an amazing thing to see; but I wasn't fooled. Behind the strength was weakness, and fear.

Schwarzkopf, almost pleading, said, "Don't you want to help Mr. and Mrs. Lindbergh get their baby back?"

She lowered her head and nodded. Sighed. "Go ahead, then. Ask your questions."

Welch nodded to the stenographer to start, then said, "State your name and age, please, and place of birth."

"My name is Violet Sharpe. I was born in England in 1904 in Berkshire. About two and a half years ago, I went from England to Canada. I stayed there about nine months and moved to New York."

"And went to work for the Morrows?"

"Well, I registered at Hutchinson's Employment Agency on Madison Avenue, and was interviewed there for Mrs. Morrow, and received a position as maid, which I still occupy."

"Have you made any friends, male or female, in New York, or New Jersey?"

"No. None."

She was too good-looking a girl for that to ring true.

Exasperation distorted the inspector's voice. "Since the time that you arrived in New York from Canada, you've been out in company of *no* friends, male or female?"

"No. I have nobody here other than my sister, Emily."

"Where does she reside?"

"In Englewood. A friend of the Morrows employs her."

Welch moved to the other side of her. He tried again. "Have you at any time since your arrival in this country been to *any* social functions, public gatherings, theater, dinners, or dance, with *any* man or woman?"

She paused.

Then she said, "Yes."

Welch, with studied sarcasm, said, "Why don't you tell us about it, then, Miss Sharpe?"

"My sister and I were walking through the village of Englewood on a Sunday afternoon . . ."

"What Sunday afternoon?"

"February twenty-eighth."

"Of this year?"

"Of this year. We were walking along when a man passed us on Lydecker Street in an automobile and waved his hand at us. I mistook him for one of the employees at the Morrows', and waved back. He stopped his car and I went over to him, but realized my error—explained that I had taken him for someone else."

"What did he say?"

"He said, 'That's all right, where are you going?' And I said,

'Just to the village.' He invited my sister and myself to ride there in his car, which we did. During the ride we had a friendly conversation and the gentleman said he'd like to take me to the movies some night, if I would like to go."

"What did you say?"

"I said okay."

She was a pretty easy pickup for a girl who'd been here for years without making a single male or female friend.

"And what did he say?"

"He asked for my phone number and I gave it to him."

"The phone number of the Morrow house, you mean?"

"Yes. He wanted to know who he should ask for when he called, and I told him to ask for Violet."

"Did he call?"

She nodded. "At about ten minutes of eight on the evening of March first."

The day of the kidnapping.

"What did he say?"

"He asked if I would care to go out with him that evening. I said I would, but that I wouldn't be ready for a while, as I hadn't yet finished with serving dinner. Before long, he came to the back door of the pantry of the Morrow house."

"What did you do?"

"I got my hat and coat and went out. He had another couple with him, who I'd never seen before. The four of us went to a movie house in Englewood and after the show, he drove me back to the Morrow home. It was then, I think, eleven P.M."

"Have you seen your date since?"

"No. I made a second date with him, for March six, but I couldn't get away from the house. I haven't spoken to him or seen him, since then."

Schwarzkopf stepped in and smiled warmly. "You're doing fine, Miss Sharpe. Just fine. Now, if you can just fill in a few blanks . . ."

She turned snippy again. "What sort of blanks?"

"Names would be a good start."

"I told you before! I don't remember any names."

"You don't remember the name of your date? You went for a

ride with him on that Sunday afternoon, spent an entire evening with him . . ."

"I can't remember."

"Look," Welch said, "we know you're nervous. Just relax and the name will come to you."

"I am *not* nervous, and I can't remember his bloody name!"

"What about the other couple?" Schwarzkopf asked. "Can you remember who they were?"

She cocked her head and smiled with tight sarcasm. "No. I can't remember their names, either."

"You were out with these people a little over a week ago," Welch said, "and you can't remember their goddamn names?"

The steno paused, wondering whether to record "goddamn."

Violet folded her arms across her chest, and her chin was raised high; but she was trembling. And she didn't dignify Welch's badgering with a reply.

"What movie did you see, Violet?" I asked.

Welch and Schwarzkopf looked at me, a little surprised that I'd get into this.

"Who are you?" she asked.

"My name's Heller. I'm a police officer, like the rest of these men."

"You have no business prying into my private life. None whatsoever!"

"Take it easy," I said. "Just tell us what the movie was about. Something, anything, about the movie you saw—the actors in it, anything."

Red Johnson had passed a similar test with flying colors.

But Violet Sharpe said nothing.

"What was the name of the theater?" I asked.

"It was in Englewood. That's all I know."

Welch and Schwarzkopf looked at me and I shrugged. I wasn't doing any better than they were.

"Thank you, Miss Sharpe," Schwarzkopf said. And to Welch, he said, "Send her back to Englewood."

Schwarzkopf left, and I went along, following him back into the bustling garage command post.

"I have half a mind to turn her over to Welch," Schwarzkopf said, "and let him work his magic on her."

"If you do that," I said, "you do have half a mind."

"What would you suggest?"

"No rubber-hose technique—just some in-depth, sustained questioning. She was frustrating to interrogate, I'll grant you, but you shook her loose when we'd barely begun."

Schwarzkopf stopped in his tracks; sighed. "She's one of Mrs. Morrow's favorite maids. We push her too hard, we'll get in trouble with the Morrows."

"So fucking what?"

Schwarzkopf made a face. "If we get in trouble with the Morrows, we'll get in trouble with Colonel Lindbergh."

"Hook her up to a lie detector, then. Hell, hook up all the Lindbergh servants, and all the Morrow servants, too."

"Don't you think I've thought of that? Colonel Lindbergh won't have it. It's an invasion of privacy, and an insult, to his employees, he says."

Half an hour later, Constable Willis Dixon of the Hopewell P.D. showed up, grinning. He reported to Schwarzkopf.

"Some interesting items in that maid's room," he said, with his gap-toothed grin.

So Schwarzkopf had sent Dixon, not his own men, to do a search of Violet's room at Englewood, while she was here being questioned. Schwarzkopf was smart, in his weasel way: why get his own people in trouble, if the Morrows got owly about harassment of their favorite servant?

"First of all," Dixon said, "the servants over there say Violet's been havin' an affair with an older man—a butler, they say. I figure it's this guy Septimus Banks."

"Who's that?" I asked.

"The Morrows' head butler," Schwarzkopf explained. "History of drunkenness."

"Anyway, I sure found some good stuff in her room, gents," Dixon said. "A handwritten book of dirty stories. An address book with twenty-six names. And a savings book on a New York City bank."

"You didn't take any of these with you, did you?" Schwarzkopf asked, anxiously.

"No! But I did do some browsing. You know, Violet makes a hundred bucks a month, and's been working less than two years. And I was told she sends a good chunk of her pay home to her folks in Great Britain."

"So?" I asked.

"So," Dixon asked in return, "why does she have almost two grand in her savings account?"

Chapter 11

Bonfires burned orangely against the night, flames fighting the icy wind, kindled by troopers keeping vigil on the periphery of the Lindbergh estate.

Inside the command-post garage, two members of the New Jersey State Police were keeping vigil with a deck of cards. The two troopers—a kid named Harrison and a guy about thirty named Peters—had joined Constable Dixon and myself for a quiet game of poker. At a little after midnight, the rest of the skeleton crew of troopers were stretched out and snoring on army cots.

The only guy on duty was a fellow named Smith who was on the switchboard; but he was slumped and sleeping, too. The only calls that came through were those directed to the troopers themselves; Lindbergh had rejected Schwarzkopf's request that calls to the house be routed here first for monitoring purposes. Every call, crank or otherwise, from anybody savvy enough to wrangle the unlisted number of the Hopewell estate, went straight to the phones inside—one on Lindy's desk, another in the hallway, another upstairs (though at night the latter was disconnected).

Once Inspector Welch had answered the hall phone and Lindbergh snapped at him, "What the hell are you doing?"

And it was fucking rare that Lindbergh cursed.

"It rang and I answered it," Welch had said.

Lindbergh's expression and tone rivaled the weather in coldness. "I want it understood very clearly, and right now, that neither you nor any other policeman is to touch that phone for any reason. You are here through my courtesy and I ask you not to interfere with my business."

On the other hand, Mickey Rosner, pride of New York's underworld, frequently answered the phone and had full access to it.

Dixon, the two troopers and I were sitting at one of the tables where mail was sorted; bags of the stuff were crowded up against the wall behind us, like Moran's men in that Clark Street garage where Capone held his St. Valentine's Day dance. The picnic-type table was littered with nickels and dimes and quarters. The majority were piled before me. It was my deal.

"Black Maria," I said, dealing them down.

"What the hell is Black Maria?" Peters wanted to know. A chain-smoker, he was a brown-haired, rosy-cheeked guy whose eyebrows were almost always knit, as if he were suspicious people smarter than him were taking advantage. Which they often were.

"Seven card stud," I said. "High spade in the hole splits the pot."

"Oh," Peters said, and sucked in some smoke.

Dixon seemed to know the game and, from the forced poker face he maintained glancing at his two hole cards, probably had the ace of spades down. Harrison was the youngest man at the table and he was just playing, and losing, without comment.

I had barely finished the deal when Colonel Breckinridge came bustling in. The usually dignity-personified Breckinridge was wearing a plaid dressing robe and in stocking feet, legs bare and white and hairy.

"Heller," he said, relieved. "You're still here."

Normally I was gone by nine at night, heading over to Princeton in the flivver Lindy loaned me. I had hung around tonight to take money from these eastern hick cops.

"Yeah," I said, checking my two hole cards. Queen of spades. All right. "What do you need?"

"You," he said, and grabbed me roughly by the arm and pulled me away from the table.

"Hey!" I said, cards spilling from my hands.

"Come along," he said, and I was following him back into the house, leaving the cards and my money behind.

"I was winning," I said, indignantly. "I must have been up three bucks . . ."

"Never mind that," he said. "I need you to be Colonel Lindbergh."

"What?"

Breckinridge led me to the hall phone outside the study. The receiver was off the hook.

"There's an elderly fellow named Dr. John Condon on the line," he said. "Claims he's received a letter addressed to him, with an enclosure addressed to Colonel Lindbergh."

"So?" Calls like this came in all the time.

"Dr. Condon says he doesn't know if there's anything to it—the letter may be from a hoaxer or a crank; but recently he sent a letter to the Bronx *Home News* offering a one-thousand-dollar reward to anyone who returned little Charlie safely. And they printed the letter, and he thinks this may be an answer to that."

"What the hell is the Bronx *Home News*? Sounds like some bush-league suburban rag."

Breckinridge shrugged. "It is."

"Then it's not very likely the kidnappers would've seen his letter, there."

"I know—but this man is no crank—he's a professor at Fordham University. At least he says he is—and the credentials and degrees he reeled off sound legitimate."

I made a farting sound with my lips.

"But," Breckinridge continued, "he refuses to speak further unless he's speaking to Colonel Lindbergh himself—who I'm not *about* to disturb . . . Charles has only begun sleeping again, these last few nights."

"Oh. Well, fine. Sure, I'll play Lindy."

Breckinridge smiled. "Thanks, Heller. You know the Colonel wants every lead, every call, taken seriously."

"Sure," I said, picking up the receiver. Queen of spades down. Damn! "This is Colonel Lindbergh. What is it?"

"Ah, Colonel! I'm so relieved! I've just received a letter, which may be of importance to you."

His voice was well modulated but blustery.

"Do they usually deliver your mail at midnight, Professor?"

"I didn't get home until ten—I had classes today. I was sorting through perhaps twenty pieces of correspondence when I came upon this one. Shall I read it?"

"Please, Professor."

He continued in a declamatory style. "It says—and I must make allowances for misspellings and poor syntax—'Dear Sir: If you are willing to act as go-between in Lindbergh case please follow strictly instruction. Hand enclosed letter personally to Mr. Lindbergh. It will explain everything. Don't tell anyone about it. As soon we find out the press or police is notified, everything are cancel and it will be a further delay.' Atrocious spelling!"

"Is there more?"

"Yes."

"Well, Professor, you can flunk the guy later. Finish reading the thing, please."

"Certainly. 'After you get the money from Mr. Lindbergh, put these three words in the New York *American:* Money is ready.' "

I covered the mouthpiece and spoke to Breckinridge. "I think this old boy's just after some easy dough."

" 'After that we will give you further instruction,' " Condon continued. " 'Don't be afraid, we are not out for your one thousand—keep it.' That's a reference to the one thousand dollars I offered for the baby's safe return, in my letter to the Bronx *Home News*. I wish I could have offered more, but it was all I could scrape together in my hope that a loving mother might regain her child."

"You're too generous," I said, stifling a yawn.

" 'Only act strictly,' " he went on. " 'Be at home every night between six and twelve—by this time you will hear from us.' That last isn't quite clear."

"How is it signed?"

"With the mark of the Mafia!"

Right.

"Is that it, Professor?"

"Well, the letter is postmarked Station T, New York City; it came in a long, plain, white envelope. Inside is a smaller envelope, also plain white, which says: 'Dear Sir: Please hand enclosed letter to Colonel Lindbergh. It is in Mr. Lindbergh's interest not to notify the police.' I did not open this enclosure, sir."

Pompous ass.

"Well, open it and read it to me."

Like a sound effect on a radio program, the tearing of the envelope found its way to me over the phone.

" 'Dear Sir,' " he read, " 'Mr. Condon may act as go-between. You may give him the seventy thousand dollars.' "

I perked up a little: the seventy-thousand figure was correct—it had been fifty, but the most recent note had raised it.

" 'Make one packet,' " he said. " 'The size will be about . . .' There is a drawing of a box, here, Colonel. Its dimensions are indicated—seven by six by fourteen inches. Shall I continue reading the letter?"

No, stand on your head and whistle "Dixie," dickhead.

"Please," I said.

"The rest reads: 'We have notified you already in what kind of bills. We warn you not to set any trap in any way. If you or someone else will notify the police there will be a further delay. After we have the money in hand, we will tell you where to find your boy. You may have a airplane ready—it is about one hundred-fifty miles away. But before telling you the address, a delay of eight hours will be between.' "

"Is that it?" Despite hitting the ransom figure right, this guy seemed an obvious fraud, looking to pick up a fast dollar. Seventy thousand fast dollars.

"Well, as I told you, it's signed with what I believe is the mark of the Sicilian Mafia. There are two circles intersecting . . ."

"Circles?" Now I perked up a lot. Breckinridge saw that, and leaned forward. "Intersecting?"

"I would call them secant circles, if I might be permitted . . ."

"Yeah, yeah, you're permitted. Keep describing."

"There are three dots or holes across the horizontal diameter of the intersecting circles. The circles are tinted—one red, one blue."

Shit.

"Is this letter important, Colonel? I hope I have not wasted your valuable time, sir."

"It's very important, Professor," I said. "Where are you? We'll come for you, right away."

"I'm in the Bronx. But suppose I come to you, Colonel. You have anguish enough and are needed at home. I'll come to you—to Hopewell."

"When, Professor?"

"At once," he said, melodramatically, and hung up.

I stared at the phone a moment.

Then I looked at Breckinridge, whose eyes were wide.

"Better get Slim out of bed," I said.

An hour and forty-five minutes later, I was standing with my hands in my topcoat pockets, leaning against the whitewashed stone wall, near the locked gate where Featherbed Lane turned into the Lindberghs' private drive. I was hiding from the wind, waiting for Condon to show. A trooper stood in front of the nearby weathered contractor's shack with a rifle cradled in his arms; he looked like a prison guard. There were no reporters this time of night.

I heard footsteps crunching the cold ground behind me and my hand drifted toward the nine millimeter, which I'd taken to wearing under one shoulder, lately; but when I turned, I saw Breckinridge approaching in a topcoat, but bareheaded.

He stood with his hands tucked in his pockets and said, "I woke up the chancellor of Fordham University and he confirmed Condon's credentials. Seventy-two years old, retired grade-school teacher. Teaches part-time, physical fitness buff, coached football, still gives swimming lessons."

"At seventy-two?"

Breckinridge raised an eyebrow. "He's apparently quite a character. A real self-styled patriot—featured at public events singing 'The Star-Spangled Banner,' bringing himself to tears each time."

"I may cry, myself."

The night was crying already, moaning like a sick trapped beast. I pressed against the wall, turned up my topcoat collar to shield my face; even a guy from Chicago could die in this icy wind.

"I also rang up the editor and publisher of the Bronx *Home News*," Breckinridge said.

"Colonel, you're turning into a better cop than Schwarzkopf."

He paused, wondering if that was much of a compliment. Then he said, "The editor, a Mr. O'Flaherty, said he was an 'old dear friend' of Condon's, and that the good doctor had contributed poetry, essays and letters to the *News* over the years, on current topics of many a stripe . . . signing them P. A. Triot and J. U. Stice, among other quaint noms de plume."

I snorted a laugh. "He sounds like a crank and a busybody to me. Why the hell would the kidnappers pick a goof like this? All kinds of big-shot public figures have offered their services as go-between."

"I can't begin to answer that. Nor could editor O'Flaherty— who said the circulation of the *News* was less than one hundred thousand."

Headlights cut through the darkness and up Featherbed Lane. As the car drew to a stop, an elderly, walrus-mustached fellow climbed quickly out, nimble for a man his age and size, at six feet something and maybe two hundred-some pounds. No topcoat in sight, he wore a neat, dark, out-of-fashion three-piece suit with a golden watch fob and speckled tie, and a bowler hat, which he was even now removing politely; he looked like somebody who'd gone to a party in 1912 and arrived a few decades late.

"Would this be the Lindbergh home?" he said. It was the voice I'd heard on the phone two hours before.

Through the barred gate, Breckinridge said, "It would. Are you Dr. Condon?"

The old man bowed, making a sweep with the bowler. "I am Dr. John F. Condon."

Two other men were in the car. I unbuttoned my topcoat; I had a clear path to the nine millimeter.

"You have a letter for the Colonel?" Breckinridge asked.

"I do, sir. I prefer to deliver it to him, personally."

From just behind Breckinridge, I called out, "Who's that with you?"

Condon squinted; he had apple cheeks and stupid eyes. "Colonel Lindbergh?"

"No," I said. "I'm a cop, and I'm armed. Who's in the goddamn car?"

Condon lifted his chin and his eyes and nostrils flared. "Language of that sort is unnecessary, sir."

"Who's in the goddamn car?"

"Heller," Breckinridge whispered harshly. "Please!"

Condon stepped gingerly forward, hat in his hands. "I was accompanied by two friends, one of whom was generous enough to drive me here. When I called I was in Max Rosenhain's restaurant, and Max came along with me; our mutual friend, Milton Gaglio, a clothier, was also present. He drove."

"Tell 'em to get out of there and put their hands up," I said.

"Really," Condon said stiffly, head high, "this is most undignified."

"It gets worse if your friends don't get out of the car."

They got out of the car; a small dark man, about thirty, and a stockier guy in his late fifties. Both wore topcoats and hats.

The smaller, younger one said, "I'm Milton Gaglio. Sorry it took us so long to get here. We got lost. Had to stop at the Baltimore Lunchroom to get directions."

That was at the Hopewell crossroads.

"I'm Max Rosenhain," the older man said, with a nervous smile. "We're kind of a committee—a wop, a Jew and a harp."

Nobody laughed.

"Put your hands up, gentlemen," I said.

They looked at each other, more surprised than anything; only Condon seemed offended.

"I can understand your concern for security . . ." he began.

"Then shut up," I said, "and do as you're told."

Breckinridge, who seemed slightly taken aback by my police tactics, unlocked and swung open the gate, and I went out and frisked the three men. Condon's two pals took it stoically, but the professor made little huffing and puffing sounds.

"Let's see the note, Professor," I said.

"I prefer to show it to Colonel Lindbergh."

"Just show me the signature."

He breathed heavily through his nose, thought my request over, then dug a white envelope out of his suitcoat pocket, removed from it a second, smaller envelope and held the note up. The familiar blue and red circles and punched holes were there, all right.

"Stand away," I told him, and then nodded to the other two, to communicate the same thing. I looked inside the car, a black Chevy; poked at and looked under the seats, checked the glove compartment. I asked Gaglio to open the trunk and he did; it was empty but for a spare tire and a jack.

"Okay, boys," I said, gesturing grandly. "Get back in your buggy."

Condon nodded stiffly and with silly precision returned the letters to their envelopes and walked with exaggerated dignity to the black Chevy. The other two moved quickly, like the soles of their feet were hot.

I called over the trooper from the contractor's shack and had him and his rifle climb aboard the running board, to accompany them to the house.

Then I said to Gaglio, who was behind the wheel, "Drive around back. Park near the garage. And wait for us."

The car pulled away and eased up the dirt lane as Breckinridge swung the gate shut and locked it again. The red eyes of their taillights moved slowly toward the mostly dark house, a few rectangles of yellow light glowing on the first floor; the trooper rode along the side of the car like a stunt pilot riding the wing of a plane.

"You were a little rough on them, weren't you?" Breckinridge asked.

"That professor is either a con man or a jackass," I said. "And I got no patience with either."

Breckinridge had no reply to that; we walked up to the house, nodding as we passed to two troopers who stood forlornly near a dwindling bonfire.

The trooper who'd ridden the running board had the three men grouped at the door that led through the servants' sitting room. Breckinridge sent the trooper back to his post, and opened the door for his guests. We gathered in the kitchen, where only one small light over the stove burned. The little terrier, Wahgoosh, came scrambling in from the living room.

"Breckinridge is my name," the Colonel said, talking over the dog's incessant barking. "This is Detective Heller of the Chicago Police."

"Chicago?" Gaglio said. "What are you doing here?"

"That's none of your business," I said affably, kicking the dog. "But I'm making why you boys are here, mine."

"You're a crude, rude young man, Detective Heller," Condon said.

"When visitors drop by at two in the morning, I am."

Breckinridge said, "Colonel Lindbergh is waiting to see you, if you're ready."

"I'm always ready," Condon said, with a smile.

We walked through the living room, while Wahgoosh trailed along, going completely fucking berserk; if anyone was still sleeping in this house before, they weren't now. Breckinridge sat Gaglio and Rosenhain down on the sofa, where the dog snarled at them and they sat looking at it with wide frightened eyes, hands in their laps like wallflowers at a cotillion.

Lindbergh was not behind his desk; he was pacing in his study looking even more haggard than usual. He had not brushed his hair and his baby face was darkly unshaven; he wore brown slacks and a brown leather flight jacket thrown over an undershirt.

"Good evening, Colonel Lindbergh," Condon said, stepping forward grandly, offering his hand as if bestowing a medal. "I would recognize you anywhere, sir."

That put Condon in the select company of everybody in the United States over the age of three.

"Allow me to say that all patriotic Americans are grateful to you, sir, for your pluck and daring . . . and our hearts go out to you in this your time of need."

Lindbergh twitched a smile and said, "Dr. Condon, I'd like to see these notes you received."

"Certainly, sir. It is my great pleasure."

It's always a pleasure to hand ransom notes over to a tortured parent.

Lindbergh studied the notes and then spread them out on the desk. "Nate," he said. "Henry?"

We gathered around and looked at them. Their content reflected what I'd heard on the phone, but the spelling and form and signature were those of the notes previously received.

"They're authentic," Lindbergh said.

We didn't disagree.

Then he smiled, sincerely, at Condon and said, "Doctor, it was kind of you to come out here. I hope we haven't caused you too much trouble."

Condon gave me a sharp sideways glance, but then beamed at Lindbergh. "It is no trouble whatsoever, Colonel. I want you to know, now, that my only purpose is to serve you. I am completely at your disposal."

Lindbergh glanced at me; I rolled my eyes.

"Tell me something about yourself, Doctor," Lindbergh said.

"I am professor of education at Fordham, and principal of Public School Number Twelve in the Bronx."

"Been teaching long?"

"Fifty years," he said proudly. "And in that time I've lost only nineteen hours."

Oh, brother.

"That's an excellent record. And your birthplace?"

He stiffened, as if trying to grow. "The most beautiful borough in the world—the Bronx! I've lived there my entire life."

I sat down. I wondered if they'd divided up my three bucks out in the garage, or if there was any chance Dixon saved it for me.

"Family?" Lindbergh asked him.

"A wife and three splendid children."

Lindbergh looked at me. I shook my head. He looked at Breckinridge, who shrugged.

"Professor," Lindbergh said, "we would be delighted if you would assist us in turning the ransom requested over to the kidnappers, to obtain the return of my son."

Oh, Christ!

"I'd be honored, sir—but I am a stranger to you. I would much prefer that you verify my standing."

"We will," I said.

"You'll stay tonight?" Lindbergh asked. "It's late, and I'd like to talk to you tomorrow, at length."

"Certainly. I'll be delighted to, if it can be arranged for me to return to Fordham by four in the afternoon. I have a lecture."

"You'll be there by four."

"I have two good friends waiting in the living room, Colonel . . ."

"I'm afraid we don't have accommodations for them. I'm sorry."

"Before they go, they'd appreciate meeting you."

"Fine," Lindbergh said, and we all walked out into the living room, where Lindbergh politely shook hands all around, to the accompaniment of Wahgoosh's yapping. Lindbergh offered his thanks, and Gaglio and Rosenhain assured us all they would say nothing to anyone about the events of the night. On their way out, I told them pointedly that that would be a very good idea.

Lindy, Condon and Breckinridge were chatting quietly in the living room when suddenly a woman in a pink silk robe floated in like an apparition.

Anne Lindbergh, her face pale as chalk, eyes large and luminous, said, "Is there news?"

Lindbergh went to her, took her gently by the arm and walked her over to Dr. Condon. He explained that the professor had received a note from the kidnappers in reply to a letter he'd written a newspaper, offering to serve as intermediary.

"Dr. Condon," Lindbergh said, "is going to deliver the ransom, so we can get Charlie back."

"Thank you, Doctor," she said, studying him with moist eyes. "You seem very kind."

"My dear," he said, sidling up to her, "you must not cry—if one of those tears drops, I shall go off the case immediately."

She smiled—at the absurdity of it, I think—and the professor took that as an invitation to slide his arm around her shoulder.

"Child," he said, "I shall do everything in my power to return your boy to you." He raised the forefinger of his free hand like a politician making a point. "You're talking to a man who once won a twenty-dollar prize for submitting to the Bronx *Home News* the following New Year's resolution: 'That I shall, to the best of my ability, and at all times, help anyone in distress.' "

"Uh, really," Anne said.

"I swear it is true," he said gravely.

Lindbergh delicately moved Anne out of Condon's grasp, and the professor said jovially, "Look at the Colonel, here! I believe he's jealous of an old fellow like me!"

Anne laughed nervously. "Good night, Doctor," she said. "Good night, Henry. Nate."

Lindbergh walked her to the stairs.

When he came back, he said, "Thank you, Professor—my wife hasn't laughed since the night they took Charlie."

Condon bowed again; he was just in front of me, and you don't know the restraint it took, not kicking him in the ass.

"I'm afraid I can't even offer you a comfortable bed," Lindbergh said. "Every bedroom in the house is taken."

"I quite understand."

"If you can manage camp style . . . ?"

"Perfectly."

"Henry," Lindbergh said, "take the doctor up to the nursery, if you would. That cot Nate was using is still up there."

Breckinridge nodded and ushered the professor upstairs.

"Nate," Lindbergh said, quietly, taking me by the arm, "do you mind staying over?"

"No. Technically, it's been morning for several hours now."

"If I round up some blankets for you, will you sleep in the nursery?"

"Keep an eye on that pompous old goat, you mean?"

"Something like that. I think he's sincere."

"He's also a pain in the ass."

"Most people are. Would you share quarters with him, just for tonight?"

"Sure."

When I entered the dark nursery, some light from the hall fell in and revealed Condon on the floor on his knees in his long johns with his hands wrapped around the rungs of the crib. His voice boomed through the room.

"Oh great Jehovah, by Thy grace and that it may redound to

Thy credit and that of Thy immortal Son, I swear that I shall dedicate my best efforts and, if necessary, the remaining days of my life, to helping these unfortunate parents."

He knew I was standing there, as he continued.

"Let me do this one great thing as the crowning act of my life. Let me successfully accomplish my mission to the credit of Thy Holy Name and that of Thy Divine Son. Amen!"

He stood. He turned to me. "Detective Heller. I did not see you there."

"Right." I had an armful of blankets and a pillow. I tossed them in the middle of the room. "Make yourself a pallet, gramps. The cot is mine."

He did that, and was asleep before me; even his snoring seemed pompous.

When I woke up in the morning, he was dressed and at the toy chest by the window, going through it.

"What the fuck are you doing?" I snapped.

It frightened the old coot; he jumped, turned around and said, pointedly, "I find your language most offensive and if you don't refrain from such talk, we might have to resort to fisticuffs."

I went over and looked him right in his watery blue eyes. "I said, what the fuck are you doing?"

He had a wood-carved elephant in one hand. "I'm looking for a toy or some other item that the child might be able to identify as his."

There was a knock at the door behind us and we both turned; Lindbergh peeked in.

"Excuse me, gentlemen," he said. "It's eight o'clock. We'd like you to join us for breakfast."

"I'd be honored," Condon said, clutching the toy elephant.

Lindbergh, as before, stayed in the doorway of the nursery; he looked casual and neat at once, wearing a pair of old gray trousers and the leather flying jacket over a darker gray shirt with a tie.

I was standing there in my underwear. "He wants to borrow that toy elephant. For identification purposes."

Lindbergh seemed confused by that.

Condon held up the wooden elephant. "When I've succeeded

in establishing personal contact with the kidnappers, I shall ask to be taken where the baby is being kept. I shall show the baby this toy, and watch for his reaction."

"He can't say 'elephant,' " Lindbergh said, quietly. "He says 'el-e-pent.' "

"Splendid! I'll ask the child to name this toy, and will know what response to expect! In that way, it will be impossible for them to confront me with the wrong child and deceive me."

I was getting my clothes on while this brilliant dissertation was delivered. As far as I was concerned, you could deceive this clown with a dime-store doll.

"Take it with you, by all means," Lindbergh said.

"I've already taken the liberty of removing two other items," Condon said. "I'd like your permission to keep them—two safety pins that secured the blankets under which your son slept, to the mattress."

"I don't see why you'd want . . ."

"It's simple," Condon said, with a self-satisfied smile. "And, I believe, entirely logical. I am taking the pins so that when I meet the man who wrote to me, I can show them to him and ask him where he saw them. If he can tell me exactly where they were fastened on the night of the kidnapping, then we'll know we are dealing with the person who actually entered this nursery and took your son."

"I could use some coffee," I said.

"Let's go down, then," Lindbergh said, and led the way.

Darkly attractive Betty Gow helped horsey Elsie Whately serve us breakfast—orange juice, bacon, eggs, toast and coffee—which we took informally, at the kitchen table. Condon babbled about the Bronx and spouted homilies, showing off for Anne Lindbergh and her mother, who were breakfasting with us, as well.

After breakfast, Lindbergh hustled Condon into the study; Breckinridge and I followed.

"I am convinced," Lindbergh said, taking a seat behind his desk, "that you are in contact with the people who took my son."

Condon sat across from Lindbergh, on the edge of his chair; Breckinridge and I stood.

"Professor, I'll arrange to place fifty thousand dollars in your bank account," Lindbergh said, as he wrote something on a slip of paper. "Since the original amount asked for has been raised to seventy thousand, I'll make every effort to have the additional twenty to you within a day or two."

He handed Condon a note. I moved in and read it over his shoulder: "I hereby authorize Dr. John F. Condon to act as go-between for my wife and myself." It was signed Charles A. Lindbergh.

"This afternoon," Lindbergh was saying, "Colonel Breckinridge will insert the notice 'Money is ready' in the New York *American,* per the letter's instructions."

"It would be disastrous if the newspapers got wind you're in touch with the kidnappers," Breckinridge told Condon. "We need to find some pseudonym for you to sign the ad with."

Condon rubbed his chin; he hadn't shaved this morning, and it was stubbled with white. "By putting my initials together," he said thoughtfully, "J.F.C.—I come up with Jafsie."

I looked sharply at Breckinridge and he looked at me the same way.

Sister Sarah Sivella, two days ago, while in the sway of Chief Yellow Feather, had spoken—and even spelled out—that name: *Jafsie.*

"Fine," Lindbergh told Condon. "That's fine—use that. It'll hide your identity from everyone except whoever it was who wrote to you . . . and to me."

"Before I return to the Bronx," Condon said, "do you have pictures of your son I might study, that I might indelibly impress upon my mind his features?"

"Certainly."

I gestured to Breckinridge and he stepped out into the hall.

"One of us has to stick with the old boy," I said. "You heard him—that pen name he supposedly just made up . . ."

"Jafsie," Breckinridge said, nodding. "We heard that before, didn't we?"

"We sure did. But Lindy's liable to dismiss it as Sarah Sivella tapping into the spirit world or ESP or some ridiculous damn thing."

"True." Breckinridge was troubled. Then his expression sharpened. "Let me handle this."

We went back into the study, where Condon was studying baby photos like a student cramming for an exam.

Breckinridge touched him on the shoulder and said, warmly, "Professor, I wonder if I might stay as your houseguest, until any negotiations with the kidnappers are concluded? I'd consider it a great favor."

"My entire home and everything that is in it," Condon said grandly, "is at your disposal as long as you wish."

"You're most gracious, Professor," Breckinridge said, and the men shook hands. "We'll start today."

Chapter 12

Mickey Rosner, snazzy in a three-piece black suit with white pinstripes and a flourish of white silk handkerchief in his breast pocket, was holding court. His dark face, average in every way but for his large, flattened nose, was cracked in a smile; the little bastard was beaming like a new father handing out cigars. He was seated at a table for four in a speakeasy in the back of the Cadillac Restaurant on East Forty-First Street in Manhattan. With him were his two cronies, Irving Bitz and Salvatore Spitale, proprietors of the speak, which was suitably dark, smoky and crowded. Most of the crowd was reporters, which made sense, because the joint was right behind the New York *Daily News* building.

Spitale was perhaps forty, dark-haired, dark-eyed, dark-complected, with a round face that didn't match his slender frame, and a suit just as expensive as Rosner's. His partner Bitz was a smaller, fatter version of Spitale only with a cheaper suit, jug ears and dumb, hooded eyes.

The three men were conducting an informal press conference;

reporters juggling notebooks and beer mugs were tossing the trio of hoods questions, but not too hard: underhand softball pitches.

"Mickey," one reporter said, "you interviewed a prisoner at the Tombs last night, for Colonel Lindbergh. What did you learn?"

"Not at liberty to say, fellas," Rosner said, and he bit off the end of a fat Havana.

"What about the rumors you're holding secret talks with a top underworld figure, who's currently in prison?"

Rosner shook his head no, lit up his cigar, waved the match out.

Another reporter said, "Come on—weren't Spitale and Bitz in Chicago a few days ago?"

"Yeah, Salvy," another said, turning his attention to Spitale. "How 'bout it?"

"No comment," Spitale said, and grinned at Rosner and then at Bitz.

"Mickey," another newsman said, "how in hell did *you* end up Lindy's rep? You're still facing a grand larceny charge on that stock-kiting scam from last October."

Rosner's smile disappeared and he gestured with the fiery end of the cigar. "I'm a respectable businessman, gents. You know that—I deal in real estate."

There were some muffled laughs and some laughs that weren't so muffled.

"Mickey," said a reporter, a disembodied voice out of the swirling smoke, "why are we here? I mean, we appreciate the free suds—but you haven't given us jack shit."

Rosner grinned again. "Maybe you ain't asked the right questions."

There were mutterings and moans, mostly good-natured, from the well-lubricated press contingent.

Another reporter tried a question—for Spitale, this time. "Hey, Salvy—what's this about the cops dropping a couple bootlegging beefs against you guys? Did Lindy pull some strings?"

Spitale laughed. "I won't dignify that with a response."

"Well, tell us about your role in the Lindbergh case, then."

He splayed a hand to his chest. "It's this way, boys—I was

asked to use my influence in getting the kid back. If professionals have got a hold of him, they know where to get in touch with me in five minutes, day or night, rain or shine. Right, Irv?"

Bitz nodded dutifully.

Then Spitale continued: "But I'm not a cop, see? Get it straight—I'm no cop; I don't go snooping around."

"You almost sound sorry you got involved."

He shrugged facially. "I am kinda sorry I got mixed up in this thing, yeah. You guys are printing pictures of my kids and my family, and my policy of keepin' out of the papers has been knocked for a loop. Can't you fellas cover something else—like the Shanghai War, or wherever?"

"Have you found any trace of the baby, Salvy?"

"Well, to be honest, I have not. In fact, I'm a little discouraged."

Rosner cut in. "*I* have *better* news to report, fellas."

The reporters glanced around at each other, their expressions saying, *About damn time.*

"The baby is alive and well," Rosner said, flicking ash off his cigar onto the floor. "I give you my personal assurance that the baby is about to be returned to his folks."

Even Spitale and Bitz seemed surprised by that.

The reporters began hurling questions at Rosner, hardballs this time, but he held up a hand in a stop gesture; the hand glittered with diamond rings.

"What I'm saying don't represent my *opinion,*" he said, "but what I actually *know.*"

"Are you negotiating the return of the baby?"

"If I was, saying so would put those efforts at risk, right? So let's cut this off right here, okay? Thank you, fellas."

He rose and pushed through the reporters, leaving a confused Spitale and Bitz to field the rest of the questions. Rosner was heading toward the men's room; nobody bothered following him.

Except me.

I'd driven into Manhattan midmorning, to check in with IRS man Frank Wilson and to meet with Breckinridge after work. The plan was to spend the evening with the attorney and the eccentric

Dr. Condon at the latter's Bronx bungalow, waiting to see if the ad that ran today ("Money is ready—Jafsie") got a response.

Among a handful of other things I wanted to do while I was in New York City was check out Spitale and Bitz's speakeasy; I'd stopped in for the free lunch, heard the scuttlebutt about the "press conference" and hung around nursing beers for two hours waiting for Rosner and company to show.

Now Mickey was standing at the urinal. He and I had the small room to ourselves; I hook-and-eye latched the door, waited for him to finish, and as he turned, buttoning up, he sneered.

"What the hell are you doing here, Heller?"

"What do you think, Mickey? Checking up on you."

He started to brush past me. "Stay out of my way."

I took him by the arm. "You didn't wash your hands, Mickey. Stick around a second, and wash your hands."

He jerked loose of my grasp. "I'll wash my hands of you, flatfoot."

But I was blocking the way. "Tell me, Mickey. What was that bullshit about being sure the kid was safe? That he'd be returned any second now?"

He straightened his suitcoat, tried to summon some dignity. "Just tossin' the newshounds a bone."

"Are you, or any of your people, negotiating with Capone?"

"Maybe."

I unbuttoned my coat, put my hands on my hips, letting him get a look at the nine millimeter under my shoulder. "That's not much of an answer, Mickey."

"Fuck you. You don't know who you're messing with. You can wake up dead, messing with me."

I grabbed him by his tailored lapels. "Don't get tough with me, you greasy little fucker. You're going to spill, or drown."

"Drown?"

"Guess how."

Rosner licked his lips, and said, "I don't know a goddamn thing, goddamnit! Now, back off, Heller—or I'll tell Lindy you been shovin' me around."

I let him go, roughly.

"Why don't you do that?" I said. "And I'll tell him why."

I let him pass. He never did wash his hands.

I'd met with Wilson earlier; the T-man had had little to report on his end: no news on Capone's missing man Bob Conroy; Agent O'Rourke had infiltrated the Marinelli/Sivella spiritualist church, but had nothing yet to report.

I'd filled the agent in about Condon, and he was furious Lindbergh hadn't brought him in on it.

"Maybe you ought to shadow the professor," I said. "He may be tied in with those spiritualists—unless you think Sister Sarah really did pull the name 'Jafsie' out of the spirit world."

"The Bronx and Harlem are next-door neighbors," Wilson said, reflectively. "You don't need a Ouija board to get from one to the other."

"If Lindbergh finds out I tipped you, I'll be persona non grata. So keep it under your hat."

Condon lived in the Bedford Park section of the Bronx, just west of Webster Avenue, in a neat, modest two-story white clapboard on quiet, tree-lined Decatur Avenue. Shrubbery hugged the house and the well-tended lawn was brushed with snow.

It was a little before six o'clock when I found myself on Condon's front porch, knocking on a door inset with stained glass. Darkness had already settled upon the Bronx—the most beautiful borough in the world!—and the night air was nippy. I was just about to knock again when the door was answered by a dark-haired, dark-eyed attractive woman in her mid-twenties; her eyes were tense as she asked me who I was.

"Detective Heller," I said, not bothering to mention what police department I was attached to. "I'm expected."

She nodded tiredly and opened the door.

As inconspicuously as possible, I traced the trim lines of her figure in the brown dress with white collar. "And you are?" I asked.

She smiled with quiet irony. "Married, for one thing. Dr. Condon's daughter, Myra, for another. And disgusted with this whole affair, for one more."

"Well, we have the latter in common anyway," I said, handing her my hat and coat, which she didn't seem particularly inclined to receive. We were in an entryway that faced the second-floor staircase. She listlessly led me through a nicely but not lavishly furnished parlor so old-fashioned the doilies had doilies. Then she summoned me into an adjoining living room where a grand piano was covered by a paisley shawl like somebody's grandmother; sitting on the brocade davenport were the professor and a pleasant-looking, plump woman in her late sixties wearing a floral print dress and a concerned expression.

Condon was patting her hand and saying, "There, there, Myra . . . nothing to worry about."

"I thought *you* were Myra," I whispered to my reluctant hostess.

"That's my mother," she said, blandly. "I was named after her."

"Oh," I said.

She sat on the couch next to her parents and crossed her nice legs but made sure I didn't see much.

"Good afternoon, Detective," Condon said, hollowly.

"Good afternoon, Professor," I said. "Good afternoon, ma'am. Don't believe we've had the pleasure."

Condon uncharacteristically skipped the formalities. "Mrs. Condon had a phone call earlier today."

I pulled up a chair; it looked like something Marie Antoinette might have sat on, eating cake. "Tell me about it, please," I said to Mrs. Condon.

"Someone called on the telephone for my husband," she said, in a warm alto, the faintest vibrato of nervousness coloring it, "around noon."

"Man or woman?" I asked.

"It was a man. I told him that my husband was giving a lecture and would be home between six and seven. He said he would call again about seven this evening." She looked at the professor, who had a sick-cow expression. "He said you were to stay in and wait for his call, dear."

Condon's expression turned shrewd and he said, "And what was his name?"

"Why, dear," she said, "he didn't give it."

No shit.

"That 'money is ready' ad of yours appeared in the morning edition," I said. "That's pretty quick action."

Condon's eyes tightened in attempted thought. "You think this phone call, then, was a message from the kidnapper in response to the ad?"

I sighed. "Gee, Professor. It just might be."

Any irony I allowed to show in my voice was lost on Dr. and Mrs. Condon, but Myra the Younger smirked at me mirthlessly.

"Dad," the daughter said, sitting forward, "I'd like to see that baby returned as much as anybody. But don't you think you should withdraw, graciously, and just let somebody else take your place as intermediary?"

He raised his chin. Where was Dempsey when you needed him. "I've sworn to see this thing through to the bitter end."

"But, Dad—you're not a young man. This is dangerous for you . . ."

"We can't think of that," he said. "When the time comes that a respectable man cannot walk out of the door of his own home merely because he is attempting to assist one of the greatest heroes of all time, well, then . . . then I do not care to live a day longer."

Was he trying to cheer me up?

"Are you all right, Mrs. Condon?" I asked.

"Yes. Thank you. I didn't get your name, young man . . . ?"

"My name's Nathan Heller. I'm a police officer from Chicago. I appreciate your hospitality."

"Actually," she said, a hand to her generous chest, "I've been a bit shaken up. Luckily Myra stayed over, and fixed a nice supper. Plenty for everyone."

I turned to Myra. "You don't live here?"

"No," she said, and smiled at me tightly, the sort of smile that contradicts itself.

"It is typical of little Myra," Condon said, "that though she thoroughly opposes my determination to enter this case, she made arrangements to be here with me, in the Bronx, to absorb some of my routine duties."

"Such as?" I asked her.

"Father received several hundred letters today," she said, "in response to that letter to the editor he wrote to the *News*. It's been like that every day since it appeared."

"You should save those letters," I said, "and give them to the cops."

"Colonel Schwarzkopf, you mean?" Condon asked.

"That would be better than nothing," I said. "But this is New York. You got cops in this state, too, you know."

There was a knock at the door; Condon's daughter rose languidly to answer it, and moments later she was ushering Colonel Breckinridge into the living room.

I filled him in, quickly, about the telephone call Mrs. Condon had received earlier.

"It's almost six-thirty now," Breckinridge said. "No call yet?"

"Not yet," I said. "Why don't we eat?"

"Sir!" Condon said, sitting up straight. "How can you think of food, when a child's life hangs in the balance?"

"Well, if we eat," I said, "it won't tip the scale, one way or the other. Or, we can all sit around jumpy as cats in a rainstorm."

We ate. The dining room was behind the living room, and Myra—a sour hostess but a sweet cook—served up a pot roast with oven-browned potatoes, carrots and onions.

"Colonel," Condon said, working on his second helping of everything, baby in the balance or not, "as you may recall, I mentioned that the distinctive red-and-blue-circle signature of the kidnappers reminded me of a Sicilian Mafia sign."

"Yes," Breckinridge said tentatively. He was picking at his food.

"Well, I replicated the symbol and began showing it around Fordham today."

"You what?" I said.

He sipped his drink—a big wholesome glass of milk—and repeated his sentence word for word.

I just shook my head. His daughter Myra glared at me.

Proud of himself, a forkful of food poised in midair, Condon said, "Mind you, I've said nothing to anyone of my trip to Hopewell the other night. But I've been determined to learn, if possible, the meaning of that mysterious symbol."

"Professor," Breckinridge said, his face whiter than Condon's cow juice, "that really may not have been wise."

Condon didn't seem to hear; his eyes and smile were glazed and inwardly directed. "I sketched it on a piece of paper, that symbol, and carried it with me these last two days. I've been showing it to everyone I meet, asking them about it."

"Swell idea," I said.

"Finally," he said, raising a significant forefinger, "this afternoon I found someone who recognized it—a Sicilian friend of mine."

Breckinridge touched a napkin to his lips and pushed his plate of mostly uneaten food away.

"As a result," Condon said, "I'm convinced our kidnappers are of Italian origin. My Sicilian friend confirmed my suspicion, explaining that the symbol was that of a secret criminal organization in the old country—the symbol is the *trigamba,* or 'three legs.' "

"Three legs?" Breckinridge asked.

"My Sicilian friend explained that two legs were fine, but 'when a third leg walks, beware.' "

"Let me write that down," I said.

"Its symbolic meaning," Condon continued, "is that if a third leg, a stranger, enters into the province of the secret society, the Mafia, that intruder can expect a stiletto through the heart."

His daughter Myra, cutting her meat, dropped her own knife clatteringly. "Daddy," she said. "Please don't do this. Please withdraw from this silly dangerous escapade."

Colonel Breckinridge looked at the young woman with mournful eyes. "Please don't ask that, miss. Your father may be the only honest person on earth actually in contact with the kidnappers."

"Excuse me," Myra said stiffly, "I think I'll pass on dessert," and hurled her napkin to the table and got up and went out through the front parlor; her footsteps on the hall stairs, several rooms away, conveyed her annoyance.

After apple pie, Breckinridge stepped out onto the porch for a smoke—the professor allowed no tobacco of any kind in his "domicile"—leaving Mr. and Mrs. Condon to keep watch by Mr. Bell's invention, which was on a stand in the hallway outside the living room.

"Can you believe that man?" Breckinridge said bitterly, pulling greedily on a cigarette. "Showing that signature around the Bronx! To some 'Sicilian friend'!"

"He's a dunce, all right," I said. "Unless he's very clever."

"Clever?"

I nodded, tapped my temple with one finger. "Something clicked in this hat rack I call a head, while he was babbling about that Mafia sign. When I first talked to him on the phone, back at Hopewell, Condon told me that the letter to him was signed with 'the mark of the Mafia.' "

"Yes. I remember. So?"

"He went to great lengths to assure me that he hadn't opened the interior envelope, the one addressed to Slim."

"Right."

"I even heard him rip it open, over the phone."

"Yes. I recall."

"Well, the note to Slim was signed with the 'mark of the Mafia,' all right—but the note to Condon was unsigned."

Breckinridge thought about that. "But how could the professor know about the signature before he opened the letter . . . ?"

"Exactly. Of course, he may have already opened that inner letter, and just ripped some other piece of paper for the benefit of my ears. But either way . . ."

"Yes. Worth noting, Heller. Worth noting. And there's something I might tell you."

"Well, hell, go ahead."

Breckinridge drew on the cigarette, exhaled a wreath of smoke. "Last night Condon was, as usual, running off at the mouth. He was talking about his daughter, Myra, how she'd been a teacher before her marriage. And then he got into a spiel about how 'the love of teaching runs strongly' in his family. That Mrs. Condon had been a 'splendid schoolteacher herself,' that he and she had first met when they were teaching at the same public school."

"Yeah. So what?"

"Heller, they taught at Old Public School Number Thirty-Eight, in Harlem."

That hit me like a sack of nickels. "Harlem! As in Sarah Sivella and Martin Marinelli, Harlem?"

"Exactly." He pitched his cigarette into a small bank of snow on the lawn. "Shall we go in?"

But before we could, an eager Mrs. Condon appeared in the doorway and said, "The phone is ringing, gentlemen . . . my husband is about to answer it."

We moved quickly through the house and saw Condon pick up the phone in the midst of a ring.

"Who is it, please?" he said formally; he stood with chin high, light-blue eyes about as alert as a Chinese opium addict's.

After a beat, he said, "Yes, I got your letter."

I stood close to him and bent the receiver away from his ear, so that I could hear, too. Condon gave me a reproving look but didn't fight me.

"I saw your ad," a crisp, clear voice said, "in the New York *American.*"

"Yes? Where are you calling from?"

Brilliant question! Fucking brilliant!

"Westchester," the voice said.

Condon's brow knit as he tried to think of something else incisive to ask.

"Dr. Condon, do you write sometimes pieces for the papers?"

That seemed to take the professor aback. After a moment, he said, "Why yes—I sometimes write articles for the papers."

A pause was followed by the voice speaking in a dim, muffled tone to someone standing by: "He says sometimes he writes pieces for the papers."

The voice returned, strong and clear and a bit guttural. "Stay in every night this week. Stay at home from six to twelve. You will receive a note with instructions. Act accordingly or all will be off."

"I shall stay in," Condon said, putting his hand on his heart.

"*Statti citto!*"

Another voice on the phone had said the latter, cutting in.

Almost half a silent minute crawled by. Then the crisp, guttural voice said, "All right. You will hear from us."

Condon blinked at the click of the phone, then said, self-importantly, and pointlessly, "They have severed the connection."

He severed his own connection—that is, he hung up—and I said to Breckinridge, "Could you hear all that?"

"Yes," Breckinridge said. "What was that foreign phrase?"

"*Statti citto,*" I said. "It means, 'shut up,' in Sicilian. My guess is they were using a public phone, and someone was walking by."

"I think," Condon said, thinking deeply, "he may have been deceiving us when he said he was calling from Westchester."

"No, really?" I said archly. "That hadn't occurred to me."

"We'll have to get the money together quickly," Breckinridge said, distractedly, pacing in the small area.

"The kidnappers' last letter was quite specific as to the dimensions of the money box," Condon said. "Might I offer to have such a box built, tomorrow?"

Breckinridge looked at me and I shrugged.

Condon went on, raising a lecturing forefinger. "Upstairs, in my study, I have the ballot box of the Lieutenant-Governor of the State of New York in eighteen hundred and twenty."

Whoop-de-doo.

"It has a lid, two hinges and a casement lock. The box I shall have constructed will duplicate that ancient ballot box."

"What's the point?" I asked.

Condon's apple cheeks were a pair of pink balls in his ludicrous smiling face. "I'll specify that it is to be of five-ply veneer. We'll use different types of wood in its construction. Maple, pine, tulipwood . . . and a couple of other varieties. Five different in all."

"Which will make the box easy to identify," I said.

Breckinridge looked at me, curiously.

"It's not a bad idea," I said, surprising us all.

"Doctor," Breckinridge said, putting a hand on the old boy's shoulder. "I'm not unaware of the sacrifice you're making. I'm aware that members of your family don't look favorably upon your participation in this case. But some day, I hope, you'll in some way be rewarded for what you're doing."

"I do not expect a small reward for anything I might do," Condon said, with the usual pomp and circumstance. "Perhaps the reward I intend to ask for is too large."

I didn't for one second think Condon was going to ask for dough, though. He was either too square a john or too crooked a one to do that.

He didn't disappoint me.

"I ask only," he said, "that when that little baby is recovered, I be the one to place him back in his mother's arms."

Breckinridge bought it, apparently; he shook Condon's hand and said, warmly, "You'll deserve that. And I'll see to it that you get what you deserve, Doctor."

My feelings exactly.

Chapter 13

The bronze Tiffany clock on the mantel in the dining room of the Condon home chimed seven times. In the adjacent room, the living room, the shades drawn, we sat: Condon, his wife, Breckinridge and me. Tonight the daughter was back in New Jersey, having had enough of this intrigue.

"My friend is a first-rate cabinetmaker," Condon said, hands on his knees. Then he added, "A *Bronx* cabinetmaker," as if that made all the difference.

"This ballot box you're having duplicated," I said, "how long will it take your Bronx cabinetmaker to do the job?"

"He promised delivery within four days," Condon said, as if sharing something miraculous with us. "The cost will be three dollars—materials and workmanship included!"

"Well, that's swell," I said, "but suppose they ask for delivery of the dough sooner than that?"

Colonel Breckinridge said, "I hope to God they do. We'll have the money together by Monday afternoon."

"Perhaps I should call my cabinetmaker friend," Condon said, thoughtfully, "and bid him hasten."

"If they contact us tonight," Breckinridge said to me, "it will be to arrange the money drop, correct?"

"Probably," I said. "But you guys did run an ad saying 'Money is ready'—and it isn't."

"But that was the specific language," Condon said defensively, "the kidnappers required!"

"I know," I said. "I was here. But you shouldn't have run it before the money *was* ready."

That shut Condon up; and Colonel Breckinridge sank into a gloomy silence.

I'd already had a confrontation with Lindbergh over this earlier, at Hopewell.

"I thought you had the money together," I'd told him.

We were walking with the leashed Wahgoosh around the barren outskirts of the yard of the house; it was midmorning and windy and cold.

"Frankly, Nate," he said, "I'm a little stripped for ready cash."

"Well, hell, your credit's good—wasn't your father-in-law a partner at J. P. Morgan's banking house?"

Lindbergh nodded. "My wife's mother has offered me the money, but I refused it."

"Slim! This is no goddamn time to stand on ceremony . . ."

He raised a hand. "I've been liquidating stocks. The ransom's damn near raised."

"These are stocks you bought before the crash, huh?"

"Yes."

"What did they cost you?"

He took a moment or two to answer; without looking at me, he said, "Three hundred and fifty thousand."

"Which you're selling to raise seventy."

He shrugged with his eyebrows. "Actually—fifty. I'm still working on the other twenty."

The wind nipped at my face. "I had no idea . . . they really got you over a barrel, don't they?"

"They do. I hope we can arrange for proof that I'm not being hoaxed. . . . Nate, I've kept you in the dark about it, and for the time being I still have to: but Condon isn't the only party who can make a convincing case for being in touch with the kidnappers."

"What?"

"I can't say any more right now. I'm looking into these other claims. In the meantime, Condon seems perhaps the most reliable option."

My eyes rolled like marbles. "If Condon is the most reliable option, God help you with the others."

He said nothing. We paused while Wahgoosh pissed.

I turned my face away from the March wind. "I heard Schwarzkopf say something about keeping Condon's house under surveillance, and shadowing him to any ransom drop point."

"Yes."

"Well, I'm glad. There's hope for Schwarzkopf yet."

"Perhaps, but I've forbidden it."

"You've what?"

"Colonel Schwarzkopf withdrew his proposal to stake out Condon's house, when I objected."

"On what goddamn grounds did you object?"

"That it might endanger the safe return of my son."

What could I say to that? Other than it was fucking nuts. I could only hope Frank Wilson had taken my advice and put Condon under government surveillance. We walked. The dog crapped.

"You have to call Wilson in, Slim."

"Pardon me?"

"Agent Wilson of the IRS. And his boss Irey. Especially his boss Irey."

"Why?"

"You've got to record all the serial numbers of the ransom money, before you pay it out. Irey can help you with that, and he's the guy who can track the money, once it's started getting into circulation."

Lindbergh shook his head, no. "I made a statement to the press that I wouldn't pay the kidnappers in marked bills. I won't break my word."

"Oh, for Christ's sake," I said. I shook my head, said, "That tears it," turned and headed for the house. The wind pushed at my back, encouraging me.

"Heller!" Lindbergh called. "Where are you going?"

"Chicago," I said, over my shoulder. "We got a more normal brand of insanity back there."

"Wait. Wait!"

I stopped and he walked up beside me, the dog frisking at his heels.

"I'll talk to Irey," he said. "But no promises."

"Okay."

"I'd like you to stick around a while longer."

"Why?"

"There are gangsters in this, obviously. They may be Capone people."

"You've got Irey and Wilson on the case; they know Capone better than I do."

"They're not from Chicago. And they're not street cops. They don't know the breed of crook Capone uses, like you do. Nate, we need your expertise."

I was flattered. I couldn't help it. Lindy was behaving stupidly in many respects, but he was still Lindy. Saying no to him was like saying no to Uncle Sam.

"No," I said.

His cheek twitched; his eyes were desperate. "Will you at least stay till we play out the Condon hand? Just that long?"

I sighed. "Sure. Why not. It beats chasing pickpockets around LaSalle Street Station."

He offered me a hand to shake and I shook it. Wahgoosh growled at me.

The bronze Tiffany clock chimed seven-thirty just thirty seconds before the doorbell rang.

"This is it," Breckinridge said, standing. His eyes were hard and tight.

"Perhaps I should answer it," Condon said, standing. His eyes were soft and loose.

"There's an idea," I said.

Condon moved quickly for his size and age, and I was on his heels, Breckinridge on mine. The nine millimeter under my arm kept us all company.

The old professor threw open the door, like a ham actor in a bad play, and on his front porch were two spear-carriers in our little melodrama.

"Hiya, doc," the older of the two men said. "We thought we'd drop around and find out what's new on the case."

"Yeah," the younger, shorter one asked. "Any word?"

It was Max Rosenhain the restaurateur, and Milton Gaglio the clothier, respectively, the professor's two pals.

"Ah, my friends!" Condon said, spreading his arms. "How wonderful to see you. Please do step in."

And step in they did, hats in hand, nervous smiles taking their faces upon seeing me. I shut the door, damn near slamming it.

"Gentlemen," Colonel Breckinridge said, "we're grateful to you for your concern, and interest, but . . ."

"But get the hell out of here," I said.

"Mr. Heller!" Condon said. "I will not countenance your foul language and rude behavior in my house!"

"Shut up," I said to him. To the other two, I said, "We're waiting to hear from the kidnappers, you jack-offs. What do you think this is, a radio show?"

The two men swallowed and exchanged embarrassed glances.

Condon was glaring at me. "Really, Detective Heller. Your conduct is unconscionable."

We were in the Bronx, so I gave him his city's namesake cheer. Then I said to his dumb-ass pals, "If the kidnappers are watching this house, as I suspect they are, waiting for the right moment to make their move, then you two clowns may have just scared 'em off."

"We didn't mean any harm . . ." Gaglio began.

"We didn't think . . ." Rosenhain said.

"Right," I said, and the doorbell rang.

We stood there looking wild-eyed at each other, clustered as if in a football huddle, only there was no quarterback.

So I called the play. In a harsh whisper, I said, "Everybody but the professor, get into the living room. Go. Now. But quietly."

To their credit, they did just that.

Condon looked at me, his eyes sharper than usual. I put my back to the wall, to the left of the door, and got the nine millimeter in hand; I nodded to him. He nodded back, swallowed, and opened the door.

"You Dr. Condon?"

Peering around the edge, I could see a man standing in the doorway: a little guy with round wire-rim glasses and a ferret face; he wore the cap and coat of a cabbie.

"I am Dr. Condon."

"Here you go, pal."

And the cabbie, if that's what he was, handed an envelope to the professor; the envelope bore the bold, childlike block printing and numerals we'd seen before.

The apparent cabbie was still standing there, waiting for a tip, I guess.

With my left hand, I reached out and grabbed him by the lapel of his uniform and pulled him into the entryway and kicked the door shut. I shoved him up against the nearest wall, his back to me, and patted him down with one hand, keeping the nine millimeter in the other.

"Hey!" he said. "Hey! What's the big idea?"

"You ain't heeled," I said. "That's a start. Turn around and put your hands up. Colonel!"

Breckinridge came in, his eyes bugging a bit as he saw me holding the gun on the little cabbie.

"Usher our caller into the living room," I said. "He seems clean." To the cabbie, I said, "What's your name?"

"Perrone," he said, loudly, almost proudly. His voice was indignant, but his eyes were scared shitless.

"Put your hands down, Mr. Perrone, and behave yourself."

Wordlessly, Breckinridge led the cabbie into the dining room.

Condon was standing there stupidly with the letter in his hands, looking at the thing as if afraid of it. I took the envelope from him, tore it open and read to myself:

> Mr. Condon.
> We trust you, but we will note come
> in your Haus it is to danger. even
> you cane not know if Police or
> secret servise is watching you

follow this instuction.
Take a car and drive to the last
supway station from Jerome Ave
line. 100 feet from the last station
on the left seide is a empty frank-
further-stand with a big open Porch
around, you will find a notise in
senter of the porch underneath a stone.
this notise will tell
you where to find us.

Here, in the right margin, the by-now familiar interlocking-circles signature appeared, and the note continued:

Act accordingly.
after 3/4 of a houer be
on the place. bring the mony with you.

"May I read that?" Condon asked, and I handed it to him. It was his mail, after all.

He read it over several times and looked at me with worry in his watery blue eyes. "Bring the money?"

"That's what it says."

We joined Breckinridge in the living room. Mrs. Condon had left the room and the cabbie was seated on the couch between Gaglio and Rosenhain. Breckinridge was pacing. He grabbed for the note like a starving man for a crust of bread.

"Bring the money!" he read. "Judas Priest! We haven't *got* the damn money . . ."

"What do we do?" Condon asked desperately. "I assumed we would work out the details for the ransom exchange, but now . . ."

"What's important now is to make contact," I said. "Explain that the money really will be ready soon. Make the best of it."

Condon was shaking his head; he seemed confused, disoriented.

Hell with him. I turned to the cabbie, bookended on the couch by Condon's two cronies.

"What was your name again?" I asked him.

"Joe Perrone. Joseph."

"Where did you get that letter?"

"Guy hailed me and handed it to me over on Gun Hill Road at Knox Place."

"How far is that from here?"

"Don't you know?" the cabbie asked.

"No," I said. "I'm not from here. I'm a tourist. With a gun."

"It's about a mile from here."

"What did the guy say? What did he look like?"

The little cabbie shrugged. "He asked me if I knew where Decatur Avenue was, where twenty-nine seventy-four would be. I said sure, I know that neighborhood. Then he looked around, over this shoulder and that shoulder, and stuck his hand in his pocket and gave me this envelope and a buck."

"What did he look like?"

"I don't know. He was wearing a brown topcoat and a brown felt hat."

"Any physical characteristics about the guy that were noticeable?"

"No. I didn't pay any attention."

"Nothing about the man that fixes itself in your mind?"

"No."

"You wouldn't know him again if you saw him?"

"No. I was looking at the buck he gave me. George Washington, him I can identify. What's this all about, anyway?"

Breckinridge chimed in. "I'm afraid we can't tell you that just now, Mr. Perrone. Rest assured it's most important."

"Let me see your badge," I said.

"Sure." He unpinned it from his uniform coat.

I wrote the number down in my notebook. Then I wrote it down on a separate page which I tore out and handed to Gaglio.

"Make yourself useful," I said. "Go out to that cab parked in front and check this number against the ID card in the backseat. Then write down the license plate number, too."

Gaglio, glad to be of help, nodded, got up, took the sheet of paper and scurried out.

"What now?" Breckinridge asked.

"The professor keeps his appointment," I said. "I'll drive."

"There were to be no police," Condon said.

"I'm not a cop in New York State," I said. "Just a patriotic concerned citizen."

"With a gun," the cabbie said.

"Right," I said. "We'll take my flivver."

By "my flivver," of course, I meant the one Lindy loaned me.

Gaglio came back in and said, "It checks out."

"Good," I said. I turned to Perrone. "You go on about your business. You may be hearing from the cops."

"What should I say?"

Condon covered his heart like a school kid pledging allegiance. "Tell the whole truth and nothing but the truth."

"Except for my pulling a gun on you," I said.

"Right," he said, and he was up and out.

"What about our friends Max and Milton?" Condon asked.

"They stay here," I said. "And they're not my fucking friends."

The night was nobody's friend. The sky was black and the city was gray. A cold wind blew leaves and rubbish and scraps of paper across the all-but-deserted streets of the most beautiful borough in the world.

As I got behind the wheel, and Condon slid his big frame into the rider's seat, I said, "I'm a stranger to this part of the world, Professor—you'll have to navigate."

"I can do that ably," he said cheerily. Then, turning suddenly somber, he said, "I trust, despite our differences, we can join forces in this just cause."

"We'll do fine, Professor. I'm just here to back you up."

Placated, Condon folded his hands on his lap and I pulled away from the curb, heading west.

Eight solitary blocks later, he said, "Turn north on Jerome Avenue—just up ahead."

I turned onto the all-but-deserted thoroughfare, gloomy and gray under the subdued glow of the street lights. Condon pointed out the last subway station on Jerome Avenue, and I slowed.

"There's the hot-dog stand," I said.

On the left side of the street was the sagging, deteriorating shack, a summertime operation that had missed a couple summers. The sad little booth was fronted by an equally sad, sagging porch. I pulled a U-turn and stopped before it.

"Allow me," Condon said, and got out.

He climbed several steps to the porch, each step giving and groaning under his weight. In the middle of the porch was a big flat rock, which I could see Condon stoop to lift. He returned quickly, an envelope in hand.

We were almost directly under a street lamp. He tore the envelope open and read the note aloud to me: " 'Cross the street and follow the fence from the cemetery direction to Two Hundred Thirty-Third Street. I will meet you.' "

"How far is that, Professor?"

"About a mile. The fence mentioned is the one enclosing Woodlawn Cemetery to the north—Two Hundred Thirty-Third Street runs east-west and intersects Jerome Avenue about a mile north of this frankfurter stand. It forms the northern border of the cemetery."

"Which means?"

"You'll have to swing the car around again."

I pulled another U-turn. We couldn't have had less traffic if the world ended yesterday. On our one side was the rolling wooded acreage of a park, on the other a sprawling, iron-fenced cemetery.

"That's Woodlawn," Condon explained. "And that park is Van Cortlandt."

"You'd be better off if that cab driver had driven you."

"Perhaps, Detective Heller—but if pressed I'll admit I like having you, and your gun, around."

We kept going along Jerome, parallel to the cemetery, stopping about fifty feet short of the 233rd Street intersection. Ahead was a triangular plaza that was the entrance to Woodlawn Cemetery, with heavy iron gates, shut and undoubtedly locked.

I pulled over. "Go on up and stand by that gate."

"You think that's the location the kidnappers meant?"

"Yes. Go on. I'll cover you."

"I suppose that's wise. They'll not contact me unless I'm alone."

"I'm here if you need me."

He nodded and strode over to the plaza, looking around brazenly. Inconspicuous he was not.

But that was okay. We wanted the kidnappers to see him.

He paced. He dug the note out of his pocket and read and reread it—in an apparent attempt to signal any representative of the kidnap gang who might be watching. Nothing. He paced some more.

Ten minutes of this went by before he came marching back to the car. He got in.

"I don't know what's wrong," he said. "There's no one out there. Were we on time?"

"It's nine-fifteen," I said. "Maybe we're early. It's warmer in here. Sit for a few minutes."

We sat. The wind out there did all the talking.

Then Condon said, "There's someone!"

A short, swarthy man in a cap and with a handkerchief covering his face was walking toward us along Jerome Avenue.

Condon got out of the car, quickly. He walked toward the man. The man walked toward him.

And passed the professor by.

Condon turned and stood in the middle of the sidewalk, scratching his head, watching the guy walk away. The old man looked in my direction, shrugged, and headed back for the area by the iron gates, where he again began to pace.

At nine-thirty, I was getting restless. I was beginning to think nothing was going to happen—perhaps because I was along. I was also wondering where Wilson's man was hiding himself; I assumed Wilson had put a man, or men, on Condon's house, and that we'd been trailed here. But the shadow man must have been goddamn good. Because I felt alone. Just me, Condon, the night, the wind and half the corpses in the Bronx.

Condon, rocking on his heels, was standing with his back to the iron gate.

And now, like something in a haunted-house movie, a hand was extending itself through the iron gates toward the professor.

I sat forward, about to call out, but the professor began to pace again. He moved well away from the extending ghostlike hand, looking everywhere but in that direction.

And now the hand withdrew, only to return seconds later, with something white in it. The white thing began to flutter like a bird. A handkerchief, waving. Whoever it was, in the cemetery, was trying desperately to signal the professor, without calling out to him.

Finally Condon noticed it, and moved quickly to the gates, where he began to speak to somebody on the other side. I rolled my window down, and the window on the other side, as well, but I could hear nothing but the wind.

They spoke for perhaps two minutes, and then Condon abruptly backed away.

"No!" I heard him say.

I reached for my gun.

Then I saw a figure, a man in a dark topcoat and hat, climb up, over and down the gate and land almost at Condon's feet. For a split second the two men faced each other, the one who'd jumped remaining in a catlike crouch.

"It's too dangerous!" the man said, and began to run.

The guy, who was about a head shorter than Condon, ran across the street, diagonally—right in front of me, though I got no sort of look at him at all, his dark felt hat brim pulled down, obscuring his face.

A cemetery security guard had appeared at the gate—his presence, apparently, had spooked the man in the dark topcoat—and was shouting, "Hey! What's going on?"

But Condon was ignoring that. The old boy was hoofing it across the street after the man. I had them both in sight. And I could have joined in the chase. But the professor was doing all right, at the moment. I stayed a spectator—for now.

The man ran north into the park; Condon followed, calling out to him: "Hey! Come back here! Don't be a coward!"

The guy slowed, and turned, and waited for Condon. They were only a few hundred feet into the park. The cemetery security guard hadn't even bothered to come out; he'd stayed inside to protect the dead. Condon and his companion were standing by a clump of trees near a small groundskeeper's hut with a park bench in front of it.

Condon gestured to the bench and the guy thought about it, and sat. And then so did Condon.

They sat and they talked. For a long, long time.

I thought about getting out of the car and finding my way to those trees and bushes and eavesdropping. But the guy's compatriots might be watching me, and I might queer the whole deal. And I could see both Condon and the man in the dark topcoat just fine. I could be there in seconds if trouble developed.

But it didn't. They just sat and talked.

While I sat stewing, my gun in my lap, looking around for signs of anybody else, kidnappers, T-men, innocent bystanders, anybody. Tonight the Bronx was as dead as Woodlawn Cemetery.

Finally, after an eternity, they stood.

And shook hands.

The man in the dark topcoat turned away and walked north, disappearing into the wooded park. Condon watched him go, then walked slowly toward my car. He was smiling.

"That went well, I think," he said, getting in.

"I'd have opened the car door for you," I said, "but my hands are numb from the cold. You talked to that guy for over an hour."

"There's no longer any possibility of doubt," he said. "We're in touch with the right ones. Those who have the baby. It's only a question of time, now."

"And money. You'll never know how close I came to following you. I should have grabbed that son of a bitch."

"What good would that do? You'd spoil everything!"

"Maybe," I said. "But I'm starting to think these bastards are playing us for suckers. That kid could be dead, you know."

Condon blanched, but recovered, a silly grin peeking out under the walrus mustache. "No, no. Everything's fine. The child's being fed according to the diet."

As we drove back to his home, an animated Condon told me about his meeting with the man, who gave his name as "John." And then he told it to Breckinridge, and the next day to Lindbergh. I heard it three times, and each time it was a little different.

The man in the dark overcoat and dark soft felt hat had held the white handkerchief to his face as he spoke to the professor through the bars of the iron gate.

"Did you got it, the money?" the man had asked.

"No," Condon said. "I can't bring the money until I see the package."

By "package" the professor meant the child, of course.

At this point the snap of a breaking twig had broken the gloom like a gunshot, startling both men.

"A cop!" the man said. "He's with you!"

At this point the man had climbed the gate and, for a moment, sans handkerchief mask, faced Condon.

"You brought the cops!"

"No! I wouldn't do that . . ."

"It's too dangerous!"

I interrupted Condon's story to ask him to describe the man.

"I only saw his face for a fleeting moment," Condon said.

"Well, you sat and talked to him for an hour!"

"In the dark, with his hat pulled down and his coat collar up," Condon pointed out. "But I would venture to say he was about five foot eight, aged thirty to thirty-five, weighing perhaps a hundred sixty pounds. Fair to chestnut hair."

"You said he never took his hat off."

"Yes, but that nonetheless is the coloration, judging by his sideburns, and the hair around his ears. He had almond-shaped eyes, like a Chinaman."

"Any accent?"

"Yes. Pronounced his *t*'s as *d*'s, and his *c*'s as *g*'s."

"German?"

"I would say Scandinavian."

After their brief face-to-face confrontation, the man had run across the street (in front of me in the parked flivver) into the park, and Condon—after assuring the approaching security guard that there was nothing wrong—followed him there, both of them settling on the park bench near the hut.

Condon claimed he had scolded the man, telling him not to behave so rudely: "You are my guest!"

Following that berserk lesson in ransom etiquette, they sat in silence, which the "guest" broke. "It's too dangerous. It would mean thirty years. Or I could burn. And I am only go-between."

Condon hadn't liked the sound of that. "What did you mean, you could 'burn'?"

"I would burn if the baby is dead."

"Dead! What are we doing here, if the child is dead!"

"The baby is not dead," the man had said with reassuring matter-of-factness. "Would I burn if the baby is *not* dead?"

"I'm a teacher, sir, not a lawyer. Is the child well?"

"The baby is better than it was. We give more for him to eat than we heard in the paper from Mrs. Lindbergh. Tell her not to worry. Tell the Colonel not to worry, either. Baby is all right."

"How do I know I am talking to the right man?"

"You got it, the letter with my singnature. Same singnature that was on my note in the crib."

Here I interrupted Condon again to say: "But it wasn't in the crib—it was on the windowsill."

Condon gestured dismissively. "That small discrepancy is negligible, compared to the confirmation I *did* receive."

Seated on the bench with his "guest," Condon had removed from his pocket a small canvas pouch, opened it and extracted the safety pins he'd taken from the Lindbergh nursery.

"What are these?" Condon asked.

"Pins from the baby's crib."

I shook my head hearing this, as Condon said to me, "And thus I proved, beyond a shadow of a doubt, that I was indeed talking to the man who stood in the nursery and lifted that child from his crib!"

"Professor," I said, "it doesn't take a genius to identify safety pins as coming from a baby's crib."

"But these were identified as being from the *Lindbergh* baby's crib!"

"Yeah, right. He might've guessed Baby Snooks, instead. Go on, go on."

Condon had asked the man his name.

"John," he'd said.

"My name is John, too. Where are you from, John?"

"Up farther than Boston."

"What do you do, John?"

"I'm a sailor."

"Bist du Deutsche?"

Condon's question got only a puzzled look in return; the professor asked again, in English.

"Are you German?"

"No," John said. "I'm Scandinavian."

Condon then took time to explain to John that his (that is, John's) mother, if she were still alive, would no doubt disapprove of these sordid activities. Then, because it was cold, Condon wasted even more time trying to convince his "guest"—who had a bad cough—to take his (that is, Condon's) topcoat.

The baby, John told the professor, was on a boat ("boad," he pronounced it). The boat was six hours away and could be identified by two white cloths on its masts. The ransom had been upped to seventy thousand because Lindbergh had disobeyed instructions and brought in the cops; besides, the kidnappers needed to put money aside in case they needed lawyers. The kidnap gang numbered six, two of whom were "womens." John's boss was "Number One," a "smart man" who worked for the government. Number One would receive twenty grand of the seventy sought, and John and the other two men and the two nurses would each receive ten grand.

"It seems to me that you are doing the most dangerous job," Condon said, sympathetically.

"I know it."

"You're getting a mere ten thousand dollars. I don't think you're getting your fair share."

"I know it."

"Look, John—leave them. Come with me to my house. I will get you one thousand dollars from my savings and see if I can get you more money from Colonel Lindbergh. That way, you'll be on the law's side."

John shook his head and said, "No—I can't do that. The boss would smack me out. They'd drill me."

"You'll be caught, John! Think of your mother!"

"We won't be caught. We plan too careful—we prepared a year for this."

Condon then offered to exchange himself as a hostage for the child; and when John turned him down, Condon asked to at least be taken to the baby. Surely John didn't expect that the Lindbergh forces would pay the money without first seeing the child.

"No!" John said. "Number One would drill us both, if I took you there. But I will send by ten o'clock Monday morning proof we have the boy."

"Proof?"

"His sleeping suit."

Then, Condon claimed, John spent several minutes assuring the doctor, who brought up the subject, that Red Johnson and Betty Gow were not involved in the kidnapping; that they were innocent.

"This," Condon said to me, "should be a relief to the Lindberghs and the police as well."

I didn't respond. My thoughts didn't exactly mirror the old goat's: I found it suspicious as hell that Condon would ask John about Johnson and Gow, and ridiculous that a kidnapper would 'heatedly' stick up for these strangers . . . unless of course they weren't strangers to him.

John, rising to go, had asked a final question. "You will put another ad in the Bronx *Home News?*"

"I will," Condon said.

"Say 'Money is ready,' " John said, walking backward, lifting a finger. "And this time, it better be."

And he turned and slipped into darkness.

"You shook hands with him," I said, "before he went off into the woods."

"Yes," Condon said, "but not as friends. Rather as negotiators who have come to a preliminary meeting of minds."

Any meeting of minds with Dr. John F. Condon was a poorly attended affair.

But the professor was tickled with himself and his adventure—delighted that channels were open for continued negotiations that would lead to the boy's safe return.

I was hoping Wilson's men had followed us here, had been silently watching, and had shadowed "John" home.

Yet I couldn't help feeling I'd fucked up, that I should have got out of the car to eavesdrop and either follow this bastard "John," or just nab him and beat the life, or the truth, out of him.

Whichever came first.

Chapter 14

The sleeping suit, which "John" had promised would be in Condon's hands by ten o'clock Monday morning, did not arrive until Wednesday's mail.

The days between were both tedious and tense, though the weather had turned pleasant. Overnight winter had transformed itself into spring, which wasn't entirely good news, as it heralded a new, worse-than-ever tourist assault on the Lindbergh estate. The New Jersey State cops were in their element, for a change, finally doing what they were qualified to do: direct traffic. Schwarzkopf's boys in their spiffy uniforms manfully warded off the sightseers, although—somewhat ironically, considering whose estate it was—the interlopers who could not be curtailed were the airplane pilots who, at $2.50 a ticket, were flying over the house and grounds all the sunny day long, to the delight of their rubbernecking passengers and the annoyance of all us on the ground.

On Tuesday, two weeks since the kidnapping, Colonel Schwarzkopf held a press conference about, among other things, Henry "Red" Johnson; seemed the sailor had been deemed innocent of any wrongdoing in the Lindbergh case, but was in federal custody awaiting deportation for entering the country illegally. What Schwarzkopf didn't tell the newshounds—because he didn't know it—was that I'd suggested to Frank Wilson of the IRS that Johnson's deportation proceed at a snail's pace, in case later on Johnson turned out not to be quite so "innocent."

Wilson continued to be cooperative with me, and I with him, but he had confirmed my suspicion, the night of the cemetery rendezvous with "John": nobody had trailed Condon and me, and nobody had, accordingly, been able to tail and trail John home.

"The orders come straight from the top," Wilson told me. "Lindbergh and Mills are pals, you know."

Wilson meant Ogden Mills, Secretary of the Treasury.

"That's insane," I said.

"We've been told to lay off," Wilson told me gloomily. "No stakeout on Condon, no interference in any way in how Colonel Lindbergh wants the case handled."

Hamstrung as they were, Wilson and the IRS agents were continuing their own investigation, including the ongoing search for Capone's man Bob Conroy; but Jafsie, John and the whole sorry crew were getting a free ride.

Around ten-thirty Wednesday morning at his house in the beautiful borough of the Bronx, Professor Condon received a pliant oblong brown-paper package, obviously the sleeping suit, though the old boy didn't open the bundle. Instead he called Breckinridge, at the attorney's office, to arrange for Lindbergh himself to come do the honors. Condon said he had his reasons for this, and one of them was obviously a desire to have Lucky Lindy as a houseguest.

But it was well after dark before Lindbergh and I were able to sneak away from the estate. The place was still crawling with reporters and sightseers. I drove the flivver, and Lindy crouched in back, wearing a cap and large-lensed amber glasses and a flannel shirt and well-worn, faded denim pants; it was a cool night, but he wore no topcoat—he looked like a delivery boy. He had the baby face for it.

We arrived at Condon's Bronx bungalow a little after one A.M. The professor answered the door and, for a moment, didn't know who Lindbergh was, till the amber glasses were removed. Not that Slim's disguise was impenetrable: I figured Condon gave himself the same puzzled expression every morning in the mirror.

"I have something for you," Condon told Lindbergh archly, as we followed him through the hallway and into the living room, where Colonel Breckinridge—still Condon's houseguest—waited.

The brown-paper bundle was on the grand piano, on the paisley shawl.

"Are you quite sure," Condon said, touching Lindbergh's arm, "that you wish—that you can *bear*—to inspect the contents of this package?"

Lindbergh said nothing; he just reached for the package and began to carefully unwrap it, like a fussy woman undoing a Christmas present, wanting to save the colorful paper for next year. A note had been enclosed, which he set aside. He lifted out a small woolen garment—a gray sleeping suit. A red label in the back collar identified it as a Dr. Denton's, size two.

Lindbergh looked at it curiously. He sniffed it. "I think it's been laundered," he said.

"Let me have a look," I said.

He handed it to me hesitantly, as if the slack suit were the child itself.

"It could've been washed," I said, taking it, examining it. "Or it could be new. Whoever sent it might've had to go out and buy it."

Lindbergh's face squeezed in on itself. "How would they know what to buy? The description we gave the papers was purposely misleading."

That was true: the press had been told, and printed, that the sleeping suit was a "fine, white balbriggan" that buttoned in front with a backflap. This one buttoned in back, and was gray, with a breast pocket.

"Somebody who worked around your kid would know," I said.

He grimaced irritably and said, "I'm convinced this is the sleeping suit."

"Well, then. You're convinced. Better have a look at the note."

He did. We all did. It was signed with the by-now-familiar interlocking-circles signature. It said:

> Dear Sir: Ouer man fails to collect the
> mony. There are no more confidential

conference after the meeting from March
12. Those arrangements to hazardous
for us. We will note allow ouer man
to confer in a way like before.
Circumstance will note allow us
to make a transfare like you wish.
It is impossibly for us. Wy should we
move the baby and face danger to
take another person to the plase is
entirely out of question. It seems
you are afraid if we are the right
party and if the boy is alright. Well
you have ouer singnature. It is always
the same as the first one
specialy these three hohls

It continued on the reverse:

Now we will send you the sleepingsuit
from the baby besides it means 3 $ extra
expenses because we have to pay
another one. Pleace tell Mrs. Lindbergh
note to worry the baby is well. We only
have to give him more food as the diet says.
      You are willing to pay the 70000
note 50000 $ without seeing the baby first
or note. let us know about that in the
New York-american. We can't do it other ways.
because we don't like to give up
ouer safty plase or to move the baby.
If you are willing to accept this deal
put these in the paper.
      I accept mony is ready
            ouer program is:
after eight houers we have the mony receivd
we will notify you where to find the
baby. If thers is any trapp, you will be
                  responsible what
                  will follows.

"What does this mean," Breckinridge asked, taking the note. "This business of 'Circumstance will not allow us to make a transfer like you wish.' "

"I pleaded with him," Condon said, "that I might be taken to the place where the child was being kept, to ascertain the boy's health and safety."

"If he won't let us see the child before the money is paid," Lindbergh said glumly, "we'll pay it anyway."

"Well, after all," Condon said, cheerfully, "this fellow has kept his word with us throughout. And we've kept our word with him."

"Yes," Lindbergh said, eyes at once haunted and bright. "There's no reason to think they won't deliver my son as soon as they get their money."

I didn't say anything. There was nothing short of a couple of straitjackets that would straighten this pair out on this subject.

"We'd best draft our response to the kidnappers," Condon said, putting a grandfatherly hand on his famous guest's shoulder. "For the newspaper ad."

We sat in the living room and Condon, Breckinridge and Lindbergh hashed it out. I didn't contribute. I was thinking about Chicago, now that the snow would be thawing.

"We can't let negotiations drag on too long," Lindbergh was saying. "If the kidnappers get impatient, or the newspapers get wind of this, my son could pay with his life."

"Sir," Condon said, "I think it's important for us to at least try to see the baby before the money is paid."

I almost fell off the couch: the old boy had said something that actually made sense.

"No," Lindbergh said. "We're in no position to make demands. It's their game: we play by their rules. Run the ad they want."

A little after three in the morning, Condon's pretty, sullen daughter Myra entered and offered us a light meal in the dining room. I didn't know why she was here, and I didn't ask. But she was marginally friendlier this time around, probably because of the famous presence of Colonel Lindbergh; and her chicken-salad sandwiches and lemonade were fine. Half an hour later we began to leave, and Lindbergh paused at the grand piano in the living room, where on the paisley shawl the unwrapped brown-paper package had been set.

Lindbergh reached for the package, quickly, impatiently, and handed it to me, like it was something hot.

"We'd better get back," he said to me, "and show this to Anne."

I drove—the most famous pilot in the world my passenger. We rode silently for a good long time. We approached the George Washington Bridge, its silver arc indistinct against the night, a parade of flickering lights moving across it over the Hudson. We joined that parade and when urban New Jersey faded into rural New Jersey, he began to speak.

"You think I'm foolish, don't you, Nate?"

"I think you're human. The problem is, most of the people you get advice from don't."

He was looking absently out the side window, into darkness. He was still wearing the amber glasses and cap; he wore them all the way home. "I'm anxious to have this over."

"Don't get too anxious."

He looked at me. "Do you trust Condon?"

"Not particularly."

"Do you think he's an accomplice?"

"Maybe. Or a dupe."

"Or exactly what he seems to be?"

"Which is what, Slim?"

"A good-hearted old patriot who wants to help out . . ." And he trailed off.

"Who wants to help out the 'Lone Eagle'? Maybe. A bigger question is, are these extortionists the people who have your son?"

"You don't think they are?"

"They could be operating off inside information from servants, or from Mickey Rosner. They don't know anything I don't know, for example. And what the hell do you know about me?"

"I know I trust you."

"Well, you shouldn't. You shouldn't trust any fucking body."

"I trust my own instincts."

"And your instincts tell you that 'John' is one of the kidnappers?"

He shook his head from side to side, but it was not in a "no" gesture. "I'm not closing off any avenue I can go down to find my son. And this sleeping suit . . ."

"This sleeping suit is standard issue, Slim. Store-bought, lacking in laundry marks, or any other identification. There are thousands, tens of thousands, like it."

"I gave the newspapers a false description of the garment, remember?"

"I remember. So the extortionists could have got lucky, or they could have had inside information. Here's another thought—doesn't your son have his own bedroom at your wife's mother's house, at Englewood?"

"Why, yes."

"How many of these sleepers, how many sleepers just like this one, are there in a drawer in that Englewood nursery?"

"I don't know. I don't believe we have an exact inventory for such things."

"Right. And how many servants do they have in that joint? Around thirty—any one of whom could have provided a description, or plucked a sleeping suit from a drawer. That would explain why it took several days for Cemetery John and crew to deliver those pj's. And why it's freshly laundered."

He didn't say anything.

"For that matter, Condon himself could've taken a sleeper from your son's drawer."

"Are you serious?"

"He could've, just like I could've. We both slept in that room. I caught Condon going through your kid's toy box, remember?"

He said nothing; he was frowning.

I shook my head and drove. We were driving through farm country, now, that might well have been Illinois. I wished it were.

"Anne will know," he said.

"What?"

"If it's Charlie's sleeping suit. Anne will know."

I knew enough not to respond to that one.

We drove in silence again. I mulled a few things over that I didn't share with him. How phony the German phrasing of the

notes seemed to me, particularly in light of the Sicilian phrase—
statti citto—in the phone call to Condon, and Condon's own discovery of the Black Hand meaning of the "singnature" on the notes.
This latest note again contained a suspicious number of correctly
spelled, difficult words, among the misspelled smaller ones. And
John in the cemetery used gangland phrases—"The boss would
smack me out," "drill us both." I supposed a Scandinavian immigrant could have picked up such talk. But somehow it just didn't
ring true.

"The other day," I said, breaking the silence as the black sky
began turning gray, "you indicated there were other 'parties,' besides the professor, who might be in contact with the kidnappers.
You wouldn't want to let me in on any of that, would you?"

He didn't hesitate in his response. "Actually, you should know.
It involves your specialty: gangsters. It's one of the reasons why I
asked you to stick around."

It seemed there was a socially prominent individual in Norfolk,
Virginia, a certain Commodore John Hughes Curtis, who'd been
approached by a bootlegger who claimed to be one of a gang of six
who kidnapped Lindbergh's son.

"Curtis is the president of one of the largest ship-building
companies in the South," Lindbergh said. "He has impeccable
credentials—Admiral Burrage called me, in fact, to arrange a meeting between Curtis and myself."

Now, added to the endless list of colonels, were an admiral
and a commodore.

"Admiral Burrage," Lindbergh explained almost defensively,
reading my cynical expression no doubt, "was in command of the
cruiser *Memphis,* the ship that brought me back from Paris."

Back from his legendary solo transatlantic flight to Paris, he
meant.

"Besides," he said, "the Very Reverend H. Dobson-Peacock
has vouched for Curtis, as well."

Now we had a Reverend on the list. A Very Reverend.

"Who is this Peacock, anyway?"

"Reverend Dobson-Peacock is an old friend of the Morrow
family. The Reverend was in charge of a church in Mexico City."

The late Dwight Morrow had been Ambassador to Mexico; it was during that period that Anne Morrow and Charles Lindbergh met, wooed and fell in love.

"I've agreed to meet tomorrow afternoon with the Admiral, the Reverend and the Commodore," he said. It sounded like a nursery rhyme. "I'd like you to sit in."

I turned onto the rutted dirt road that was Featherbed Lane. Dawn was starting to sneak through the thickets on either side of us, like another nosy sightseer.

Suddenly, Lindbergh burst out with something as if both eager and embarrassed to say it. "Did you ever hear of a man named Gaston Bullock Means?"

I snorted a laugh. "Are you kidding? Sure I've heard of him. Biggest con man who ever lived, in a couple senses of the word 'biggest.' Chicago is one of that fat bastard's favorite sucker ponds."

There was a faint defensiveness in Lindbergh's soft response: "My understanding is that he's a former Justice Department operative."

"Yeah—he worked for Burns, before J. Edgar Hoover cleaned house. Hoover's an ass, but he's not a crook like Burns and his boys. Gaston Means was the Ohio Gang's bagman, during the Harding administration. What in hell are you asking me about that son of a bitch for?"

Lindbergh was silent for a moment. Then he said, "Means also claims to be in touch with the kidnap gang."

"Oh, Christ."

"I had a call from Admiral Land . . ."

Another admiral!

". . . who's a relative of mine. My mother's cousin. Anyway, Admiral Land was approached by Mrs. Evalyn Walsh McLean, the Washington society woman."

"The Hope diamond dame?"

"That's the one. She lost her own son a few years ago—whether it relates to the Hope diamond curse is anybody's guess—but at any rate, she's sympathetic to Anne and my situation. Means is in her employ."

"Why?"

"I don't know exactly. He's done some private detective work for her before. But through her he passed along two pieces of information that make me think we shouldn't rule him out."

"Which are?"

"He says the kidnappers have raised their ransom demand from fifty thousand to one hundred thousand dollars. That ties in, at least roughly, with the notes we've received, from Cemetery John and his gang."

"And the other?"

Lindbergh seemed hesitant to share that. But finally, as we were drawing up to the closed, locked gate, he said, "He told Mrs. McLean the description in the papers of the sleeping suit was a false clue." Lindbergh pointed to, but did not touch, the loosely wrapped brown-paper package next to him. "And he described the sleeping suit Charlie was really wearing."

"A lot of that going around," I said, "wouldn't you say?"

He frowned, but not in anger. Frustration.

It was light out by the time we reached the house. Anne Lindbergh, in a thin blue robe, met us at the door to the servants' sitting room; her face was pale, bare of makeup, her hair drawn back tightly. She looked haggard but hopeful.

I was carrying the package. Lindbergh nodded to me and I handed it to her.

She drew out the sleeping suit and held it in her hands out away from her, like something both precious and terrible. Then she clasped the package to her bosom, the paper crackling, one arm of the garment slinging itself over her shoulder.

Her eyes were glittering and her smile was a tragic fucking thing.

"It's his," she said. "It's Charlie's."

"It's a good sign," he told her, with a deathly smile. "It means the kidnappers can be trusted. It means negotiations are finally, truly, fruitfully, in full sway."

She hugged the brown paper and the Dr. Denton and said, again, "It's Charlie's. It's his."

And after that, there was never any doubt of it.

Slim wouldn't allow any.

Chapter 15

Late the next afternoon, Lindbergh, Schwarzkopf and I met a black touring car that rolled to a stop near the garage command post. The car had Virginia license plates and a small American flag on its radio antenna. Three men stepped out.

The driver was a long, lean man in his late sixties wearing a well-tailored navy-blue suit under a tan camel-hair topcoat; his face was hawklike, with a trim gray mustache, his stone-gray hair parted neatly in the middle. In the backseat had been a stocky, balding fellow in black and his vague fifties, several chins rubbing his clerical collar, his eyes wide-set and buggy. Riding in front had been the most prepossessing of this singular trio, a big, tanned, muscular-looking man with a round, pleasant face under a jaunty bowler; he wore a gray topcoat over his dark suit, a red-white-and-blue tie peeking out from under.

Lindbergh greeted them, speaking to the thin, mustached hawk-faced man first. "Admiral Burrage," he said. "Good of you to come."

"Pleasure to see you again, Colonel," he said, his smile somber.

"Sorry the circumstances are such as they are. Is your mother well?"

"She is, thank you."

"Good. Good." Burrage introduced the clergyman as the Very Reverend Dobson-Peacock, and the tanned hail-fellow-well-met as Commodore John Hughes Curtis.

"This is Colonel Schwarzkopf of the New Jersey State Police," Lindbergh said, gesturing to the impressively uniformed police official, and the men began shaking hands all round. "He'll be sitting in with us. So will Detective Nathan Heller, of the Chicago Police Department."

They looked at me curiously, as well they might, and Curtis said, with a pixie smile, "Have you wandered off your beat, son?"

"Not really," I said, shaking the hand he offered. "From the first day of this affair there've been indications the Capone outfit may be involved. I'm here to check that angle out."

Curtis nodded somberly. "That certainly doesn't contradict what I've experienced, Detective Heller."

"Just out of curiosity, Commodore," I asked, "what are you commodore of?"

"The Norfolk Yacht Club."

"Why don't we all step inside," Lindbergh said, gesturing toward the house. "We have much to discuss."

In the study, Elsie Whately brought in a tray of tea and coffee, and we got settled around in chairs all cozy with our cups in hand, the fireplace going. Lindbergh, who was drinking milk, took his position behind the cluttered desk and said, "I'm sorry if there were problems getting in touch with me."

Dobson-Peacock spoke up; his voice was as British-sounding as his name.

"Frankly, Colonel," he said, not hiding his exasperation, "it's been a frustrating experience, getting through. I left a message with a gentleman . . ." The word "gentleman" was invested with considerable sarcasm. ". . . who identified himself as your 'secretary'— a Mr. Rosner. This was some *days* ago, Colonel."

Lindbergh lifted one eyebrow, barely, and set it back down. "I'm sorry, Reverend. But things have been harried here. It took me two days to return a call to the White House, last week."

"Charles," the admiral said gently, "I hope you know that I would go to the ends of the earth to help you get your boy back."

"Thank you, Admiral."

"Then forgive me for asking, but have we spoken recently?"

"Why, no. I received your letter, and had Colonel Breckinridge contact you. . . ."

"Well, when I called here, I spoke with someone who identified himself as you—but clearly wasn't."

I'd played that game once myself, but wasn't the guilty party this time.

Burrage was saying, with stiff formality, "At first I spoke with this fellow Rosner—who said, and I quote, 'Oh, another admiral, huh?' Soon I spoke to someone who identified himself as 'Colonel Lindbergh,' and met my information with utter indifference. I'm not convinced it wasn't the same man."

"Gentlemen," Lindbergh said, his weariness apparent, his embarrassment, too, "I'm sorry you were inconvenienced, and treated disrespectfully . . ."

"Charles," Burrage said, "no one is looking for an apology, good Lord, not at all. We merely want to make clear to you why it's taken us so long to put this possibly vital information before you."

"We would hate," Dobson-Peacock said, teacup daintily in hand, "to be found negligent, when in fact we've made every reasonable effort to . . ."

Lindbergh raised a palm. "You're here. The delay, whoever's fault it may have been, is behind us. Commodore Curtis, I'd appreciate hearing your story."

Curtis beamed. "I'm relieved to be here, at last, Colonel. So very relieved." He swallowed, and began: "On the night of March ninth I was attending a meeting at the Norfolk Yacht Club. Every yachtsman in the club was there, it was urgent business—winter storms were raising hell with our piers and moorings. You know how it is."

Lindbergh, hands folded before him prayerfully, nodded.

Curtis went on: "I was one of the last to leave the meeting. And I'd had a little to drink, frankly, but what happened in the parking lot sobered me up immediately."

An old Hudson sedan had pulled alongside Curtis, actually blocking the path of his green Hudson, making him stop. At first he'd assumed it was one of his yachting friends, but then he recognized the driver as Sam, a rumrunner for whom Curtis had on several occasions arranged boat repairs.

"Sam jumped out of his car," Curtis said, gesturing with both hands, his eyes intense, "and jumped onto my running board. He leaned in the window and said, 'Don't get sore, Mr. Curtis! I gotta talk to you.' "

Sam had slipped into the front seat and was "shaking like a leaf." The normally "cool as a cucumber" rumrunner made Curtis promise he would not tell anyone what he was about to reveal. Curtis promised. Sam said he'd been sent to Curtis by the gang that stole the Lindbergh baby.

"He said they wanted him to contact me," Curtis said, gesturing to himself, as if he couldn't believe his own words, "to form a small, select committee of prominent Norfolk citizens who would act as intermediaries . . . to arrange the ransom payment and the return of the child."

Curtis had asked, Why me? And why Norfolk, Virginia, of all places? Sam had answered the latter question by saying that the kidnappers feared a demand for a split, or a flat-out hijack, from Owney Madden's New York mob; and as to the former, well, Curtis was known to be a "square john." He'd repaired boats for rumrunners—like many a dockyard man along the coast—but was at the same time a pillar of society.

"I asked them why they didn't deal with these appointed underworld go-betweens the papers were talking about," Curtis said, "Spitale and Bitz. And Sam said the gang wrote them off as small-timers, a joke."

I interrupted with a question. "How reliable is this guy, this 'Sam'?"

Curtis shrugged. "I've never caught him in a lie or an attempted fraud. I'd say, for a man in a shady line of work, he's a square-dealer. I've even put a good word in for him with the Coast Guard, occasionally."

"What's his last name?"

"I don't know. He has a lot of aliases."

Lindbergh said, "Can you get in touch with him?"

Curtis nodded. "Yes. But I feel I must protect Sam, at this juncture, to better protect your son. If anyone but me contacts him, it might be risky."

"I agree," Lindbergh said.

Here we go again: playing by the rules in a game set up by cheats.

"I told Sam, emphatically," Curtis said, emphatically, "that under no circumstances would I ask you for any money, Colonel Lindbergh. Sam claimed that the gang understood this, and that they wanted the ransom deposited in a Norfolk bank and only paid *after* the child had been returned safe and sound."

Lindbergh's eyes narrowed.

"At any rate, that was what Sam said on the first meeting," Curtis said. He almost whispered the next, milking the melodrama: "Sam called again, four days ago. He told me the kidnappers are getting 'antsy'—though the baby is all right. They hired a special nurse and are following the diet Mrs. Lindbergh published in the papers. They also say they bought a new outfit for the little boy."

All of the latter tallied with Condon's cemetery contact: the nurse following the diet; buying a new outfit, after the sleeper had been sent along.

"Sam told me," Curtis said, "that you're negotiating with another member of the same gang up here. Sam says the man up here wants fifty thousand dollars, maybe as much as one hundred thousand dollars. But Sam says he can deliver your son for twenty-five thousand dollars."

Lindbergh and I exchanged sharp glances. Not a word about Condon had leaked to the press—yet the Norfolk gang seemed to know about Jafsie's negotiations, and the increased ransom demand.

"The token of good faith the kidnappers are demanding," Curtis said, "is that sum—twenty-five thousand dollars—deposited in a Norfolk bank in the name of the three of us . . . Reverend Dobson-Peacock, Admiral Burrage and myself. We have been accepted as the committee of intermediaries."

Curtis sat back, finished with his tale, and Lindbergh sat and stared at his folded hands. The fire crackled and snapped. The three gents from Virginia exchanged uneasy glances. Silence hung in the room like steam.

Awkwardly, Curtis broke the silence. "Colonel—how much ransom are you willing to pay? Is that figure too high . . . ?"

Without looking up, Lindbergh said, "I can't agree on any sum, until I have positive proof that I'm dealing with the right people."

Of course, he couldn't tell these three that he was already deep in negotiations with Condon's Cemetery John. Even if their contact, Sam, already seemed to know as much, it was clear that Curtis, Dobson-Peacock and Burrage didn't.

"If they really have my child," Lindbergh said, "they can prove it by describing certain physical characteristics the boy has, which haven't been shared with the press."

Curtis, obviously disturbed by the tentativeness of this, said, "Colonel, I've told Sam repeatedly that under no circumstances will any money be handed over until you hold your boy in your arms . . ."

Lindbergh rose. "I have no doubt, gentlemen, of your good intentions." He looked at Burrage and said, "Admiral, I know you want only the best for Anne and Charlie and me."

The three men, sensing their imminent dismissal, stood. They looked crestfallen to a man.

Lindbergh came around and placed a hand on Burrage's shoulder. "But, gentlemen, I'm in no position right now to deposit that twenty-five thousand dollars."

Curtis said, "If that's the case, Colonel, I'm sure I could raise the money myself, among my friends at the club . . ."

Lindbergh raised a hand, gently. He said, "I'm not closing any doors, Commodore. Tell your friend Sam that if he can give you—or the Admiral or the Reverend—a photo of Charlie taken since the night he disappeared, I'll be convinced."

Curtis nodded, apparently pacified.

"Or," Lindbergh said, "get a few words in writing from them, and tell them to sign the note with a certain symbol."

"Certain symbol?" Curtis asked.

"They'll know," Lindbergh said. "At least they will, if they're for real. I want to thank you for your trouble, for your concern, for your long trip north . . . could I invite you to stay for dinner?"

"We'd be honored," Curtis said, quickly.

Reverend Dobson-Peacock, who clearly loved to eat, was nodding his second. Burrage seemed vaguely embarrassed, but he thanked Lindbergh and also accepted.

Lindbergh showed them into the living room, gesturing to Schwarzkopf and myself to stay in the study. We could hear the dog's bark echoing out there.

Lindy returned without them, shortly, and said, "Well?"

"I can't read it," I said.

Schwarzkopf laughed shortly. "That's not like you, Heller. You always have an opinion. Particularly, a negative one."

"Not this time. The Admiral and the Reverend are legit—Curtis is maybe a wild card. He seems a little full of himself."

"He's a successful shipbuilder," Lindbergh said.

"These are hard times," I said. "A check on his financial status wouldn't hurt."

"I agree with Heller," Schwarzkopf said, a little surprised that he did.

Lindbergh nodded his assent. "But some of what Curtis said does jibe with information from Professor Condon's contact."

"Except his 'Sam' is willing to settle for twenty-five thousand," Schwarzkopf pointed out. " 'John' wants seventy."

Lindbergh sighed. Shook his head. "I don't know what to think. Hell. Maybe we should be encouraged that a gang member is offering my son's return at a bargain rate."

"This half-price sale," I said, "may not be a good sign."

They both looked at me.

"It may mean there's dissension in the ranks. If this is the same group, and different members are approaching different parties to sell the kid to, well . . ." I shrugged.

Lindbergh went over and poked at the fire. It was dying. His mouth was drawn tight.

"By the way, Colonel," Schwarzkopf said, "I want to make it clear that I was not the one who gave Admiral Burrage the runaround on the phone."

"Mickey did that," I said, "dollars to doughnuts."

"Certainly at the very least," Schwarzkopf said, "that little hoodlum was goddamned rude to the Admiral."

Lindbergh said nothing. Just poked the fire.

"You know that splash in the papers the other day," I said, "where Rosner and Spitale and Bitz spouted off to the press? Well, it wasn't quite how it played in the papers."

"What do you mean?" Lindbergh asked.

The papers had indicated each man had been tracked down at his home or business, for interview; I explained that in fact the three had held a press conference in their speakeasy, which catered to the yellow press.

"Colonel," Lindbergh said to Schwarzkopf, rather distantly, "I notice you've sent some of your men home." He stirred the glowing ashes. "How should I interpret that?"

Schwarzkopf stood as if at attention. "Strictly a budgetary measure. I'm afraid we've exhausted the five thousand dollars in the State Police Emergency Fund."

"I see."

"We've cut off the catering from New York, and are now having meals prepared at Lambertville Barracks, and shipped here by car every day."

Lindbergh nodded. He looked at Schwarzkopf; the fire glowed orangely on the young Lindbergh's rather bland face. He said, "I wish I could afford to feed your men myself, Colonel. God knows I appreciate what they, and you, have done."

"And will continue to do. I'm simply curtailing all unnecessary expenses. I'll be appearing before the State Finance Committee next week, looking for more funds."

"I'm sorry you've run through your emergency kitty."

"Colonel, we've already spent far more than that."

"How much has this effort cost, thus far?"

Schwarzkopf swallowed. "Fifty thousand dollars, Colonel."

Lindbergh looked blankly into the fire. "Fifty thousand dollars. The initial ransom figure. There's an irony in that, somewhere."

"If there is," Schwarzkopf said, "I'm sure your friend Mr. Heller will find it."

Schwarzkopf nodded curtly to Lindbergh and went out, revealing Mickey Rosner leaning against the wall, reading the *Daily News*.

"Step in here, Mr. Rosner," Lindbergh said.

"Sure, Colonel."

Mickey, wearing a cocky little smile, stood and rocked on his heels.

"I want you to do something for me."

"Just name it, Colonel."

"Take Spitale and Bitz off the case."

"Well . . . sure. But, why?"

"They aren't acceptable intermediaries."

"Well . . . you're the boss. Anything else?"

"Yes. Clear out."

"Clear out? You mean . . . clear out?"

"Clear out. You're off the case, too."

Rosner looked at me and sneered. "Thanks for nothing, Heller."

"Any time, Mickey," I said.

Rosner breathed through his nose, nodded to Lindbergh and shut the door behind him.

"No answer to our ad," Lindbergh said, turning to me, what just happened with Rosner already forgotten, or anyway, filed away.

"Give it time," I said. "These boys have moved slowly all the way. No need to read anything into it."

"I suppose. Anyway, this time the money *is* ready. Fifty thousand of it, at least. This afternoon armed guards from J. P. Morgan brought the cash to the Fordham Branch of the Corn Exchange Bank, where I've arranged for Professor Condon to have twenty-four-hour access to it."

"You've made a list of the serial numbers, surely?"

"No."

I didn't know what to say to that.

"You think I'm botching this, don't you, Nate?"

"What I think isn't important."

"It is to me."

"Then let Frank Wilson and Elmer Irey and the rest of the T-men take the gloves off."

He said nothing.

Then he put a hand on my shoulder and said, "I just want Charlie back. I want this to be over, and Charlie to be back with his mother. Understand?"

I understood. You didn't have to be a father to understand that.

He removed his hand; smiled awkwardly. "Join us for dinner?"

"Thanks. I'd like the chance to study those three Virginians a little more."

"I may have you look into Curtis—discreetly."

"That would be my pleasure."

"But I have something else I'd like you to do, first."

"Oh?"

"Would you take a trip to Washington, D.C., for me? I want you to meet this Mrs. McLean."

"The society dame who's hired Gaston Means to play private eye?"

"That's right. Apparently Mrs. McLean has put together one hundred thousand dollars in fives, tens and twenties to give Means to give the kidnappers. I'd like you to find out if she's spending her money wisely."

Chapter 16

ashington, D.C., was as cold and gray as its granite memorials; what I'd heard about our nation's capital and cherry blossoms in the springtime remained a rumor. I'd taken the train from Princeton, arrived at Union Station and let a taxi carry me out into the bleak wintry afternoon. No point in trying to maneuver a car around these streets myself; I'd had a look at a D.C. map back at Hopewell and knew it was hopeless: wheels within wheels with stray spokes flung here and there.

As the taxi drew away from the train station plaza, a modest little collection of fountains and monuments and statues overseen by the Capitol dome, I straightened my tie and pulled up my socks, thinking about the million-some bucks I was about to call on.

Million-dollar destination or not, it was just a fifty-cent ride, including tip, down Massachusetts Avenue to Dupont Circle. My cabbie, a redheaded kid who looked Irish but had a Southern accent, pointed the sights out to me lethargically as we crawled through traffic as thick as any in Chicago or New York. I was less interested in the Government Printing Office or the row of redbrick buildings "built for Stephen Douglas back in the 1850s" than the stream of pretty young female office-workers getting off work, pouring out of the various government buildings like coeds heading for the big game. Here and there tattered unshaven guys selling apples or just looking for some buddy to spare them a dime leaned in the shadows of massive, unheeding buildings they probably helped pay for, back when they were making a living. Soon those buildings briefly gave way to colored tenements, until poverty again slipped into the shadow of limestone and white marble. After about the sixth statue of some distinguished dead guy—a Civil War hero or Daniel Webster or whoever—I informed the cabbie, "The commentary won't buy you a bigger tip. Do I look like a big spender?"

Actually, I almost did. I was manicured, cleaned, pressed, pomaded, perfectly presentable from my topcoat to my toenails. I had clean underwear on and everything. Lindbergh had slipped me fifty extra bucks expenses, and asked me to pack my bag so I could stay as long or short as this took.

The cabbie drew up in front of a building slightly smaller than Chicago's City Hall. I knew there had to be some mistake.

"This isn't it," I said, half out of the cab, half in.

"Sure it is," he drawled. "2020 Massachusetts."

"But I'm supposed to be dropped off at a residence. This is a damn embassy or something."

The building before me was a four-story brick building that looked regal in a vaguely Italian way, its walls curving, black latticework and white columns dressing the many windows; but despite the gingerbread, the joint seemed institutional, somehow, a cross between a villa and a public school—a big public school.

"Who are you callin' on?"

"Mrs. Evalyn Walsh McLean."

"That's where Mrs. McLean lives, all right," he said. "You figure her for a bungalow, bud?"

The black iron-spike fence was unlocked. Detective that I am, I found my way up a winding walk through an evergreen-landscaped yard to an elaborate inset pillared front porch, sort of a portico that got punched in. Massive dark-wood-and-cut-glass doors were framed by smooth, round, green-veined marble columns. Wearing clean underwear suddenly seemed less than impressive.

The butler who answered the doorbell certainly wasn't impressed with me, clean underwear or not. He was tall, beefy, pale, cueball-bald and perhaps fifty, with a lumpy blank face and contempt-filled eyes.

I didn't wait to be asked in. I was used to servants who didn't like me, and brushed by him, saying, "Nathan Heller. Mrs. McLean is expecting me."

That display of cockiness got knocked right out of me as I moved into a reception area you could've dropped my residential hotel on Dearborn in and still done plenty of receiving.

"Your coat, sir," the butler said. "And your baggage?" Clipped British tones, but this bloke was no Brit.

I climbed out of the coat, handed it and the traveling bag to him, trying not to scrape my jaw on the floor as I took everything in. The reception hall rose four stories to a vast stained-glass window that bathed the rich dark-wood room in golden dappled light. An impossibly wide staircase rose under the golden window to a landing where two marble classical statues did a frozen dance; on their either side, a stairway rose to promenade galleries on successive floors.

So deep into the afternoon, on an overcast day like this one, it struck me as weird that the stained-glass skylight could still turn this room into a golden shrine. Then it hit me: not the how, but the why—Evalyn Walsh McLean's father, Thomas F. Walsh, had been a Colorado mining millionaire. A gold miner who struck it rich.

The butler returned without my coat and bag, but with the same air of superiority.

"Was this by any chance the Walsh family home?" I asked.

"Yes, sir."

That explained the gold motif, all right.

"Who lives here now?"

"Mrs. McLean, sir, and her three children, when they're not off at school, sir."

"And Mr. McLean?"

He pursed his lips. "Mr. and Mrs. McLean do not live together, sir. Please come with me. Mrs. McLean is waiting."

Our footsteps echoed and reechoed across the oak parquet floor. The door he opened for me, over to the left, was small; one would not expect it to lead anywhere grand.

One would be wrong.

We were now in what seemed to be a ballroom: an elaborate mural of angelic babes—both the bosomy and cherubic varieties—playing musical instruments on a curved plaster sky; the walls were surprisingly unostentatious plaster, but the wood trim was all gilt-edged. There was a cut-glass chandelier, and a stage behind which sheer-yellow-curtained windows bathed the room golden.

"What is this?" I asked him, working to keep up with him, as we cut diagonally across the smooth wood floor. We seemed to be heading toward a gold-veined marble fireplace.

"The Louis XV ballroom, sir."

"I've never been in a house with a ballroom before."

"There are several more upstairs, sir. Not to mention the roof garden."

"Not to mention that."

He opened a door just past the fireplace and indicated I should go on in.

The half-circle sun porch I stepped out onto seemed small in comparison to where I'd just been, but in reality was bigger than a suite at the Palmer House. Horizontal golden stained-glass panels above the windows painted the white room yellowish. This whole goddamn house had jaundice.

There wasn't much furniture: just a few hard-back plush-seated chairs here and there. She wasn't using one of them. She was standing, staring out at the street, across the snow-smattered and surprisingly meager brown lawn. She was small, and she was wearing a brown-and-yellow plaid woolen housecoat, the kind you could get for under a dollar at Sears Roebuck. Her back was to me, but her hand was turned toward me, away from her, diamonds and rubies on the fingers, a cigarette trailing smoke toward the doves in the stained glass above.

The butler cleared his throat and, with an expression he might have used while disposing of a dead rat by its tail with two fingers, said, "Mr. Heller to see you, madam."

Her back still to us, she said, "Thank you, Garboni."

I knew he was no limey.

"Leave the door open, Garboni. I'm expecting Mike any minute." Her voice was husky; a sensual, throaty sound, two parts sex, one part chain-smoking.

He left us and I stayed planted well away from her, waiting for her to recognize my presence.

She turned slowly, like a ballerina on a music box. She was a morosely beautiful woman, with sad blue almond-shaped eyes, a slender, gently aquiline nose, lips neither thin nor full, painted blood-red. Her hair was short and dark brown, several curls studiously poised on her smooth, pale forehead. The dowdy bathrobe was floor-length but sashed around her small waist rather tightly; silver slippers peeked out from under. She was slim, almost tiny, but her breasts were large and high, a Gibson Girl figure, and she had that kind of face as well. She looked perhaps thirty, though forty was more like it.

She smiled but it only made her eyes sadder. "Mr. Heller," she said, and moved toward me quickly, extending a red-nailed, bejeweled hand. "So kind of you to come. So kind of Colonel Lindbergh to send you."

I took her hand, wondering if I was expected to kiss it, which I wouldn't have minded doing—you got to start someplace. But before I could make up my mind, she tugged me over to one of two chairs on either side of a small glass-topped table where an overflowing ashtray sat next to a square, silver, sleek decorative lighter and a flat, square, silver decorative cigarette case on which "EWM" was engraved in a modernistic flourish.

She perched herself on the edge of the chair across from me, crossing her legs, robe falling away enough to reveal gams that were smooth and white and shapely. Being rich agreed with her.

"Excuse my appearance," she said, shaking her head of curls, smiling ruefully. "Around the house, I'm a regular slob."

"You look fine to me, Mrs. McLean."

"If I'd known you would turn out to be such a handsome

young man," she said, her smile turning wicked, "I might have tried to dazzle you. I was expecting a policeman."

"That's what I am."

"But not the rumpled, potbellied kind." She flicked ashes into the tray. "You're from Chicago?"

"Yes, ma'am."

"I understand Gaston Bullock Means is well known there."

"Yes he is. I've never met him myself, but I work pickpocket detail, and we frequently link up with the bunco boys. And they know Means very well indeed."

"You may think me foolish," she said, with a smirk directed at herself, "for calling upon that blackguard. But I understand Colonel Lindbergh himself has sought assistance in the underworld."

Her arch phrasing should have seemed ridiculous to me; but for some reason I found it charming. Or maybe it was her legs I found charming. Or her breasts. Or her money.

"Colonel Lindbergh," I said, "*has* tried going the underworld route—but recently he fired those bootlegger would-be go-betweens of his."

"But he didn't fire you."

"No. But I'm not a gangster."

"You're a Chicago policeman."

"Yeah, but that's not exactly the same thing. Sometimes it's a fine line, I admit. . . ."

Her eyes narrowed; either my humor eluded her or she was too preoccupied to notice it. "I have been of the belief, from the very beginning, that this was an underworld job. Specifically, that your fellow Chicagoan Al Capone had a hand in it."

"Well, there are people who might agree with you. Or who at least wouldn't rule that out."

"Which is why you've wandered so far off your beat?"

"Yes it is. But, frankly, this little shack of yours is the farthest I've wandered yet."

I heard the sound of a dog's claws scrambling on the wooden floor out in the ballroom. A big dog. I turned to see a Great Dane come hurtling into the room, saliva on his pink jowls. If I'd worn my gun, I'd have shot the son of a bitch.

But the dog put on the brakes and skidded to a stop at Mrs. McLean's side; he curled up on the floor next to her chair and she leaned a hand down and began to scratch behind his ears, under a collar that glittered with rhinestones.

"This is Mike," she said. "He's a Great Dane."

"I didn't take him for a poodle."

"My poodle died several years ago," she said, absently. She smiled, wanly. "I do miss my other pets. Mike's the only one I keep in town."

"Really."

"The monkey and llama are at Friendship. The parrot, too."

"Friendship?"

"That's the McLean family estate. Country estate. That's where Ned is staying, these days."

"Your husband."

"Yes." She twitched a smile, and it was nearly a grimace. "Friendship was a monastery, once, but I doubt Ned's leading a monastic existence." A sigh. "Things are a bit bitter at the moment, Mr. Heller. We're separated, you see, Ned and I. We're bickering over just who will divorce who. Or is it whom?"

"Whoever," I said.

"I wouldn't really care, except he'd like custody of our three children. And he's a very sick man, Mr. Heller. Mentally ill. Alcoholic. Well, his little chippie can have him. But he can't have the boys and Evalyn."

"Evalyn? Your daughter's name is Evalyn, too?"

Her smile was thin and proud. "Yes. That wasn't the name we gave her—she was christened Emily, but several years ago, when her father and I began having our little problems, she turned against that name and declared she simply must have another. Mine."

She petted the dog again. The big brown beast was plastered to the floor, his big jeweled collar sticking up stiffly, like a hoop his neck was caught in.

"Mrs. McLean, why did you get involved in the Lindbergh case? I know you have a reputation as something of a philanthropist, but . . ."

Her smile was one-sided and self-mocking; so was her cigarette-in-hand gesture. "But I'm also a silly, shallow, publicity-seeking society woman, correct, Mr. Heller? Both assessments are true. However my concern, my sympathy for the Lindberghs runs deeper than any social considerations, pure or self-interested. You see, Mr. Heller, their baby was, at the time of this crime, the most famous baby in the world. I was once the mother of the child who occupied that unhappy position. You're just young enough not to remember."

"Actually, I think I do. They called your son the 'million-dollar baby,' right?"

" 'One-hundred-million-dollar baby,' to be exact. But I called him Vinson."

"An unusual name."

"It was my brother's name. That, really, is where it all begins, Mr. Heller. My brother died young. He was barely seventeen."

"I'm sorry."

An eyebrow arched in a fatalistic shrug. "It was an automobile accident. No one's fault, really. Vinson loved to race—it seems to me his favorite car, that year, was his Pope Toledo. He had one that he could change, in a jiffy, from a roadster with bucket seats to a sedate-looking family car with a large tonneau. One time he screeched in . . ." She gestured out toward the street and the driveway. ". . . slid the tonneau in place, and when the traffic cop who'd been chasing him spotted the buggy and pulled in, the officer scratched his head, saying he could swear this was the car he'd been chasing, but this one had a different kind of hind end."

I smiled politely.

She laughed a little, sighed. "Vinson liked my red Mercedes almost as much. Used to wear racing goggles when he drove it, and he could make that car deliver all the speed it had in it. I was with him when . . . when the tire blew. It was like a pistol shot. We were going down the grade toward Honeyman's Hill, toward the creek, and went right through the side of the bridge. I nearly drowned. I'm still something of a cripple . . . one leg shorter than the other." She shook her head. "He did love to race."

I didn't know what to say; so I didn't say anything.

She looked at me with eyes that were deeply blue, in several senses. "So—I named my first son after Vinson. It seemed a good way to keep my brother alive, after a fashion. My Vinson was born in this house. Immediately the newspapers began calling him the 'hundred-million-dollar baby.' Even the *Post*—our own paper."

This was all vaguely familiar to me. "Didn't he have a solid gold crib?"

"It wasn't solid gold at all," she said, crankily. "It was a present to Vinson from our good friend, King Leopold. Of Belgium?"

"Oh. That King Leopold."

"A handsome and generous gift, but it was just gold plating . . . yet the reporters made it out to be the crib of Baby Midas. That was when the notes began."

"Notes?"

She waved her cigarette-in-hand in the air, impatiently, smoke curling. "Letters, telegrams, even anonymous phone calls despite our unlisted number, from criminals willing to accept the 'golden crib' as payment for not kidnapping my baby."

"Oh."

She shook her head. "Little Vinson couldn't lead a normal life; he was virtually imprisoned. We had an electric fence, and armed guards patrolling the grounds. Even so, with all of that, an intruder sneaked past the guards and placed a ladder at the nursery window—just as at the Lindberghs' estate—and was working on the heavy metal screen with wire-cutters when Vinson's nurse spotted him and screamed."

"Did your men get the guy?"

"No. They fired shots in the air, and he scurried off into the night. Left a ladder, some footprints, untraceable. This kind of thing went on for years. Kidnap threats on their part, increased security on ours. Finally it ended."

"How?"

She looked toward the street. "Ned and I were away. At the Kentucky Derby, at Churchill Downs. You know, I had a premonition . . . or at least a sense of foreboding. It's a peculiar sensitivity; I can't define it, really. But from time to time, I feel I know that death impends. I thought it was my *own* death—and at the hotel I wrote Vinson a long letter, telling him how much I adored him."

"What happened?"

"One of the servants, a valet, was looking after Vinson that morning. Sunday morning. Vinson crossed the street, to talk to a friend; they began playing tag, the two boys, and Vinson was dodging his friend, and he stepped in the path of a tin lizzie. The funny thing was, the lizzie was going at a slow pace, I'm told. Did little more than push Vinson so that he fell down. The driver braked, didn't run over him. Vinson seemed not badly hurt, at all."

"You don't have to go on, Mrs. McLean."

She was still looking at the street; a single tear ran down her powdered cheek, glimmering like a jewel. "They picked him up and brushed the dust from his clothes. The doctors said there was nothing to be done—as long as there'd been no internal injury, he should prove none the worse for wear. But a few hours later my boy became paralyzed. And at six o'clock Sunday night, with me still away, he died. He was eight years old. He never saw the letter I wrote."

I didn't offer my sympathy; it was too small a bandage for so deep and old a wound.

She turned her head away from the street and looked at me and smiled tightly, politely. She didn't wipe the tear away—she was proud of it, like all her jewels. "That, Mr. Heller, is why I am interested in helping the Lindberghs. As much pleasure as I've had giving various functions, or buying baubles, or contributing to charity, I tell you it's meaningless, it's empty, compared to the inner satisfaction I will feel if I can restore that baby to its mother's arms."

She sounded damn near as silly as Professor Condon; but it hit me a different way. Maybe she was a spoiled, pampered society woman and about as deep as a teacup; but she was acting out of her own pain, and that touched even a jaded cynic like yours truly. Even if this image she had of herself was silly-ass ridiculous— appearing out of the mist with the baby in her arms, presenting it to its mother, like something out of the last reel of an old D. W. Griffith silent—it was obvious she had a good heart.

She lit up another cigarette with the decorative silver lighter. "Do you believe in curses, Mr. Heller?"

"I believe in tangible things, Mrs. McLean. If you mean, do I think your son died because you own the Hope diamond, no. At least not in the way you mean."

"Well, in what way, then?"

"Only somebody as rich as you could afford that diamond, and could attract the publicity that would go with it, gold baby cribs and so on."

"Which attracts the attention of the underworld."

"Something like that."

She shrugged. "I don't know—perhaps the stone *is* 'evil.' I had it blessed by a priest, and I like to think it's brought me good luck. I've had some of that, too, you know."

"You've got it better than some people I know."

"They say that three hundred years ago the blue diamond was stolen from the eye of an idol in India. Marie Antoinette wore it as a necklace . . . and it was stolen in the aftermath of the revolution."

"Well, once she was guillotined, Marie would've had a hell of a time keeping the thing on, anyway."

She laughed; the first time. A good laugh, full-throated and as rich as she was. "Legend has it you're not supposed to even touch the thing. I don't encourage my friends to handle it, and for years I kept it away from my children."

"That sounds like you do take the curse seriously."

"But I don't really. Hell, I've grown casual with it. I do love the silly thingamabob. I wear it almost all the time."

"I don't see it now."

"Don't you? Haven't you noticed? Mike's wearing it today."

The Great Dane lifted his head at the sound of his name and looked at me like I was the dumbest shit on the planet. He had a right to feel highfalutin, for a hound, considering the simple necklace of "rhinestones" looped around his stiff collar bore the most famous diamond in the world, an indigo blue stone, in a diamond setting, about the size of a golf ball. It winked at me.

So did Mrs. McLean.

"Stay for dinner, Mr. Heller," she said, rising, "we'll have drinks and talk of Gaston Means and kidnappers and ransom money, afterward."

Chapter 17

The butler, Garboni, showed me to my room, so I could freshen up before supper. It seemed I was staying overnight.

"People may talk," Mrs. McLean had said, as we exited the sun porch, taking my arm rather formally, as if she were attired in the latest Hattie Carnegie creation and not a housecoat, "but hell, let them. I hardly think with a staff of twenty, and sixty rooms, I need worry about you compromising what little remains of my virtue."

"Like the white slaver said to the schoolgirl, you can trust me, Mrs. McLean."

She smiled at that. "You'll be staying in Vinson's room. It's been kept just the same, since his death."

"You've put me in your son's room?"

"No. My brother's. My son's room has been preserved, as well. It's a luxury of a house this size. But I never allow anyone to sleep there."

Brother Vinson's room, my room, was on the third floor—and we, the butler and me, went by elevator. I tried to remember when

I'd ever been in a private residence that had elevators before, and couldn't. The hallway Garboni led me down was wide enough to accommodate an el train and still take passengers on from either side. Persian rugs underfoot, brocade wallpaper surrounding me, I gaped like a rube at oil paintings and watercolors that looked European and venerable in their elaborate gilt-edged frames, noting my slack-jawed expression in the mirror of dark-wood furniture that was polished past absurdity. I felt about as at home as an archbishop in a brothel; but like the archbishop, I could adjust.

Garboni opened the door to Vinson's room—actually, it was a suite of rooms—and we entered a sitting room a little smaller than the deck of the *Titanic*. The butler dropped my traveling bag with a clunk.

"Take it easy, pal," I said irritably. "There's a gun in there."

His eyes flared a little bit; that threw him. "Sorry, sir."

"And here I was getting ready to give you a nickel tip."

He took that at face value, or seemed to. "No gratuities are necessary, sir."

"I'll say. Scram."

He scrammed; without a word, without even a nasty look. For a burly-looking wop, this bird was pretty easily spooked.

And so I was alone in Vinson's digs. Sort of.

Just me and the stuffed alligator. And the two sets of armor. And the waist-high ivory elephant. And the six-foot bronze horse. I sat on a plush red couch with a half dozen red pillows, the sort of thing you might find yourself sitting on in a San Francisco whorehouse, and took in the goddamnedest, god-awfulest assembly of mismatched junk I ever saw. A Navajo blanket covering a table; an oversize anchor clock on the wall; a portrait of a Madonna and Child; a Hindu bust; a combined bookcase and gun case; seven pieces of old armor on the wall and a shield, too; a carved bellows; several red throw rugs; a slinky-looking sofa that looked like something a Turkish harem girl might lounge on. Vinson might've been dead, but his bad taste lived on.

The bedroom itself was almost spartan in comparison—a bookcase filled with Horatio Alger, a cabinet with mirror, a single bed of rough rustic wood that seemed a relic or reminder or something of Colorado.

I used the bathroom—I had my own private one, no bigger than your average Chicago two-flat—and, as Mrs. McLean requested, freshened up. As I splashed water on my face, I wondered what to make of this—specifically, of her. She seemed silly but smart; self-absorbed but caring. A vain rich woman in a 98-cent housecoat.

I didn't like her exactly—but she fascinated me. And she was attractive; probably ten or fifteen years older than me, but what the hell—older women try harder. Even wealthy ones. Especially wealthy ones.

The room had its own phone, which would allow me to check in with Lindbergh and Breckinridge at my convenience. On the other hand, I could be listened in on, so I'd edit whatever I said with Mrs. McLean in mind.

Freshened or not, I wore the same suit down to dinner—I only had two along; in fact, I only owned two—and, for fifteen minutes or so, sat alone under a cut crystal chandelier at a table for twenty-four, at which there were two place settings, directly opposite each other, midway. I was served a thin white wine that the thin black server, who was dressed far more formally than I, informed me was a Montrachet, as if I should have been impressed, which I wasn't. He should have known better than to try to impress a guy who had a stuffed alligator in his room.

Mrs. McLean's entrance, however, did impress. She had traded in the dowdy plaid robe for an embroidered gown, its delicate lacework dark red against a soft pink that at first seemed to be her flesh; but her flesh was whiter, creamier, as was attested to by the low cut of the gown, the white swell of her breasts, and they were indeed swell, providing a resting place for a string of perfect pearls so long it fell off the cliff of her breasts and dropped to her lap. There were worse places to fall from and to. She'd relieved Mike of the Hope diamond, which was around her own neck now, dangling just above the cleft of her bosom. In her hair was a feathered diamond tiara and her earrings were pearls that dwarfed the ball-bearing–size ones of the necklace.

Her smile was amused and pleased. "I told you I could dazzle, if I chose."

"You look great," I said, lamely, getting up.

She gestured for me to sit and soon we were enjoying her chef's filet of lemon sole ("with Marguery sauce").

"Maurice," she said, referring to her chef, "is the most priceless gem in this house."

"I hope he doesn't come with a curse."

"No," she said, smiling a little, more relaxed now despite her more formal attire, "just with the pedigree of the best cafés in Paris and London. He trained as a caterer. That's the only sort of chef to go after."

"I'll keep that in mind. I suppose tartar sauce is out of the question."

She laughed; I was glad she was finally getting my jokes—too bad I hadn't been joking.

"You know," she said, reflecting a while later over Maurice's "patented" parfait, "money is lovely to have and I do love having it—but it doesn't really bring the big things of life. Friends, health, respect. And it's apt to make one soft, selfish, self-indulgent."

"You mean, while we're eating parfaits in this palace, people are out there scrounging for scraps, living in shacks made out of tin cans and cardboard."

She nodded, sadly, even as she tasted a bite of parfait. "If only I'd had the courage, years ago, to lead my own life . . . apart from Ned and his family and my parents and my family . . . I might by now have helped so many poor souls. . . . I might have done infinitely more good with my life."

She licked ice cream from her lips as she shook her head regretfully.

"Well, you are trying to do some good," I said. "For the Lindberghs and their boy."

"Yes. In my small way. If you're finished, Mr. Heller, we can move to the sitting room, and I'll explain everything."

I took her by the arm and we moved through that excessive, magnificent house through the Louis XV ballroom, not to the sun porch this time, but to a room nearly as large as the ballroom where plush comfortable furnishings crouched in the golden glow of a massive marble fireplace.

"I've had two glasses of wine already," Mrs. McLean said, standing at a liquor cart about the size of a Maxwell Street pushcart, only mahogany and gold-inlaid. "That is my limit. But if you'd like more . . ."

"No, that's fine," I said, settling down into an oversize sofa opposite the glowing fire. This modest little drawing room was paneled in mahogany, had a twenty-foot ceiling, a massive pipe organ built into one wall, and a Persian rug smaller than Lake Michigan partially covering its parquet floor.

She sat next to me, pulled up an ottoman, kicked off her shoes and put her silk-stockinged feet up on it. A thick arch support tumbled out of her right shoe. She noticed me noticing that and tugged on my arm and pointed to her tiny feet; she wiggled the toes of her right foot.

"See," she said. "Shorter. From that accident, years ago. I told you."

"They look fine to me."

"Mr. Heller, you're a charming man."

"Everybody says so. Why don't you break your rule and let me get us a couple of drinks."

Her smile was impish. "Why don't I?"

I poured myself some Bacardi, no ice, and some sherry for her.

"Thank you, Mr. Heller," she said, sipping hers.

"Why don't you call me Nate?"

"Why don't I? Why don't you call me Evalyn?"

"Why don't I. And why don't you tell me all about Gaston Bullock Means."

"All right." Her lovely features were serene in the firelight; she was looking into the flames, held by them, as she spoke. "As I said, from the beginning I felt the Lindbergh kidnapping was an underworld job. But I could hardly offer myself as an intermediary—what self-respecting criminal would deal with a flighty society woman like Evalyn Walsh McLean! Besides—they say it takes a crook to catch a crook—and Gaston Bullock Means was the perfect crook for what I had in mind."

"What made Means the 'perfect crook' for the job?"

She raised an eyebrow, sipped her sherry. "I knew he'd done

a lot of dirty work for the Harding administration—he certainly knew his way around the capital, from the back alleys to the front parlors."

"He did time, didn't he?"

She nodded. "Until recently, he was in the federal penitentiary at Atlanta, on prohibition charges, stemming from abuses when he was a Justice Department agent."

"Taking bribes from bootleggers?"

"That's right. Anyway, I first met him several years ago, when some friends of ours in the administration were reluctant to contact Means directly about some documents he'd pilfered. They seemed in mortal fear of the barrel-bellied blackguard. So I called him up, arranged a meeting and picked the papers up from him, myself— as a favor."

Evalyn Walsh McLean seemed an unlikely bagman for the Ohio Gang; but there it was.

"At our meeting," she said, with a self-satisfied smirk, "Means made some threatening remarks aboout several friends of Ned's and mine—Andrew Mellon, Harry Daughtery—and I put him in his place."

Andrew Mellon was then Secretary of the Treasury; Daughtery had been Harding's Attorney General.

"How did you do that, Evalyn?"

She shrugged, but her nonchalance wasn't convincing. "I told Means I'd always been curious to know what it would be like to meet a murderer. And now I knew."

"And what did he say to that?"

"He asked me what I meant by that, and I said, 'I think you know,' and he said, 'Oh . . . Maude King.' And then he paused— such an innocent-looking, dimpled, moon-faced miscreant—and said, 'Accidents will happen.' "

I knew about Maude King—she was an eccentric, wealthy widow from Chicago, the kind the papers like to call a "madcap heiress," and Gaston Means had wormed his way into her confidence by foiling some thugs who accosted her on a street corner in the Loop. He became her financial adviser, and bilked her out of an estimated $150,000, before taking her on a hunting trip in North

Carolina, where Mrs. King was "accidentally" shot to death.

It seemed Means had taken the target pistol the two of them had been using and left it in the crotch of a tree while he wandered off for a drink of spring water. Somehow the gun had discharged in Means's absence, and Mrs. King managed to get shot behind the left ear. The North Carolina jury acquitted Means; the Chicago press had not.

"Means has a history, obviously," I said, "of taking advantage of attractive, wealthy women."

Her smile was as many-faceted as the gleaming jewel that rode her gently moving bosom. "Attractive wealthy *older* women, don't you mean?"

"Not really. I remember seeing photos of Maude King—she didn't look any older than you. Which is to say, not old at all."

"That's diplomatic, Nate. But I'm at least ten years your senior. . . ."

"The point is," I said, "Means has fixed his sights on women with money before. Are you sure he didn't seek you out?"

"Absolutely not. I called him. He came here, to my home."

"When was this?"

"The fourth of March."

Hell, that was several days before I even got involved in the case.

She pointed off vaguely to the rest of the house. "There's a drawing room on this floor, with a balcony overlooking it. I met Means there, while my friend Elizabeth Poe, a reporter from the *Post*, hid above with a revolver."

It was obvious from the sparkle in her eyes that she loved the intrigue.

"I asked him point-blank if he knew anything about the Lindbergh kidnapping. Without hesitation, he said, 'It so happens that I do. Why?' I might have asked, is it true blue is your favorite color?"

"Evalyn, a good con man never misses a beat. You toss him a curve, he'll bat the ball out of the park."

"Perhaps. At any rate, I told him of my concern, my sympathy, for the Lindberghs, and said I wanted to aid in effecting the boy's return. Then I asked him what he knew about the kidnapping, warning that if there was any funny business, I'd see him sent to prison."

She tried to sound stern and tough, but it was about as convincing as Means's story about the pistol in the crotch of the tree.

"He said he didn't blame me for being skeptical about him. He said he'd committed just about every kind of sin under the sun. But what he said next convinced me."

"What was that?"

"He said, 'I haven't come forward to the police or press with what I know about the Lindbergh case because of the tissue of lies that my life has been so far.' That phrase struck me: 'tissue of lies.' "

"Con men always have a way with words, Evalyn."

"He claimed he'd been in a New York speakeasy about ten days before, where he'd run into an old cellmate of his from Atlanta. The old friend asked Means, or so Means said, if he was interested in playing ransom negotiator in a big kidnapping that was going to be pulled around March first."

"Did Means say his friend specifically mentioned Lindbergh?"

"Means said he'd been told only that it was a 'big-time snatch.' But Means turned down the opportunity, saying that 'napping' was one crime he wouldn't touch."

The fire crackled.

I sat sideways and looked right at her, getting her attention away from the flames. "So then when the Lindbergh kidnapping broke on the radio and in the papers, Means figured it must be the 'big-time snatch' his pal mentioned."

She nodded; her eyes looked unblinkingly my way, the fire reflecting in them, the stone on her chest doing the same. "Means claimed he'd contacted several prominent men here in Washington, including Colonel Guggenheim, but hadn't gotten anywhere. Means was viewed as the little boy crying wolf. I later ascertained from Colonel Guggenheim and a prominent local judge that this was quite true."

I'd lost count of the colonels in this case, a long time ago.

"Means offered to get in touch with his old cellmate, and I urged him to do so. The next morning he told me he'd succeeded in contacting his old friend, and that the man was indeed the 'head of the Lindbergh gang,' and eager to open negotiations for the baby's return. Then began the continuing succession of meetings, including several with Jerry Land present, working with Means as the intermediary with the kidnappers."

Jerry Land was Admiral Emory S. Land, the Lindbergh relative who'd conveyed word of what Mrs. McLean and Means were up to, to Slim.

"Where do things stand now?" I asked her.

"Last Monday, I gave Means a big pasteboard carton filled with bills in denominations of five, ten and twenty dollars."

"You gave that to him already?"

She nodded. "One hundred thousand dollars."

I sighed. "Have you seen him since?"

"Oh yes. He lives over in Chevy Chase with his family. He has a wife and son, you know—the son is his motivation, he says. He says he hopes to atone for his past and make his boy proud."

"Yeah, well, that's touching. But that was days ago. Has he delivered the ransom to the 'gang'? He obviously hasn't delivered the baby to you."

"It's supposed to happen soon. I'm going to Far View tomorrow—that's where the kidnappers have agreed to make delivery. Means is meeting me there."

"Where and what is Far View?"

"My country home. In Maryland. I've made arrangements with a doctor friend of mine for anyone who might inquire, that for the next few days to a week, I'm at Union Memorial in Baltimore taking a rest cure."

"There's a lot of intrigue in this thing, isn't there?"

She shook her head, laughed a little. "Yes there is. And Means insists on using code names and numbers . . . he was a double agent at one time, you know."

"Yeah. He worked for the Germans just before the World War."

"I'm Number Eleven. The baby is referred to, always, as 'the book.' Means himself is 'Hogan.' Admiral Land is Number Fourteen. And so on."

"I need another drink." I got myself one. "How about you, Evalyn?"

"I shouldn't."

"Anybody who can hand Gaston Means a cardboard box with one hundred grand in it can risk a second glass of sherry."

"Valid point," she said, and took the sherry. "I've involved you, I'm afraid, in the intrigue."

"Oh? How in hell?"

"Well, I knew Colonel Lindbergh wanted me to meet with you, but if Gaston Means, or the kidnappers, knew I was dealing with a policeman . . . even one so far off his beat . . . it might prove disastrous. I can trust my staff—they've all been with me for years. But if anyone, Gaston Means in particular, should ask them—you came here today to be interviewed for a position."

"What position is that?"

"Chauffeur."

I snorted a laugh, finished my Bacardi. "That's rich. I couldn't find my way across the street in this town. Well, I'd like to meet Means. And maybe it *would* be best if I did it undercover."

"Undercover?"

I pointed to myself with a thumb. "Meet your new chauffeur. Who's going to escort you to your country place—where I'll size Means and his story up for myself."

Her smile was almost demure. "That would be wonderful, Nate. You think . . . you think I'm a foolish old woman, don't you?"

"You're not old at all."

"The fire's dwindling. Would you put some wood on?"

"All right."

When I returned to the couch, she was sitting with her legs tucked up under her, illuminated by the blaze I'd rekindled. I sat next to her and she moved closer.

"I haven't been with a man since my husband and I separated," she said.

I didn't believe that, but I said, "A lovely girl like you?"

She was amused. "You think calling me a 'girl' is going to win me over?"

"You look like a girl to me."

The amusement dropped like a mask; something was smoldering in her expression, and the fire had nothing to do with it. "Nate. Nate. Why don't you just kiss me?"

"We just met. You don't know anything about me, Evalyn."

"You have a dry wit. You have a gun in your suitcase. You have nice eyes, a little cruel, but nice. Your hair looks red in the firelight. I know all that, and more."

"More? What else do you know?"

"I know you have a gun in your pocket, too."

"That isn't a gun."

"I know."

I kissed her. Her mouth was wet and warm and tasted like sherry. Her tongue flicked my tongue.

"More," she said.

I kissed her some more; it was nice and got nicer. Hot and got hotter. I slid my hand up the slope of her bosom—I felt the chill cut stone of the Hope diamond and pulled my hand away like I'd been burned. I drew the rest of me away, too, head reeling from rum and where I was.

"Let me get this off," she said hastily. She removed the diamond necklace, and the pearls, too, and tossed them on an overstuffed chair nearby, as casually as if she'd slipped off her shoes. The diamond was catching the fire and flashing.

"Help me with this," she said, reaching behind her, and I did, and soon the gown was around her tiny waist and her breasts, perfect, high, full, enormous, were basking in the golden glow of the fire. I put my hands on them. I put my mouth on them. Sucked the tips till they were hard.

"What about your servants?" I asked, gasping, my face half-buried in her treasure chest.

"They'll only come when I ask them," she said.

"Me too," I said.

Chapter 18

We arrived at Far View after dark the next night. Behind the wheel of Evalyn McLean's powder-blue Lincoln Continental, I was every bit the perfect chauffeur, wearing a spiffy gray woolen uniform with shiny black buttons and matching cap, bequeathed by a driver who'd recently retired from the Walsh family's employ after thirty faithful years. He'd been heavier than me, but Mrs. McLean had someone on her staff take it in. Evalyn and Inga—her fortyish, blonde maid, a dourly attractive woman who'd been with her "mistress" over twenty years, and who was aware of my true identity— sat in the backseat and directed me; I didn't mind having two backseat drivers: my only flaw as a chauffeur, after all, was my complete lack of familiarity with Washington, D.C., and its environs.

From Massachusetts Avenue, we had headed in the direction of Baltimore, then doubled back; we were soon off the main highway and exploring the wilds of Maryland via narrow, rutted back roads, occasionally gravel, usually dirt. The private drive to Far View was gravel, but neglected, weeds overtaking it; the same was true of the grounds, where weeds poked up between the patches of snow. Nonetheless, the house itself—which I had foolishly pictured as the modest "country place" Evalyn had casually mentioned—was impressive in the moonlight, a sprawling Southern mansion of the plantation variety, pillars and all, ghostly white amidst tall skeletal trees.

"My mother spent a lot of time here," Evalyn said, leaning up from the backseat. "I haven't been out here, since she died."

"When did she die?" I asked.

"Last month."

It was the first she'd mentioned it, but I found that telling. She'd jumped on the Lindbergh bandwagon within weeks of her mother dying. Evalyn—a woman in mourning, her emotions frazzled, looking to do something meaningful with her rich, empty life—made easy prey for a shark like Gaston Means.

"I'm sorry about your mother," I said.

"Another victim of the Hope diamond curse?" she wondered aloud wryly. "She was a Christian Scientist, actually . . . wouldn't stand for medical help. Thank God I'm a heathen."

"You never liked this house anyway," Inga said.

"True," Evalyn said. "I don't like its history."

"What history?" I asked.

Evalyn leaned back. "A man and wife lived here, a long time ago. They fought continually—he beat her for her supposed faithlessness, and on nights when the wind was blowing a certain way, her screams could be heard for miles, it's said. Finally he knocked her over the head and put her down a well, here."

"I wonder if it's safe," I said.

"The house?" Inga asked.

"To drink the water."

Nobody in the backseat laughed, but I caught Evalyn's tiny smile in the rearview mirror. That dry wit of mine again.

As we drew nearer to the house, I could see that its windows were boarded up.

"Looks deserted," I said, pulling up near the garage and stables in back. This surprised me, because she'd said the phones would be working.

"It is deserted, virtually," she said. "There's an elderly caretaker I've kept on."

"Does he like growing weeds?" Inga asked sarcastically.

"The place does look a little raggedy," Evalyn said to her maid, "but winter hasn't quite left us. Gus'll tend to things in due time, I'm sure."

Inga grunted. She was very pretty, in a peasanty sort of way, but she was sour; the kind of woman whose time of the month was all month.

I helped the mistress and her maid out of the car—Inga wore her black-and-white uniform under a simple wool overcoat, while Evalyn wore a mink coat over a dark brown angora frock trimmed white, her belt white, her beret brown with a white band. I got the suitcases, including my traveling bag, out of the trunk; there were four bags, all of which I managed to carry. Neither woman made a move to help me, including waiting for me to put the bags down so I could open the side door, which was unlocked. Evalyn had called the caretaker in advance.

But that didn't mean anything homey was waiting for us. We moved from the smallish kitchen through the big, dark, cold house where only the occasional piece of furniture remained, in every case shrouded with a sheet. The air was stale, musty, but the house wasn't dirty; caretaker Gus had done *some* work. The bedrooms were on the second floor. The third floor was closed off.

Evalyn did not allow me to switch on any of the lights.

"Means's instructions," she said, "as per the kidnappers' orders, are that lights are forbidden. The idea is that Far View should continue to look unoccupied."

"Cold in here," Inga said, patting her arms, though still in her overcoat.

"The furnace isn't in working order," Evalyn said.

"The fireplaces are," I said.

She waggled a jeweled finger. "Means said not a single light— including the fireplaces."

"Where *is* Means?" I asked.

"He said he would come," Evalyn said. "Let's go to the kitchen. Inga, see if you can whip something up for us."

Inga grunted.

We huddled around the wood-burning stove—which Evalyn permitted us to get going—and I held a flashlight for Inga, who morosely prepared a meal that did not include Maurice's filet of sole with Marguery sauce or his patented parfait. Canned pork and beans was the extent of it; that and coffee. But it tasted fine to me. Evalyn seemed satisfied by the fare, as well—though I had a feeling it was the evening's main course that she found filling: intrigue.

We were sitting drinking coffee, shivering despite the blankets around us Indian-style, when the lights of a car coming up the driveway slanted through the cracks of the boarded-up windows.

Several minutes later a big man—both tall and fat—entered; he wore a dark heavy topcoat, under which a blue bow tie peeked, and a homburg, which he immediately removed, revealing himself to be nearly bald. He had a flashlight in one hand. He clicked the flashlight on and held its beam under his chin.

"It's me," he said. "Hogan."

Gaston Bullock Means had a puckish smile and a deeply dimpled baby face. Washed with the flashlight light, that face was at once sinister and benign.

Then the light was suddenly in my face; I squinted into it, grinding my teeth, remaining servile.

"Who's this?" Means said.

"My chauffeur," she said. "His name is Smith. I've just hired him."

"Nobody's name is Smith," Means snapped.

"Look in a phone book," I said, pulling my head out of the light. "You'll find you're mistaken."

He dropped the beam to the floor, where it pooled whitely. "His credentials are sound, Eleven?"

Evalyn, a.k.a. Eleven, said, "Indeed."

"All right, then," he said to me, grandly, "henceforth you're Number Fifteen."

Inga spoke up, huffily. "I thought I was Number Fifteen."

"Ah, yes . . . that's right. Smith—you're Number *Sixteen*."

"Swell."

He walked over to Evalyn, but did not sit, though there was an extra chair immediately handy. "Can I speak candidly in front of these people?"

Sure he could—we had numbers, didn't we?

"Yes," Evalyn said. "I brought only this skeleton staff, as per your request."

"Good. Good." He snapped off the flashlight and sat. He was an enormous man, as big as the wood-burning stove. "I have good news for you, Eleven. The Fox was waiting for me when I got home last night."

"The Fox?" she asked.

"My old cellmate. The leader of the kidnap gang. The Fox. That's how his men know him."

The bad guys had their own code names, too, it seemed.

Means leaned forward conspiratorially. "He asked me if I had the ransom money. I told him I did. I told him to wait outside until I made sure my family was asleep, and then I would let him in, and let him see his money."

I probably shouldn't have spoken up, but I did. "Wasn't that foolish?" I asked.

"Foolish?" Means looked at me as he might regard a buzzing fly.

"Foolish," I said. "What was to keep him from stealing the money?"

He lifted his chin nobly. "The Fox was my cellmate. There is such a thing as honor among thieves!"

No there isn't.

"Oh," I said.

"I took him downstairs, to the basement, and took the cardboard box of money from its hiding place and piled the bills on a table. I let him examine them for himself. He was pleased right off the bat that the denominations were small and the bills old and worn, the serial numbers nonconsecutive. In other words, Eleven, the Fox is convinced that you're going to play fair. He counted the money twice, and was delighted to find it totaled precisely one hundred thousand dollars."

I spoke again. "Where's the money now?"

"No longer in my home," Means said irritably. "Locked in a safe, pending further developments."

"Inga," Evalyn said, sensing Means's growing irritation with me, "get Mr. Means some coffee."

Inga did.

"That's 'Hogan,' Eleven. Always Hogan." Means sipped his coffee with great satisfaction, saying, "We should have delivery of the book any day now. As soon as the Fox and his people are convinced the police are not watching us."

"The book?" I asked.

"The baby," Evalyn reminded me.

Means looked at me sharply; his eyes, which usually twinkled Santa Claus-style, narrowed and grew colder than the room, and the room was an icebox. "You ask a lot of questions for a chauffeur," he said.

"I used to be a cop," I said.

Evalyn blinked.

"Mrs. McLean thought," I said, "her new chauffeur ought to be something of a bodyguard, as well as a driver, considering current circumstances."

"I see," Means said, his puckish smile returning, but his eyes remaining ice-cold. "And where were you a police officer?"

"You ask a lot of questions yourself, Hogan," I said.

Means looked at me with bland innocence. "It's the way I learn things, Fifteen."

"*I'm* Fifteen," Inga said crabbily.

"I'm Sixteen," I said. I smiled at him. "And never been kissed."

He beamed at that. "I like you, Sixteen. I really do. We're going to be great friends."

"That's peachy. Have you seen the baby?"

"No—but by tomorrow this time, with God's help, we all will."

Evalyn splashed coffee from the cup in her hand.

"Or the next day," Means said, with a shrug. "The Fox promises delivery soon."

"What about the money?" I asked.

"What money?"

"That's code," I said, "for one hundred thousand dollars ransom in a cardboard box."

"Oh, yes," Means said. "I've told the Fox he will not receive his booty until the book is safely in Eleven's arms."

"And he accepts those terms?" I asked.

"Certainly. He trusts me implicitly. I was his cellmate, remember."

Means stood; he was as big as a grizzly bear, and every bit as dependable. "I leave you to your vigil."

With that, and a tip of his homburg before placing it on his big bald head, Means slipped out into the cold night, where the wind howled, shaking the brittle trees like a faithless wife.

Chapter 19

The furniture in my corner room was sparse—bed, nightstand, small table, dresser. There were faded places on the wallpaper where framed photos, paintings, mirrors or whatever had once hung. Wind rattled the boarded-up windows, fighting to get in, somewhat successfully. Cozy it wasn't, but the bed had clean sheets and sufficient blankets, so I thanked God and Gus the caretaker for small favors. I stripped to my underwear—wishing I'd worn long johns—and settled in. I had a lot on my mind, but it had been a long, strange day, and sleep took me quickly.

I awoke just as quickly, when—how long after, I'm not sure—my door creaked open and a small female figure stood there; light from the hall made a shapely silhouette through a sheer nightgown, a nicely top-heavy silhouette that I recognized, even sleep-dazed, as Evalyn's.

"Nate," she whispered. "Are you awake?"

"Sure," I said, sitting up. Actually, I *was* awake—the kind of wide awake you can be when you're startled into it.

She shut the door and the room went nearly black. I could

barely make her shape out in the darkness; she was standing next to me, next to the bed, but I sensed her more than saw her. For one thing, she smelled good, cloaked in a perfume that suggested night-blooming jasmine. Then light flashed—a match—as she lit a red candle on my nightstand, a nightstand incidentally that bore no lamp.

In the flickery light from the candle, she stood before me with her beautiful breasts outlined under the sheer black nightgown, their rosy tips staring at me like wide eyes. Speaking of which, Evalyn's eyes were themselves round and staring—in a pale, haunted face.

"Nate," she said, "forgive me for this intrusion."

I threw back the covers. "You're forgiven."

She climbed in bed and I threw the covers back up over her, and me. She was shivering.

"You've caught a chill," I said.

"No," she said.

"What is it then?"

"You'll think I'm foolish."

"No I won't."

"I . . . I was in bed, almost asleep. I heard footsteps on the stairs. I wondered who might be coming up. First I thought it might be Inga, but the sounds went right by Inga's room and came toward mine."

She pulled the covers around her, tighter. I slipped my arm around her; she was trembling like a frightened deer.

"As they . . . they reached my door, these footsteps, they stopped. I thought that any moment, whoever it was would enter my room. I thought, perhaps, it was you . . . after last night, perhaps a midnight rendezvous. . . ."

"I haven't been out of my room, Evalyn."

She nodded, as if she knew that already. "Across from my room is a doorway to the stairs to the third floor—which is shut off. I don't even know where the key is. I heard footsteps going up those stairs. Then I heard the footsteps above me. Above the ceiling of my room."

"Maybe it's Inga."

"I don't think so. I got up, went into the hallway. The third-floor door was locked."

"It wasn't me up, wandering. You don't think Means doubled back, for some reason?"

She shook her head. "I don't know. The caretaker doesn't live on the grounds; he has a little place in Bradley Hills. Why would he be stalking around?"

"If you're concerned . . ."

"It could be one of the kidnappers, checking us out, couldn't it?"

"It's possible."

She turned to me; her eyes were as frightened as they were lovely. "Can I stay with you tonight?"

"You talked me into it. What about Inga? Are you concerned about what she might think . . . ?"

"I have no secrets from Inga. Could we block the door?"

I told her we could; I got out of bed, moved the dresser in front of the door, and got my nine millimeter out of my travel bag and put it on the nightstand.

"Slide over," I told her. I wanted to be next to the gun.

She slid over. "I'm a damned fool."

"This house would give Frankenstein the willies." I climbed in bed next to her. "Look, it could've been your imagination. You might've been dreaming, or hearing night sounds . . ."

"It is a noisy night."

"Sure. Why don't you get some sleep?"

"Hold me, would you, Nate? Hold me."

I held her.

"Don't blow out the candle," she said.

"I won't."

"Why do you put up with me?"

"I like women with big money and big breasts."

"You're terrible."

"You really think so?"

"No."

The wind shook the windows, boards and glass alike; she grabbed me. She was terrified. So I kissed her, just to settle her down. It led to more.

"You must think *I'm* terrible," she said, later.

"Not at all."

"You think I'm shallow. You think I'm silly."

"Sure. But not terrible."

She laughed; it was a husky laugh. "I'm getting old, Nate. These breasts of mine are starting to droop."

"Not that I can see. Anyway, I'll be glad to lift 'em for you—anytime."

"You. You."

I kissed her again. She seemed to have forgotten about her kidnapper or ghost or whatever-it-was making footsteps in the hall and above the ceiling. Or had she invented that to find a way into my room, without looking "terrible"?

"That's an ominous-looking thing."

"I'll take that as a compliment."

"I mean the gun."

"Oh. Well, ominous is a good way for a gun to look."

"Have . . . have you ever killed anyone with it?"

"Yes. I killed a kidnapper not so long ago. That's why Lindy thinks I'm a prince."

"You talk about it so . . . casually."

"I'm not really casual about it, Evalyn. I don't ever mean to use a gun casually. That gun of all guns. . . ."

"What about that gun?"

I didn't say anything.

"What is it, Nate?"

"Evalyn, I . . . nothing."

"What?"

"Well. Look, I'll be frank with you. I might've dismissed you as a silly, shallow woman, if it weren't for some of what you've been through. If you don't mind my saying."

"Such as?"

I swallowed. "Losing your son."

She touched my face.

I touched her face.

She said, "You lost somebody, too, didn't you?"

I nodded.

"Nate . . . are you . . . ?"

I wiped my face with my hand; the hand came away wet. "No. Sweating. These blankets."

"Who, Nate? Who did you lose?"

And I told her. I told her slowly, and in detail, about my father. About what I'd done to make him use my gun on himself. About how I carried that gun so I wouldn't forget.

"But I do forget sometimes," I admitted. "Life and death are cheap in this lousy goddamn world. Particularly in this lousy goddamn depression."

"I'm not by nature contemplative," she said, hugging my arm, staring into the near-darkness. "But the thing I wonder about most is why the universe is geared so to cruelty."

I kissed her forehead.

The wind was settling down, now; it was making a whistling, almost soothing sound.

"Why don't you tell me about your son? Tell me about your little boy."

She did. For perhaps an hour, she told me of her "sweet and preternaturally wise" little boy. Little Vinson was the only ghost in the house, as the candle burned down and night turned to morning, and he was not a sinister presence.

A few hours later, the footsteps in the hall and the thought of ghosts seemed foolish to us as we went down for breakfast. Evalyn was wearing a casual black-and-white frock; I'd been allowed to abandon the chauffeur's uniform for one of my two suits. Inga was fixing bacon and eggs—Gus the caretaker had dropped off some fresh supplies, it seemed—and the smells of the food and the morning were refreshing.

But Inga seemed even gloomier than usual.

We sat at an unpretentious square table in the kitchen as Inga served us our eggs and bacon and toast with a side order of bloodshot, black-circled eyes.

"My dear," Evalyn said to the maid, "you must have had a dreadful night!"

Inga said nothing.

"Serve yourself, dear," Evalyn told her, "and join us."

Sullenly, Inga did. Her blonde hair hung in strings as she

poked at her food. Suddenly she looked up, her eyes as wide and haunted as Evalyn's had been when she entered my room the night before.

"Madam, if it is just the same to you, could I please change my room tonight?"

"Why, dear?"

"Somebody kept pulling the sheets off my bed every time I went to sleep."

"Inga," I said, "is there a lock on your door?"

"Yes—and I used it."

"And your windows are boarded up, like mine?"

"Yes."

Evalyn leaned forward, her blue eyes piercing. "You mean to say, Inga, that someone pulled the sheets off your bed when you were alone in the room, with the door locked and the windows boarded up?"

"Yes. Several times this happened. I hardly sleep."

"You don't think anybody was hiding in your room or anything?" I asked.

"I had a flashlight," she said. "I looked under the bed, and in the closet. I was alone."

"I'll take that room tonight," I told her.

For the first time Inga smiled at me. "Thank you, Mr. Heller."

"With any luck," Evalyn said, cheerfully, "before then, Means will show up and we'll take delivery of 'the book' and be well out of this funhouse."

But Means didn't show.

We spent most of the day, Evalyn and I, walking the weedy, snow-patched grounds, threading through the tall bony naked trees, following paths Evalyn's mother had traced. Often we held hands, like kids going steady; maybe, in a way, that's what we were.

That afternoon, elderly, lanky, grossly mustached Gus—who chewed tobacco that he smelled just a little worse than—opened the door to the long-unused third floor. Gus claimed to have the only key, and the door seemed not to have been used in a while— and the caretaker had a hell of a hard time working the key in that rusty lock.

There were no ghosts on the third story other than a few more pieces of sheet-covered furniture. A layer of dust coated the floor, undisturbed by footprints.

Evalyn, standing just behind me, her fingers on my arm, said, "I must have just heard noises the wind made."

"Must have," I said.

I didn't believe in haunted houses, of course; but then lately I'd been exposed to the likes of Edgar Cayce, Sister Sarah Sivella and Chief Yellow Feather, and I was starting to think we ought to start looking for Lindy's kid in a magician's top hat.

That evening was just as cold as the previous one, and we again huddled in the kitchen, drinking coffee, wearing blankets, waiting for either Means to show up or the phone to ring or at least some goddamn ghost to materialize. Nothing did.

Evalyn and I spent the night in the room Inga had abandoned. We sat up virtually all night, when we weren't otherwise entertaining ourselves; Evalyn smoked a pack of cigarettes, and I ran out of Sheiks. It was a long, tiring, memorable night, but no ghosts showed, no footsteps sounded in the hall or on the stairs or on the ceiling, and nobody, flesh or vapor, pulled the covers off.

She had fallen asleep in my arms, both of us half-sitting up, pillows behind us, blankets sheathing us. Light seeped through the cracks of the boarded-up windows. The long night was over.

As I was getting out of bed, I heard something fall heavily to the floor; I jumped, and Evalyn jumped awake.

"What . . . ?" she began.

I stood, frozen, looking at a small table against the side wall, where four or five books were in the process of tumbling to the floor, from between two secure bronze horse-head bookends.

I looked at her.

She looked at me.

Our eyes would've been right at home in a minstrel show.

I walked slowly over to the table. The books were on the floor, in an ungainly heap. The bookends stood alone, on the table but flush against the wall, as had been the books, before they fell. It was as if someone had shoved them on the floor; only the wall was where the books would have to have been shoved from.

I shrugged, said it was nothing, started getting my clothes on.

Evalyn nodded, shrugged, padded down the hall to her own room to dress. We said nothing more about it, not over breakfast anyway; we said almost nothing at all, actually, except to comment on what a nice sunny day it was for a change.

Shortly after breakfast the phone jangled out in the hall and scared the hell out of all of us. The rings echoed through the big, mostly empty house, as Evalyn rushed to answer.

She held the receiver sideways so I could stand next to her and listen.

"Hogan speaking," said the voice of Gaston Means. "Who is this?"

"This is Eleven," Evalyn said.

"Eleven, we couldn't get through with the book last night. We had a close call."

"A close call?"

"Listen carefully: come to my home at Chevy Chase this afternoon. Be very, very careful of your movements; make certain you're not followed. I'll see you there at half past two."

And we heard the click of him hanging up.

She looked at me, phone still in her hand. "I'm going, of course."

"Not alone." I touched her shoulder, firmly. "This could be a replay of the Maude King 'accident.'"

"Come with me, then. He didn't say I couldn't bring my chauffeur."

So early that afternoon I put on my chauffeur's uniform and, with her navigating, found my way to Chevy Chase, in Maryland just across the state line from the District of Columbia. The neighborhood was residential and affluent, albeit not affluent in the Evalyn Walsh McLean sense. The house at 112 Leland was a big white two-story pillared number with a spacious, sloping lawn behind a wire-mesh fence—a comfy castle with the prisonlike touch of the fence and, here and there, floodlights mounted to posts. My guess was alarms and switches were hooked up, as well—Means had invested in a considerable security system.

The gate was open, however—we were expected, at least Evalyn was—and I stood behind her with my chauffeur's cap in my hands as she rang the bell. A tall, slender youth of perhaps sixteen, neat as a pin in a diamond-patterned sweater and gray slacks, answered the door.

"We're here to see Mr. Means," Evalyn said, smiling.

The boy nodded; his eyes were large, brown, guileless.

"Please come in," he said, and we did.

The house was as neat, as orderly, as the boy's apparel. Well furnished, in the Early American mode. The people who lived here weren't rich exactly, but they were clearly successful.

"I think my father is expecting you," the boy said.

Means's voice boomed down. "Hello there! Come on up!"

We went up the staircase, leaving the boy behind, and there, on the landing, stood Means—as disheveled as his house wasn't. His brown suit rumpled, his tie loose, his eyes bloodshot, his breath boozy, his face sweat-slick, Means ushered us into a cluttered den past a table on which was a Rube Goldberg contraption consisting of a long board with four dry-cell batteries, a big light bulb and a reflector.

The big moon-faced bastard fell heavily into the chair behind his messy desk. "God, Eleven! What a close call we had last night."

"What do you mean, Means?"

"Call me 'Hogan,' Eleven. I must insist. Should we talk in front of your chauffeur?"

"I'm agent Sixteen," I said, "remember?"

"If you're a police spy," Means said enigmatically, "the Lindbergh boy will bear the burden."

"Tell us about your close call," I said. I found Evalyn a chair, clearing off some letters and old newspapers. I stood, cap in hand. The cap was covering the nine millimeter in my waistband.

"I went to the place the baby is being kept," Means said darkly, sitting forward, hands locked prayerlike.

"Where was it?" Evalyn asked.

"I can't divulge that," Means said, with a regretful wag of his massive bald noggin. "I gave my word to the criminals I wouldn't share their location with anyone. But I will say it's within a hundred miles of Washington."

"Did you see him?" Evalyn asked, breathlessly. "Did you see Charles Augustus Lindbergh, Jr.?"

"Yes," Means said, matter-of-factly, his dimples cute as a

baby's behind. "I held the boy in my arms. He had blue eyes, blond hair, was dressed in a knitted cap, buff coat, brown shoes and white stockings. The age and appearance tallied with everything I've seen and heard about the child."

Evalyn looked at me yearningly; she longed to believe this.

"What about the close call?" I said.

Means narrowed his eyes, cocked his head, sat forward. "Last night, sometime after midnight, we started out from the gang's headquarters in two cars. I was traveling in the lead car. The Fox, with the baby in tow, was in the second. I was to keep an eye out for police. If I saw the police were stopping cars and searching them, I was to use my invention . . ." He pointed to the Rube Goldberg contraption with the light bulb. ". . . and signal the car behind, where the Fox was with the baby. I was to flash the light three times."

Evalyn glanced at me; she seemed excited. She was buying this.

"Along toward three in the morning," Means continued, "we were nearly to Far View when I saw a car stopped by a policeman up ahead. I flashed my light three times, and the car behind me turned and went back."

"Back?" I asked.

"To the hideout," he said, melodramatically.

This guy ought to have been on the radio.

"Back at the hideout," he went on, "the Fox and the rest of the boys were jittery as june bugs. The Fox said the deal was definitely off, as far as Far View being the drop point was concerned."

Evalyn looked at me anxiously and saw my skepticism. She turned back to Means and said, "This sounds pretty queer to me. . . ."

Means affected a hurt expression. Grandly, he opened a desk drawer and removed a brown-paper package fastened with red sealing wax.

"There's your hundred thousand, Eleven," he said. "Take your money back, if you want to pull out."

Evalyn shook her head no. "I don't want to pull out—as long as there's the slightest chance we'll get that baby back, I'm in."

He plucked a letter opener from the mess on his desk and cut the cord on the package; the paper came loose and revealed green bills on top. Then he plucked from the package a tag, which he handed toward Evalyn. She took it. Read it. Handed it to me.

It said:

GASTON B. MEANS
Property of Mrs. Evalyn Walsh McLean

"I put this on the package," he said, taking back the tag, "for your protection. Should I meet my death in this endeavor, your money will be returned."

I knew just eyeballing it that that package wasn't big enough to hold one hundred grand in small currency; but I would have to tell her later. And was his desk drawer the "safe" he'd told me the money was locked away in?

"I'll resume negotiations," he said to her, "if you wish."

"Do that," she said curtly. "I'm leaving Far View and returning to 2020. Keep me informed—we'll work out a new drop point. But if you're not on the level, you'll finish your days behind bars."

She sounded as melodramatic as Means; but she wasn't lying.

"Eleven," he said somberly, "you saw that fine boy of mine downstairs, didn't you? The very thought of him would prevent me from doing anything wrong—that boy's my life, now."

We left Means and his messy den and his neat house and fine boy and we sat in the powder-blue Lincoln, talking.

"You think he's lying, don't you, Nate?"

"I know he's lying. The trouble is, with a con man like him, he's probably building on *some* truth. He's had a few kernels of inside information—the question is, where has he gotten it? How close is he to the actual kidnappers?"

Her mouth was a thin determined line. "I have to follow this out to its conclusion."

"Why don't you let me put the Treasury boys on this? Tracking this cellmate of his, the 'Fox,' if he exists, would be a snap."

"No! No. That might spoil everything . . . the child might suffer . . ."

She sounded like Lindbergh now.

"These T-men are the boys who got Capone," I said. "They can . . ."

"No. If you do, I'll call Ogden and quash it, Nate, I really will."

"Ogden?"

"Ogden Mills. Secretary of the Treasury Mills."

Now she really sounded like Lindbergh.

"Okay, Evalyn. Okay. But I'm afraid this is where I get off. I'll drive you back to Far View, but my advice to you is to turn Means over to the authorities. You might still get your money back, and some information about the kidnapping, to boot."

"No," she said, firmly.

I spoke through a strained smile. "You know what today is, Evalyn? April first. April Fool's Day."

"That's cruel."

"You said it yourself: it's a cruel universe."

"Promise me, Nate. Promise me you won't interfere."

"Evalyn—"

"Promise me. Promise!"

She touched my cheek; her eyes mingled hope and despair.

"All right," I sighed. "All right."

So I drove her back to Far View. We didn't speak. We weren't mad at each other, exactly. But we didn't speak.

In the second-floor room, where Evalyn and I had sat waiting for ghosts the night before, I packed my clothes and my gun and left the room to the poltergeists. As I came down the stairs, Inga said I'd had a phone message while I was away and handed me a small folded piece of paper; I slipped it in my pocket without glancing at it, as Evalyn was approaching.

"Why don't I drive you and Inga back to 2020?" I asked.

"I can drive myself," Evalyn said, without rancor. "I don't really need a chauffeur, you know. It's just another of the empty luxuries in my life."

"Evalyn—I know you mean well in this. But you're in over your head."

"It's only money, Nate. If I can save that child . . ."

"Evalyn . . ." I looked around; we were in the kitchen, alone, waiting for Gus the caretaker to collect me and take me to the train. I gave her a long, lingering kiss.

"I'll be back," I said.

She touched my face again.

"I'll be waiting," she said.

As I went out to get in Gus's pickup truck, she stood watching me from the back doorway, like another ghost in that damn haunted house.

In the pickup, I unfolded Inga's message; it was from Breck- inridge.

It said: "Jafsie has heard from John."

Chapter 20

I sat in a comfortable chair near a crackling fire emanating from a marble fireplace in an expensive, high-ceilinged library worthy of Evalyn Walsh McLean's Massachusetts Avenue mansion; but I was not in Washington, D.C. I was in Manhattan, in a stately graystone townhouse just off Central Park on East 72nd, the New York residence of the late Senator Morrow, Lindy's father-in-law.

Nearby, at a long mahogany conference table, sat Elmer Irey and Frank Wilson, the dour frick-and-frack IRS agents whose mutual round black-rimmed glasses and black suits and dark ties made them humorless mirror images. Wilson was the more clearly restless of the pair, drumming his fingers, searching his balding scalp for clues of hair. Irey was as immobile as the face on a coin. But both were worried.

So was I.

We were waiting.

I'd been with Lindbergh and Breckinridge at Professor Condon's bungalow all afternoon; Irey and Wilson had stayed away, in case the house was being watched. Final preparations were made at Condon's, including stuffing the two cord-and-brown-paper-wrapped packages of cash—one containing fifty thousand dollars in the various denominations specified by the kidnappers, and the other containing the additional twenty thousand—into Dr. Condon's duplicate antique ballot box, an oblong wooden affair with brass hinges and clasps. Work of a first-rate Bronx cabinetmaker or not, it didn't hold up under the bulk of the bills: one side split. The twenty-grand packet had to be carried separately, and the box wrapped with cord.

We were responding to the note that had arrived with Jafsie's April Fool's Day mail, while I was away; it read:

> Dear Sir: have the money ready by Saturday
> evening. we will inform you where
> and how to deliver it. have the money
> in one bundle we want you to put
> it in on a sertain place. Ther is
> no fear that somebody els will
> tacke it, we watch everything
> closely. Please lett us know if
> you are agree and ready for action
> by saturday evening.—if yes—
> put in the paper
>   Yes everything O.K.
> Is a very simble delivery but we
> find out very sun if there is any trapp.
> after 8 houers you gett the adr, from
> the boy, on the place
> you finde two ladies. they are
> innocence.

The message was signed with the familiar symbol.

"If the ransom drop comes off tomorrow night," I'd told Slim, "I'll go with the professor."

We were sitting in Condon's living room, sipping tea served by the professor's shell-shocked wife; the pretty, pretty unfriendly daughter was lurking, too, worried about her father. Right now she was helping her papa and Breckinridge with the ransom package.

The ad—saying "YES. EVERYTHING O.K. JAFSIE."—had appeared in the morning New York *American*.

"I don't want you going along, Nate," Lindbergh said. "They might recognize you from last time. They might know, by now, you're a cop."

"You can't let the professor handle this by himself."

"I won't. I'll go myself."

"Is that smart? You're a prime kidnap target yourself."

"In that case, you can do me a favor, then."

"Yes?"

He shrugged. "I knew Anne would be disturbed if she happened to see me leave the house with a gun."

"I guess she might at that."

"So I didn't bring one. Can I borrow your nine millimeter?"

"Why, sure."

"And shoulder holster?"

"Of course."

"You don't mind?"

"Hell, Slim. I'm honored. It'll almost be like being there."

He sipped his tea. He smiled slyly at me, his eyes narrow and shrewd. "Tell me, Nate. Did you work on Irey? And Wilson?"

"What do you mean?"

He nodded sideways toward the other room. "Those bills in there. That money. Wilson spent the morning recording all the serial numbers at J. P. Morgan and Company."

I grinned. "Well, that's swell. It really is. You won't be sorry."

He shook his head, sipped more tea. "I guess it took over a dozen clerks to help get the job done. Five-thousand-some items of currency, with no two numbers in sequence."

"Don't look at me, Slim—I didn't put the pressure on Irey. He's capable all by himself of figuring out that recording those bills is the thing to do. But what made you change *your* mind?"

Lindbergh's mouth twitched. "Irey," he said, and then added, admiringly: "He's a hard-nosed bastard."

I didn't push him, and Slim didn't elaborate further, but that evening, as I waited with the two IRS agents in the Morrows' vast library, I asked Irey how he'd convinced Lindbergh.

"He gave me some noble malarkey," Irey said, "about wanting

to keep his promises to the kidnappers, to encourage them to keep their promises to him."

"Slim doesn't know much about crooks, I'm afraid."

"When it comes to being a detective," Irey said, "Lindbergh makes a damn fine airmail-pilot. At any rate, I told him that unless he allowed us to record the serial numbers of the bills, the Treasury Department would play no part in the case."

"But what about his pull with your boss?"

Irey's smile was as thin as a stiletto blade. "Even the Secretary of the Treasury knows that his department damn well better not compound a felony. Which is what we'd have been guilty of, if we allowed those bills to go out unrecorded."

"And that sold Slim."

"Not immediately," Irey said, with a shake of his head. "We withdrew—from his home and from the case—and didn't hear from him till this morning."

"He must have checked with Secretary Mills, after all."

"Maybe. But it didn't do him any good. He gave us the go-ahead."

"Mills?"

"Lindbergh. And that second packet, the one with twenty thousand in it, is strictly gold certificates."

"Gold certificates?"

"Yes. Fifty-dollar ones. Four hundred of them. Those will be child's play for bank tellers to spot."

"Nice thinking, Elmer."

"Thank you, Mr. Heller—but the gold-certificate notion was Frank's work. The smaller-denomination bills are mostly gold certificates, as well."

I nodded and smiled at Wilson, who nodded and smiled back at me. We were one big happy family—three cops sitting in a posh townhouse library, while an eccentric professor and a stunt flyer were off in the night somewhere with seventy grand to turn over to some self-proclaimed kidnappers.

Earlier that afternoon, when Lindbergh and I had spoken about the marked bills, I'd attempted to make another point, with considerably less success.

"Why don't you," I'd suggested, "let Irey and maybe the New

York cops follow you to wherever the ransom drop is, then pull in undercover men to throw a net over the area?"

He shook his head sternly, no. "That's out of the question. That would be much too dangerous. . . ."

"No it wouldn't. You'd have cops acting as cabbies, drunks, truck drivers, washerwomen, priests . . . undercover cops do that kind of thing all the time, and well."

"The kidnappers wouldn't be that easily fooled, Nate. They'll go into this thing suspicious as hell."

"Slim, it's not suspicious to be passed on the street by a milk wagon or a bunch of college whoopee boys . . . it's natural to have people on the streets, even at night, especially at night, when this ransom drop will probably come off."

But he wouldn't hear of it.

Later Irey confirmed that he'd made a similar plea to Lindbergh to no avail; and in this case, the word from above was to stay out of Lindy's way.

So those of us who were thinking like cops were one for two—and batting .500 in the Lindbergh game was a goddamn good average.

I'd been at Condon's most of the day and into the evening, when the doorbell rang around a quarter to eight; the daughter, Myra, answered the door and a cabbie—she described him as young, thin, dark—handed her an envelope and scurried back to his cab and was gone before any of us could stop him or even get his license number.

Lindbergh tore open the envelope, read the note, with Condon and Breckinridge looking on.

When I made a move to look at it, Slim's boyish face was cold; he shook his head, no.

"You're not part of this, Nate," he said. "We'll take the professor's car. You drive into mid-Manhattan and join the IRS boys. And wait."

I sighed, irritably. "You don't usually order me around, Slim. I'm not sure I like it much."

He lifted a hand, as if about to place it on my shoulder, then saw from my expression that it wouldn't be appreciated.

He said, "I know you don't approve of how I'm going about

this. But you're just a consultant—you're not really part of the police, here. I don't want you knowing where we're going . . ." He was clutching the note, wadding it a bit. ". . . and I don't want you following us."

"What good would it do me? You've got my gun."

He smiled shyly, embarrassed, and went ahead and put the hand on my shoulder and squeezed. "Promise me, Nate."

People kept asking me to make promises I didn't feel like keeping. But I nodded anyway.

"Thank you." He looked at Breckinridge. "Would you stay here, with the professor's family, Henry?"

Breckinridge nodded in his sad, dignified way.

Condon's daughter brought her father his coat and hat and helped him into them, telling him to be careful. The professor, bug-eyed, red-faced, calm as a walrus in heat, said, "Allow me to handle the parcel," and grabbed up the cord-wound, split-apart, jam-packed ballot box, as well as the separate package with the twenty grand in gold notes.

That was fine with Lindbergh, who viewed the money with disinterest and even disdain, and the two men hurried out to the Ford coupe and, Lindbergh behind the wheel, Jafsie with the loot on his lap, disappeared down the street and turned south.

Now it was almost midnight; four hours later, in the Morrow library, and no sign of Lindbergh or the professor.

"They could be dead in a ditch somewhere," I suggested.

"If they are," Wilson said, "it won't be our fault."

"Tell that to the press," Irey said glumly.

"Success, gentlemen!"

The booming, overly well-modulated voice belonged to none other than Professor John F. Condon, who entered the chamber with his arms outspread as if looking for someone to embrace. I wasn't volunteering.

Lindbergh and Breckinridge came in on the professor's heels; all three men were still in their topcoats and hats, except for Slim who was hatless to begin with. Two Morrow butlers hurried after the men, who had burst into the apartment without any of the usual amenities, and began collecting coats and hats.

"We delivered the ransom," Lindbergh said, digging in his

jacket pocket, "and we have been given directions." He smiled, and the smile mingled joy with desperation. "We can find Charlie if we follow this."

He placed a small note on the conference table, and we all gathered round. It said:

> the boy is on Boad Nelly
> it is a small Boad 28 feet
> long, two person are on the
> Boat. The are innosent
> you will find the Boad between
> Horseneck Beach and gay Head
> near Elizabeth Island.

It lacked the usual circles and holes signature, but the handwriting was as before.

"I've already called for an amphibian," Lindbergh said, eyes bright as glowing coals, "and as soon as it's light, we'll take off."

"Sit down, gentlemen, please," Irey said, gesturing to the table, looking first at Lindy, the professor and Breckinridge, but at myself and Wilson, too. We all gathered around the table, and sat.

Lindbergh and Condon told the story, the former doing most of the talking, but the latter taking over at the points when center stage of the melodrama became his.

The note the cabbie had delivered directed them to follow Tremont Avenue east until they reached 3225, a nursery, J. A. Bergen Greenhouse and Florist. There they would find a table outside the florist shop entrance, and underneath the table would be a letter covered by a stone. The letter directed them to cross the street, walk to the next corner and follow Whittemore Avenue to the south. They were to bring the money. Condon was to come alone. He would be met.

"As we approached Whittemore Avenue," Condon said, leaning forward, his eyes rheumy but intense, "I realized that these wily kidnappers were duplicating their precautions from the previous meeting."

"Why is that?" Irey asked.

Wilson was taking notes.

"Whittemore Avenue," Lindbergh said, "is a dirt road running parallel to St. Raymond's Cemetery."

Another graveyard.

The professor raised a finger in the air like a Bible-beating preacher making a point about heaven, or hell. "For the second time," he said, "our meeting was on a Saturday night. And for the second time, our rendezvous took place . . ." He looked at each of us significantly; his expression, in the orange reflection of the nearby fireplace, was that of a senile scoutmaster telling a singularly unscary ghost story around a campfire. ". . . in the city of the dead."

And me without any marshmallows to roast.

"As I told the Colonel," Condon confided, winking at Irey, who acknowledged the wink not at all, "I have heard that Italian gangsters frequently frequent graveyards. . . ."

Frequently frequent? What was this clown a professor of, anyway? Redundancy?

"And our pair of cemetery conferences," Condon continued, "would tend to confirm my belief that the gang is a mixture of Mafia members and the Scandinavian, 'John.' "

Lindbergh, thankfully, picked up the story at that point.

Condon had stood outside the car, reading the note by flashlight, hoping to attract the attention of any lookout that the kidnap gang might have posted. A man in a brown suit approached, brim of his brown felt hat pulled down; he walked with a decided stoop. When he passed the car, he covered the bottom half of his face with a handkerchief, eyeballing the two men.

When the apparent lookout was out of sight, Lindbergh began to climb out of the coupe, but Condon stopped him: the note had said that the professor must come alone.

But Jafsie was less of a stickler about the note's other directions: he left both the ballot box and the separate packet of money behind, telling Lindy, "I want to talk to John first." And he had walked east, not south, on Whittemore—"This enabled me to look behind most of the tombstones and bushes that fronted the avenue."

Peering into the "eerie semidarkness" of the cemetery, however, Condon saw nothing but shadows.

When he had walked past the cemetery gates, Condon turned and walked slowly back; he called out to Lindbergh, "There seems to be no one here, Colonel."

A voice called, then, from behind a tombstone: "Hey, Doctor!"

A figure rose specterlike from behind a gravestone.

"Hey, Doctor—over here!"

Both Condon and Lindbergh heard the voice, which they described as "guttural."

Condon moved toward the tombstone, but the figure moved away, and the professor followed him into the cemetery, where, after zigzagging among the graves, the figure crouched behind a hedge.

"I said to him, 'What are you doing crouched down there—stand up if you want to talk to me!' " Condon was gesturing theatrically; Lindbergh didn't seem to mind, but Wilson looked up from his note-taking to roll his eyes at me, discreetly. Condon was saying, "He asked me if I remembered him from that other Saturday night, at Woodlawn Cemetery. I said I did. He asked, 'Have you got it, the money?' And I said, no, I didn't bring any money. That it was up in the car."

Cemetery John had then asked if Colonel Lindbergh were armed, and the professor had said no ("I lied," he said, proud of himself), and then John demanded his money.

"I refused," Condon told us. "I said, 'Not until you give me a receipt!' "

"A receipt?" I said. "You asked the kidnapper for a *receipt?*"

"It was a business transaction of sorts," Condon said, stiffly, defensively. "I was well within my rights to demand a written receipt, paying over such a sum."

Irey looked stunned; Wilson, frozen in his note-taking, had the expression of a man examining shit on his shoe.

"Further, I demanded a note specifying where the baby is—and that, gentlemen, is the very note." He pointed to the small note, which still lay on the table, like a cocktail napkin.

"Yeah," I said sarcastically, "but where's your receipt?"

The professor ignored that. He went on to say that John had said he would have to go and get a note ready; he'd be gone a few minutes, during which time Jafsie could go to the car and come back with the seventy thousand dollars.

"And here," Condon said, regally, "was my masterstroke—I talked him out of twenty thousand dollars."

"You *what?*" Irey said; his eyes popped behind the black-rimmed lenses.

Condon beamed, in his apple-cheeked way, saying, "I told him, 'John, Colonel Lindbergh is not so rich. These are depression times—he couldn't raise that extra twenty thousand. But I can walk up to that auto right now and get you fifty.' "

Wilson was slumped over his notebook, covering his eyes with one hand. Irey's face remained stony, but red was rising out of his neck like a metal poker getting hotter. Slim, who seemed to sense a major blunder had been pulled, was shifting uneasily in his chair.

Condon didn't read any of this; he was wrapped up in his own wonderfulness. "And John said, 'All right—I suppose if we can't get seventy, we take fifty.' "

"Do you know what you've done?" Irey said.

"Why, yes. I've saved Colonel Lindbergh twenty thousand dollars."

"I could shoot your head off," Irey said.

Condon blinked; his expression was as innocent as it was stupid. "Have I done something wrong?"

"The little package you left behind," I said, "was full of fifty-dollar gold certificates. Big bills—easy to trace. The largest bills in the ballot box were twenties—not near as conspicuous."

Condon thought that over. Then, summoning his dignity, he said, "I would do it again if I had the chance—I would save Colonel Lindbergh every possible penny." And he smiled at Lindy, who smiled back, wanly.

Approximately fifteen minutes after Condon had headed back to the car for the money, while Cemetery John headed wherever for some notepaper and a pencil(!), the two men met again at the same spot in "the city of the dead." Condon passed John the ballot box of money, and John passed the professor a sealed envelope, instructing him not to open it for six hours. John looked at the money, pronounced it satisfactory; Condon pledged to John that if this were a "double cross" he, Condon, would pursue the gang to the ends of the earth, if necessary!

That must have scared shit out of him.

"While the professor was in the cemetery," Lindbergh told us, Wilson taking notes fast and furious, "that same fellow in the brown suit we'd seen before came running down the other side of the street, from the direction of Whittemore. He covered his face again, with his handkerchief, as he passed by the car—and blew his nose so loudly that it could've been heard a block away."

"Did you see his face?" Irey asked.

"Not directly," Lindbergh said. "He ran to a spot some distance away, but I saw him drop the handkerchief—like a signal of some kind."

"Colonel, you heard Cemetery John's voice," Wilson said, looking up from his note-taking. "Could you identify him by it, do you think?"

Without hesitation Slim shook his head, no. "Oh, I remember the voice clearly enough. But to say I could pick a man out by that voice . . . I really couldn't."

"Well, I could," Condon said, slapping his hand on the table. "My hearing *and* night vision are excellent. I can describe him to a T . . . a hatchet-faced individual with almond-shaped eyes. . . ."

"Get a sketch artist over here," Irey told Wilson, who nodded, pocketed his notebook and went out. Irey began questioning Condon about various details; Slim got up and moved around and sat next to me.

"Nate," he said, "are you going with us?"

"To search for the Boat *Nelly*? Sure, if you want me to."

"I want you to. Maybe you should grab a nap on a couch. It's after one A.M., now. We'll be leaving at dawn."

"Okay," I said, yawning, stretching as I pushed away from the table. I got up. "You know, one thing surprises me."

"Oh?" Lindbergh said.

"Yeah." I grinned. "The way you been playing fair, playing by the rules, I'm halfway surprised you didn't wait six hours, like you were told, before you opened that envelope."

"Oh, I was going to," Slim said. "But Dr. Condon talked me out of it."

Chapter 21

It was still dark when we reached the airstrip. We'd left Manhattan around two A.M., bound for Bridgeport, Connecticut, Lindbergh driving, Breckinridge in the front, Condon, Irey and me in back. Wilson stayed behind "coordinating," whatever that was. I fell quickly asleep against the locked door as Jafsie, sitting between Irey and me like an oversize child, his cow eyes glazed, alternated between chortling over his triumph of depriving the kidnappers of four hundred fifty-dollar gold certificates, and spouting Shakespeare.

I awoke, briefly, when the car came to a stop, saw Lindy conferring with airport officials and some Navy men, and quickly surmised that our plane hadn't arrived yet. I saw a middle-aged fellow in civilian clothes, apparently an airport manager, hand Lindy a small but bulging bundle and Lindy smiled at him gratefully, taking the bundle, shaking the man's hand. I went back to sleep, Condon next to me in the car's backseat, as alert as a watchdog, and nearly as smart.

A whirring roar, louder than Judgment Day, awoke me. I sat

up sharply; Condon was gone. I got out and saw, across the airfield, the rising sun glittering on the blue-gray surface of Long Island Sound. Above, a huge silver flying boat wheeled in the sky, making its approach.

"A Sikorsky amphibian," Irey yelled, above the din. He was standing just behind me, his topcoat flapping in the wind, as he held his hat on with one hand. Some of it was the breeze; most of it was the airplane, coming in for her landing.

Irey moved closer to me. "That's perfect," he shouted, almost directly into my ear. "We can spot the Boat *Nelly* from the air and put down right beside her."

I nodded. I wondered what he meant by "we." I'd never been up in a plane, and had no intention of starting now.

As the huge silver bird set down, slowed, and swung gently around, its propellers turning from a blur into blades, Lindbergh walked into, and seemed to enjoy, the wind the props manufactured. I kept my distance while he, Colonel Breckinridge and Irey gathered near the plane. Slim inspected the ship, talking casually but intently with the pilot who brought her in.

Condon was next to me, looking with some trepidation at the big silver bird.

Lindbergh opened up a cabin door and stowed inside the bundle the airport official had given him. Then he strolled over to us and smiled in his boyish way. There was something in his face today I hadn't seen before. I couldn't quite put my finger on it.

"All right, gents," he said brightly.

Hope. That was it: there was hope in his face, the crinkles around his eyes, the tug at the corners of his smile.

"I'd like you to go along, Doctor," Lindy said to Condon. "You're not afraid of planes, are you?"

Jafsie raised his chin and said, "Sir, I will go anywhere you go."

Lindy turned to me. "How about you, Nate?"

"Slim, if God had wanted me to fly, I'da been born with a parachute . . . and I still wouldn't go."

"Well, God isn't asking you—I am."

I sucked in some air and blew it out. "What do you want me along for? Somebody ought to stay with the car."

"We can use another spotter. Besides, you've been in on this since almost the beginning. You deserve to be in on the finish." He squeezed my arm; he squeezed it hard. "We're going to bring Charlie back, Nate. Come along."

I went along.

Lindbergh took the controls, of course, and Breckinridge— who was also a pilot, as were so many of Slim's pals—took the copilot's chair. Condon and Irey sat behind them, and I sat behind Condon and Irey. In one corner of the plane was Lindbergh's bundle, loosened enough to reveal its contents: a blanket around some baby clothes and a bottle of milk.

Lindbergh placed his hands on the wheel and sighed, contentedly, and then he gunned the Sikorsky's engines and I felt my stomach fall to my shoes as we lifted off. In retrospect I realize the takeoff was smooth, but it seemed to me at the time that every nut, bolt and screw holding this mechanical beast together was shaking apart. The bellow of the twin engines was deafening and as Lindbergh swung the ship around, slowly circling the field, I was thankful I hadn't eaten lately.

Lindbergh pointed the plane toward the climbing morning sun, as we skirted the Connecticut shore. I sat, the seat beneath me rumbling, my eyes closed. We were soon heading toward Martha's Vineyard, over the northern end of Long Island Sound. But I didn't know that.

I told myself if I had to fly, what better pilot could I have for my first air voyage than the most famous pilot in the world? At the same time I realized that this particular pilot was one of the most reckless daredevils ever to take flight.

Finally, as the hum of the plane and even the vibration of my chair began to lull me, I looked out my window at the placid blue glimmering surface of the Sound. It, too, lulled me. From up here, the world became something abstract—colors, shapes, patterns. The day couldn't have been a clearer, more perfect one. It was even cold enough, in the cabin, to keep that damn milk from going sour.

Just as I was getting comfortable, Condon began talking. I couldn't quite make it out, at first, but he seemed intense, serious.

After a while I tapped Irey on the shoulder and he leaned

back and I said, "What's the old fart babbling about, anyway?"

"Excerpts," Irey said with a glazed expression.

"Excerpts?"

"From the Song of Solomon."

Suddenly the rumble of the Sikorsky's engines seemed a blessing.

I had a clear view of my two pilots, despite my rear seat, and I noticed, after a while, Lindbergh turning the controls over to Breckinridge. That was almost a relief, as of the two colonels, Breckinridge struck me as the staid one—no stunt-flying from him.

But almost immediately we began to lose altitude.

The fucking ship was sinking like a stone!

"Slim!" Breckinridge said, trying not to panic. "I'm trying to pull up, but . . ."

Lindbergh reached over and took the wheel momentarily, got it back on an even keel, and returned the controls to Breckinridge. Lindy was smiling, faintly. Breckinridge swallowed, his expression baffled.

I, of course, had died of a heart attack long before.

Not long after, Breckinridge shouted again. "I'm trying to turn right, and it's turning left! What in hell is wrong. . . ."

Lindbergh again took the controls and banked the plane to the right, without problem.

Breckinridge was looking carefully at his friend. Then he slowly began to smile. "You rascal."

Rascal?

And Lindbergh began to laugh. I'd never heard him laugh, not like that.

Breckinridge was grinning. "You crossed the wires on this crate, when you looked it over. . . ."

Lindbergh's laughter filled the cabin, drowning out even the drone of the twin engines. He was like a college boy watching a frat-house friend open a door and get drenched by a bucket of water. Irey looked back at me, whiter than his shirt. Condon seemed to be praying.

Lindbergh reached beneath the control panel on Breckinridge's side, laughing softly as he did, and made some adjustments and said, "I got you, Henry. I got you."

"You rogue. You rascal."

"You fucker!" I said.

Lindbergh looked back, startled, then embarrassed. "Didn't mean to scare you, Nate. I just like to put one over on Henry now and then."

"Keep in mind I didn't bring a change of underwear, okay?"

"Okay," Lindy called back to me, shyly smiling. "Sorry. Forgot this was your first time up."

I supposed the reemergence of Slim's notorious practical-joker side was a good thing. But I couldn't work up much enthusiasm about it. I shut my eyes. Actually slept a little.

Irey's voice woke me, as he called back to me: "We're getting there."

I looked out the window at a blemish on the blue mirror below.

"That's Cuttyhunk Island," Irey said, turning toward me. "First of the Elizabeth Island group."

The plane swooped low and my stomach did a flip. Nonetheless I kept my eyes on the window where I saw half a dozen specks turn into trim Coast Guard cutters; a Navy man-of-war steamed into view, as well. Lindbergh throttled down, dropping us near a few boats bobbing gently at anchor near the shore. Soon we were flying so low we were almost skimming the sea; then the twin engines would gather volume as Lindy would pull us up, swinging wide, turning to again swoop low.

I got used to it; I did get used to it. And I never again, as long as I lived, felt uneasy in an airplane—after all, I had survived "hedgehopping" with a daredevil stunt-pilot, as we played tag with the tips of swaying masts.

For better than six hours, we roared over and swooped down near dozens of boats, fishing boats and pleasure craft alike, never seeing Cemetery John's "small boad."

Around noon, Lindbergh turned away from the search area and the seaplane roared steadily ahead for a while and then swooped down again, and out the window I saw the sea, churning whitely as we settled down in Buzzard's Bay. We taxied to Cuttyhunk Island, and I was eager to place my feet on the relatively solid, dry land that was the bouncy wooden dock.

A swarm of reporters awaited. They called questions out to

all of us, trotting along beside us as Lindbergh walked stoically forward; they badgered him, trying to find out who Condon was, who Irey and I were, Lindy never acknowledging their presence with even a glance.

"Now, now, boys," Breckinridge said, waving them off. "Please leave us alone. We've nothing to tell you."

They backed off long enough for us to have a quiet lunch at the old Cuttyhunk Hotel. Condon chowed down; I was able to eat a little. Breckinridge and Irey had modest appetites. Lindbergh, his face pale and his eyes dead, ate nothing; when any of us asked him a question, he'd grunt a monosyllabic nonresponse.

After lunch we went back to the Sikorsky and the afternoon was a replay of the morning, minus the joking: in silence, Lindy swept the sea off southern Massachusetts. No boat resembled the "boad" *Nelly*. We looked out the windows mutely, our eyes burning from looking.

Night began to settle in on us.

"Something's gone wrong," Lindbergh finally admitted. "Maybe the Coast Guard activity spooked them."

Breckinridge, in the copilot's chair, cleared his throat and said, "There seems little point going on with the search, for the time being."

Lindbergh answered him by making one last swing through the Sound at near sea level; then the plane picked up altitude, leveling out, and turned homeward, to the southeast.

We landed on an airstrip in Long Island. Lindbergh had arranged for a car to be waiting at the Aviation Country Club at Hicksville. We piled in and rode in silence to Manhattan. The bundle of blankets, baby clothes and milk had been left behind in the seaplane. The milk was probably sour by now, anyway.

Lindbergh spoke for the first time as the car was stopped at a light in the Thirties on Third Avenue. "I'll take you home, Professor."

"Please don't, Colonel," Condon said; he was sitting between Irey and me, again, in the backseat. "Let me out here—I can get home very nicely on the subway."

"I'll take you." Slim's voice was strangely cold.

"It isn't necessary," Condon said, a certain desperation in his voice.

"All right." Lindbergh swung over by the stairway of an uptown station. He turned and looked at us. His face was gaunt and grim. "We've been double-crossed, you know."

Condon said nothing. His lips were trembling under the walrus mustache.

Lindbergh got out and let Condon out; in doing so, I had to get out as well, and I heard Slim coldly say to the professor, "Well, Doctor—what's the bill for your services?"

I thought Condon was going to cry. His face fell farther than my stomach had on takeoff. Unbelievable as it seems, I felt sorry for the old boy.

"I . . . I have no bill," he said.

Lindbergh seemed a little ashamed, suddenly. "I'd feel better if you let me reimburse you for . . ."

"No," Condon said, with some dignity. "I never accept money from a man who is poorer than myself."

With a nod to Lindbergh, and another to me, he descended into the subway station.

After Lindbergh dropped Irey and Breckinridge off at their respective stops in Manhattan, I shifted to the front seat and we began the ride back to Hopewell. Again, I slipped off into sleep. When I awoke we were in the wilds of New Jersey.

Lindy smiled sadly over. "Among the living again, Nate?"

"Technically," I said. "How are you doing?"

"Been thinking. Do you think the old boy took us for a ride?"

"Condon? I don't know. I keep thinking about those Harlem spiritualists who knew about him before we did."

Lindbergh nodded. "I'm not writing him off, just yet, or that ransom I paid. I'm heading out again, tomorrow. For another look."

I shrugged. "Like you said, maybe all that naval activity frightened 'em off. Maybe they disguised the *Nelly*, stuck her in some secluded cove somewhere."

"It's possible," he agreed, a little too eagerly. "I'll call Newark airport when I get home—arrange for a monoplane."

"Good."

We rode in silence; the woods were on our either side.

Then he said, "Could you join me on the search, tomorrow? It would be just the two of us."

"Well . . . okay. But no practical jokes, okay?"

He managed a smile. "Okay."

He turned off Amwell Road onto the dirt of Featherbed Lane. Soon the big house came into view; though it was nearing midnight, a scattering of lights were on. People were up.

"Oh God," he said. "This is going to be hard. Look at that."

"What?"

"The nursery."

The lights were on in that second-floor corner room, glowing like a beacon. A mother was waiting to welcome her baby.

Chapter 22

For the mansion on Massachusetts Avenue, this was a small draw-ing room—almost intimate, its several couches grouped around another of the omnipresent gold-veined marble fireplaces, in which a fire was lazily crackling. The room had a sunken effect, an open stairway along one wall leading up to a balcony that looked down on us from four sides.

Evalyn was draped against one end of one couch, as if posing for a portrait in the classical style, only she was wearing the simple brown-and-yellow plaid bathrobe she'd worn the first time I saw her. The Hope diamond was nowhere to be seen. Maybe Mike the dog was wearing it; he was nowhere to be seen, either. In the shadows of the reflecting fire, her face was lovely, but she looked tired, and sad—or anyway melancholy, which is the wealthy's way of feeling sad.

I was sitting nearby, enjoying her company, morose though it might at the moment be. Despite her eccentricities, I liked this woman. She was a good person with a good heart, and she smelled good, too. She had large, firm breasts and was very, very rich. What wasn't to like?

But her melancholia was catching. I had the nagging sense that all of us—from Lindbergh to Breckinridge to Schwarzkopf to Condon to Agents Irey and Wilson to Commodore Curtis to Evalyn Walsh McLean to Chicago P.D. liaison Nathan Heller—were on a fool's errand. I simply could not feel that child's presence out there. After a month and a week, the idea of getting that kid back safely seemed about as likely as Charles Augustus Lindbergh listening to reason.

I had gone up in the sky with Lindbergh again, at daybreak Monday, on the heels of the unfruitful Sikorsky search Sunday; smoothly guiding a Lockheed-Vega monoplane, the Lone Eagle combed the coastal waters of the Atlantic, and the Lone Passenger—me—helped him look. I was no longer bothered by flying—or maybe it was that Slim was taking it so much easier, not swooping down so suddenly, or skimming the sea's skin so recklessly. He brought with him another blanket and a small suitcase of Charlie's clothes; no milk this time. We flew over the Elizabeth Islands and Martha's Vineyard, Coast Guard cutters still patrolling the Sound, the surface of which was as dark blue that day as Evalyn's famous bauble.

No craft resembling the *Nelly* turned up, and by noon Lindy's face had taken on a stony despondence. He didn't say so, but I knew he was thinking of Commodore Curtis and the Norfolk contingent when, as afternoon blurred into evening, he swung as far south as Virginia.

The night before, Slim had come home to Hopewell empty-handed to comfort his waiting wife in the doorway; this night, the house again blazing with light, the nursery once more waiting for its tiny charge, Lindbergh met Anne in the doorway and fell into her arms. The tiny woman was patting the tall man's stooped back like a child when I slipped silently away, feeling an intruder, finding the flivver I'd been given to use and heading to my suite at the Old Princeton Inn, knowing that this was over, but also knowing no one was quite ready, or able, to admit it. Certainly not Slim Lindbergh.

In the days that followed, Lindbergh allowed Condon to place another ad ("What is wrong? Have you crossed me? Please, better directions—Jafsie") that brought no response. I spent several evenings at Condon's, with Breckinridge, waiting for nothing. The professor's spirits were low.

Condon had made a positive contribution, it seemed, by leading a federal agent to a shoe impression in the dirt of a freshly covered grave at St. Raymond's, where "John" had jumped a fence along the cemetery's access road. A moulage impression was made, waiting for eventual comparison to any captured suspects.

As the week wore on, Elmer Irey asked, and got, Lindbergh's permission to distribute to banks a fifty-seven-page booklet listing the serial numbers of the 4,750 bills Jafsie had paid John. This seemed to me relatively pointless: bank tellers aren't in the habit of noting the serial numbers of the bills they handle, and the booklet made no mention of the Lindbergh kidnapping.

A few days later, however, a bank teller in Newark figured out the booklet's purpose, proposed his theory to a reporter and it was soon all over the wire services. Now that the list of numbers was labeled "Lindbergh" and published in the papers, shopkeepers started posting it near their cash registers. The first bill spotted, a twenty, turned up at a pastry shop in Greenwich, Connecticut.

"Now we've had it," Lindbergh had said glumly, the day the wire services ID'ed the serial numbers list. "The kidnappers will never resume negotiations."

"Slim," I said. "They got their dough. Days ago. There aren't going to *be* any more negotiations." We were sitting in the kitchen of the house, both of us covered with soot and smelling of smoke. My morning as a detective had been spent helping Lindbergh, a dozen or so troopers, and butler Ollie Whately beat out a brushfire. We were alone—the smoke had sent the women of the house retreating to the Morrow house in Englewood. I was drinking a cold-sweating bottle of bootleg beer. Slim was drinking ice water.

"Besides," I continued, "these may not even *be* the kidnappers—this could be an extortion scheme, plain and simple."

"You saw the sleeping suit yourself, Nate. . . ."

"Right! You got sent a standard-issue pair of kid's pajamas to prove Charlie's identity. Why not a photo? Or a lock of hair? Or something with your boy's fingerprints on it?"

"We've been through that," he said softly, unsurely.

I sighed heavily, sat forward; the backs of my hands were black. "Do you remember why I'm here? The name Al Capone ring a bell? You wouldn't play Capone's game, remember? And now he's sitting back in Cook County Jail, waiting for his last appeal to be turned down."

Face smudged with soot, Lindbergh gave me a testy look. "What's your point?"

I spread my white-palmed black hands like Jolson singing "Mammy." "If Capone took your boy, using his East-Coast bootleg gang connections to do so, he had to figure out *long* ago that he fucked up."

His eyes were slits. "What do you mean?"

"I mean, if the initial idea was, 'Snatch Lindy's kid and deal myself outa stir,' Capone knew *weeks* ago he failed. So none of these so-called kidnap gangs—not Jafsie's, or the Commodore's, or god-damn Gaston Means's—may have your kid. All Jafsie's 'kidnap-pers' most likely have is somebody on the inside—some servant who's feeding them information, a sleeping suit, a copy of the first note that Capone's kidnappers left behind . . . which gave 'em something to pattern the later notes on, and which got 'em fifty grand from you. And now Jafsie's 'kidnappers' are as gone as your dough."

"I don't believe any of that."

I shrugged. "It's just a theory. But it's as good as any."

"If you're right, Charlie is . . ." He couldn't say it.

I patted the air, gently. "He could be. He could be. On the other hand, suppose Capone had Charlie snatched, then faded when he saw his get-outa-jail plan go south. He's not going to . . . excuse me for even bringing this up . . . but he's not going to murder your boy and have a capital rap hanging over him."

"So where would that leave Charlie?"

"Well, maybe with the people Capone contracted to do the kidnapping. Some bootleg bunch really might have the boy. They might be playing out the ransom hand, too."

"In that case," Lindbergh said, perking up, "maybe the real gang *is* trying to contact me . . . through Commodore Curtis, or even Means!"

I swigged the beer. "Anything's possible in this crazy enterprise."

He nodded, raised an eyebrow. "Well, I've been in contact with Commodore Curtis. And *he* says he's in contact with his bootlegger friend, 'Sam.' "

"You want me to check Curtis out? Not to mention Sam."

He shook his head curtly. "No. I'll follow that lead myself. All I'd like from you is to get a bead on this son-of-a-bitch Means. What about Mrs. McLean?"

"I've been calling her home. She's away on a trip somewhere—due back late tonight or early tomorrow. The butler wouldn't say, of course, but my hunch is Means has her chasing her tail."

"I feel terrible about her hundred thousand dollars."

"How do you feel about your fifty?"

He smiled a little, like a mischievous kid. "Worse than I do about her hundred thousand. Would you go down and see her?"

So here I was again, in Washington, D.C., in the pleasant if quirky company of Evalyn Walsh McLean.

"I know I look like hell," she said, sitting up. She lit herself a cigarette from a gold box on a nearby glass-and-mahogany coffee table; she used a matching gold decorative lighter. Exhaling smoke grandly, she said, "Forgive the robe. Even though I was expecting you—and you *know* how pleased I am to see you again—I just couldn't make myself spruce up, somehow. Nate, I've been through the mill."

"What mill, exactly?" I sipped a Bacardi I'd made myself. "Where *have* you been, Evalyn?"

Her smile was self-mockingly thin. "To hell and Texas, and various purgatories between. After Far View was deemed inappropriate by the 'kidnap gang'—as I'm sure you'll recall, darling—Means arranged for a new 'drop point,' at Aiken."

"Aiken?"

"It's not a condition, dear. It's a town in South Carolina. I have a place down there—it's where my son Ned is in school. Means told me the gang was willing to attempt a delivery of the 'book' there, so I went down with Inga and, not wanting my son to walk in on this Gaston Means-directed tragicomedy, rented a little cottage. Means came down and had a look around, seemed to approve of the setup, said he'd let the gang know I was there. The next morning he reappeared, and informed me dramatically that one of the kidnappers wanted to meet with me—that very afternoon!"

I had gotten up and gone to the liquor cart and was pouring her some sherry. "Face-to-face with one of the kidnappers, huh?"

She arched an eyebrow ironically. "Not just any kidnapper—the mastermind himself: the 'Fox.' At two o'clock that afternoon, a car stopped in front of the cottage—Means walked in, all smiles, followed by a stranger right out of *Little Caesar*."

I gave her the sherry. "How so?"

She painted an image in the air. "He was tall, thin, wore his hat low over his forehead, wore an expensive-looking camel-hair overcoat. He kept that coat on all the while—hands jammed in his pockets, as if he had a gun in either pocket. But he *spoke* well—he seemed to be an individual of some polish and education." Her face looked angular and lovely in the fire's shadowy flickering. "The Fox said he wanted to look through the place, make sure there were no hidden microphones. Means and Inga stayed in the living room, while I showed our guest around. He looked in closets, under beds, wiping off everything he touched with a handkerchief. Odd."

"What made that odd?"

"He was wearing thick gray suede gloves at that time."

"Oh."

She inhaled smoke; let it out. "After he'd searched the house, the Fox asked if he might have a look around the grounds; I consented, sent him off alone. When he returned, he told Means that he was satisfied I was playing it straight with the gang. Then the Fox turned to me and said that within forty-eight hours, the 'book' would be handed over to me, personally, on a side street not far from the cottage."

"Yet somehow it never happened."

She smiled ruefully. "The arrangements were typically Means-baroque. Four automobiles would be waiting, two on one side of the street, two on the other, the child would be handed over in the middle, with machine guns trained on me from every car."

I had to smile. "Means does like his melodrama."

"I do wish you'd been there, Nate. I wish you'd stayed with me through all this."

"So do I. I would've grabbed that goddamn Fox and skinned him. Then we'd be somewhere."

She nodded, putting out one cigarette, getting another going. "Well, the Fox may have spoken like an educated man, but he was as big a scoundrel as Means. Before he left, the blackguard made a veiled threat about my children, should I 'cross' him. Then he left, and Means left with him."

"And what happened, to prevent the 'drop' from taking place, machine guns and all?"

"Means arrived the next day, and said it was all off. Things were in an awful mess, he said. The gang members were quarreling amongst themselves. Lindbergh had apparently paid 'fifty grand' through that other negotiator . . ."

I sat up. "What? What's this?"

She raised both eyebrows in casual surprise. "Didn't I ever mention that? Means said, oh, weeks ago, that Lindbergh was working through another negotiator, when of course Gaston *Means* was the only appropriate negotiator. . . ."

Jesus. Had Means known about Jafsie, weeks ago? And had he known about the ransom payment in St. Raymond's Cemetery, before the papers guessed it?

Her expression sharpened, now, in response to my reaction. "From what I'm seeing in the press," she said, "about lists of marked bills, that much of his story is true, isn't it? There *was* a ransom payment, through another negotiator?"

I nodded.

"Means claims the gang was arguing about whether to turn the baby over to Lindbergh, through this other negotiator, or to me, through Means. Making matters worse, they were squabbling over how exactly to divide the spoils."

"Where was the baby supposed to be, at this point? Aiken?"

"Not specifically. The boy could have been brought there, easily enough, Means said. He said the child was now being kept on a boat, at sea."

"A boat? At sea?"

"Yes. Means claimed a fast launch was keeping the kidnappers informed as to what was going on, on land. He felt the boat was in the vicinity of Norfolk. Nate—what's wrong? You're white as a ghost."

I was shaking my head. "Means knows too much. He knows about things he should have no way of knowing."

Was there *really* a "boad *Nelly*"? Was Commodore Curtis, of Norfolk, really in touch with the kidnap gang, via the rumrunner "Sam"?

"All I know," she said, "is that Means told me that the Aiken delivery was off—that the child was being taken by water and land to a point near Juarez, Mexico."

"Mexico?" My head was reeling.

"He said the gang felt safer out of the country. They felt if they were ever caught, that they'd be torn limb from limb."

"That much is the truth, anyway." I gulped down the rest of the Bacardi. I could've used another, but I didn't get myself one; Evalyn's words were making me woozy enough. "And that's what you meant by, 'to hell and Texas'?"

She nodded. "Means said if I went to El Paso, just across the border from Juarez, he could arrange that the gang would bring the baby to me."

"And you went."

"Inga and I, yes. To the Paso Del Norte Hotel in El Paso, where Means met us, at four in the afternoon. He assured us the 'book' was 'across the river,' as he always referred to Mexico. He went across the border and returned that night with bad news: the gang was still quarreling over the division of the spoils. This went on for another day, with Means going 'across the river,' and returning, with nothing developing; he even brought the Fox back around—who seemed nervous, kept saying he had to protect his gang, couldn't take a chance on turning the baby over unless they were 'protected on every angle.' I blew up at them both, stormed out, took the next train home."

"Did Means try to stop you from going?"

"He did, until I told him that any prolonged, unexplained absence on my part would make my lawyers and friends suspicious, and that the first thing they'd think of would be to go straight to J. Edgar Hoover."

"And you returned home."

"Yes. Arrived late the night before last."

"Have you heard from Means, since?"

"Oh yes. He called this afternoon. Claimed he'd flown from El Paso to Chicago, with the Fox, shortly after I'd taken my leave from them. That he had just returned to his home, at Chevy Chase, from the airport, and would call on me soon."

I got up and began to pace. "Do you expect him this evening?"

"Possibly. At this point, do we care? I'm convinced Means is perpetrating the biggest hoax of his career. You were right all along, Nate. I was a fool."

Suddenly I wasn't so sure who the fool was. If I'd stayed with Evalyn, and not gone back to reenter the Jafsie sweepstakes, maybe I'd be on top of things, instead of underneath the weight of it all.

"What *is* it, Nate? What's wrong?"

"Call Means. Get him over here. Now."

I was perched out of sight in the balcony, from which that reporter friend of Evalyn's had supervised her first meeting with the notorious Gaston Bullock Means. And like Evalyn's reporter friend, I was armed. The nine millimeter was snugly beneath my left shoulder.

Below me, in a room lit only by the fireplace, Evalyn—still wearing the dowdy robe, smoking yet another cigarette—paced. Before long, Garboni announced, and ushered in, her awaited guest.

Massive Gaston Means, who had rushed here to see Mrs. McLean, eager to be of help, stood before her like a shaved bear in a suit. That suit was dark blue and vested with a blue-and-red tie; he looked like a Southern senator, the kind a lobbyist could buy for a cigar, a drink and a whore.

"I was afraid, Eleven," Means said in his mellow manner, "that you had lost faith in me."

"Please sit down, Means."

" 'Hogan,' my dear. I must insist."

Their voices rose to me, echoey but distinct.

She sat; arms folded, head erect. "Let's dispense with the melodrama for once. Tell me the truth, Means. Tell me how much more money you want."

"I don't want anything," he said, sitting on the nearest couch, homburg in hand. "The four thousand expenses you gave me is sufficient."

Evalyn hadn't mentioned that, though later she confirmed it: Means had asked for, and gotten, four grand from her as an expense account, above and beyond her hundred grand he was "holding."

"You look tired, Eleven. Are you well?"

She was lighting up a fresh cigarette. "Is the 'book' well, is more to the point. What news do you have?"

He gestured broadly. "As you know, I've just been in Chicago. A member of the gang was sent there, a few days ago, by the Fox, to unload the fifty grand Lindbergh paid that other negotiator. But the Fox's man hasn't had any luck—no buyers. The banks have the serial numbers, you know."

"So I've read in the papers."

"The gang is pretty sore at Lindy for marking that money. I'm trying to convince them that your one hundred thousand isn't marked."

"Thank you. So what's our next move?"

Means leaned forward conspiratorially, clutching his homburg like a tiny shield. "The gang wants clean money to replace the marked stuff they got from Lindbergh. They're willing to sell that marked fifty thousand back for thirty-five thousand, unmarked."

"And I suppose that thirty-five thousand is to be taken out of my hundred thousand?"

He leaned back, surprised, almost insulted. "Oh no—that hundred thousand is not to be touched under any circumstances. The moment a deal for the marked money goes through, the hundred thousand might be needed on a moment's notice, for the return of the book."

Evalyn blew out smoke. "Means, have you still got that money of mine?"

"Your money? Why, of course!"

"Where is it?"

"In a safe down at my family home in Concord . . . and has

been since right after you saw it in my home that day. Surely, Eleven, you can't imagine I would've taken that money with me to Aiken or especially to Texas—and run the chance of having it hijacked!" Smilingly, he patted his chest. "You don't know Gaston Means."

"Sometimes I wish I didn't. This thirty-five thousand—who's going to put that up? I haven't got that much in cash."

"I tried to raise it myself, my dear, from a bookmaker friend of mine. But, alas . . ."

That was it; that was all I could take.

I came down the stairs. My footsteps were like gunshots. Means looked around, startled. He rose from the couch, turning, his moon face intense, his hand drifting toward his coat pocket.

But I already had the nine millimeter in hand.

"Don't," I said without enthusiasm.

He didn't. His face was slack, the dimples lost in fleshiness; his tiny eyes were wide.

Evalyn's eyes glittered; she seemed a little afraid, and a little excited by my entrance. She liked melodrama, too.

"I'll need a few moments alone with Mr. Means," I told her. She'd been warned I might do this. She nodded and went quickly out.

"Eleven!" he called after her, pawing the air. She didn't answer. A door closed, heavily.

I walked over to him. "Hands up, Means. You know the procedure."

"What's the meaning of this, Sixteen?"

"You remembered my code number. I'm flattered." Patting him down, I found a small automatic, a .25. In his fat hand it would have looked like a party favor. I tossed it gently on the couch.

"Who *are* you?" he asked indignantly.

"Not the chauffeur. What do you *really* know, Means?"

He gave me his innocence-personified expression; he looked like a dissipated cherub. "Know?"

With measured sarcasm, I replied, "About the Lindbergh case."

He shook his head, dignified, stubborn, idealistic. "I'm sworn to secrecy."

"I want names. I want to know who engineered this thing."

"What thing?"

"The kidnapping, you fat bastard. The kidnapping."

He held his chin up; it was shaped like the end of a small garden shovel. "I don't know anything more than I've told Mrs. McLean."

"Would you be willing to take a lie-detector test, Means?"

He snorted. "I don't believe in those things. Wires and electrodes and needles. Poppycock."

"I didn't mean that kind of lie detector."

He snorted again, skeptically. "What kind *did* you mean?"

"The Chicago kind."

"And what, pray tell, is the Chi—"

He didn't finish the question, because I'd stuck the barrel of the nine millimeter in his mouth.

"We use this kind of lie detector in Chicago," I explained.

His eyes were as wide as Mickey Mouse's, and just as animated. His dimples had returned but, with his mouth full like that, he wasn't smiling.

I was. "Get down on your knees, Means, and do it smooth. This has a hair trigger, and so do I."

Carefully, he got down on his knees, a kneeling Buddha on an oriental carpet, unwillingly suckling the Browning all the way.

Once he was settled in his prayerlike posture, he made some sounds; he seemed to want to know what I wanted.

"Names, Means. I want the names of the people that did the job."

He made more sounds around the gun, apparent protestations of innocence, of ignorance. I pushed upward, so the gunsight would cut the roof of his mouth. He began to cough, which was dangerous. His spittle turned reddish. He began to cry. I had never seen a man that big cry, before. I would have felt sorry for him if he weren't the scum of creation.

"Nod," I said, "if you're ready to tell the truth."

Choking a little, he nodded.

"Okay," I said, and slid the gun out of his mouth. It dripped with his reddish saliva, and I wiped it off on his suitcoat, disgustedly.

"Max Hassel," he said, breathing hard. "And Max Greenberg."

"Are you making that up?"

"No! No."

"They're both named Max?"

"Yes! Yes."

"Who are they?"

"Bootleggers."

They would be.

"Where can I find them?"

"Elizabeth."

"New Jersey?"

"New Jersey," he nodded.

"Where in Elizabeth?"

"Carteret Hotel."

"Be specific."

"Eighth floor."

"Good. More names."

"That's all I know. I swear to God, that's all."

"Hassel and Greenberg are the kidnappers?"

"They engineered it. They didn't do it themselves. They used their people. People who were selling beer to Colonel Lindbergh's servants, and the Morrow house servants."

"Was one of the servants in on it?"

He nodded. "Violet Sharpe—but they just used her. The little bitch didn't know what she was doing."

I slapped him. Hard. I slapped him again. Harder.

"What . . . what else do you want to know?" he asked, desperately.

"Nothing," I said. "I just want to slap you around some, you fat fuck."

His cheeks were red and burning and tear-streaked; he looked pitiful, on his knees, the world's biggest altar boy, caught with his hand in the collection plate.

"If Hassel and Greenberg aren't for real," I said, "you're going to take the lie-detector test again, Means—and you're going to flunk."

"They're . . . they're for real," he said, thickly.

"If you say a word to them, or anyone, about our conversation, I'll kill you. Understood?"

He nodded.

"Say it," I said.

"If I say a word to anybody, you'll kill me."

"Do you believe me?"

He nodded; there was still red spittle on his face.

"Good. Are you really in contact with the kidnap gang?"

Without hesitation, he nodded.

"Is the boy alive?"

Without hesitation, he nodded.

"Do you know where he is?"

Now he hesitated, but he shook his head, no.

"Who is the fellow the Fox?"

He swallowed. "Norman Whitaker. A friend of mine. Old cellmate."

"He's not in on the kidnapping?"

"No. He's with me."

"What's his function?"

Means shrugged. "Color."

"Color. What about Evalyn's dough?"

"I still have it."

"You still have it."

"I swear. I really have been trying to negotiate the return of that dear child."

"Stop it or you're going to get slapped some more. What's the extra thirty-five grand for?"

He pressed his hands over his heart. "That was true, all of it . . . I *did* go to Chicago, the gang *can't* move that marked cabbage . . . I swear to God."

I smacked him along the side of the head with the nine millimeter; he tumbled over, heavily, like something inanimate, and the furniture around him jumped.

But he wasn't out, and it hadn't cut him; he'd be bruised, that was all.

"All right," I said, kicking him in the ass. He was on his side. He looked up at me with round hollow eyes. There was something childlike in his expression. I gestured impatiently with the gun.

"Get up," I said. "Go home. Talk to fucking no one. Wait for Evalyn to call."

He got up, slowly. His face was soft, weak, but the eyes had turned hard and mean. If he was like a child, in his endless self-serving fabrications spun from fact and fancy, it was an evil, acquisitive child, the kind that steals another kid's marbles, the kind that steps on anthills.

I'd gone to great lengths to prove to him I was dangerous; but despite his tears and cowardice, Means remained goddamn dangerous himself.

I gave him his hat and, sans slugs, his gun.

"Who *are* you?" Means said, thickly.

"Somebody you never expected to meet."

"Oh, really?" he said, archly, summoning some dignity. "And who would that be?"

"Your conscience," I said.

He snorted, coughed, and lumbered out.

I sat on the couch, waiting for Evalyn. I didn't have long to wait: she came down the stairs as if making a grand entrance at a ball, despite her dowdy bathrobe. She'd gone around somewhere and come out on that balcony and eavesdropped the whole encounter.

She moved slowly toward me; the shadows of the fire danced on her. Her face was solemn, her eyes glittering.

"You're a nasty man," she said.

"I can leave," I said, embarrassed.

She dropped the robe to the floor. Her skin looked golden in the fire's glow; nipples erect, delicate blue veins marbling her full ivory breasts, a waist you could damn near reach your hands around, hips flaring nicely, legs slender but shapely.

"Don't dare leave," she said, and held her arms out to me.

"Why, Evalyn," I said admiringly, taking that smooth flesh in my arms. "You're a nasty girl."

Chapter 23

Toward the middle of the next afternoon, uptown in the rail-and-harbor city of Elizabeth, New Jersey, a powder-blue Lincoln Continental drew up along the curb of the posh Carteret Hotel. The grandly uniformed doorman moved swiftly down the red carpet in the shadow of the hotel canopy to open the rear right door for the Lincoln's solitary passenger, beating the chauffeur to the punch. The chauffeur, however, in his neat gray wool uniform with black buttons, was there in time to help the stately lady passenger, Mrs. Evalyn Walsh McLean, out of the backseat. She wore a black velvet dress with a large quilted black-and-white scarf tied stiffly, squarely around her neck, and a black velvet conical hat, an outfit whose festive styling clashed interestingly with its mournful coloration; but for diamond earrings and a diamond bracelet on one of her white gloves, Mrs. McLean's jewelry was uncharacteristically absent. Her thin, pretty lips were blood-red. The chauffeur, a rather handsome young man in his twenties with reddish-brown hair, allowed the doorman to usher lithe, lovely Mrs. McLean into the hotel lobby. The chauffeur, by the way, was me.

I got our luggage out of the trunk of the Lincoln—my simple traveling bag and a big heavy leather number for Evalyn; I told her we'd only be one night, and shuddered to think what she'd bring for a weekend away. I turned our things over to the bell captain, who told me I could for a fee park in the private lot behind a nearby bank. On my way back, on foot, I cased the exterior of the hotel a bit.

The Elizabeth Carteret Hotel was a nine-story, heavily corniced brick building between a massive Presbyterian church and various storefront businesses; the Ritz Theater was diagonally across the way. Narrow alleys were at the left and right of the hotel, with a service-and-delivery-only alley in back, a side entrance with a bellman on the right-hand alley, and no outside fire escapes. An exclusive, expensive hotel, with relatively tight security. I was glad I'd come in undercover.

Evalyn was waiting in the marble-and-mahogany lobby, where businessmen and bellboys mingled with overstuffed furniture and potted plants.

"We have separate rooms," she said quietly, handing me a key, "on the ninth floor."

"Adjoining?" I asked.

"No. Traveling together like this, just the two of us, is dangerous. If my husband found out, it could be used against me, in court."

"I get it."

"But I have a suite." Her smile was tiny and wicked. "Plenty of room for company."

Soon I was in my own small but deluxe room on the ninth floor, getting out of my chauffeur's uniform and into my brown suit, as well as my shoulder holster with nine-millimeter Browning. I really should have boiled the latter, after sticking it in Gaston Means's yap, but somehow I hadn't got around to it. I'd had my hands full since yesterday.

First they'd been full of Evalyn, of course, in her gigantic canopy bed with its pink satin sheets that matched the sprawling bedroom's pink satin walls. Mike the Great Dane, incidentally, who I hadn't seen much of this trip, I saw plenty of that night: he slept at the foot of her bed. He snored. I let him.

In a way, it was okay, because I had to think. I had to figure out exactly what to do about the lead Gaston Means had literally spit up.

The next morning we'd had an egg-and-bacon soufflé in a breakfast nook a family of six could've lived in. I sipped my fresh-squeezed orange juice, and asked, "Will you stake me to a couple long-distance calls?"

She looked at me over her coffee cup, a bit surprised. "Well, certainly. Something to do with Means?"

"Yeah."

"What should I do about that scoundrel?"

"Keep playing along with him, for the time being. Only don't give him another red cent! I'm an inch away from having you demand your dough back, and then, when he doesn't cough it up, call in the cops."

"You think my money's gone?"

"Is Hitler a stinker?"

She sighed. "It's not the money. It's the child. I thought we might get that child."

"We still may. With Means, it's hard to know the truth, even when he's telling it. His wildest stories have twenty or thirty percent reality in them. The rub is narrowing down and identifying that percentage."

She nodded, with a frustrated smirk. "He knows enough about the kidnapping, then, to make you think he's had at least *some* contact with the kidnappers?"

"That would be my guess. With his government and socialite connections in D.C., and his underworld ties, he's the ideal bagman for a job like this. Only, choosing Gaston Means to collect and deliver money really is, as we say in the Middle West, putting the fox in charge of the henhouse."

She nodded, wearily. Then she brightened, rather unconvincingly. "Do you want to make those calls? I can have the phone brought to you."

"Why not."

I tried to get Elmer Irey at his temporary office in New York, but got Frank Wilson instead. Quickly, and with few details, I revealed that Gaston Bullock Means had passed himself off as a negotiator for the kidnap gang. I did not mention Evalyn's one hundred grand. This was not quite the moment when the boom— whether federal or local—ought be lowered on Means.

"Means is the biggest damn liar," Wilson said calmly, "on the face of the earth."

I agreed. "But he *is* connected to half the bootleggers in the U.S."

"That's true enough," Wilson said reflectively. "Back in the twenties, when he was a Justice Department man, he sold 1410-A's right out of his office."

Form 1410-A was a federal government permit to deal in alcohol, meant for druggists and other legitimate users.

"Well," I said, laying it out on the table, "Means says two bootleggers engineered the kidnapping."

"Really." Wilson's voice had turned as flat as last night's beer.

"They're both named Max. Max Greenberg and Max Hassel. Heard of 'em?"

"Waxey Gordon's two top boys?" His sigh conveyed boredom and irritation. "I hardly think two of the biggest beer barons on the East Coast are going to mess around with kidnapping the goddamn Lindbergh baby."

"Why not?"

His voice had a shrug in it. "They don't need the money, Heller. They're businessmen, and kidnapping is not their racket. Besides which, they're up to their asses in a beer war."

"Yeah?"

"Yeah. Dutch Schultz and Waxey Gordon's respective hoodlums have for several months been shooting at each other with some regularity—which as long as innocent bystanders don't get killed, is fine with me."

"Well, I think Greenberg and Hassel are worth looking into."

"They already are being looked into."

"In relation to the Lindbergh case?"

"Hell no. In relation to income-tax evasion. And we're working on their boss Waxey, too."

"You mean, that's a case you're working on personally?"

"No. I mean the Intelligence Unit of the IRS."

I had to try one more time. "Well then, will you alert the

agents handling the case that there may be a Lindbergh connection?"

There was a long pause. Finally, he said, "I appreciate your efforts, Heller. I know you feel frustrated, as do I, as does Chief Irey. And you've kept us informed about things that Colonel Lindbergh has unwisely kept to himself. I appreciate that. We appreciate that."

"I sense a 'but' coming."

"But . . . I'm not going to interfere in another agent's ongoing case. Not on the say-so of Gaston Bullock Means, for Christsake! Heller, you're a police liaison from Chicago. Stay out of federal business."

"What about New Jersey business?"

"When did they move Cook County to New Jersey? Why don't you call up Colonel Schwarzkopf? I'm sure he'll be thrilled to hear from you. Is there anything else?"

Fucker.

"What about Capone's boy, Bob Conroy?" I asked. "You guys were going to track him down."

"Well, we haven't. If he's on the East Coast, he's well hidden. Maybe he's taking a swim in cement overshoes."

Wilson was probably right on that score. "What about the spiritualist church? I would think the Marinellis—who seemed to know about Jafsie before Jafsie knew about Jafsie—would be a hell of a good lead, now that the old boy has paid fifty grand out to God knows who."

"Heller, Pat O'Rourke joined that church, stayed undercover and joined in on their mumbo-jumbo for three weeks, but found not a damn thing."

I didn't know what to say. O'Rourke was a good man. Maybe there wasn't a damn thing to find.

"So what do you suggest?" I asked Wilson.

"I suggest you think about going back to Chicago. We've got fifty grand in marked bills floating around out there, and that's going to lead us to our kidnappers."

I thanked him sarcastically and he said "you're welcome" the same way and we both hung up. Evalyn had listened to my half of the conversation, and seemed to have gotten the drift. She was wide-eyed and astounded, whereas I just felt beaten down.

She was holding her cup up for a colored maid to fill with coffee. "I can't believe the government won't follow up on these two Max fellows!"

"I can. You got red tape on the one hand, and the word of Gaston Means, who makes Baron Münchhausen look like Abraham Lincoln, on the other."

"What now?"

I made another phone call. To Colonel Schwarzkopf at the Lindbergh estate. But I didn't say a word about the two Maxes.

"I've had an anonymous tip," I told him. "About Violet Sharpe."

"Reliable?" Schwarzkopf asked skeptically.

"Very," I said, realizing I must have been the first man in history to refer to Gaston Means as a "very reliable" source.

"She's apparently the inside man on the kidnapping," I said, "though she may have been an unwitting one."

"I'll put Inspector Welch on it."

"All right, but tell that son of a bitch to use a little finesse, will you?"

Schwarzkopf said nothing in reply; neither one of us chose to fill the silence with anything, and just hung the hell up.

"One more call," I said to Evalyn, who was still breathlessly listening. I got the long-distance operator again and caught Eliot Ness at his desk at the Transportation Building back home.

"What can you tell me," I asked, "about Max Greenberg and Max Hassel?"

"Hassel's real name is Mendel Gassel, Russian immigrant, career rumrunner who paid a big income-tax fine six or seven years ago," Eliot said matter-of-factly. "Greenberg is a thug from St. Louis made good. Or bad, depending on how you look at it. They're both dangerous, but Greenberg's got the brains."

"Anything else pertinent?"

"Usual stuff," he said blandly. "Our Narcotics Unit indicted Greenberg for shipping two trunkfuls of heroin to Duluth, back in '24 or '25. They didn't get a conviction. He beat several arson raps, assault raps, too. Then Big Maxie ran prostitutes out of a hotel he owned in New York somewhere, till bootlegging beckoned."

"He sounds like quite the capitalist. You guys probably would get along great—you're both Republicans."

"You must be doing pretty good out there, if you can afford to insult me at long-distance rates."

"It's not my nickel. Look, why are Waxey Gordon and Dutch Schultz mixing it up? I thought they were allies."

"Irving Wexler and Arthur Flegenheimer," Eliot said archly, using their real names, "are both anticipating the relatively imminent unemployment of yours truly."

"Huh?"

"They both know beer's going to be legal, before long, and they've set their beady eyes on a big, legitimate market, meaning more customers than they can supply from their present breweries. Schultz has breweries in Yonkers and Manhattan, and Waxey has 'em in Patterson, Union City and Elizabeth. Each wants the other guy's facilities, and territory."

"So they're shooting holes in each other's gang."

"Yes. Which is good."

"Frank Wilson would agree. Why aren't those breweries you mentioned shut down?"

Eliot laid the sarcasm on with a trowel. "Why, Nate—they're making *near* beer there, didn't you know that? Brewing 'round the clock—even though only a truck or two leaves each brewery each week."

No doubt hundreds of gallons of real beer flowed via sewer pipes to hidden bottling and barreling plants.

"Eliot, who would Capone be friendlier with, Schultz or Gordon?"

There was a pause. "Funny you should ask. I honestly don't know if Snorkey has any ties with Wexler, though I'd be surprised if he didn't." Then, with studied blandness, he added, "But Flegenheimer was up to the Cook County Jail, not so long ago, visiting Al."

That made me sit up. "What?"

"Yeah. Lucky Luciano brought the Dutchman around. I understand there was quite a shouting match. Al was serving as mediator for some East-Coast squabble—jail officials let the boys use the execution chamber for their confab . . . Al sat in the hot squat, like a king on his throne."

"Jesus." Even for Chicago, this was beyond the pale.

"Well, Snorkey isn't going to win his final appeal," Eliot said edgily, "and he won't find the federal pen so accommodating. Why are you asking these questions?"

"I have reason to believe Lindbergh's kid was snatched by Greenberg and Hassel."

"And you were wondering if it's within the realm of possibility that Capone's reach could extend to them?"

"Yes," I said.

"Yes," he said.

There was a brief crackly silence.

Then I said, "Okay. Only now I'm not sure what I should do about it."

"Telling Irey and Wilson is your best shot."

"Right. Well, thanks, Eliot."

"Is there anything I can do?"

"Sure. You can apologize for getting me in this shit."

He laughed, but said, "I do apologize. You've been out there a hell of a long time. Maybe it's time to come home."

"Soon," I said, and thanked him and hung up.

So I had decided to talk to Greenberg and Hassel myself.

Evalyn wanted me to approach them and see if I could negotiate the safe return of the baby for her. I said I had the same idea, only if the two copped to the snatch, I'd pull in the feds and we'd nail the bastards.

"No more money gets thrown away," I said. "Grab the sons of bitches responsible, and let 'em know if their people don't hand over the kid, they take a hard fall."

"Can you scare them, men like that?"

"When you put a gun in their mouth, you can."

"But would the police do that?"

"Evalyn, I am the police."

It was a little before four when I took the stairs at the rear of the hotel down to the floor below, the eighth, where Means said I'd find the two Maxes. I figured there would be bodyguards posted, who'd take me where I wanted to go, one way or the other, particularly with a beer war in progress. I took a deep breath and withdrew the nine millimeter, and hid it behind me before I pushed open the door marked "8"—I knew there'd be muscle to deal with. No way around it. . . .

Only the hall was empty.

For a moment, I was confused; then, slowly, like a heat rash, disgust spread over me.

Had Gaston Means done it again? Sent me, like Evalyn to El Paso, on another wild goose chase? I holstered the nine millimeter and slowly, pointlessly I was sure, prowled the hall.

Then I noticed a door, room 824, on which hung a sign that said "Old Heidelberg." The lettering was Germanic and I was clearly looking at the logotype of a brand name of beer. Or anyway, "near beer."

But, again, there were no men posted outside the door. I got the gun out, held it behind me, and knocked. There was no answer, so I tried again, and finally the door cracked open and a pasty pockmarked face looked at me past a night-latch chain, skeptically, with eyes blacker and deader than a well-done steak.

"What?" he asked. The single word conveyed both menace and distrust.

"Police," I said. "I have a warrant."

The black, dead eyes narrowed and I slipped my toe in the cracked door and shouldered it open, popping the night latch.

My host backed up. He was heavyset and short but with a thin man's face; his lips were the color of raw liver and his hair was cropped, white and ungreased, and as dead-looking as his eyes. He wore a light-brown, expensively tailored suit with a white shirt, the dark-brown silk tie loose around a loosened collar, suit coat open. He didn't seem to be armed.

"Let's see the warrant," he said doubtfully, and loudly, as if trying to warn somebody in the next room.

"It's right here," I said, and showed him the nine millimeter; it felt a little unsteady in my hand, but not so you'd notice.

"Shit," he said, making a three-syllable word of it, rolling the dead black eyes. He put his hands slowly, grudgingly, up.

Shutting the door behind me with my heel, I took in a vast living room appointed in plush modern furniture, in various shades of green, from pastel lime to money-color.

He was shaking a little, but mostly he looked coldly, quietly pissed-off. "How did you get past Louie and Sal?" he wondered.

"I didn't see Louie," I said, patting him down with one hand, confirming his lack of hardware, almost choking on his pungent after-shave lotion, "and I didn't see Sal."

That confused him a little. "What about Vinnie?"

"I didn't see Vinnie, either."

"That's impossible."

"This is America. Anything is possible. You Hassel or Greenberg?" It sounded like a Jewish fairy tale.

He licked his liver lips. "Hassel. Maxie's in the office."

"Let's go say hello."

He led me through the endless living room—a wet bar in one corner was stocked better than a Rush Street speak, and against one wall leaned several fancy pigskin bags of golf clubs. We moved through a bedroom to a closed door, which Hassel grudgingly opened, glancing back unhappily at me.

He went in first, the nose of my nine millimeter in his back, as I followed him into the adjoining, smaller bedroom which had been converted into an office with several desks and filing cabinets. A big fleshy man in his shirtsleeves and suspenders, his suit coat draped over the back of his swivel chair, was hunkered over a ledger book at a rolltop desk against the far left wall, on which an Old Heidelberg neon sign, unlit, mingled with various black-and-white business-related photos. The man at the desk had shiny black hair and a big flat head.

"Maxie," Hassel said, tentatively.

Maxie waved at him impatiently, without looking back. "Just a minute, just a minute."

"Maxie . . ."

Maxie sighed, pushed away from the desk, and without looking at us, said, "Where's the fuckin' money *go*?" Then he turned and blinked twice, as if that was all the sight deserved, his partner with his hands in the air and a stranger with an automatic pointed in both their general directions. "What the hell's this about?"

"Put your hands on your knees," I said.

Maxie's eyes were dark and mournful, his mouth a thin cold line in a face that was puttylike, unlined, unused, as if no emotions had left their tracks. As he slowly lowered his hands toward his knees, one hand lingered near the right-hand pocket of the draped-on-the-chair suit coat, a pocket with a revolver-size lump in it.

"You could die in that chair," I pointed out.

Maxie blinked again, swallowed, and put his hands on his knees.

I moved slowly over there, my back to a wall so I could keep my eyes on both Maxes, and flipped the suit coat off the chair; it dropped to the floor with a clunk. Lucky for us all, his coat didn't go off.

"Is this a rubout?" Maxie asked, like he was asking the time.

"Not necessarily," I said, moving back near the doorway, just inside of which I'd left his partner. "We're just going to talk."

"If the Dutchman sent you," he said reasonably, "you're working the wrong side of the street. We pay *real* dough. And we can protect you."

"Listen to Maxie," Hassel advised, with a nervous sidelong glance.

They didn't seem to see the inherent fallacy of telling a guy holding a gun on them that they could "protect" him.

"The Dutchman didn't send me," I said. "A rich lady from Washington, D.C., did. Named McLean."

The two men exchanged glances. I couldn't read anything in it. God knows I tried.

"You fellas look smart enough to know Gaston Means can't be trusted," I said.

Maxie Greenberg nodded thoughtfully.

"That bastard lies when he prays," Hassel confirmed.

"You boys need a new man in the middle," I said. Which was where I was, keeping the gun on them both, Hassel with his mitts up, Greenberg hands on knees. "I'll give you the money, you give me the kid."

Hassel gave me another sidelong nervous glance.

Eyes boring into me like a sniper sighting a victim, Maxie said, "Who are you?"

"A guy looking to make a few bucks and put a kid back in his own crib."

"What makes you think we got Lindy's kid?" Hassel said.

"I don't remember mentioning Lindy's kid," I said.

A loud banging out in the other room scared shit out of me; I damn near started firing.

"That's the door," Hassel said, flatly. "The one you come in."

The banging continued, and a voice said, "Boss, it's Vinnie! It's Vinnie, boss! Let me in."

Hassel smiled smugly. "Well, there's our boy Vinnie. I better let him in, don't you think?"

"If he's your boy," I said, "why doesn't he have a key?"

"Somebody might take it off him," Maxie said.

"You gotta be named 'Max' to get a key," Hassel said. Private club.

"*Boss!*" the voice called.

"We don't answer it," fat Maxie said with the faintest of smiles on his thin lips, "he'll bust it down."

I took Hassel by the arm; it was fleshy but there was muscle under there. "Get rid of him. No need to get cute—we're going to make a straight business deal, here. Fewer faces that see me, the better."

He looked at me with those black dead eyes, and nodded.

I went over to Maxie, and stood just to his left, between several wooden four-drawer filing cabinets and the corner of the wall the desk was up against.

"If this is business," Maxie said, hands on his knees, his head tilted to one side in a gesture of reasonableness, "why have any guns at all?"

"I like negotiating from a position of strength."

There was the garbled sound of conversation out in the living room, then the sound of running, the sound of furniture being knocked over. Maxie started to move, started to rise, but I swung into his gut with the nine millimeter, knocking the wind out of him, sitting him back down, sending him· in his chair rattling back against the desk.

And the gunshots started.

They were muffled shots, silenced shots, WHUP! WHUP!

WHUP! WHUP!, but they were gunshots all right. Some of them were happening in the connecting room, and Maxie, still doubled over, glanced at me with round accusing eyes and I ducked down and flattened back against the wall, using the wooden filing cabinets for cover, and saw Maxie drop his hand toward that coat on the floor, fumbling for the gun in that coat pocket, getting it in hand, a .38 Police Special, sitting on the edge of his chair and looking up toward the doorway, at something and somebody I couldn't see, looking as if he were about to rise his fat ass up out of that chair, only he never did.

He sat back in the chair, leaning back like a man getting a close shave, but this was no close shave: he was getting bullets pumped into him, into his chest, into his neck, into his face, the top of his head erupting and spattering the Old Heidelberg neon, his legs and feet tap-dancing while the silenced bullets softly sang.

Then the gunshots stopped and left him sitting with his head back and emptying out, blood dripping on the carpeted floor like red rain. Cordite stench scorched the air, gun smoke mixing with blood mist.

And I was cowering against the wall, in the corner made by the wall and the wooden filing cabinet. Unseen, I thought. They didn't know I was here—did they?

"Phil," a voice called from the other room. It was a whiny voice, high-pitched. Then, closer: "I did mine."

"Mine's done, too, Jimmy." This voice was a baritone with gravel in it.

The nine millimeter was tight in my hand; my breath was sucked in hard, my heart pounding in my ears. I moved my head, my shoulders carefully, oh so slowly, forward, just barely glancing a sliver's worth around the edge of the filing cabinet.

I could see them, one standing over by, and the other in, the doorway: the one inside the room must have killed Greenberg; he was wearing a brown topcoat and hat, was average in size and build, but his face was distinctive—as flat as a jockey's ass, no cheekbones at all, eyes tiny, slitted, oriental-looking. The other guy, the one in the doorway, Hassel's dispatcher, wore a mustard-color tweedy-looking topcoat and was small; his face was round and his nose pug and his eyes round and bright and cheerful.

These were not faces I would forget.

Neither would I forget their guns, though I couldn't actually see them: they were big automatics, mostly hidden by fuzzy white towels that had been wrapped turbanlike around the barrels and over the muzzles; both towels, around the nose of each gun, were on fire, orange flames flittering on the scorched area around the nose of each automatic. Neither man seemed to notice.

They were talking softly, laughing lightly as they moved into the outer suite.

I waited ten seconds, then carefully stepped past Maxie, who was draped back across the desk, bloody gray matter seeping out his skull onto the ledger book; well, Eliot said the guy had brains.

I moved quickly, quietly, across the room, the nine millimeter in hand. Slowly, I stalked after the torpedoes, but as I was coming out of the office into the adjoining bedroom, I damn near tripped over Hassel, who was on the floor, his face turned to one side, his dead eyes even deader now, his head cracked open like a melon draining its seeds and pulp.

That stopped me a second. And by the time I was out in the living room, they were almost to the door.

"Police!" I called, and shot at them, specifically at their backs. That's the best place to shoot a man, after all.

But that goddamn living room stretched out forever, and I missed one guy, and only winged the other, the cheerful one, but he wasn't so cheerful now, yowling like a dog that got its tail stepped on, mustard-color topcoat splotched with ketchup-red, and the other one, the flat-faced fucker, turned and shot at me, no towel on the gun anymore, a big humongous Army Colt, and the room exploded with noise.

I dropped to the floor, and behind me a pigskin golf bag took a slug like a man and clattered on top of me, pinning me, but I squeezed off three more, as they were bolting out the door, my slugs chewing up wood and plaster.

And they were gone.

For perhaps two seconds, I considered pursuing them.

Then I got out from under the golf clubs, stepped past the still-smoldering burnt towels they'd discarded along the way; the makeshift silencers had been effective—the gunshots had obviously attracted no attention outside the suite itself, although these latest, louder ones no doubt would. I had to get the hell out.

In the hall, gun still in hand, I met no one. Later, I learned that Hassel, Greenberg and Waxey Gordon had rented out the entire eighth floor, which explained why no one had reacted to the gunshots yet. As for Louie, Sal and Vinnie, and any other body-guards, they were either deceased or paid off; maybe that had actually been Vinnie's voice, in the hall, as he played Judas for an unspecified number of gold coins.

I could have stuck and talked to the local cops. After all, I could describe the gunmen who shot Greenberg and Hassel. But I didn't give a fuck who shot Greenberg and Hassel—who were, after all, just victims of this goddamn beer war; maybe Lindy's kid was now another (inadvertent) victim of that war.

And I wasn't about to become the next victim, either, which is what I would be if I went around identifying and testifying against mob torpedoes. Mrs. Heller's little boy didn't get to be a cop be-cause he was stupid.

Yes, they'd seen me, but I was nobody out east, nobody they'd know, or ever recognize.

Eliot was right: it was time to go home.

All of these thoughts took approximately three seconds, as I rushed toward the door to the rear stairs and went up them, two at a time, my gun still in hand; I didn't slip it into its holster till just before I went through the door to the ninth floor, where I found a wet-eyed, nearly hysterical Evalyn waiting breathlessly.

"I heard gunshots! Nate, are you . . ."

"I'm swell," I said, grabbing her by the arm, walking with studied calmness down a hall where various guests had stepped from their rooms with looks of alarm and confusion. We went inside her suite but I didn't tell her what happened, not at first. I just lay on her bed and she held me and patted and smoothed my hair while I trembled like a frightened child.

Chapter 24

On the following Monday, I played chauffeur for Evalyn one last time. Midafternoon, I was tooling the powder-blue Lincoln up rutted Featherbed Lane to the whitewashed stone house where a child, not so long ago, had been stolen. Evalyn rode in front this time, and I wasn't in the natty gray uniform with the black buttons. She was a little depressed and, frankly, so was I.

"Not a word to Colonel Lindbergh," I cautioned, "about Hassel and Greenberg. I don't want to go making any more accomplices-after-the-fact than I already have."

She nodded. She looked with hooded-eyed interest at the bleak, weedy grounds of an estate that to her must have seemed modest indeed.

"Look at the hillside beyond the house," she said, distractedly, searching out some beauty in the barrenness. "The white and pink dogwood against the dark cedars . . . lovely."

The thought didn't seem to cheer her up much. She wore a black fox stole and a smartly cut black suit with a white silk blouse and pearls, dark silk stockings, and a soup-dish black hat with no veil; she looked like a wealthy widow, in token mourning.

I pulled around by the garage, where a modest level of police activity continued; the weather today was almost warm, and the doors were up, and the handful of troopers dealing with mail and phone calls seemed to be moving at half-speed, in a sluggish, dream-like state. Schwarzkopf didn't seem to be around.

I ushered Evalyn from the Lincoln as if we were both approaching a graveside ceremony. Halfway to the side door, however, Lindy—wearing a dark-blue sweater over an open-collar shirt, his brown pants tucked into his midcalf leather boots—came out to greet and meet us halfway. He smiled at us, shyly friendly, but the dark circles under his eyes would rival a raccoon's.

"Mrs. McLean, it's an honor," he said, warmly—in fact, his voice was at that moment as warm as I think I ever heard it. "I'm so pleased you've come."

"The honor and the pleasure are mine," she said, with dignity, extending a gloved hand rather regally, which he briefly took. "It was kind of you to suggest we meet."

That seemed to embarrass him a little.

"Nate," he said, acknowledging me with a nod and smile. And to us both, with a stiff gesture, said, "Let's go inside."

He took her by the arm, and I trailed after.

We moved through the servants' sitting room; the desk Schwarzkopf had set up out there, making it an informal office, was empty. I asked Lindbergh where the state police colonel had gone, and was told Trenton—Schwarzkopf was spending less and less time here. In the kitchen, we found homely Elsie Whately chopping vegetables with a sharp knife, preparing to do her reverse magic on perfectly edible provisions; she portioned out one minimally civil nod for us all to share, as we passed through.

In the large living room, Anne Lindbergh—wearing a simple dark-blue frock with a lace collar, looking like a schoolgirl, albeit a five-month pregnant one—rose and moved toward Evalyn with a warm, wide smile and an arm extended for a handshake in a manner about as dainty as a longshoreman's. The brown-and-white terrier, Wahgoosh, who'd been asleep on the couch, uncoiled like a cobra and began barking with his trademark hysteria.

Lindbergh spoke sharply to the mutt, silencing him, but Evalyn, still shaking hands with the grateful Anne, merely said, "I like dogs—please don't scold him on my account."

Hell, in Evalyn's house, Wahgoosh would've been wearing the Star of India.

Anne was clasping Evalyn's gloved hand, holding it with both of her bare ones as if it were something precious.

"You've done so much," Anne said. "You've tried so hard."

Evalyn swallowed. "And accomplished so little, I'm afraid."

Anne's smile was tight yet soft; her eyes were tired, but they sparkled—with tears, perhaps. "You're a wonderful person, Mrs. McLean. I'm aware that you . . . lost your own little boy. And so, I do understand, and I do appreciate, all you've done. All you've tried to do."

"You're very kind."

Anne released Evalyn's hand, but stood very near her. What Lindbergh's wife said next was spoken softly, and not meant for anyone's ears but her guest's. Detective that I am, I heard every word.

"I think," Anne said, "analyzing it, that women take sadness . . . and conquer it . . . differently from men. Don't you?"

Evalyn said nothing.

"Women take it willingly, with open arms. Men try to lose themselves, in effort. Would you care to walk with me? The dogwoods are blooming, and you can see the occasional wild cherry tree. . . ."

They exited arm-in-arm, Anne playing gracious hostess and tour guide, and Lindy said to me, "Someone you should see."

"Oh?"

He didn't explain—just led the way.

In the library, with Breckinridge seated near the desk, Commodore John Hughes Curtis stood straight as a ship's mast, hands locked behind him. His two previous companions—Reverend Dobson-Peacock and Admiral Burrage—were conspicuously absent. He remained an impressive, immaculately attired Southern gentleman, well over six foot, his hair iron-gray, features regular and tanned.

"Commodore," Lindbergh said, "you remember Nate Heller, with the Chicago Police Department?"

"Yes," Curtis said, with a big, affable smile, offering a bear's-paw hand for me to shake. "The Capone mob expert."

"That may be stretching it," I said. "But none of us can deny that bootleggers seem to be all over this case."

Curtis nodded, solemn now, and Slim said, settling himself behind the desk, "Since you saw him last, Nate, the Commodore has had much more contact with *his* group of bootleggers and rumrunners. Commodore, would you mind repeating your story for Detective Heller?"

"Not at all," Curtis said, reasonably, and as I found a seat, he finally sat, too. Breckinridge and I had already exchanged small smiles and nods of greeting; the gray, loyal attorney and I had come to share a measure of respect and even friendship.

"Several weeks ago," Curtis said, fixing his steady gaze on me, "I was approached again by 'Sam'—that rumrunning, fleeting acquaintance of mine, whose 'fishing smack' I repaired once or twice. . . ."

"I don't remember you describing 'Sam' in much detail," I said, noncommittally.

"Well, he's a big, lumbering individual . . . usually wears flashy clothes, like some gangster in a moving picture. He's decidedly Jewish in appearance, his English broken."

Being half-Jew myself, I wondered how anybody's appearance could be "decidedly Jewish," but I decided to let it pass.

"At any rate," Curtis continued, "he called me, several weeks ago, and asked if I could meet with him in Manhattan, the next day. With some urgency in his voice, he suggested we meet at a cafeteria near Forty-First Street, at one A.M. Sunday morning."

Admiral Burrage had arranged for a Navy pilot to fly Curtis to New York, where he checked in at the Governor Clinton Hotel under an assumed name.

"I walked uptown, in the middle of the night, to the cafeteria. Only one side of the room was in use, porters already at work cleaning the other side for the early morning trade. Chairs were piled high, the floor was being swabbed."

"Commodore," I said. I was tiring of people who savored melodrama. "Could you get to the point?"

"Detective Heller, I found only one other customer in the

cafeteria: Sam, who was sitting at the very last table eating a plate of wheat cakes with some relish."

Pickle relish, maybe. God, these people.

"Sam claimed the boy was with a German nurse—that he himself had never seen the child. But that he could get her, the nurse, to write out a description for me to give the Colonel. I told him that that was okay, but that I wanted proof, personally, for my own satisfaction, that his crowd really stole the child."

"And what," I asked, "did Sam say to that?"

Curtis smiled. "He offered to take me to meet the rest of his gang—to which I immediately said, 'Let's go, then!' But he made me wait two more days—and the night of the second day we met again. I was told to follow Sam's vehicle through the Holland Tunnel . . . then to the Hudson-Manhattan train station in Newark. And that was where I came face-to-face with the four men who, if they're to be believed, masterminded this kidnapping."

Well, the melodrama of that did have some effect, even on me.

"They were waiting there, on the train platform. No one else was around; the lighting was minimal. One of the men I'd seen before, in the Norfolk shipyard, though this was the first I'd heard his name: George Olaf Larsen. He's in his early forties, medium height, drab-colored hair combed straight back from his forehead. Sam always addresses him as 'boss.' "

The second man, Curtis said, was introduced simply as Nils— a Scandinavian in his early thirties, blond, with a florid complexion. The third man was called Eric, another blond but in his mid-forties.

The fourth man was named John.

"He's a handsome man," Curtis said, "with the physique of a physical culturist. From his accent, I'd say he was either Norwegian or Dutch."

I glanced significantly at Lindbergh and then at Breckinridge; Lindy flicked an eyebrow up, while Breckinridge maintained a lawyer's poker face.

But we all knew the same thing: while a *New York Times* reporter had, last week, identified Professor Condon as "Jafsie," and Jafsie as the Lindbergh ransom negotiator, the story of "Cemetery John" was not yet public knowledge.

All five of the gang had piled into Curtis's car and headed for

Larsen's house in Cape May, at the southern tip of New Jersey.

"Along the way, John said, 'Sam, he says you want some proof we do this job.'" Curtis was imitating the man's Norwegian accent; it was pretty hammy. "'Suppose I tell you exactly how we do it. One night, about one month before kidnapping, I go to some party with a girl friend of mine, a German trained nurse, at roadhouse outside Trenton.'"

The cadence reminded me a bit of the ransom notes Lindbergh and Condon had received.

"'At roadhouse I meet a member of Lindbergh and Morrow household,'" Curtis continued, still mimicking "John." Then he interrupted himself to say: "John didn't say which servant. But he said he recruited this person—he wasn't even specific about the gender—and promised 'plenty good money for the trouble...'"

"My servants," Lindy broke in, rather coldly, "are above suspicion."

I bit my tongue; I wondered idly how Schwarzkopf and Inspector Welch were faring with the Means tip about Violet Sharpe—which Curtis seemed to be substantiating.

"I'm just telling you what I was told," Curtis said, quietly defensive. "John's story was interrupted by our arrival at the Cape May cottage. A woman named Hilda—identified as Larsen's wife—met us and led us into a brightly lit dining room. We sat around a table, and John finished his story."

The night of the kidnapping, Nils, Eric, the German nurse and John had driven a green Hudson sedan and parked three hundred feet or so away from Featherbed Lane. Sam had followed in another car, and parked farther away still, on a high spot near the main road, where he could signal if another car pulled into the lane. Nils and John, with a three-sectioned ladder, went to the nursery window. They climbed through the window, with a blanket, a rag and some chloroform. Because the ladder was so unsteady, they exited with their human parcel via the front door.

"The front door?" I asked.

"They knew the layout of the house," Curtis explained. "They showed me a map, a huge floor plan, which judging from my two visits here would seem to tally. They knew how to lock the pantry door, to keep everyone in the kitchen and the servants' quarters away from the front hall, if anybody heard anything. There was a key on a nail for them to use—the servant they bribed had told them where to find it."

I looked at Slim.

"That key does exist," Lindbergh admitted.

Curtis said, "They had a letter for Colonel Lindbergh, describing the child. I didn't read it, but I saw it—it seemed to be sort of half-printed, half-written."

The notes Lindbergh and Jafsie received did mingle printing with cursive, somewhat.

"I was of course ecstatic that they'd finally provided the proof of identification the Colonel sought. And I suggested that one of them accompany me, that very moment, here to Hopewell, to present the letter to Colonel Lindbergh."

"But they refused," I said.

"Quite the contrary," Curtis said. "Larsen went with me. We drove through the night. At Trenton, the next morning, first thing, I attempted to call Colonel Lindbergh, and finally did get through to him, but was unable to arrange the meeting—the Colonel had a pressing engagement."

I glanced at Lindbergh, finding it hard to believe that he'd decline a chance to meet with Curtis and someone who claimed to be one of the kidnappers.

Lindbergh shrugged. "That was the day you and I went out in the Lockheed-Vega, Nate."

The second day of searching for the "boad" *Nelly*. No wonder Curtis and his possible kidnapper fell through the cracks.

"Larsen was pretty jumpy," Curtis said. "He insisted I drive him back."

"What about the letter," I asked, "with the physical description of the kid?"

"He wouldn't hand it over to me; he hung onto it."

"Why in hell?"

"He was angry with Colonel Lindbergh, and suspicious."

"Have you had any contact with Sam or John and company, since?"

He nodded. "Yes. There has been one subsequent meeting."

After the papers had been filled with lists of serial numbers and speculative stories about "Jafsie," Curtis was contacted by Sam for another meeting at the Newark train station. He found all of the self-proclaimed kidnappers but Larsen squeezed into Sam's car, and was told to join them. He did, and was driven to a three-story house in the Scandinavian section of Newark. In a small, sloppy one-flat serving as a bedroom, dining room and sitting room, the men found chairs and Curtis asked John about Jafsie.

Curtis continued his impression of John's accent. "He said, 'Sure, I did the work with Condon. That was the idea all along—to chisel this Lindbergh through Condon, then turn the boy in through you. That's why we were willing to let the kid go cheap to you.' I told him I didn't call twenty-five thousand dollars 'cheap,' but John said the Lindberghs were 'rolling in dough.' "

Curtis asked for the letter, describing the boy, and John bragged that he'd torn it up—"Do you think we're fool enough to keep something that hot around?"

"I was getting skeptical," Curtis admitted. "So I demanded hard proof. They gave it to me."

"Yeah?"

"They showed me some of the ransom money."

I looked sharply at Lindbergh and Breckinridge.

"Fifteen hundred in fives, tens and twenties," Curtis continued. "They gave me a list of the bills, in a newspaper clipping, and I checked several against it." He took a breath and nodded, once. "These are the men who have the Colonel's money, all right."

Silence hung in the room like humidity.

Then Lindbergh, clearly sold, said, "I think we can proceed with depositing that twenty-five thousand and arranging the safe return of my son."

Curtis sighed in relief. "Thank God, Colonel. Of course, you know I'm at your service."

Lindbergh rose. "I need a few moments, in private, with my attorney and my police consultant. If you don't mind."

"Not at all," Curtis said, heartily, rising.

"I would like you to stay for supper, of course, and we'll talk this evening." Lindy reached his hand across the desk.

Curtis, beaming, shook Lindbergh's hand, then did the same

with Breckinridge and myself, as we stood briefly, politely, till he was out the door.

"What do you think, Nate?" Slim asked, sitting back down.

"Much of what he says does jibe with things that the man on the street couldn't know."

Breckinridge, who'd been quiet, said, "Much of it jibes with Condon."

"And even with Gaston Means," I said. "And Curtis—despite a flair for theater that rivals the Great Jafsie—seems a reliable go-between. Did you check up on his financial standing?"

I was asking Lindy, but Breckinridge answered. "His shipping firm has had its ups and downs, in these hard times. But he appears solvent. And his social standing is unquestioned."

Lindbergh was nodding. "And his fellow go-betweens Dobson-Peacock and, of course, Admiral Burrage are unimpeachable."

"Well, then," I said, "play out the hand—but, of course, you'll bring in Irey and Wilson."

"What do you mean?" Lindbergh asked, as if the concept I'd suggested were arcane.

"Slim—if we've learned anything from Condon, not to mention Gaston Means, it's that we can't play by the rules in a game set up by cheaters. Curtis is running around with these 'kidnappers' like a freshman on a fraternity hazing. You need to have the authorities in on this—carefully, secretly, without Curtis's knowledge—but in on it. He has to be shadowed, and when the ransom payment is made, you follow the fucker who gets the money to wherever he goes and . . ."

"No," Lindbergh said, shaking his head vigorously. "Nate, no. We play it straight."

I looked at him the way you look at a driver who signals right and turns left. "What do you mean, 'straight'?"

"Curtis is honest, and reliable. I trust him. I think he can get Charlie back."

"That isn't the point!" I was on my feet now, leaning my hands on his desk. "If these are in fact the same sons of bitches who took that fifty grand from Condon, then they've *already* screwed you, once! And if they're just some interloping extortionist gang, then you're going to just throw *more* goddamn dough out the window." I took my hands off his desk; I was shaking my head, frustrated, disgusted. "You can't be serious, Slim—you *have* to have learned *something* from the Condon experience. . . ."

His face was stone.

Breckinridge seemed sympathetic to my stance, or at least his expression said so, even if he didn't.

I backed away from the desk. I tried to keep the irritation out of my voice. Summoned a sense of calm and crawled inside. "Well, then, that's it, Slim. This is where I get off."

"I'd like you to stay." His voice was earnest; his eyes were hurt. "We're still dealing with bootleggers, rumrunners . . . we can't rule out the Capone connection."

"I don't rule that out. But I can't be party to this any longer. It just goes against my grain as a cop. All due respect."

"If that's how you feel . . ."

"It's how I feel."

He stood. "I do understand, Nate." His words were cordial, but his tone was tense. "I . . . respect what you're saying. But you know how I feel about getting my son back."

"I know," I said, trying to sound at least a little conciliatory. "My point is, you've been going about it all wrong."

A frown grazed his face—nobody talked to him that way—but it was gone as he came out from around the desk. "Then, uh . . . you'll be heading back for Chicago soon?"

"I'll drive Mrs. McLean back to Washington, tonight. I'll catch the train there, tomorrow."

"Fine." He dug in his pocket. "Here's some expense money." He peeled off five twenties.

I had a hunch I was supposed to feel insulted. Maybe I did feel a little insulted. But I put the money in my pocket.

"Thanks," I said.

"You'll stay for supper?" he asked.

"Yes. And we'll have to talk to Evalyn, about Means."

"The Means information was a dead end?"

He didn't know how dead.

"Slim, Means is a completely unreliable go-between. Don't ask how I know, but any lines of communication he may have had with the kidnappers have been severed."

He wondered about that, but I'd asked him not to ask how I knew, and he was goddamn good about playing by the rules some other asshole imposed on him.

"What I'd like you to do," I said, "as a favor to me if nothing else, is encourage Mrs. McLean not to pursue Means as a go-between, any longer. To encourage her to have the son of a bitch arrested, which after all might uncover some worthwhile information. She's inclined to do that herself already. But she needs to hear it from you."

"That's why you suggested I invite her here?"

"Yes. That, and I think she deserved to meet you and your wife. To hear you thank her. I think she's got that much coming, for her hundred grand, rich though she is."

Lindbergh, chagrined, nodded his agreement.

During dinner, amidst my social betters talking about politics and coming-out parties and yachts, I noticed something odd. We were having the usual dreadful English cooking, courtesy of Elsie Whately—mystery stew, tough bread, murky coffee and cardboard pie—and butler Ollie, Elsie's better half, was serving us. But he seemed very ill at ease. The presence of either Curtis or Evalyn or the both of them seemed to get on his nerves. The table service, which Ollie had set, was missing the knives. Anne Lindbergh herself got up and provided them.

Why in hell would a servant trained in household duties since he was knee-high to a fetus forget so ordinary a piece of table service as a knife?

After dinner, Slim did indeed encourage Evalyn to cut Means loose, turn him in and do her best to get her money back.

It was perhaps eight-thirty when we walked out into a cool, overcast night, Evalyn and I followed by Slim and his pretty Anne, who held hands like young lovers. They looked like the perfect American couple they'd been, not so long ago, the circles under their eyes, the redness of those eyes, the lines worry was etching in their faces, smoothed by the night's cool half-light.

That was my last image of them, their smiles slight and shining, like slices of the moon, Anne delicate and waving from the hip, her other hand resting gently on the rise of her tummy, where a new child grew, Slim raising a hand in goodbye, shy, modest, his stubbornness not showing.

As we drove away, the ruts of Featherbed Lane challenging even the Lincoln's suspension, Evalyn seemed at peace; even happy.

"They're wonderful people," she said. "Wonderful."

"They're nice," I agreed. "Damn shame."

"So in love."

"Definitely."

We were moving through the dark woods, moonlight filtering through the trees, when Evalyn said, "Pull over. Pull off."

"Why?"

"Just do it."

I did as I was told, the Lincoln's wheels crunching leaves and twigs as we rolled to a stop. I shut the car off and looked at her; for a woman who'd had a big meal recently, she sure looked hungry. She was unbuttoning the white silk blouse, breathing heavily, her breasts heaving. The fox stole was curled up between us on the seat as if asleep, the black jacket of her suit draped over it like she'd covered it, to keep it warm.

"Fuck me," she said.

I love it when rich women talk dirty.

Then we were in the backseat, her black dress hiked up, my trousers around my ankles, her silk stockings rubbing smoothly against my bare legs, the sounds of animals outside the car counterpointing the sounds of animals within.

Later, as I drove, she slept much of the time, cuddled up against me. She smelled good; her jasmine perfume was mingling with a natural muskiness from our coupling.

At one point, half-asleep, she said, "How would you like a full-time job?"

"Huh?"

"I really could use a sort of bodyguard, chauffeur, security chief . . . it would pay nicely, Nate."

"Well, uh . . ."

"There'd be fringe benefits."

"Gee, Evalyn."

"Double your salary," she said, and began to snore.

I thought about it all the way to Washington, D.C. Was she

serious? After all, I had a career. Hell, I wasn't some male concubine. I was a cop, I was a detective; not a kept man!

"Evalyn," I said, the next morning, in her mammoth breakfast nook, drinking coffee from a china cup worth more than any single possession of mine, "I accept."

"You accept what, Nate?"

"Your offer. I'd love to come to work for you."

She smiled sadly; she looked older this morning—pretty, but every year her age. She wore a pink silk robe—not her dowdy plaid number. And the Hope diamond was around her neck; it winked mockingly at me. She was sipping tea.

"That, I'm afraid, was just wishful thinking on my part. I can't have you around. You're too dangerous."

"Don't judge me by the other day," I said, nibbling buttery toast. "I hardly ever get in shoot-outs."

"It's not that." She had a tiny, bittersweet half-smile. "Frightening as that was, I will treasure the memory. The fear will fade, the romance will sustain."

"Evalyn, I'll go back to Chicago if you tell me to."

"Go back to Chicago, Nate."

"Oh. Well. Sure."

Her eyes glistened with regret. "Nate—my husband wants my children. And my children are the most important thing in my life. If Ned found out about us, about you and me, he could use it against me, and could have them. He could win them. And I can't have that." She shook her head, with a look of unmistakable finality. "We mustn't see each other again."

She reached across the table and touched my cheek.

"It's been wonderful," she said. "A real adventure. But it's over."

I got up and went over and gave her a kiss; a nice fat buttery smooch.

"Let me know if you ever need me," I said.

Then I wiped off my face with a fancy napkin, went upstairs, got my bag, caught a cab and hopped a westbound train. The only thing this detective hoped to find, right now, was Chicago, Illinois.

INTERIM

APRIL 1932–SEPTEMBER 1934

witnessed the rest of it long-distance, via the newspapers and an occasional on-the-qt call from Colonel Henry Breckinridge, who had come to agree with me that Slim's no-cops-allowed approach was (as Breckinridge put it) "counterproductive."

The only other difference, this time around, was that Colonel Schwarzkopf was kept abreast of the Norfolk ransom negotiations (though the Virginia authorities weren't). Not that it mattered much: Schwarzkopf and his spiffy state police continued to obey the Lone Eagle's hands-off orders and stayed well away from Curtis and the supposed kidnap gang he was dealing with.

For the rest of April and well into May, Lindbergh followed Commodore Curtis's lead and boarded first a small rented vessel, then the yacht *Marcon*, belonging to a hotel-owner pal of Curtis's, and finally the eighty-five-foot ketch, the *Cachalot*, belonging to another Curtis crony, for various attempted sea rendezvous with the kidnappers. Raging storms, rough sea and dense fog seemed to conspire with heavy boating traffic to keep any meeting from occurring. Between outings, Curtis—all by his lonesome—would rush ashore for phone calls and meetings with Hilda, Larsen and sundry others of the kidnap gang members, who seemed eager to return the little boy to his weary parents. Detailed descriptions of several boats the kidnappers were using were provided by Curtis, as were various specific rendezvous points.

On May fifth, while Lindy and Curtis and crew were searching for kidnappers off the coast of Virginia, Gaston Bullock Means was getting arrested by the FBI on an embezzlement charge—specifically, "larceny after trust." Immediately after I suggested it, and Lindbergh himself okayed it, Evalyn had first fired Means, demanding the return of her money, and then—after Means gave a typically wild excuse for not being able to do so—she tipped the feds to him.

But the crime having been committed in the District of Columbia meant Means had to be arrested in D.C. And his home in Chevy Chase was just over the Maryland state line. The feds shadowed him till he drove those few blocks into federal territory, got pulled rudely over and found himself deposited in the office of old J. Edgar himself, who despised former-agent Means for the black eye he'd given the bureau.

And to Hoover, Gaston Bullock Means told a story which he had already tried (unsuccessfully) out on Evalyn and her lawyers.

It seemed when Mrs. McLean requested the return of her one hundred thousand dollars, Means had picked up the money in his brother's home in Concord, North Carolina, and was on his way to Washington to hand it over when, just outside of Alexandria, a man waving a red lantern flagged him down. This fellow (who Means hadn't seen all that well) had put a foot on Means's running board and said, "Hello, Hogan—Eleven told me to take the package from you, here."

And of course Means had turned the money over to this stranger, because, after all, the stranger knew Means's code name and Evalyn's code number.

Later, it came as a devastating shock to Means to discover that the stranger had not really been a representative of Mrs. McLean's; that her money had never been returned to her. Unfortunately, nobody questioned Means about this story with the aid of a Chicago lie detector.

And so, naturally, Means pleaded not guilty, and served six days in the redbrick D.C. jail before a bondsman put up the $100,000 bail—a fitting amount, I thought.

The afternoon of the day Means got out of jail—May 12—a colored driver hauling a load of timber pulled his truck alongside a narrow, muddy back road between Princeton and Hopewell and wandered into the underbrush, braving a steady rain, to take a leak. But before he could, he noticed something half-buried in dirt and leaves.

A small, decayed corpse.

Colonel Lindbergh was at the time on the *Cachalot,* just off the New Jersey coast, trying to make contact with another boat, called (Curtis said) the *Mary B. Moss.* Curtis was ashore trying to make contact with the kidnappers through "Hilda." The yacht eased into Cape May Harbor that evening, after another day of miserable weather, though prospects for a better day were imminent. Lindbergh remained aboard ship, where he'd been sleeping nights of late; hopeful that tomorrow the rendezvous would finally be made.

But a naval officer and a Curtis associate boarded the ketch and discovered that the news that had already been on the radio and in headlines had not reached the storm-tossed ship. Gingerly, they told Lindbergh, but I'm told that Slim knew at once from their faces that his son was dead.

The next afternoon—Friday the thirteenth—Lindbergh spent three minutes in the morgue identifying the decomposed body as his son. Anne stayed home.

A few days later, Commodore Curtis—who'd failed to provide either Treasury Agent Frank Wilson or Schwarzkopf and Inspector Welch with any conclusive proof of the existence of Sam, John, Hilda, Larsen, et al.—confessed that it had all been a hoax. Investigators said Curtis's business was in trouble, and that the year before he'd had a nervous breakdown; also, in the thick of his "negotiations" with the "kidnappers," he'd signed with the New York *Herald-Tribune* to tell his story.

The yacht-club commodore was tried for obstructing justice and fined a grand and sentenced to a year in the pokey, though the latter was suspended.

Gaston Means got fifteen years. Nobody could find Evalyn's

hundred thousand (actually one hundred and four thousand, including Means's "expense account"), though feds ransacked his Chevy Chase home and checked several safety deposit boxes.

The feds also checked the safety deposit boxes of the late Max Hassel and Max Greenberg, who Means in court fingered as the real kidnappers. Nearly a quarter of a mil in cash was found in Hassel's safety deposit box, but the denominations were fifties and up, whereas both Evalyn and Lindbergh had paid out fives, tens and twenties.

Meanwhile, the "Fox" turned out to be a disbarred lawyer named Norman Whitaker who had indeed been Means's cellmate; he claimed never to have laid eyes on the Lindbergh boy, that he had assumed the role of "mastermind kidnapper" to help out his old swindler pal. He was in fact in jail at the time of the actual kidnapping. And now he would be in jail again, for two years.

Evalyn wasted no time finding a new cause. In June of '32, to the dismay of her socialite friends, she began championing and funding the "Bonus Army," the depression-racked World War veterans who were seeking aid from the government; the government, of course, responded with tear gas and terrorism. But God bless Evalyn and her good heart for trying to help. And the Bonus Army was a hell of a lot better place for her to spend her money than Gaston Bullock Means.

As for the Means tip about Violet Sharpe, Inspector Welch followed up on it, all right. Welch had already been suspicious, as Violet's stories had continued to shift—the movie theater she said she'd attended March first evolving into a roadhouse called the Peanut Grill, the boyfriend's name finally coming back to her—Ernie—but leading to her falsely identifying a cabbie named Brinkert when the real "Ernie" was a beau of hers named Miller.

Not surprisingly, Welch questioned Violet repeatedly, particularly in the month following the discovery of the corpse of a child, and on June 10—the day after a particularly pointed interrogation—Violet reacted with panic and anger to the news that Welch was on his way back for another round. At Englewood, she apparently poisoned herself, rather than be questioned by the persistent Welch again. Cyanide.

I felt a little bad about that. I'd helped focus Welch—a thick-headed third-degree artist if ever I met one—on the girl. Not that I figured she was blameless; but so much information died with her.

Professor Condon was considered a suspect, grilled by the cops, humiliated by the public (one letter promised Condon a look at a picture of the child's kidnapper, and the enclosure was a small mirror); but he held up far better than Violet Sharpe. And much of the press attention he seemed to thrive on, pontificating at the drop of a hint.

Betty Gow's beau, Red Johnson, was deported; Betty herself, when the Hopewell household broke up, went back to Scotland. The Whatelys stayed on, maintaining the estate for the eventual return of the Lindberghs, who had moved "temporarily" to Next Day Hill, the Morrow estate at Englewood, shortly after the discovery of the little body less than two miles from their Hopewell house.

But butler Ollie took sick—he became increasingly nervous, and troubled by internal pains; he survived an emergency operation for a perforated ulcer, then died four days later. His widow stayed in the Lindberghs' employ, though her employers forever abandoned the unlucky Hopewell house, donating it to be a welfare center for children.

In mid-August, Anne Lindbergh gave her husband a second son. Lindy beseeched the press and public to allow the boy to "grow up normally"; at the Englewood estate, the cranky fox terrier Wahgoosh was made second-in-command to a surly police dog named Thor, who was known to shred the clothing and flesh of intruders. Kidnap threats against the infant were an everyday occurrence, the notes now requesting money to *prevent* a kidnapping; in one case kidnap notes and a ransom drop led to the arrest of two suspects—both of whom had alibis in the previous kidnapping, however.

There was something else, which struck me as very strange: when the name of the boy was finally released to the press, it turned out Anne and Charles had christened him "Jon."

Even without the "h" out, that seemed a hell of a choice.

I quit the force and went into business for myself in December 1932. The Lindbergh case had long since become something I followed in the papers, like everybody else. I began to wonder if they'd ever find the kidnappers. If Capone had really been behind it—he was in the Atlanta pen, now, as Eliot predicted—I didn't figure they ever would.

On the other hand, that ransom money was out there, and in 1933, the country went off the gold standard, meaning anybody with gold certificates had to turn them in by May first or face the legal consequences. That, thanks to Frank Wilson and Elmer Irey's insistence on paying out the ransom in gold notes, ought to flush out the kidnappers.

Or the extortionists.

I continued to think it might have been an interloping group with inside info that had contacted Jafsie; with that kid buried in so half-ass a fashion, so near the estate, in woods that had been searched time and again, the kidnappers themselves seemed unlikely to risk going after any dough. They had fucked up that night, accidentally killing the kid maybe when the ladder broke, or when they were fleeing the house, and faded into the night and history.

At least, that was my theory. And when the gold notes were tracked, I'd be proven right or wrong.

A New York City dick named James Finn, a lieutenant, had been keeping in his Manhattan precinct office a large city map charting the path of the surfacing gold notes for over a year, when the gold-standard situation started crowding his map with pins.

I had never met Finn, but apparently he was in touch with Schwarzkopf and even Lindbergh in the early days—just another cop being kept at arm's length.

Anyway, it was Finn who made the bust. September 19, 1933.

They only got one guy: a German carpenter in the Bronx. Following it from Chicago, in the papers, I figured Finn and the feds would soon shake the rest of the gang out of this Hauptmann guy.

The papers claimed he was Jafsie's "Cemetery John."

I had thought about calling Slim with my condolences, when I first heard about the body of his little boy turning up in those woods; but I figured I was the last person he'd want to hear from. I'd got very drunk, sitting by the phone, making my mind up, and got a little weepy, which was the rum talking.

Lindbergh called me, but better than two years later. Not long after they caught the kraut, in fact. A long-distance call so crackly it might have been from another planet, not New Jersey. On the other hand, my experiences in New Jersey led me to believe it just might be another planet.

"Nate," Slim said, "I've been negligent in thanking you."

"Don't be silly," I said. "I wish I could have done more."

"You wanted to. Sometimes . . . I wonder how things might be different, if I'd listened to you."

"Not much. Frankly . . . if you'll forgive my bluntness, Colonel, it's obvious your son died the night of the kidnapping. Nothing we could have done differently would change that."

"Those evil bastards would be in jail now."

"Maybe. But this clown Hauptmann will cough up his accomplices. Wait and see."

I heard him sigh. Then he said: "That's what we're counting on. I understand you're in private practice, now."

"That's right. A-1 Detective Agency. I'm the president. Also the janitor."

He laughed. "Same old Nate. If I ever need a detective, I know who to call."

"Right," I said. "Frank Wilson."

He laughed again, wished me well, and I wished him and Anne and their new son the same. And that was that.

It felt strange, sitting on the sidelines, after having been in the midst of this famous affair, early on. Not that I minded. Sometimes I thought about Lindbergh; fairly frequently I thought about Evalyn. Bittersweet memories.

Nonetheless, it was reassuring knowing that this case was behind me—that it was, in fact, virtually solved.

II

The Lone Wolf

MARCH 13 – APRIL 4, 1936

Chapter 26

It was a little after nine o'clock on a morning that, judging by what I could see past my scenic view of the el, was overcast and unpromising. Friday the thirteenth—not that I put much stock in luck, bad or good or otherwise. Looking back, though, I'd have to say that this particular day lived up to its reputation.

When the phone rang on my desk, however, right next to my crossed feet in their argyle socks with holes that only showed when my shoes were off, which they were, I was blissfully unaware of anything except the sports section of the *Trib* and the paper cup of coffee I'd brought up from the deli downstairs.

I damn near spilled the coffee and about knocked the phone off the desk with my feet. That misshapen black object didn't ring that often. I had a large office, but it was just the one big room, which I also lived in, on the fourth and final floor of a building at Van Buren and Plymouth that additionally housed a palm reader, an abortionist and two or three shysters, among other agents of free enterprise, with a flophouse next door. Most of my business, these days, was established—primarily retail credit checks for the suburban financial institutions who were the backbone of my bank-book. There was also the occasional divorce job, but for some psychological reason, those were almost always walk-ins: some sad man, or woman, but usually man, would stumble in red-eyed, feeling guilty as Cain, and hire me to confirm his or her worst fears. With photos.

I slipped my feet into my shoes—wouldn't do to greet business in my socks, even over the phone—and said, "A-1 Detective Agency, Nathan Heller speaking."

Before I'd even gotten those words out, I realized the static in my ear was announcing that rarity of rarities: a long-distance call.

"Mr. Heller," a female voice said, operator-efficient, "can you hold the line? We have a call for you from the governor."

"The governor?" I sat up and straightened my tie. I had no respect for any politician, but I didn't get calls like this often. Make that, ever.

"Hold please," she said again.

And I listened to the scratchy sound of taxpayers' money drifting carelessly away. What the hell would Governor Horner want with me?

"Mr. Heller," a reassuring baritone voice intoned; even over the crackly wire, it was an impressive voice. "This is Governor Hoffman."

I'd heard him right, but nonetheless, stupidly, I said, "Governor Horner?"

"No," he said, with the faintest edge of irritation. "Hoffman. I'm calling from Trenton."

"Oh! Governor Hoffman."

I wasn't speaking to the governor of Illinois; I was speaking to the Governor of New Jersey. I recognized his name not because I was politically astute, but because I'd seen it in the papers recently.

"As you may know, Mr. Heller, an inordinate amount of my time and energy, over the past several months, has been wrapped up in the Lindbergh case. Or, to be precise, the Hauptmann case."

"Yes, sir."

Governor Hoffman was the center of a controversy that extended well beyond New Jersey state lines. The convicted kidnapper—actually, convicted murderer—found responsible for the Lindbergh crime had been taken under the governor's wing, so to speak. A month or so back, Hoffman had granted Bruno Hauptmann a thirty-day reprieve.

"The prisoner's reprieve ran out several days ago," Hoffman said; his voice conveyed both sadness and frustration. "And I'm not going to issue another one."

"I see," I said, not seeing at all.

"The new date for execution has been set for March thirtieth. I intend to see that the time we have remaining is well used."

"Uh . . . how so, Governor?"

"I've had several independent investigators working on this case, for several months, and I don't intend to stop my efforts. In fact, with your help, I intend to step up those efforts."

"My help?"

"You've come highly recommended, Mr. Heller."

"Surely you haven't run out of investigators out on the East Coast, Governor Hoffman. Unless there's something that needs doing on the Chicago end . . ."

"You're one of the few people alive aware that there *is* a Chicago 'end' to this case. And I'm well aware of your role in the early days of the investigation. You witnessed a lot. You came into contact with Curtis, Means, Jafsie, Marinelli and his common-law wife Sarah Sivella, and so many others. You're the ideal person to conduct this eleventh-hour inquiry."

Eleventh-hour inquiry!

"Governor . . . if I may be frank."

"Certainly."

"The Lindbergh case was one of the most frustrating, convoluted, hopeless affairs I ever came in contact with. I've considered myself damn lucky to be out of that stew."

There was a crackly pause on the line.

Then the baritone voice returned, stern now: "There is a good chance, Mr. Heller, that Bruno Richard Hauptmann is innocent. And it is a damn-near certainty that he was *not* the lone kidnapper."

"Maybe so . . . but from what I read, he probably was involved. Could be he'll still talk, when all his legal parachutes have folded up. And finger the rest of his mob."

The words came quickly now: "Mr. Heller, come to Trenton. Allow me to make my case. You're under no obligation. I'll wire you the money for your train tickets. You can settle your affairs in Chicago and travel on Sunday. We'll meet in my office first thing Monday morning."

"Governor, the Lindbergh case is the last thing I want to get involved with."

"I can offer you a retainer of one thousand dollars against your standard fee. Which is?"

"Uh, twenty-five dollars a day," I said, doubling it and then some, "and expenses."

"Done," the governor said.

"Done," I said, and shrugged.

We both hung up.

I put my feet back up on the desk, loosened my tie, and said to nobody, "Isn't this the damnedest turn of events?"

After spending the rest of the morning doing credit checks by phone, I treated myself to the finnan haddie at Binyon's around the corner, heading down around eleven-thirty to beat the luncheon crowd. That was where I ran into Hal Davis of the *News*.

"Hey, Heller," Davis said, cheerfully. "Eating regular and everything." He was a small man with a big head and bright eyes; he looked about thirty, though he'd never see forty again. "Who died and left *you* money?"

"I got a client."

"That is news," Davis said. He took off his fedora and joined me, even though he was on his way out, raincoat over his arm. "Buy me a cup of coffee?"

"Yeah," I said, "if you'll buy me a beer, after."

"Sure." He waved a waiter over. Binyon's was all dark paneling, wooden booths and businessmen. "So—what do you hear from your pal Nitti?"

I grimaced; the sweet taste of the fish went sour. "Davis, I told you a hundred million fucking times. I am *not* connected."

Davis smirked. "Yeah, yeah. Everybody knows Frank Nitti likes you, Nate. You done him favors."

"I'm an ex-cop," I sighed. "I know some Outfit guys. Don't make a big deal out of it."

"Ever since you testified in Nitti's favor that time . . ."

"Drop it, Hal."

"Okay, okay! What do you hear from Barney?"

He meant Barney Ross, the boxer, welterweight champ in fact, who was a friend of mine since we were kids together on the West Side, and who incidentally was my landlord. We discussed Barney's flourishing boxing career—he had just KO'ed Lou Halper in Philly in eight—and half an hour later we were in the Shamrock, the bar next to the Dill Pickle. Barney used to own the place, and boxing and other sporting-world pics still decorated the dingy walls.

Davis must have smelled a story, because he bought me a total of four beers. And on the fourth, something in the back of my mind clicked—or maybe snapped—and I decided to let him in on my new client. The thought of the publicity, and what it might do for my business, suddenly sounded as good as the hardboiled egg I was eating.

"Governor Hoffman, huh," Davis said, his eyes glittering. "You don't really think that kraut Hauptmann is innocent, do you?"

"Watch your language," I said. "I'm of German heritage myself."

"You're awful sensitive today, for a half-mick, half-hebe."

"The kraut probably isn't innocent," I admitted, "but I'm gonna keep an open mind. Besides, anybody who thinks that clown pulled the kidnapping *and* the ransom scam, all by his lonesome, is playin' with the squirrels."

Davis drank that in and then his face crinkled with amusement. "You know what I heard?"

"No. Illuminate me."

"You know how one of the big pieces of evidence against Hauptmann was they found that old coot's phone number written on a wall inside his closet?"

Jafsie's phone number had indeed been found in that manner at Hauptmann's apartment.

"Yeah," I said. "So?"

"So I hear a reporter on the New York *Daily News*, Tim O'Neil, wrote that."

"What do you mean, wrote it?"

Davis grinned, shrugged. "After they took Hauptmann away, the cops confiscated his apartment, and gave the press free and easy access. It was a slow news day, so O'Neil writes old Jafsie's number on the closet-trim and calls the inspector on duty over and says, look what I found. Bingo! Front page of the *Daily News* that night. Is that sweet or what?"

"Would *you* do that for a story?"

"Hey, if the guy's fuckin' guilty, what's the difference?"

"Maybe nothing," I said. "But it just shows how from day one everybody's been awful goddamn anxious to slap that poor bastard in the chair. Yet nobody seems to give a damn about his accomplices."

"That's 'cause this story needs an ending, Heller," Davis said, matter-of-factly. "America's had its fill of this one. Even Lindy flew the coop."

Charles and Anne Lindbergh had taken their young, press-besieged son Jon to Great Britain late last year, in self-imposed exile.

"The New Jersey cops and prosecutors," Davis said, "would rather let Hauptmann go to the chair and take the names of his accomplices with him, than let him miss out on a punishment he so richly deserves. And a lot of people in this country agree."

The little reporter, who'd had only two beers, took his leave with a nod of his fedora and a wink of one tiny eye, and I knew he was going to write me up for the late edition. I wasn't drunk, after all. But I might've been a hair less than sober, and as I wandered back up the three flights of stairs to my office, I began to wonder if being tied to what the public might perceive as an effort to clear Hauptmann could really do anything at all positive for my less-than-flourishing one-man business.

I set up a couple of credit-check appointments in Evanston for Saturday afternoon, and called a couple of people I regularly do work for to tell them I'd be out of town for two or three weeks. Nobody seemed put out, and somewhere approaching midafternoon, I pulled the Murphy bed down and flopped out in my shirt and trousers for a nap. The four beers had taken their toll.

A sharp rapping at the door woke me; I came instantly awake, sitting up as if by spring action, surprised a little that the room was so dark, that the world beyond my window was lit only by neon. The day had slipped away. Evening or not, I had serious morning mouth, and as the rapping continued, I crawled off the bed, shouting, "Just a minute, will ya!" and eased the bed up inside its wardrobelike cabinet.

I went into the john, rinsed out my mouth, pissed like a son of a bitch, straightened my tie but didn't bother with my coat. It was a little late for a client, after all. Whoever it was could take me as I was or leave me.

I cracked the door and saw a slender, white-haired, pock-marked individual who looked a little bit like a LaSalle Street broker and a little bit like the angel of death.

"Yes?" I said, timidly, as if I didn't recognize him, but I did.

"Mr. Heller," Paul Ricca said politely. He was a man of forty who looked older than time. "Could I step in." It wasn't a question.

"Yeah, certainly, Mr. Ricca."

Everything he said had a slight accent: "Could-a I step-a in." But faint. He was as soft-spoken as a funeral director.

Paul "the Waiter" Ricca had high cheekbones and dark black eyebrows over placid dark eyes; his mouth wasn't much wider than his nose and his nose wasn't all that wide, for an Italian. He wore an exquisitely tailored sky-blue double-breasted topcoat under which a dark-blue silk tie was neatly knotted; his navy homburg probably cost more than my couch.

"Frank would like to see you," he said.

"Me?" I said.

The faintest hint of irritation was in his nod, and in his words: "Get your coat."

I got-a my coat.

Paul the Waiter Ricca, a.k.a. Paul DeLucia, a.k.a. Paul Maglio, was Frank Nitti's second-in-command. Nitti, of course, took over the Chicago Outfit when Capone was sent up; and Ricca, word had it, was Capone's choice to keep an eye on Nitti. The story was that Ricca, when he was a teenager in Sicily, had killed a man in a family feud, and that he served two years and on the day he got out shot and killed the witness who ID'ed him. He'd fled to America and, after working as a theater usher and waiter in New York, wound up one of Snorkey's top enforcers. Capone had even been best man at Ricca's wedding.

"Mr. Ricca," I said, my hat in my hand, "would I be out of line asking what this is about?"

"Yes," he said. He gestured to the door. I opened it for him and he went out first. They called him the Waiter, but he waited on, or for, nobody.

I wished I had my gun, though if the Outfit had my number, there really was no way out of it. I followed Ricca down the stairs of my nearly seedy building; in his fancy clothes, he seemed very out of place. Actually, he seemed out of place in many respects. Why was he alone? Where were the two requisite goombahs with metal lumps under their armpits? Ricca was high up—second-in-command, according to some—so why in hell was he playing gopher for Nitti?

A black Lincoln limo was waiting. And no one was behind the wheel. Ricca really had come alone.

I stood awkwardly at the curb by the car; the neons and street lights of Van Buren reflected off its shiny roof. A wino approached us, asking for a handout; Ricca froze him with a look. Then the bum stumbled away looking for a more sympathetic mark.

Above us the el rumbled by. I raised my voice above it: "Where do you want me?"

His blank expression somehow conveyed contempt; he didn't want me at all. But he said, "In the front. I'm not your goddamn chauffeur."

But that is exactly what he was—which might mean somebody was insulting him by giving him such a lowly task. And if there was anywhere I did not want to be, it was in the middle of some Outfit political gesture.

I didn't speak to Ricca as he drove me. My mind continued whirring, wondering why in hell we were alone; there wasn't even a fucking driver! Ricca had, once upon a time, been a driver, however, and the ride was as smooth as it was surprising. I expected to be taken to the Capri Restaurant, or the Bismarck Hotel or maybe the Congress, all frequent sites for Nitti holding court. Instead we took Monroe over to the near West Side.

To Jefferson Park Hospital, where Nitti's father-in-law, Dr. Gaetano Ronga, was chief of surgery.

Was Nitti sick? I'd been summoned here before, by two lesser Outfit lights than Ricca, in December of '32, in the aftermath of an assassination attempt on Nitti at an office in the LaSalle-Wacker Building by two cops who'd been Mayor Cermak's personal hitmen. Those cops had dragged me along when they went to hit Nitti, without telling me that that was on the agenda, and I'd double-crossed them eventually, by telling the truth on the witness stand. By backing Nitti's story. Which was why Nitti felt he owed me one, and why newsguys like Davis and certain cops like Captain John Stege considered me to be in Nitti's pocket.

My first meeting with Nitti—not counting the few minutes in the LaSalle-Wacker when Cermak's two cops had shot Nitti full of holes—had been in this same hospital, in Nitti's private room, where he was surprising Cermak, Cermak's killer cops and probably God Himself by surviving multiple close-range bullet wounds to the neck and back. Nitti was a hard man to kill. Cermak had proved less hard, when Nitti's one-man suicide squad, Giuseppe Zangara, hit His Honor out in Miami. But that's another story.

We were on the third floor. It was after visiting hours and the corridor was dark; what little light there was reflected off the shining waxed hardwood floor. An occasional nurse or doctor drifted by, faceless in the dimness. Ricca was walking quickly, his steps echoing, and sick people in their white beds and dark rooms glimpsed at left and right made a sort of morbid, moving and occasionally moaning tapestry. I kept up with Ricca, but stayed behind him, following like a kid being led to the principal's office by a strict and pissed-off teacher.

Then we went around a corner and moved away from hospital rooms into what seemed to be an administrative area. At a door marked Dr. Gaetano Ronga, Ricca knocked; his lips were pursed with quiet annoyance.

"Yes?" said a confident male voice from within.

"It's Paul," he said. "Your package is here."

"Send him in," the voice said.

And Ricca, for once, did wait on me: he opened the door. The look on his face was glazed and quietly contemptuous. I went on by him, into the room, and the door shut behind me. Ricca had not followed.

In a medium-size office, filled with dark wood filing cabinets, its walls hung with diplomas, family pictures and prints of flying fowl, behind a big desk on which various manila folders were neatly arranged, sat Frank Nitti.

"Nate Heller," Nitti said, with a generous gesture of one hand and a smile, but not getting up, "sit down. Nice to see you again. Thanks for comin' around."

"My pleasure, Mr. Nitti," I said, finding a hardwood chair and sitting across from him.

"You know better than that," he said, mock-scoldingly. "It's 'Frank' and it's 'Nate.' Right?"

"Right," I said. We were old friends, after all; ask anybody.

Nitti was a small, well-groomed man in his early fifties, damn near handsome, his face flecked with scar tissue here and there, his lower lip particularly. His hair was slicked back, dark with a little gray, and very neat; he was a former barber and fussy about his appearance. He seemed uncharacteristically casual in dress tonight, a white shirt open at the collar, sleeves rolled up.

"I hope you're well, Frank," I said.

"Just in for a checkup. Ever since Cermak's sons of bitches pumped that lead in me, I gotta come in all the time and get this and that checked." He shrugged dismissively, but I'd heard about his bleeding ulcers and back problems. "I take these physicals at night. It's more private that way. So. How's business, Heller?"

"Not bad. Little divorce work. Some retail credit accounts."

"I see in the paper you picked up a client out east."

I figured that was it. Davis's story about me working for Governor Hoffman on the Lindbergh case was undoubtedly all over the evening edition of the *News*.

"Yeah," I said. "Hell of a thing. Governor of New Jersey, no less."

"You worked the Lindbergh case as a cop, didn't you? Back in '32?"

"I was the Chicago police liaison, yes. I was just on the fringes. No big deal."

"That was when Al said he could get Little Lindy back. Right?"

"Uh, right, Frank." Where the hell was this going?

Nitti folded his hands; he looked strangely thoughtful. "I'd like you to do a job for me, while you're out there."

"A job?"

He shrugged. "Nothing hard. Just, if you turn anything up that would be of interest to me, I want you to let me know."

"Of interest to you . . . ?"

He looked at me pointedly. "Heller, don't make me spell it out."

I wasn't "Nate" anymore, I noticed.

"Okay," I said tentatively. "But I'm not quite following you."

He lifted a hand and one finger of that hand. "If this thing comes back to Chicago . . . if it comes back to the Outfit . . . I want to be the first to know."

I shifted uncomfortably in the chair. "Frank, maybe I better call Governor Hoffman and just back out of this thing. I don't want to be put in a position where I'm working at cross-purposes for two clients."

Nitti stood and I damn near jumped. He walked past me to the door and opened it. Ricca was waiting out there, across the hall, a sentry in a tailored topcoat.

"Paul," he said, gently. "See if you can find me a glass of milk."

Ricca nodded and disappeared and Nitti shut the door.

He began to pace, saying, "You know, I was the first of the boys to take a tax-rap fall. They got me before they got Al, you know."

I nodded.

"I hadn't been outside so very long, when they put Al away. While I was gone, Al moved the Waiter up in my place—temporarily of course."

I said nothing.

He stopped pacing, stood before me. He was not a big man; and he was slender. But his presence was towering. He said, "Al and the Waiter always been tight. They got tighter when I was away. I feel they could be . . . reckless, at times. One thing you know about me, Heller, is I don't like attracting the heat. If something has to be done, then you do it in such a way it don't come back to your doorstep."

What Nitti was talking about was his disagreement with Capone over such PR catastrophes as the shooting of reporter Jake Lingle and the St. Valentine's Day Massacre. Not that Nitti was nonviolent. But Nitti was a master manipulator, a cunning impresario of events. When he took Cermak out, it looked political; when he got rid of John Dillinger, it was the feds who took the rap. Just last month, "Machine-Gun" Jack McGurn—longtime Outfit guy who'd reportedly gone disloyal—was gunned down in a bowling alley, on St. Valentine's Day. The hitters left a comic valentine on the corpse, leading the cops and press to assume that this was some long-overdue revenge upon McGurn by remnants of the old Bugs Moran gang for McGurn's role in the famed Clark Street massacre seven years before. To me the slaying had Nitti's chessmaster fingerprints all over it.

"I think Al and the Waiter may have done this Lindbergh thing," he said. Shrugged. "That is, had it done, through their East-Coast contacts. Ricca spent as much time out there as he did Chicago, in those days; he was Al's contact with Luciano and Gordon and Schultz and the rest."

I didn't know if I liked hearing Nitti talk this openly. But I didn't seem to have any other choice than to listen.

"If Al did this—had this done—to try and buy himself out of stir, I want to know."

"Wouldn't you have been . . . consulted?"

"Jesus, Heller! Are you kidding? You think I'd let them pull a crazy fucking stunt like that? It would've been from Capone's lips to Ricca's ear. I don't know for sure that they did it, understand. It's rumor. It's just . . . what you say, supposition, on my part."

"Capone always claimed a former employee of his, name of Bob Conroy, pulled the job."

"Conroy was Al's man. No former about it."

"I don't think the feds ever found Conroy."

Nitti winced with amusement. "Oh sure, they did. Frank Wilson himself, workin' with that New York dick Finn, turned Conroy up, in August of '32."

"Really? I never heard about it."

Nitti shrugged. "Didn't make the papers out here. Nobody picked up on the Chicago angle. Conroy was found in a rundown back-room apartment he'd been hiding out in on West Hundred and Fourth in New York. Him and his pretty blonde wife. Double suicide, they called it."

"Jesus."

"There was a beer war that broke out, right about the time the body of the Lindbergh kid turned up. A lot of people in the bootlegging business was dropping like flies out on the East Coast. Waxey Gordon and Dutch Schultz was going at it. Ever hear of a pair called Max Hassel and Max Greenberg?"

"I don't believe so," I said.

"They were so-called victims in that war. So were half a dozen of their associates, over a period of six months or so. Could Al, through the Waiter, been tying up some loose East-Coast ends? If bootleggers were recruited to snatch the kid, that would make sense."

I could only nod.

Another sharp rapping made me squirm in my chair.

" 'Cusa," Nitti said. He went to the door, where Ricca was holding a glass of milk. Seeing Ricca like that, his face as white as the milk though considerably less wholesome, would have been amusing if it hadn't been so frightening.

"Paul," Nitti said with a smile, taking the milk, "thank you. Would you find my father-in-law, please, and tell him I'm ready for him."

And Ricca, with an almost imperceptible disgruntled sigh, again disappeared. Nitti shut the door and turned to smile at me like a kindly priest.

"The Waiter is very disciplined," he said, setting the milk on the desk. "And very loyal . . . to Al. In two, three years, Al will be out of stir. Meantime, I have the Waiter coming up under me, undermining my authority in little ways. Challenging me in board meetings . . ."

He trailed off, knowing that he should say no more on this subject. He went over and sipped the milk; set it back down.

But there were things I needed to know. "Frank, how does the Lindbergh case figure into any of this?"

He sat on the edge of the desk, at once casual and tightly coiled. "Couple ways, Nate."

"Nate" again.

"If I knew the Waiter and Al did this thing," he said, "it would be valuable knowledge. Something I would have over them."

"Would you expect me to . . . cover up, or withhold evidence or information from the authorities?"

"If I asked you to," he said, "wouldn't you?"

I sighed. "I'd rather not take the job, then. I'm already getting a reputation for being connected. It's not necessarily good for my business."

He shrugged. "I might throw more work your way. Put you on a nice yearly retainer."

"No offense, Frank, but I'm just enough of an ex-cop to want to keep *some* distance from your business."

He gestured with both hands in a "fair enough" manner. "Then all I ask is that you tell me what you find out. Then it's up to me to either use it, or contain it, best I can. I don't expect you to do anything but, on the one hand, serve your client, Governor Who's-It; and on the other, keep me informed."

He slid off the desk. He dipped a hand into his pocket and withdrew a thick money clip; a fifty-dollar bill was on top. He unclipped the bills and counted out ten fifties.

"Five hundred as a retainer," he said. "With a bonus, if you find something useful to me."

"Okay, Frank," I said. I took the money.

"Honest to God, kid," he said, "I don't know if Al was crazy enough to do this thing. But I know the Waiter is ruthless enough. He's made a lot of people disappear in his time."

I couldn't hold the anger back. "Then why the hell did you have him, of all people, bring me here? Do you *want* him to figure out why you hired me? He's obviously insulted at playing chauffeur to the likes of me . . ."

Nitti placed a fatherly hand on my shoulder and bestowed me a cool smile. "If you get close to something the Waiter's involved in out east, he's gonna know, anyway. He's gonna know immediately."

"Right!"

"So I had him bring you here. To send him a message."

"What message is that?"

"Not to kill you, Nate."

I just looked at him.

"I want Paul to know that you're under my protection. He touches you, he answers to me. *Capeesh?*"

I swallowed and nodded.

There was another knock on the door.

"Ah," Nitti said cheerfully. "There's Paul with my father-in-law. Time for my checkup, and your ride home."

Chapter 27

My new client, Governor Hoffman—or to be more exact, the State of New Jersey—wired me enough for a Pullman sleeper compartment, but I bought an upper berth instead and made an extra twenty bucks and change on the deal. It was the Twentieth Century Limited, that fabled fancy streamliner, which would shoot me non-stop overnight to New York, where shortly after an onboard breakfast I'd grab a less sleek train and backtrack to Trenton.

Before retiring, however, I spent some time in the dining car—the prime rib was not as good as the roast beef at the Stockyard's Inn, but the meal was on the State of New Jersey, so what the hell. Later I loitered in the lounge car, which was all chrome and mirrors and diffused lighting and, thankfully, liquor. It would have been nice to run into a beautiful lonely woman traveling alone; but I didn't. I figured a couple Bacardi cocktails would help me get over it, or anyway sleep better; but they didn't.

Even the lulling lurch of the Limited and the soothing blackness of the Pullman berth didn't put me to sleep. My mind was moving faster than the train. Partly it was worry—thinking about

Nitti and Ricca and where I might end up if Ricca deposed Nitti, at some point, like tomorrow.

But mostly I was carried back to a similar trip I'd taken on the taxpayers of New Jersey, not that much over a year before, in January of '35. I'd gone the upper-berth route that time, too—meaning I'd bilked New Jersey a little better than forty bucks on train rides alone. And they paid for a night's lodging—the Union Hotel in Flemington, where the trial was held—plus thirty-five bucks per diem, which added up.

A certain irony was not lost on me. Last year, the State of New Jersey had paid me, generously, to help put Hauptmann in the electric chair. This year, the State of New Jersey was treating me with like generosity to help keep Bruno from sitting down.

And the state had certainly spared no expense in the trial of Bruno Richard Hauptmann, even when it came to shipping in a minor witness like me from Chicago. And why not? It had been one hell of a show—a regular Broadway production, even if it had been mounted in a one-horse town.

Flemington, sixty-some miles from New York, was a roost for chicken-and-egg farmers, a village of less than three thousand Lums and Abners in the rolling hills of Hunterdon County, home of the Lindbergh estate. The little county seat suddenly had a big trial in its lap, and by New Year's Day had become host to sixty thousand "foreigners"—sightseers, reporters, telephone and telegraph technicians, swarming Main Street, clogging the roads all the way back to New York and Philadelphia.

The courthouse was a stately two-and-a-half-story white-washed stucco affair with four big pillars out front and a small, modern jail building in back. In that smaller building resided the illegal alien Bruno Richard Hauptmann. Around Christmas some compassionate locals had sung him carols outside his barred window; lately, tourists had been repeating less cheery chants, among them "Burn the kraut!" and "Kill Hauptmann!"

Hauptmann, arrested in the Bronx, had been extradited to New Jersey because in New York the only crime he could be tried for was extortion: in Jersey, he could be tried for kidnapping and murder. Attorney General David Wilentz, by defining the kidnapping as a "burglary"—hadn't the kidnapper broken and entered, and "stolen" the child away?—could in that convoluted fashion charge Hauptmann with murder. Burglary was a felony, and any killing during the commission of a felony, whether that death was accidental or intentional, was of course murder. Kidnapping could have brought a sentence of as little as five years. Wilentz and the world wanted a death sentence for Hauptmann.

From what I'd read in the papers, Hauptmann probably deserved it, though this "lone-wolf kidnapper" stuff never rang true to me. I said as much to Colonel Henry Breckinridge, who picked me up early that morning at Grand Central Station and with me made the incredibly slow journey (with snow-narrowed roads and impossible traffic, at times three miles an hour) to the Flemington courthouse.

"I can't say I buy that theory, either," Breckinridge said guardedly, studying the bumper of the buggy in front of him like a legal brief he was considering. "But my understanding is, Wilentz hasn't the right sort of evidence to prove a conspiracy, so . . ."

"They're targeting the guy they have," I said, shrugging, "using what evidence they do have. Makes sense. Have you testified yet?"

"No. But I will. It's early yet. This is only the fifth day."

"I saw in the papers that Wilentz put the Lindberghs on the stand, first."

"Yes."

Breckinridge seemed vaguely troubled.

"Must've been hard on Anne," I said.

He nodded gravely. "She stood up well. When the prosecutor handed her the little garments to identify . . . it was a tragic goddamn thing, Heller. Count yourself lucky you didn't have to witness it."

I nodded back noncommittally. "How did Slim do?"

"Fine." He turned his eyes quickly away from the road. "Why do you ask?"

"Just wondering," I said. "I understand he's attending the trial, each day."

"Yes, he is."

"What, is he staying over at Englewood?"

"That's correct. He and Anne both, though she hasn't returned to court, and has sense enough not to."

"Colonel, what's bothering you?"

"Why, nothing."

"What, you don't think it's unfair to the defendant, do you, for a martyred public figure like Lindy to be sitting in court? Where the jury can see him all the time?"

Breckinridge shook his head, no, but it wasn't very convincing. He was Slim's friend, but he was also a fair man, and a lawyer. And I knew, from what I'd read, that other aspects of Slim's performance on the stand might bother Breckinridge, as well.

For one thing, Slim had denied using his political influence to have federal officers "lay off" certain aspects of the case; and for another, he had denied that he ever expressed the opinion that a "gang," as opposed to a single-o like Hauptmann, had kidnapped his son.

These were minor lies, even mere shadings of the truth you might say; no big deal. However . . .

Lindbergh had also, on the stand, without hesitation, positively identified Hauptmann as the man in St. Raymond's Cemetery. Strictly on the basis of recognizing his voice. He had, after all, heard "Cemetery John" shout, "Hey, Doctor!"

The notion that a man could positively identify another man by having heard him say two words, four years before, was thin enough. But I remembered what Slim had said, the very night of the ransom drop, when Elmer Irey asked him in the Morrow apartment in Manhattan, if he could identify Cemetery John by his voice.

"To say I could pick a man out by that voice," he'd said, "I really couldn't."

Yet Breckinridge knew, and I knew, and Slim had to know, that the weight of Lucky Lindy providing "eyewitness identification" (make that ear-witness) would probably be all it would take to slam that German's ass in the chair. This trial, I knew with little doubt, was already over.

Flemington, even choking with outsiders, was a village not without a Currier and Ives charm in this, its winter of fame: white wood-frame cottages with green shutters behind neat wooden fences, modest yards blanketed white, shade trees grayly skeletal, gaily decorated with ice; a modest downtown where the flat rooftops of two- and three-story brick buildings wore white mantles. In the streets, however, the snow had turned black and slushy, and on the sidewalks was hardpacked under thousands of imported trampling feet.

Breckinridge dropped me off, as his car crawled along Main Street, leaving me while he went off to some distant designated parking area. I waded through the humanity (make that "humanity") where gawkers mingled with souvenir salesmen on the courthouse steps. Some pretty classy merchandise was being hawked— miniature kidnap ladders, ten cents each, in several sizes (one nifty little number you could pin on your shirt or lapel), autographed photos of Charles and Anne Lindbergh with shaky, suspicious signatures, and little bagged clumps of the late baby's hair, sold by a salesman who seemed to be prematurely balding in odd, patchy ways.

Newsreel cameramen, perched with their spidery contraptions atop cars, were churning at me; reporters attacked me like bees, some with notepads, others with microphones, asking me if I was anybody. I told them I wasn't and pressed my way inside. I showed my color-coded pass to one of several New Jersey troopers at the door, hung up my topcoat and took my hat with me up the winding stairs. I came into a big, square, high-ceilinged courtroom, with pale yellow walls and a lot of humidity-misted windows; at right was the jury box, an American flag pinned to the wall behind it, and between the judge's bench and the jury was a simple wooden chair for witnesses. Behind the judge's bench, high up, beneath Grecian trim, was the county seal, depicting a stalk of golden corn.

Right now this spartan chamber was as noisy as a stadium before the big game. Hundreds of spectators were seated in churchlike pews and several hundred more were squeezed in on folding chairs, while the rear balcony was crammed with reporters, perhaps a hundred and fifty of the fifth estate's finest, working at cramped, makeshift pine-board writing desks.

Among the spectators were celebrities: Clifton Webb, Jack Benny, Lyne Fontanne, and fat, effete Alexander Woollcott, who seemed svelte compared to rumpled, mustached Elsa Maxwell, that pear-shaped matron of café society, leading a pack of ladies in mink, bringing to mind that the mink is a member of the weasel family and that the female of that species is particularly bloodthirsty.

The crowded press box included familiar names and faces, as well: Walter Winchell, who in his syndicated column had long ago pronounced Hauptmann guilty; novelist Fannie Hurst; columnist Arthur Brisbane, who had given Capone so much publicity in the early days of the case; Damon Runyon; Adela Rogers St. John; and on and on. . . .

I took all this in as another New Jersey State cop, acting as an usher, led me to a seat behind the prosecution's bench; a small piece of paper was taped to the empty folding chair, saying HELLER. Next to my folding chair, in another, sat Slim Lindbergh. His baby face had aged, but he still looked boyish; he was dressed in a neat gray three-piece suit—without a ladder pinned to the lapel.

I nodded to him and smiled a little and he returned the nod and the smile; he didn't stand, but as I sat, he offered a hand, which I shook.

"Good to see you again, Nate," he said, over the din. "Sorry I've been such a stranger."

"Hi, Slim. Why are you putting yourself through this? You've testified."

"I have to be here," he said solemnly.

He nodded toward the prosecution's table; whether by that he meant they'd requested his presence, I couldn't say.

David Wilentz, the Attorney General, who had decided to try this case himself—because of political aspirations, the cynical said, myself among them—turned to greet me with a Cheshire-cat smile and an outstretched hand. His grip was fist-firm and his dark, smart eyes locked onto me the same way.

"Mr. Heller," he said, "thank you for coming. Sorry we haven't had a chance to talk."

"Glad to help," I said, as he released my hand.

He was a small, dark, thin-faced man with a long, thin, sharp nose and glossy, slicked-back black hair; about forty, he looked a little like George Raft, only more intelligent and shiftier. He wore a dark-blue business suit, expensively tailored, with a slash of silk handkerchief in the breast pocket. This was a guy who would never go hungry.

"Just stick to the facts," he said. "Don't offer anything."

I nodded. I'd spoken on the telephone, long-distance, to a prosecutor named Hauck, so they knew what to expect. Wilentz turned his back to me and began whispering among his fellow prosecutors.

From my seat I could see the defense table pretty well, and the person who commanded the most attention was the chief defense attorney, Edward J. Reilly. Decked out in black cutaway coat with a white carnation in its buttonhole, gray striped trousers and spats, the massive, fleshy attorney cut an unintentionally comic figure; in his mind he was Adolph Menjou, but in reality he was W. C. Fields, right down to the thinning sandy hair and alcohol-ruddy complexion. His round, thick-lensed, black-rimmed glasses gave him a further vaudeville touch.

In the papers, Reilly was reported as having two nicknames: the "Bull of Brooklyn," in reference to his younger days, when he was one of New York's most successful trial attorneys; and, more recently, "Death House" Reilly, because that was where clients of his charged with murder had been consistently ending up lately. Fifty-two (looking twenty years older), Reilly was well past his prime, and I wondered how the defendant got stuck with him.

Directly behind Reilly sat his client. Bruno Richard Hauptmann was surprisingly nondescript, a skinny, wide-shouldered man in a gray-brown suit that looked big for him. His eyes were light blue, and blank; he seemed to rarely blink, rarely to move, sitting erect and staring, not so much morose as indifferent. His hair was blond, his cheekbones high and wide, his cheeks sunken, his face an oval, his features rather handsome, and decidedly Teutonic.

The other defense lawyers (and it was only later that I learned their names) included stocky young C. Lloyd Fisher, who had (unsuccessfully) defended Commodore Curtis in this very courtroom; bespectacled, shrimpy Frederick Pope; and beak-nosed, slouchy Egbert Rosecrans. Dapper Prosecutor Wilentz and his businesslike associates were a sharper-looking bunch by far.

Bells echoing in the tower above rang the hour—ten o'clock— and the white-haired court crier announced, "Oyez, oyez, oyez! All manner of persons having business with this court on this eighth day of January in the Year of Our Lord One Thousand Nine Hundred and Thirty-five, let them draw nigh, give their attention and be heard."

The judge—Justice Thomas Whitaker Trenchard—emerged from a door behind his dais, black robes flowing; his dark hair gone mostly white, his small mustache too, he had a dignified but just vaguely unkempt demeanor, like a harried country doctor.

Soon a parade of witnesses began, police witnesses initially, and it wasn't particularly riveting stuff. Elsa Maxwell and her minks chatted amongst themselves, and occasionally the judge would sternly remind the courtroom to mind its manners.

Wilentz was smooth as a polished stone, but Reilly—who was trying to make the New Jersey police look like buffoons, which shouldn't have been that tough—was a ham actor, bouncing his voice off the rafters.

The red-flannel-faced defender did score a few points: he got a fingerprint man to admit never having even heard of the Bertillon system, and got across the ludicrously shoddy police work of the initial investigation by getting two cops to say each thought the *other* was going to take a plaster cast of the footprint beneath the child's window.

Then Wilentz got away from the police witnesses and put a frail, bearded, eighty-seven-year-old codger named Amandus Hochmuth on the stand. Hochmuth, who lived on the corner of Mercer County Highway and Featherbed Lane, claimed he'd seen Hauptmann driving a "dirty green" car on the morning of March 1, 1932. He remembered this because Hauptmann had "glared" at him.

"And the man you saw looking out of that automobile, glaring at you," Wilentz said, "is he in this room?"

"Yes!"

"Where is he?"

"Alongside that trooper there," Hochmuth said, and as he pointed a wavering finger at Hauptmann, the courtroom lights went out.

"It's the Lord's wrath over a lying witness!" Reilly shouted in the near-darkness.

The courtroom exploded in laughter. Slim didn't smile next to me, and I didn't either, because Reilly's style bored me; and Judge Trenchard rapped his gavel and threatened the gallery again.

The lights came up within a couple minutes, and Wilentz directed Hochmuth to step down and identify the man he'd seen, and, slow, wobbly, the witness did so, pointing a trembling finger at Hauptmann, and then actually placing a hand on Hauptmann's knee, fearfully, as if he might get burned.

The defendant shook his head three times and with a bitter smile said to the woman behind him (his wife Anna, I wondered?): *"Der Alte ist verruckt."*

Next to me, Slim said softly, "What was that?"

I whispered back: "He said, 'The old man is crazy.' "

Then florid defender Reilly had a crack at the old man, and did get him to confess his eyes weren't perfect, but otherwise couldn't budge the old boy.

Next came several witnesses, including a Forest Service technologist, who Wilentz attempted to use to introduce evidence about the kidnap ladder. But Reilly and his associate Pope managed to block it; the ladder had been "altered" and passed between various "hands of people not identified by the prosecution."

Following this came a familiar face, though I confess I didn't recognize him at first. The ferret-faced cab driver, Perrone, who had delivered the envelope to Jafsie's house the night of the first cemetery rendezvous, made an eyewitness ID of Hauptmann as the man who gave him the envelope. He got off the stand and placed a hand on Hauptmann's shoulder and said, "This is the man."

Hauptmann curled a lip and said, "You're a liar."

Reilly went after Perrone with a sledgehammer. He bullied the cab driver about being on relief; tested his memory about other passengers he'd had the same night; implied he'd been bought and coached by the prosecution. The tactic backfired: the courtroom hated Reilly by the time the badgering was over.

Then it was my turn. I was questioned by Wilentz about driving Condon to Woodlawn Cemetery for the first of the two "Cemetery John" encounters. I told of what I'd seen, which included the guy jumping off the cemetery gate and running into Van

Cortlandt Park, Condon following him to a bench by the shack where they sat and talked. Told all of it.

Almost all of it. There was one question, a rather key question, I wasn't asked by the slick Wilentz.

"Buy you lunch, Nate?" Slim asked, and I said sure, as we exited the courtroom for the noon break; we both had to damn near shout, because the courtroom was still buzzing.

"Union Hotel dining room okay?" Lindy asked, breath smoking in the chill air, as we pushed through a crowd that was cheering and clapping at the sight of the Lone Eagle; newsreel cameras churned and reporters called out questions—none of it registering on Slim, who carried around with him his own quiet at the center of the storm.

"Hotel dining room's swell," I said. "Where is it?"

"Right there," he said, nodding across the way. "That's where you're staying."

We moved through the car-choked street; onlookers called out to Lindy who at times bestowed them a tight glazed smile and very occasionally a nod. He seemed oblivious to the grisly goods being hawked, the little ladders and such; but he couldn't have been.

The Union Hotel was a lumbering redbrick affair with ugly gingerbread work detailing a sprawling porch over which lurked double-deck balconies. Out front a chalk sandwich board listed the fare in the dining room: Lamp Chops Jafsie, Baked Beans Wilentz, Lindbergh Sundaes, among others.

The dining room was bustling, but a few tables were reserved for celebrities like Slim and the prosecution and defense teams. Colonel Breckinridge, who hadn't made it into the courtroom, was waiting for us at an isolated table off to one side.

As we sat down, Breckinridge asked Lindbergh how the trial was going today, and he said, "Fine."

I said, "Reilly strikes me as the prosecution's biggest asset."

"How so?" Breckinridge asked.

"Well, that swallowtail coat and spats getup isn't exactly endearing him to that down-home jury. Or his loud, bullying style. He's about as subtle as John Barrymore half-in-the-bag."

A waiter handed us menus and Lindbergh examined his with

unblinking eyes, his expression not unlike the one the defendant had been wearing in court.

The middle-aged, potbellied waiter, though busy, stood attentively by while we read the menu and ordered at leisure; Lindbergh wasn't just any customer, after all.

"What are the 'Hauptmann Fries'?" I asked him.

"German fried potatoes," he said blandly.

Lindbergh ordered vegetable soup and a hard roll; Breckinridge had the Lamb Chops Jafsie; and I had the Gow Goulash (named for Betty, the nurse, who'd come from Scotland to testify a few days before).

While we waited for our lunches, I said, "I notice Wilentz didn't ask me about that suspicious guy I saw walk by Jafsie and me, at the cemetery."

"Oh?" Breckinridge said.

Lindy said nothing.

"Must not fit his no-conspiracy thesis," I said. "Slim, did he ask you about the guy *you* saw?"

"What guy?" Slim asked.

"The guy you saw on *your* cemetery jaunt. Could've been the same guy I saw on mine."

Lindbergh shrugged.

"Come on, Slim—it probably *was* the guy I saw. Walked by with a stoop, covering his face with a hanky, swarthy fella?"

"Just some bystander," he said.

"Oh, it's just a coincidence, we both saw, on our two separate trips, at our two separate cemeteries, a stooped-over wop covering his face with a hanky, while he walked by checking us out? Slim. Please."

Lindbergh said, rather tightly, "Let Wilentz do his job."

I sat forward; silverware clinked. "Why didn't Wilentz ask me anything about my *real* role in the case? There was nothing about Capone, or Marinelli and Sivella mentioning the name 'Jafsie' *before* Condon was on the scene, or Curtis or Means or . . ."

"That is not," he said crisply, "the focus of this trial. Let it go."

"Let it go? Maybe *Reilly* won't let it go, Slim."

His mouth twitched irritably. "Just use common sense on the stand, Nate. All right?"

"Common sense?"

Our food arrived; I waited till everybody was served and the waiter was gone. The Gow Goulash looked tomatoey and was steaming hot and smelled good.

"Common sense," I repeated. "You mean, lie on the stand?"

Lindbergh glared at me, but said nothing.

Breckinridge said, "No one is suggesting that, Heller, certainly."

I took a bite of the goulash; it tasted as good as it looked. Damn near as good as Betty Gow looked, for that matter.

"You know, gents," I said reflectively, "I'm from Chicago, and in many respects I'm your typical low-life greedy Chicago cop. Of course I'm private now, and part of why I left the department is that some people assumed I was for sale at any price. I'm not."

"No one is suggesting . . ." Breckinridge began, nervously.

"There's a lot of things I'll do for money, or even just the hell of it. But I make it a point not to lie on witness stands."

Lindbergh was looking at his soup as he spooned it; eating quickly, for him.

"You remember that gun I loaned you, Slim? The one you took to the cemetery that night?"

He nodded, but he didn't look at me.

"I lied on the witness stand, once. The cops and the mob had a patsy picked out. It was even okay with the patsy—he was in on the fix. I didn't see the harm of going along with it. So I lied on the witness stand."

Lindbergh touched his lips with a napkin.

"It got me ahead," I said, shrugging. "It's how I got to be the youngest plainclothes officer on the goddamn Chicago police. But it rubbed my father the wrong way. Old union guy that he was. Stuffy about things like that, like telling the truth under oath. Funny—he didn't even believe in God, yet if they put him under oath, he couldn't have told anything but the truth. Anyway. That gun I loaned you, he killed himself with it. My gun. Since then, I've been fussy about what I say on witness stands."

Slim said, "I'm sorry about your father."

"That wasn't my point."

"I know what your point is. I don't appreciate being called a liar."

"Is that what I did?"

He looked at me hard; sighed. "Nate, this man is guilty."

"I heard you say you couldn't identify 'Cemetery John' by his voice. You told the same thing to a Bronx grand jury, not so long ago. What changed?"

He gestured with a pointing finger. "I have been assured by the top police officials in this case that there is *no* doubt about Hauptmann's guilt. I have heard this from Schwarzkopf, from Frank J. Wilson, from Lt. Finn, from . . ." He shook his head, as if clearing cobwebs. "If you were able to sit in that courtroom every day, as I have, and as I *will*, you'd find that out."

"Slim, I was a cop. I am a cop. And I can tell you one thing about cops: once a cop decides a guy is guilty, that guy is guilty. And a cop will, at that juncture, get real inventive. More tampered-with and manufactured evidence, and coached and purchased witness testimony, has been presented in American courtrooms than any other kind. Trust me."

"I wish *you* would, Nate."

"What?"

"Trust me."

"Well." I smiled; dabbed my own face with a napkin. "I will let you buy me lunch. I'm not that proud."

We smiled at each other, warily, Slim and I, but Breckinridge was disturbed by all this.

After lunch I was called back on the stand and Reilly had at me. I thought, for a moment, he was getting to the heart of it.

He was asking me, in his high-handed ham-actor fashion, about the night we prepared the replica ballot box of ransom money for Jafsie and Slim to deliver to Cemetery John.

"Didn't you think it would be a good idea to go along and *capture* that person?"

"Yes," I said.

"Did the Police Department of the city of New York, and the

Department of Justice, *know* there was going to be a ransom payment that night?"

"I believe so. At least, the Treasury Department did."

"Did they know *where* the payment would be made?"

"No. Nobody knew that. Colonel Lindbergh and Professor Condon didn't know, until they got to the florist's shop, as the note directed them."

"You're referring to the note delivered by the taxicab driver?"

"Yes."

"Were the police notified, at that time? That the note had arrived, and that Dr. Condon and Colonel Lindbergh were off to make their payment?"

"No."

"Why not?"

"I don't know."

"You don't know? Mr. Heller, weren't you at the time a police officer yourself?"

"Yes. But with the Chicago Police. Just a liaison, an adviser, on this case."

"And you don't know why the New York Police, or the Justice or Treasury Departments, were not notified that the ransom payment was about to be made?"

"No, sir, I don't. I wasn't one of the big chiefs in this. I was just a dot on the 'i.' "

That got a laugh; both Lindbergh and Hauptmann smiled, strangely enough, though Judge Trenchard didn't. He rapped his gavel, demanded order, threatening to clear the courtroom.

"Mr. Heller," Reilly said, a hand on his ample side, "as a police officer, did you make any effort to follow and protect Dr. Condon and the Colonel, that night?"

"No."

Reilly smiled and looked tellingly at the jury. He'd made a point, however vaguely; but then he dismissed me!

I shuffled off to my chair, next to Lindbergh, who patted my arm supportively. My head was reeling. Shit, Reilly didn't ask me about the stooped swarthy hanky-over-the-face guy I saw; or the Capone connection; or the spiritualists; or Means or Curtis or fucking *anything*. Some of it he may just not have known. But a good deal of it had gotten into police reports and the press, in the aftermath of the ransom scam and the Means and Curtis hoaxes.

The next witness was called: "Dr. John F. Condon."

The great man had apparently just arrived, as he made a grand entrance from the back of the room.

Old Jafsie walked slowly, solemnly, to the witness chair, a tall, paunchy figure in circuit-preacher black with a crisp white hanky in a breast pocket and an old-fashioned gold watch chain draped across his breast.

Wilentz asked the witness for his age and place of residence, and Jafsie answered in a tremulous, yet booming voice, "I am seventy-four years of age, and a resident of the most beautiful borough in the world, the Bronx."

I groaned, and Lindbergh flashed me a sideways glance.

Wilentz asked for more background, and Jafsie began a yawn-inducing tale of the story of his life; I was just dropping off to sleep, when Wilentz asked him how he and Colonel Lindbergh happened to meet a man at St. Raymond's Cemetery on the night of April 2, 1932.

"And didn't you have with you," Wilentz pressed on, "a box of money?"

"Yes, sir."

"Did you give that money in a box to someone that night?"

"I did, sir."

"Who did you give that money to?"

"John."

Wilentz turned significantly to the jury. "And who is John?"

Condon turned slightly in his chair to look toward the defendant. He pointed a finger like a gun at Hauptmann and said, so loud his voice rang in the room, "John is *Bru*-no . . . *Rich*-ard . . . *Haupt*-mann!"

The court was up for grabs, the woman I took to be Mrs. Hauptmann looking at her husband with grave concern, Hauptmann himself looking stunned, defense counsel Fisher gripping Hauptmann's shoulder supportively, the gallery gasping and then jabbering, chairs scooting as news messengers scurried out.

I got up, too.

Lindbergh touched my arm and said, "Nate? You all right?"

"I've heard enough, Slim," I said, not unkindly, and went out.

That night, in the Union Hotel, I sat and drank and watched chief defense attorney Reilly laugh it up with reporters, a bosomy blonde "secretary" on either arm, drinking his red face redder. The next morning Breckinridge drove me back to Grand Central Station, where I caught the Limited. Breckinridge and I hadn't spoken much on the ride. A little small talk; the weather had turned foggy and wet—we talked about that.

At one point he did say, "Don't judge Slim too harshly."

It was a reasonable request, and I nodded, but I remember wondering if anybody on earth, besides Hauptmann's wife Anna, would grant the accused that same simple plea.

Now, over a year later, riding the Limited east once again, snug in my upper berth, I wondered if maybe, finally, somebody had.

Chapter 28

The Statehouse in Trenton, on this cold, rainy March morning (and on any other), was an ungainly affair squatting on a stretch of landscape between State Street and the Delaware River. The three-and-a-half-story wedding-cake structure seemed designed to confirm the rest of the nation's suspicions that New Jersey was innately second-rate; entry was via a ponderous two-tier porch supported by midget granite columns.

I stalked the main corridor, shaking rain off my hat, my trench-coat leaving a damp trail. As I walked I glanced at the stern faded portraits of early New Jersey patriots and statesmen, and got dirty looks in return. I moved through the cramped rotunda, festively decorated by musty, faded regimental flags from the Civil War, and found my way to the upper two floors, a gloomy maze where bureaucrats wandered aimlessly.

Somehow I managed to find the executive offices, where a male secretary took my coat and hat and showed me in to see Governor Hoffman.

The governor was on the phone, but he smiled broadly and

gestured me to an overstuffed chair opposite his massive mahogany desk, which was stacked with documents and manila folders. He was a stocky, cheerful-looking man of perhaps forty, with a round, handsome face; his blue suit and blue-and-gray tie looked crisp and neat, and so did he.

Hoffman was the youngest governor in the states, and had been sworn into office the day the Hauptmann trial began; a career politician, he was a Republican who won in a year of Democratic landslide.

"I'm glad you've arrived safely," he was saying, not to me, smiling at the phone. "Come right over. Yes, he's just arrived."

The office was a sumptuous, dark-wood chamber with an enormous oriental carpet, and a fireplace in which flames were quietly licking logs. A big, warm room, slightly cooled by formal, forbidding oil portraits of unknown past Jersey dignitaries, it nonetheless had the unlived-in, transitory feeling of the elective official's office. The huge, yellow globe near the desk seemed never to have been spun; the leather-bound books shelved behind the governor seemed never to have been cracked open; the flags—American at left, state at right—slumped on poles, never to be unfurled. The wooden filing cabinet, about ten feet away, seemed there only to provide a resting place for a silver loving cup of flowers.

"That was an old friend of yours," the governor said with a smile, as he hung up, offering no further explanation. He stood and extended his hand, and I stood and extended mine; our grips were suitably masculine and firm. We sat back down.

"I'm delighted you've come, Mr. Heller," he said, leaning back in his chair. "You're just the man for this job."

"What job is that, exactly?"

He twitched a smile, eyes twinkling; there was an endearing pixielike quality about him, a streak of unexpected mischief.

Then his expression turned solemn. "Mr. Heller, I've employed several other private detectives, and we've come up with a good deal of evidence . . . unfortunately, none of it compelling enough to get Richard Hauptmann a new trial. Nor am I in a position to grant him a pardon, or commute his sentence to a prison term."

"Oh?"

He shook his head. "I'm only one member of the Court of Pardons. In New Jersey the governor has no authority to commute a capital sentence. And I can't issue another reprieve unless you come up with something so startling that my Democratic Attorney General can't ignore it."

"Wilentz, you mean."

"That's right. We're old school pals, Dave and me. You met him, didn't you?"

"Briefly. I saw him in action at the trial. I was only there one day, but it was an eyeful. Slick operator."

He nodded, reaching for a humidor on his desk. "He is, at that. Care for a cigar?"

"No thanks."

He lit his up; a big fine fat Havana. "Funny thing is, Dave is anti-capital punishment. Me, I have no compunction about showing a murderer the door to hell."

Yes, I was back in the Lindbergh Case, aboard the Melodrama Express.

"Why," I asked, "does the State of New Jersey need private investigators?"

"I'm surprised you'd ask that, Mr. Heller, considering that once upon a time you had considerable contact with our State Police, specifically Colonel Norman Schwarzkopf."

I shrugged, nodded.

He narrowed his eyes, staring at me forcefully. "You see, I went to the death house, Mr. Heller, to see Bruno Richard Hauptmann . . . I'd heard he wished an 'audience' with me, and, rather on the sly, I granted him one, thinking, I admit, that I might hear a confession. Instead, I heard a quietly indignant man, a man of considerable dignity and intelligence, who raised a good number of questions that I had to agree needed answering."

"Ah," I said, smiling, suddenly making a connection. "So you went to the head of the State Police to find out the answers to those questions."

"Precisely. And our mutual friend Colonel Schwarzkopf ignored my executive order to reopen the investigation, sending me monthly, token notes to the effect that there were no new developments. When I granted Hauptmann the thirty-day reprieve, I began hiring my own investigators, and essentially 'fired' Schwarz-kopf from the Lindbergh case. There is, as you might imagine, no love lost between us."

"Was Hauptmann himself the reason you got involved in this?" I asked, knowing the governor had been accused of playing politics. "Was he that convincing a jailhouse lawyer?"

"He was convincing, all right. But there were other factors. I believe you've met New Jersey's answer to Sherlock Holmes—Ellis Parker?"

I nodded. "At Lindbergh's estate, in the early days."

"Parker's been conducting his own investigation," Hoffman said, "although I haven't been privy to any results as yet. He's one of the people I want you to look up, in fact; he's playing his cards a little too close to his vest, for my money."

"The old boy's a showboat," I said. "But don't be fooled by the hick veneer."

"Oh, I'm not. And I take his opinion quite seriously. He thinks Hauptmann is innocent, or at least no more than a minor figure, who is taking the fall for the real kidnappers."

"Have you considered the possibility that the 'Cemetery John' extortion group may never have had the child?"

He nodded vigorously, exhaling smoke, gesturing with the cigar. "Yes, and consider this, Mr. Heller—Ellis Parker insists that the baby found in that shallow grave in the Sourlands woods was *not* Charles Lindbergh, Jr."

"Well, I understand Slim Lindbergh's identification of the body *was* pretty perfunctory."

"Perfunctory! Are you aware that the body was examined, in the morgue, by . . . let me find it." He shuffled through some of the many documents and folders on his desk; quickly centered on the correct one and read, with rather a triumphant flourish, "The child's own pediatrician, Dr. Phillip Van Ingen, examined the re-mains. The undertaker reported Dr. Van Ingen as saying, and this is a quote: 'If you were to lay ten million dollars on a table and tell me it was mine, if I could say positively that this was the Colonel's son, I couldn't honestly identify this skeleton.' "

"Skeleton? I knew the body was decayed, but I understood the facial features were intact. . . ."

"Haven't you ever *seen* what the 'body' looked like?"

I shook my head, no.

He plucked a glossy photo from a folder. "They couldn't even verify the sex," he said, and handed the photo to me.

"Jesus," I said.

It was just a tiny black pile of bones; you could make out a skull, more or less, and a rib or two; the left leg was missing.

My mouth felt suddenly dry. "I heard that the child was identified by its toes overlapping in some distinctive way . . ."

"Well, there's only one foot there to check at all," Hoffman said. "But Dr. Van Ingen's examination of the child, on February eighteenth, ten days before the kidnapping, reported both its little toes were turned in, overlapping the next toe. The corpse, what there was of it, had overlapping toes as well—but it was the *large* toe, overlapping the second toe."

"It's hard to tell even that," I said, and handed the damn photo back to him.

"One fact is indisputable—the physician at the mortuary measured the body and found it to be thirty-three and one-third inches long. Van Ingen's measurement on February eighteenth was twenty-nine inches."

"Some of that could be attributed to growth of bones after death," I said, thinking it through. "But hell—not four and a half inches. . . ."

"Of course this all points up one of the major blunders of the trial," Hoffman said.

I nodded. "You mean, Hauptmann's defense counsel stipulating that the corpse found at Mt. Rose was Charles Lindbergh, Jr."

It had gotten a lot of play in the press. Wilentz had been questioning the woman in charge of St. Michael's Orphanage, located less than a mile from where the little corpse had been found; Wilentz wanted to dispute the notion that the body in the woods might have been one of the orphanage's charges.

But Reilly interrupted the proceedings almost immediately, saying, "We have never made any claim that this was other than Colonel Lindbergh's child."

Even the prosecution was stunned by this preposterous bungle.

There was no logical reason for Reilly to have handed Wilentz the *corpus delicti* on a silver platter like that. Reportedly, cocounsel Fisher—long Hauptmann's most staunch supporter—had stood up, shouted to Reilly, "You're conceding our client to the electric chair," and bolted out.

"Who the hell hired Reilly, anyway?" I asked.

"Hearst." The Governor said this with a quiet, ironic smile.

"Hearst! Good God, the Hearst papers crucified Hauptmann! Hearst is an old Lindbergh crony, for Christ's sake . . ."

"Well," Hoffman said, with a small shrug, playing devil's advocate, "Reilly was, at one time, a top trial attorney. You know, he got a lot of the big prohibition gangsters off, in his day."

I sat up. "Oh, really. Like who?"

Hoffman shrugged. "One of his more notorious clients, I suppose, was Frankie Yale."

Until his demise in 1927, Frankie Yale had been Al Capone's man on the East Coat. Capone had, in '27, bumped Yale and replaced him with one Paul Ricca.

Could Reilly have been in Capone's pocket? Had the red-nosed shyster thrown the case?

"You know, Mr. Heller," Hoffman said, "there are those in this state who believe I've gotten into this thing for my own glory, my own gain . . . considering the fact that I'm receiving death threats, that my home and my wife and three little girls are under twenty-four-hour guard accordingly, and that the press is demanding my impeachment, I doubt I've made a 'good political move,' in 'siding with' Hauptmann."

"What *are* you after, Governor?"

His cheerful mask collapsed. "Look—all I'm after is the truth. The people of this state are entitled to it, and Hauptmann has a right to live if he didn't murder the Lindbergh baby. This was a shocking crime—and, in the interest of society, it *must* be completely solved."

"You've let this thing get to you, Governor. You've let it touch you. That's dangerous."

With a thumb over his shoulder, he gestured at the state flag. "Mr. Heller, as Governor of this state, I have a *duty* to perform."

"No politician ever got rich doing his duty."

He flinched at that; it was barely perceptible, but it was there. He said, "I haven't expressed an opinion on the guilt or innocence of Hauptmann. But I share, with hundreds of thousands of people, doubts about the value of the evidence that placed him in the Lindbergh nursery the night of the crime."

"I'm not all that familiar with the evidence."

"Well, I'm going to make you familiar with it. But you are familiar with the role that passion and prejudice played in convicting a man that the newspapers had already convicted." He patted the folders on his desk. "I doubt the truthfulness, and the competency, of some of the state's chief witnesses. And I doubt that this crime could have been committed by *any* one man. Schwarzkopf and the rest, maybe even Charles Lindbergh himself, want this one man's death so that the books can be closed, and the pretense can be made that another great crime has been successfully solved."

I merely nodded.

He smiled, embarrassed, suddenly. "I guess I'm too much of a politician to resist climbing up on a soapbox—even when I'm sitting down. Let me fill you in on these 'witnesses.'. . ."

Turning to his folders and documents and some notes, Hoffman went down the motley group one by one.

"Let's start with the remarkable Mr. Amandus Hochmuth," Hoffman said, and I of course recognized that as the name of the Sourlands geezer who claimed Hauptmann had "glared" at him from a car the day of the kidnapping. "First of all, Hochmuth waited until two months after Hauptmann's arrest to come forward. Second of all, a friendly state trooper sent me a report of an interview conducted with Hochmuth shortly after the kidnapping, when Hochmuth said he'd seen nobody suspicious in the vicinity. Here. . . ."

"What's this?" I asked, as the governor handed across a document.

"A photostat of Hochmuth's 1932 welfare report," Hoffman said. "Look at the line on 'health status.' "

" 'Partly blind,' " I read. " 'Failing eyesight due to cataracts.' He puts the eye in eyewitness, all right." The photostat revealed him also to be Client #14106 in the Division of Old Age Security,

Department of Welfare, New York City. "This thing gives his address as the Bronx!"

"A false address," Hoffman said matter-of-factly, "so he could collect public funds from New York, while living in New Jersey."

"Well, times are hard."

"I invited Mr. Hochmuth up to my office, not long ago and, because it was at my expense I'm sure, he accommodated me. He sat where you're sitting, Mr. Heller." Hoffman pointed to the filing cabinet with the silver cup brimming with flowers. "I asked him to identify that."

"Did he?"

"Certainly. He identified it as a picture—a picture of a woman."

I laughed.

"Because of reactions similar to yours, from myself, an aide and a criminologist present," Hoffman said, "Mr. Hochmuth realized he'd guessed wrong. So he tried again—and identified that eighteen-inch-tall silver cup, filled with flowers, as a woman's hat."

"He never did get it right?"

"His third try was closest: a bowl of fruit."

"Well, law of averages. At least it didn't glare at him."

He sorted some more. "And now we come to Millard Whited, a Sourlands hillbilly who claimed he saw Hauptmann prowling near the Lindbergh estate. Mr. Whited, it seems, is on the one hand impoverished, and on the other, a liar; so say his neighbors, at any rate."

"Wasn't it Whited's testimony that got Hauptmann extradited from New York to here?"

Hoffman nodded. "Whited was brought to the Bronx courthouse to make an eyewitness identification, which he did. But I have in my possession . . ." He patted the stack of documents before him. ". . . statements Whited gave the State Police within two months of the crime that he hadn't seen any suspicious persons in the vicinity of the Lindbergh estate. So I invited Mr. Whited—at my expense—for a visit."

"Did he think your loving cup was a hat?"

"No. But he did admit he'd received a one-hundred-fifty-dollar fee, thirty-five dollars' expenses per diem and a promise of a share of the reward money. Particularly interesting, considering on the witness stand at Flemington, he denied receiving anything but dinner money."

"That thirty-five bucks per diem jibes with what I got paid for coming out." Apparently I wasn't important enough to get a fee, though.

"The other eyewitnesses are similarly suspect. The cab driver, Perrone, it turns out positively identified several *other* suspects as 'John,' before Hauptmann's arrest. The traveling salesman, Rossiter, who claimed he saw Hauptmann changing a tire near Princeton, three days before the kidnapping, is a known embezzler and thief. The movie-theater cashier, Mrs. Barr, sold tickets to over fifteen hundred people on the night of November twenty-sixth, 1933, but could pick Hauptmann out, a year later, as a man who gave her a folded five-dollar bill that turned out to be one of the ransom bills. Never mind that November twenty-sixth is Hauptmann's birthday, and that on that night he and his wife and friends were at home celebrating."

"Quite an array, these witnesses."

"Yes, but we mustn't forget the celebrity. The man who made a positive eyewitness identification of Hauptmann based upon two words he heard spoken a block away—four years before."

Charles A. Lindbergh.

"And then of course," he continued, flicking cigar ash into a silver ashtray, "there's Jafsie. That wonderful American—who when I reopened this investigation, and announced that I wanted to question him, promptly left on an extended vacation to Panama."

I had to laugh. "Is he still gone?"

"Actually, he's supposed to have returned today. And he is one of the people I want you to go around and question."

"All right, but only because you're paying me. Last I heard, old Jafsie was hitting the vaudeville circuit, with a Lindbergh lecture."

"Well," Hoffman said, "I can tell you one thing he didn't lecture about: the period when he was the chief *suspect* in the case. I have an affidavit declaring that after Condon initially failed to identify Hauptmann as John at the Greenwich Street Police Station in the Bronx . . . and he was *adamant* about not identifying Hauptmann, there . . . Jafsie was intimidated and threatened by the police."

"I'd be surprised if he wasn't."

"That was New York. Two Jersey state troopers have indicated to me that Condon was threatened by Schwarzkopf and his bullyboy Welch with an indictment for obstructing justice . . . which is what they got Commodore Curtis on, you may recall . . . if the old boy didn't recant and identify Hauptmann as 'Cemetery John.' "

"No wonder Jafsie changed his tune."

"He was quoted by a trooper as saying, 'I would not like to be indicted in New Jersey, for they would choke you for a cherry in New Jersey.' "

I laughed at that. "One of Jafsie's few intentionally humorous remarks," I said. "Sure, I'll talk to him. Who else do you want me to see?"

"Well, among others, check in with Gaston Means."

"Means! Isn't he in Leavenworth?"

"That's his official federal residence. Right now he's under observation at St. Elizabeth's in Washington, D.C. For what he himself refers to as 'high brain blood pressure.' At the same time, he's been bombarding my office with confessions; claims he's the one who engineered the kidnapping."

I sighed. "It's a waste of time, but I'll talk to him."

"I know. But these hoaxers all seem to have some element of truth, or near-truth, in their stories."

"That's how a good con is mounted, Governor. So let me guess the next name on your list: Commodore John Hughes Curtis."

"Not necessarily next, but yes, do check in with him. You do realize, Mr. Heller, that the State of New Jersey convicted Curtis on an obstructing-justice charge, on the assumption he'd had contact with the actual kidnap gang?"

"He got off with a fine and a suspended sentence, didn't he?"

"Yes, but my point is, in the same courtroom as the Hauptmann trial, one of the same prosecutors, and the same judge, convicted Curtis—why? Because, they said, he'd dealt with six persons who had kidnapped the Lindbergh baby; that by not letting the state troopers in on his actions, Curtis had prevented the apprehension of the kidnappers."

"So the Garden State is having it both ways: a kidnap gang, to convict Curtis; a lone-wolf kidnapper, to convict Hauptmann."

"Exactly. And it doesn't wash with me. There's more, there's so much more. . . ." He went riffling through the papers; he began rattling off the injustices.

A copy of a physical examination by Dr. Thurston H. Dexter on September 25, 1934, a few days after Hauptmann's arrest, showed that the prisoner had been "subjected recently to a severe beating, all or mostly with blunt instruments."

Work records at the Majestic Apartments, where Hauptmann claimed he was working during the period of the kidnapping, had been tampered with and in some cases stolen or suppressed.

A statement from fingerprint expert Erasmus Hudson, who found five-hundred-some prints on the kidnap ladder, none of them Hauptmann's, and said that Inspector Welch had asked him if it were possible to fake a fingerprint. (Hudson had said no, much to Welch's obvious disappointment.)

Judge Trenchard denying Hauptmann's request for a lie-detector test.

And there was new evidence, too: handwriting expert Samuel Small demonstrated that Hauptmann wrote in the Palmer-Zaner system and not the vertical roundhand system of the ransom notes. In his affidavit, Small wrote: "It isn't a question of *if* Hauptmann wrote those letters. It is a question whether he *could* have written them. I tell you that if you went to the prison and said to Hauptmann, 'I will let you free if you can write a single sentence the way it is written in the ransom letters,' Hauptmann would have to stay in prison the rest of his life."

Of course, I knew—like just about any cop who'd been in and around the court system in major criminal cases—that handwriting experts, like alienists, were typical, "expert" testimony. Both sides had theirs. Bought and paid.

"You realize, don't you," Hoffman said, "that the state spent more money on its handwriting experts alone than was spent on the entire Hauptmann defense."

"Even with Hearst footing part of the bill?"

"Even then. It cost over a million dollars to put Hauptmann on death row . . . but right now I don't have a single dollar of state funds available to try to get him *off* death row."

"Excuse me?" I didn't like the sound of this.

"Mr. Heller, I staked the investigators I mentioned on my own—on small sums that barely covered their expenses, out of my own meager resources."

"Governor, no offense—but the terms we discussed on the phone, those aren't negotiable."

"I'm not the one paying your fee, Mr. Heller."

"You're not?"

"No. I mentioned an old friend of yours . . . just a moment." The intercom on his desk was buzzing. A garbled voice spoke to the governor, and he said, "Fine. Send her in." He looked up at me with his ready smile; he put out his cigar. "The party who *recommended* you is paying for your services."

The door opened behind me and a small handsome woman in a black dress and a black fur and a black hat with a black veil entered; jewelry glittered amidst the somber apparel. Perpetually in mourning for who knows what, Evalyn Walsh McLean entered the room, and reentered my life.

"Governor," she said, smiling sadly, extending him her black-gloved hand; he rose behind the desk and took it, briefly. She turned to me. Behind the veil her eyes seemed tragic and delighted. "Nathan. It's wonderful to see you."

"Likewise, Mrs. McLean," I said, taking her hand briefly. I gave her my chair and got myself a new one. I was suddenly nervous.

"Mrs. McLean has never lost her interest in the Lindbergh case," the governor said.

"The official solution of this case," she said, regally, "is not satisfactory. There are loose ends to be gathered up. And I felt Nathan Heller was just the man to do the gathering."

She looked older, of course, but fine; her figure remained slender, busty, her face gaining character with the years without losing beauty.

"Mrs. McLean has rented the Hauptmann apartment," Hoffman said. "So you can have a look around there. We've already had a criminologist in, and a wood expert, to have a look in the attic."

The prosecution's star witness was a wood expert named Koehler—who'd been about to testify the day I was at the trial, but got stalled by the defense.

"It struck me as ridiculous," Evalyn said, "that a man who supposedly was so brilliant, so clever a master criminal that he could engineer the kidnapping of the century all alone, would also be so *stupid* as to fashion a single rail of the kidnap ladder from a floorboard in his own attic."

"Actually," I said, "what's really ridiculous is the notion he'd need the lumber. Hauptmann was a carpenter. He had something of a workshop in his garage, didn't he? There must've been scrap lumber all over hell."

"And a lumberyard nearby," Hoffman added, nodding.

"In any event, he wouldn't have left the ladder behind," I said. "Not a carpenter who fashioned it himself—particularly if one rail were a board from his own house. That evidence was as planted as the tree it came from."

"So said our criminologist and a wood technician from the WPA," Hoffman said, rather proudly. "The ladder rail was a sixteenth of an inch thicker than the attic boards. Also, the nail holes weren't deep enough to accommodate eightpenny nails that came from the attic floor."

"That ladder," Evalyn said bitterly, "was what Prosecutor Wilentz pledged to 'hang around Hauptmann's neck.' "

"And he did," Hoffman said. "The question is, Mr. Heller, can you give us something as major as that ladder—only favorable, and not fabricated? Something that no one, no matter how biased, could deny?"

"I don't know," I said. "I don't have very long, do I?"

"The end of the month." He shrugged. "Fourteen days."

"Hell," I said, with blatantly phony optimism, "maybe Ellis Parker is right, and the kid's still alive. Maybe I can track the boy down and sit him right there on your desk, and he can have an ice-cream cone while you phone his folks."

Hoffman smiled at that, but sadly.

"We've tried everything," Evalyn said, shaking her head, sighing. "I even hired the top defense attorney in the country, but it didn't work out."

"Who was that?" I asked.

"Why, Sam Leibowitz, of course," she said. "But the approach Sam took was disastrous."

Sam Leibowitz!

"How so?" I asked.

Hoffman sighed. "He was convinced Hauptmann was guilty. The few times he visited Hauptmann, he tried to badger a confession out of him. Felt if he could convince Hauptmann to name his accomplices, then Hauptmann's life would be spared."

"And how did Hauptmann react?"

"With his usual quiet indignation," Hoffman said. "He did not crack—and Leibowitz was off the case as quickly as he came on."

"Don't you know," I asked Evalyn, "who Leibowitz is?"

"Certainly," she said stiffly, defensively. "He's the best damn trial attorney in the country." Then studying me, she melted and said, "Why, Nathan? What do you mean?"

I looked at Hoffman. "You told me about Reilly. Now I'll tell you about Leibowitz: *he's* a mob attorney, too. Anyway, he made his mark defending guys like 'Mad Dog' Coll and a certain well-known Chicago figure with a scarred face."

"He defended Al Capone?" Evalyn asked breathlessly.

"Yes. On a triple murder charge. And got him off."

"I'm sure Sam Leibowitz . . ." Hoffman began.

But I said: "I'll tell you one thing about this case, which I learned many years ago—you can't be *sure* about *anything*. Now. Where do I start?"

The governor shrugged. "Where I did, I guess. With Hauptmann. See for yourself. Talk to Hauptmann."

Chapter 29

It was nightfall by the time I got around to visiting Bruno Richard Hauptmann. I'd spent the afternoon in an office at the Statehouse, going over the material on the case Governor Hoffman had gathered. Evalyn insisted upon coming along, though the governor had made arrangements only for me.

"Tell them I'm your secretary," she said.

"Even Rockefeller doesn't have a secretary that looks like you," I said. "You're going to have to stow all the ice in your purse."

She did, only not all of it fit; she had to stuff some of the rocks in the glove compartment. I was driving her car, a black Packard Deluxe Eight convertible, its white top up in the rain. She'd driven from D.C., all by herself. She no longer employed a full-time chauffeur.

"Death row is no place for a lady," I said.

"In my opinion," she said, "it's no place for a man, either."

The state prison encompassed a full block between Federal and Cass streets, its massive red stone walls decorated with serpents, rams, eagles and a few kneeling nudes, and studded with guard towers with quaint New England-style cupola roofs. The fortress was haloed in electric light, including opening-night-style moving beams, and loomed ominously against the black, rain-swept night.

"My Lord, what a sight!" Evalyn said.

"Damn near as big as your place on Massachusetts Avenue," I commented, swinging around onto Third Street. We parked and crossed to the gate, Evalyn taking my arm, wobbling on her heels as we navigated puddle-filled potholes.

We were met at the gate by Warden Kimberling himself, a stocky figure in a black rain slicker, his oblong, fleshy face somber, his wire-frame glasses pearled with raindrops. A prison guard, also rain-slickered, the badge on his cap gleaming with moisture, gestured us along with a flashlight in one hand and a billy club in the other. As ushers go, he was an intimidating one. The rain was coming down hard enough to limit conversation to simple shouted introductions, and the warden and his man led us quickly across a courtyard to the chunky redbrick two-story building nearby that was, I soon realized, the death house.

We stepped into the dark room, and the beam of the guard's flashlight lit on what at first looked like a ghost, but then, as bright overhead lights were switched on, became a chair. An electric chair, or to be exact, *the* electric chair. The room was surprisingly small, with smudgy whitewashed brick walls and three rows of straight-back folding chairs that faced the sheet-covered hot seat, like a meeting in a little union hall. Only if I were the guest speaker, I wouldn't sit down after my talk.

"I'm not authorized to allow your secretary to accompany you," Kimberling said. "But the prisoner's cell is just across the way. If we leave the door ajar, she can hear your conversation, and take notes or whatever."

I helped Evalyn out of her fur-collared velvet coat, which was as drenched as a well-used bath towel, and draped it and my raincoat over several of the folding chairs. I left my hat on the seat of one, and got out my notebook and a pencil and led the somewhat shell-shocked Evalyn Walsh McLean to a little wooden bench between the door and the sheeted electric chair.

"I don't suppose you know speedwriting," I said, softly.

She managed to crinkle a little smile. "No, but I have a lovely hand."

"You have a lovely everything," I said, and she liked hearing that, even after all these years. "But be careful who you show your handwriting specimens to . . . they might pin the ransom notes on you."

Warden Kimberling ordered the guard to open the steel grill-work door, and led me through. A few paces and we were standing before the bars of a cell marked "9." The only occupied cell on this floor.

Hauptmann, wearing a blue-gray open-neck shirt and dark-blue trousers, was on his feet, hands clutching the bars like a guy on death row in a bad movie; he was clearly worked up, his pale triangular face contorted, his eyes haunted. This was not the cool customer I'd been hearing so much about.

"Warden," he said, his voice tight with desperation, the pitch surprisingly high, "you must do something."

"Richard," Kimberling said, not unkindly, "you have a visitor . . ."

Hauptmann hadn't even looked at me yet. He stretched an arm out beyond the bars, pointing, pointing up.

"Look," he said. "Look!"

We looked toward where he gestured; the slanting windows of the large skylight that rose above a second-floor cellblock were getting pelted with rain, the sound echoing softly but distinctly through the corridor. One of the metal-frame windows of the skylight had been cracked open to let air in; the angle was such that no water was dripping down, but there was another problem: a sparrow had got caught between the windows and the wire-mesh-covered iron bars beneath. The bird was trapped in the cell-like area, fluttering its wings, trying aimlessly, frantically, to free itself, beating its tiny wings against the wire.

"Do something, Warden!" he said. Hauptmann was at least as agitated as the bird.

"All right, Richard," Kimberling said, patting the air, "I'll put a guard on that. Now calm yourself. You have a visitor."

Kimberling and the guard immediately moved off, Kimberling

pointing up at the skylight, where the bird fought futilely. Maybe he really was going to attend to it.

Meanwhile, Hauptmann was looking at me carefully, suspiciously, like I was a suspect in a lineup; his concern for the bird was replaced by a sudden hardness. "I know you."

"Well," I said, "we've never met, but . . ."

"You testify against me."

"Not against you. I just testified."

"You are Jafsie's bodyguard pal."

"Jafsie is not my pal. That I assure you." I extended my hand. "My name is Heller. Nathan Heller. I'm a private detective. Governor Hoffman has hired me to assist in the investigation to find the truth about this crime you're accused of."

His lips formed a faint, wry smile. " 'Accused' is a wrong word to use, Mr. Heller . . . but kind."

"Why don't you call me Nate?"

"All right." He extended his hand through the bars. "My name is Richard. Some friends call me Dick. Why don't you call me that?"

"All right, Dick," I said.

The press and the prosecution liked to call him Bruno; it made a Teutonic beast of him.

The warden approached as we were shaking hands. He said to Hauptmann, "We'll take care of that problem," meaning the bird. He looked at me. "If you need anything, at least one guard will be here at all times."

"Could you let me in there?" I asked. "I don't like having these bars between us."

Kimberling thought for a moment, then nodded, and nodded again, this time to the guard, who turned a key in the cell door and admitted me.

Then the door made its metallic whine and clanged shut behind me and the key turned gratingly and I was locked in with Bruno Richard Hauptmann.

"Won't you please sit?" Hauptmann said, and he gestured to his cot. I sat and then so did he. Near the cot was a table stacked with newspapers, magazines, various books, among them the Bible and thick paper-covered transcripts of his trial; on the wall behind the cot were pasted various pictures of his wife and his young son. There was a sink and a toilet; it was not a small cell, although tiny compared to one I'd seen Capone in back at Cook County, some years ago.

"I should explain why I've been hired," I said.

"I know why," he said.

"Has Governor Hoffman mentioned me to you . . . ?"

"No. But you were police official from Chicago who came to work on the kidnapping, in early days."

"That's right."

"So you have knowledge of this case not just anyone have."

"Well, that is right. You have a good memory."

He nodded toward the trial transcripts. "I have time for reading. I know much about every witness who spoke for, and against me. I have ask about you. You were in some things involved that the newspapers wrote up. In Chicago."

"Don't believe everything you read in the papers."

"That is good advice, Nate. Do you think Chicago gangsters do this to me?"

That caught me off guard. "Dick—stranger things have happened."

He smiled. "Strange things happen to me, often." The sound of the bird fluttering caught his attention. "Excuse," he said, and rose, and went to the bars and looked out and up. "They do nothing," he said disgustedly, sitting back down.

"I'd like to hear your side of this, Dick. That's why I'm here."

Hauptmann sighed. "Why am *I* here? That is the question I ask myself. Why does the state do to me this? Why do they want my life for something somebody else have done?"

"The court found you guilty . . ."

"Lies! Lies!" Fire lit the blue-gray eyes, though the face remained strangely placid. "All lies. Would I kill a baby?" He nodded to his son's picture; the kid looked to be about three years old. "I am a man! A father. And, I am union carpenter. Would I build that ladder?" He laughed; it echoed hollowly in the cell.

"I'll tell you this much, Dick," I said. "You were badly represented. That Reilly . . ."

"Reilly! Could a man do for one million dollars what Reilly have done to me for who-knows-why? Only once, for about five minutes, did he even speak to me about my case."

"Dick, Reilly wasn't your lawyer—he was Hearst's lawyer." And maybe Al Capone's.

He began shaking his head emphatically, no. "I did not want to take that Hearst deal—give them 'exclusive' on Annie and me. But how could I not? I have no money. The state pay forty thousand dollars to these handwriting men they bring."

"What *about* the handwriting? Those ransom notes do have some similarities to yours . . ."

"Mr. Heller—Nate—I think if you have been a man who was picked up with some of the Lindbergh money . . . even though that money might have passed through ten hands before it came to you . . . I think that these men would prove, from all your writings, that *you* were the one who have written the ransom letters."

I nodded; he was right—handwriting experts were shit. "But Dick—some of the misspellings and such, in what you wrote, *were* like some things that turned up in the notes. I saw those notes, Dick—words like 'boad' with a 'd' and 'singnature' . . ."

"They tell me to write exactly as they dictate to me," he said, quietly indignant. "This include writing words spelled as I was made to spell them."

Typical.

"This was right after your arrest?"

"Yes. I did not know at the time why specimens of my writing they wanted. If I have any idea, then I would not have let them dictate to me, so to write down *mistakes*."

"You write English pretty good, do you?"

He shrugged. "Of course I make mistakes in writing. I am immigrant. Still, not such blunders as were dictated to me. Then they took out of my writings those things which looked like the ransom notes. In the note, in the whole damn note left in baby's room, they found only one little word—'is'—that they can say look like mine."

"Did you do these specimens of your own free will?"

"At first. But then I get tired. I can hardly keep my eyes open—but they wake me up, hit me in the ribs, say, 'You'd better write, it's bad for you if you don't! You write, you write . . .' " His eyes were glazed.

This was more than believable. This was standard operating procedure for cops coast to coast.

"But why did you admit," I said, having come across this tidbit in the material I examined this afternoon, "that the handwriting in your closet was yours?"

This was the infamous "Jafsie" phone number written on the wainscoting inside a closet in the Hauptmann apartment.

"That is one of the things they have done to me!" He shook his head in stunned frustration. "A few days after my arrest, my Annie and Manfred—my child, my boy, my little Bubi—could stand it no longer. The baby could no longer sleep because of all the police and reporters and people who were there. So Annie and Bubi go to stay with relatives. Now I can see it was the wrong thing to do."

"Because that gave the cops free access to your apartment."

"This is right. Some days after I am arrested, when everything seems so mixed up in my mind, the police appear with a board on which is some writing. They say the board is from a closet in my home."

"Was it?"

"It seem so. They say is this your writing, I say it must be, because it is my custom as a carpenter to write down things on wood. But then they tell me it is Dr. Condon's phone number! Dear God! If I that number had written and knew what it was, would I have so easy told the police?"

"Maybe not," I said, with gentle sarcasm.

"With my dying breath I would have said I have never seen that number before! Besides, if I have commit this crime, would I have marked down in my own home this number?"

"Well, I was there when Condon received calls from the supposed kidnappers."

"But in my Bronx house I have *no* telephone!"

"What?"

"I must go some distance to find telephone to use. What good would to me be a number written inside this closet, very small and very dark, where I would have to get inside to see the number?"

"Wasn't it an unlisted number?"

"No! They have tried to make people think that this was a secret number. But it is not so. The number was in all the books. It was much later that Dr. Condon changed to a private number. I am certain the numbers on the closet wainscoting have been made either by police or by reporters who try to write like me."

Thinking back over what I'd read this afternoon, I'd come across an interesting point: the state's high-paid handwriting experts at the trial were never called upon to identify the closet handwriting as Hauptmann's.

"I've heard a rumor that a specific reporter did that," I told him. "I intend to try to run that down."

"Good!" Hauptmann said, and I thought he was answering me at first, but he apparently wasn't. He was looking past me and up, and standing, as he moved to the cell's barred doors.

A guard with a long pole was up on the catwalk of the cellblock tier above, trying to lift a skylight window and allow the bird to flutter free.

Hauptmann came back and sat down, looking relieved. "It's not free, but he's trying. Someone is trying. That's important. Where were we?"

"You mentioned the police had access to your apartment, because your wife and son moved out. Is that your reading of so-called rail sixteen, the piece of the ladder that's supposed to come from your attic?"

He smiled mirthlessly, shook his head. "In the first place, this 'rail sixteen' have in it some large knots which alone would prevent a carpenter from making a ladder of it. Only it is not a ladder—it is a bad wooden rack. Its construction shows that it did not come from the hand of a carpenter, not even a poor one. Wilentz, he say I am not a good carpenter. I have worked for myself and as a foreman. You ask people about whether I am a good carpenter."

"You think the wood was from your attic?"

He shrugged. "If so, they take it, not me."

The kidnap ladder had been dismantled and reassembled time and again, for various tests.

"Wilentz says I am smart criminal," Hauptmann said, with a faint sneer. "He says on these hands I must have worn gloves, because there are no fingerprints. On these feet I must have worn bags, because there were no footprints. If I was such a smart criminal, if I would do all those things, why would I go in my own house, and take up half of one board in my attic to use for one piece of this 'ladder'—something that would always be evidence against me?

"If I wanted to make a ladder, could I not get from around my yard and around my garage all the scrap wood I need? Besides, only about one block from my house is a lumberyard. Listen, I am a carpenter—would I buy wood for five rails only and not know I need wood for six?"

"This wood expert, Koehler," I said, "claims he tracked the wood the other rails were made of to that neighborhood lumberyard of yours."

Hauptmann waved a hand gently in the air, as if trying to rub out a stain there. "Koehler himself says he have traced shipments of this lumber to thirty cities. If they sell this wood in Koehler's neighborhood in Koehler's town, does that make Koehler the kidnapper?"

"I wonder where he was March first, 1932," I said. "But you're right: once the cops get a suspect, the evidence can be made to fit."

"And if they have evidence that does *not* fit," he said, "this evidence, it disappears. When I was arrested, they took among many things, my shoes. What for I at first could not imagine; but then I think: they have a footprint!"

"They do," I said. " 'Cemetery John' left one at St. Raymond's."

"Then why did they not produce the plaster model that was made?" With bitter sarcasm, he said, "Perhaps they hold this damning evidence back, out of pity for me."

Reilly should have demanded that plaster cast be produced; but then Reilly should have done a lot of things.

"Did you know they took my fingerprints not once, but again and again? Also the sides of my hands, the hollow parts of the hands. Then at the trial, when my counsel asks about fingerprints, Wilentz says, 'There are no fingerprints.' "

"There were plenty on the ladder," I said. "That's what they were checking against."

"And found not mine! In the nursery there were no fingerprints at all. Not of the parents, not of the child's nurse or the other servants. They say I wear gloves. Did the parents, then, when they go to the room to take joy in their child, and all the servants, also wear gloves?"

"It does sound like somebody wiped the room down." Somebody in the house. Somebody after the fact.

"They found a chisel near the ladder. They compare it to my carpenter's tools. My tools are a Stanley set; the one they found is a Bucks Brothers chisel. They told the jury, 'This is Hauptmann's chisel,' and the jury believed them."

"But they didn't believe your eyewitnesses, did they?"

"My eyewitnesses were good, but then Reilly *hired* more witnesses, *bad* witnesses! They were killing me! Crazy people from asylums, people with criminal records . . . and Wilentz makes of them fools. Because of that, the good people, the witnesses who tell the truth for me, they are not believed. The five people who saw me in New York in the bakery with Annie at the time of the crime, *good* people, are made out to look like liars. One of these, Manley, an old gentleman, arose from a sickbed and he swore that on the night of March first, 1932, he saw me at nine o'clock in his bakery."

I snorted a laugh. "Yet old 'Cataracts' Hochmuth and that movie cashier and the taxi driver, questionable eyewitnesses at best, *were* believed."

"Why, Nate? Why?"

"Well . . . you mentioned witnesses with criminal records. You do have a criminal record yourself, Dick."

"Yes, in Germany—after the war. Never in America." He placed a hand on his chest, fingers splayed. "I come home from the war in rags, sick with hunger. So, too, I find my mother and my brothers and sisters starving. I did steal an overcoat and I stole food. I was just a boy. These things are wrong, yes, but many times by many people were they done in my country after that war. And I have never once injured a human being."

"You broke and entered through a second-story window, once. And you held up two women wheeling baby carriages—with a gun. Add those two crimes up, and . . . "

"There were no babies in those carriages! In Germany, at that time, they use those buggies as shopping carts. You know what I stole? Nine bread rolls and some food ration cards. No babies did I frighten."

"And the second-story job?"

He shrugged. "It was the mayor's office, as much a prank as a robbery. I stole a silver pocket watch and a few hundred marks. I'm not proud of this—I knew I was doing wrong. I quieted my conscience with, 'Oh well, others do it, too.'"

Reilly should've brought this stuff out at the trial; Wilentz killed Hauptmann with the baby-buggy stickup—which shouldn't have even been the hell admissible!

"I understand all this, Dick," I said, "but *you* have to understand how it worked against you. Just being a German works against you, frankly. And hell—you were a machine gunner in the war—which makes you a killer."

He sneered a little, and his response was justifiably sarcastic: "Oh—so no American machine gunners were in the war?"

I shook my head. "When the killing's on your side, it doesn't count—particularly when you win. And I don't think your popularity's been helped by these Nazi *bund*-type rallies, either, raising money for your defense fund."

The sarcasm evaporated. "What choice have I? The state confiscated our funds, Annie and me. Are you a Jewish man, Nate?"

"My father was. I'm not very religious."

"I am." He smiled nervously. "Religious, I mean. Do you hate me for being German? Do you think I think I am the 'master race'? Do you think I would hate a Jewish man?"

Wilentz, maybe.

"I'm an American," I said, "whose forefathers came from Germany. Why should I hate you, or make such assumptions?"

Rather shyly, he touched my shoulder. "Mr. Heller—why weren't you on the jury?"

"Dick," I said, "you don't have to convince me that a lot of the evidence was tampered with or invented. You don't have to tell me that Hochmuth was blind, or that that movie cashier who said she remembered you was full of shit. I used to be a cop. I know all about that stuff."

"What *do* you want me to tell you?"

"Tell me about Isidor Fisch." I smiled gently. "Your Jewish friend."

He laughed soundlessly. "The 'Fisch story,' they call it."

"Everybody did say it smelled."

"It sounds bad. But it's true."

"Tell me. Take your time."

He drew in a breath, let it out slowly. "I meet Isidor Fisch at Hunter's Island in Pelham Park. Annie and I and our friends go there many weekends in the winter and summer both. We have enjoyed a wonderful outdoor life there, boating, swimming, fishing . . . " A small private smile appeared, and a distant look came to his eyes. " . . . cooking over a fire, playing music and singing . . . Annie bought me field glasses. I loved to watch the birds." That brought him back to reality. He got up from the cot and moved quickly to the bars and looked out.

"It's still caught," he said, shaking his head. "They give up. Damn. A free thing like that should never be in there."

"Richard," I said. "Dick. Tell me about Izzy Fisch."

He shuffled back over and sat on the cot. He said, "Fisch I meet three, four times at Hunter's Island. Once he mentions that he is interested in the stock market, like me. But he tells me he is in the fur business, and that there is good money in it. He knows of what he is talking, was a furrier in the old country. I buy some stocks and bonds for him, he bought some furs for me . . . I start with five hundred dollars I give him to buy furs, and keep reinvesting, until I finally have seven thousand dollars in furs."

"Where were all these furs being stored?"

"In the fur district in New York, Fisch said, but we never got around to going to where they were in a warehouse. Fisch was sickly, had a bad cough."

So did Jafsie's Cemetery John, I recalled.

"One day he said he was going to Germany to visit his parents. He asked me to keep four hundred sealskins at my home, while he was gone. Later on, he asks me when he goes to Germany if he can leave with me some of his belongings, and he brought to my house two satchels, a big one and a small one."

"What about the money?"

Hauptmann motioned for me to be patient. "The Saturday

before Isidor left for Germany, my wife and I give for him a farewell party. He brought along under his arm a cardboard box, wrapped up with string, and asks me to put it in a closet for him and keep it until he comes back. I thought maybe in the box were some things he forgot to put in the satchels, maybe papers and letters. I put the package for him on the upper shelf of the broom closet. It was too high there, for my wife to see, although they try to make her look bad at the trial, because they claim the shelf was low and she cleaned in there and she should see it. But she never did. Anyway. After a while there were rags and things on the shelf, covering up the box, and I forgot all about it. Fisch, he told me he would be back again in two months.''

"But you never heard from him again."

"Oh, but I did. He wrote me a few times . . . and then, in March or April, from his brother Pincus I get a letter saying Isidor have died. Pincus asked me, in his letter, as he knew I was a friend of Isidor's, to look after his brother's financial business in this country. So I wrote and told Pincus how we stood in the stock and fur business."

From the expression on Hauptmann's face, I could tell there had been discrepancies.

"Fisch have told me that he got bank accounts and a safe-deposit box and that he also got ten thousand dollars in some company that bakes pies. Also lots of furs. And that a friend owed him two thousand dollars. But when I start to look around after Isidor have died, I find that the pie company is a fake and that Fisch owes the friend eight hundred dollars, and that another friend he owes four thousand dollars. I could find no furs, except the four hundred skins at my house, which are not worth half what he told me. So I am all mixed up."

"So you opened up that little box in your closet, and . . . "

"No! I have forgot all about that box. I go to Fisch's lawyer, who tells me there is no money, nothing valuable in the safe-deposit box. And I give up."

"You gave up?"

"Yes. But three or four weeks before I get arrested, it has been raining, like tonight . . . and the water comes in the broom closet and as I am cleaning it up, I run across the box, soaking wet. When

I look, I find it is full of money! Oh ho, I say to myself—this is where Izzy's money has gone. What he has saved up, he has put in gold certificates. I put the money in a pail, and took it to my garage, where I dried it and hid it like the police found it, except for the few bills I have already spent. I did not put it in the bank, because with gold certificates, I think I should have trouble."

"You helped yourself, because Izzy was into you for, what? Seven grand?"

He nodded. "Because he owed me money and have tried to cheat me, I see that money and feel it is largely mine." He shook his head, sighing heavily. "Could I have known that money was Lindbergh baby money? No! The gas station man have testify that I say to him when I gave him that bill, 'I have a hundred more like that at home.' Would I say that if I knew that these bills maybe could take my life some day?"

"But you lied to the cops about the money."

"Because I have gold certificates, and it is illegal! I knew I would get in much trouble if they knew I had so much gold money, and besides, near the money in my garage I have hidden also a pistol which I know I am not supposed to have."

"Do you think Isidor Fisch was involved in the kidnapping, or anyway, in the extortion?"

He shook his head slowly, hopelessly. "I don't know, Nate. I wish I did. I know, when I ask around about him, I find he was not the man I thought. He was a crook. Maybe he was trading in what they call 'hot money.' "

There were footsteps in the corridor.

"Pincus, Izzy's brother, wrote me to say that shortly before Isidor died, from his bed of death, he called out for me—he seemed to want to say something about me. But he was too weak. He took to his grave that which would be of great help to me now."

Warden Kimberling's stocky figure—now in a gray business suit, the black slicker gone—appeared beyond the iron bars. "Mr. Heller, just a few more minutes."

"Would you mind checking on my secretary, Warden? See how she's doing?"

He nodded.

As he moved through the door, I saw that whenever that door

opened, Hauptmann got a nice clear view of the electric chair, covered in white.

"Six men have walked by me, going to that room, since I come here," he said with no apparent emotion. "Some of them silent, some of them crying, some even scream."

I didn't know what to say to that.

The door closed, the warden presumably having a little chat with Evalyn.

Hauptmann's hand settled on my shoulder again, less tentatively now. "Nate, I am glad you're not the pal of Jafsie."

I laughed. "That old bastard drives me bughouse."

"He came to see me, you know."

That threw me. "Here?"

"No. At the cell in Hunterdon County Jail. He ask me if I have athletic training. I tell him yes. He ask me if I have won any prizes, and I tell him sixteen or seventeen in Germany for running. Then it look like he was going to cry."

"He didn't claim to recognize you?"

"He call me 'John' many times, though I correct him. He say if I know anything, I should confess, because there was no connection between the money and the kidnapping, and I would clear myself and himself. He say the police were treating him roughly. But he never said I am the fellow—and when he left, he ask could he come see me again, and I say 'yes.' But he never did."

The door to the death chamber opened and gave us another glimpse of the muslin-covered chair as Warden Kimberling approached, saying, "It's time, Mr. Heller."

I stood. Hauptmann and I again shook hands. His eyes, which had been so cold, were warm. His smile was warm.

"I think you might help me," he said.

"I'm going to try," I admitted.

"You should believe in God, Nate. I know He will never permit some persons to commit a murder on me."

"Murders do happen, Dick."

He laughed, and some bitterness crept back in. "Yes—the poor child have been kidnapped and murdered, so somebody must die for it. For is the parent not the great flier? And if somebody does not die for the death of the child, then always the police will be monkeys." He shrugged, his smile was a humorless, fatalistic smirk. "So I am the one who is picked out to die."

There was nothing to say to that. I gave him a tight smile, a little pat on the shoulder, and got the hell out, the door clanking shut behind me.

Evalyn, sitting on the bench, all in black, truly seemed in mourning now; she'd been taking notes, my rich little secretary, the pencil worn to a nub, her face tear-streaked.

She stood, wobblingly, and came into my arms. "That poor man," she said. "That poor man."

The warden was looking on from the doorway, uncomfortably.

"Let's get our coats," I told her.

From the cellblock, I heard someone say, "Damn."

I let go of Evalyn and moved toward the warden and stood in the doorway and looked out at Hauptmann, one last time, a white face behind gray bars.

"At least he suffer not long," he said, looking up.

I stepped out into the corridor and glanced up; and saw the small gray form of the bird motionless against the wire.

Chapter 30

This neighborhood, at the far edge of the Bronx, had the small-town flavor of many a big city's outlying sections. Most of the houses were two-family, two-story wood-and-stucco jobs with neat little lawns, often with a weed-patched vacant lot next door. Hauptmann's residence—at 1279 East 222nd—was no exception: a two-and-a-half-story frame structure, its second story recessed, a stone wall bordering the front as steps rose gently to a winter-brown lawn dominated by bushes, a vine crawling up the tan stucco in front, toward the second-floor windows, like a cat burglar. At the right of the house was a vacant lot thicketed with weeds, halted at the far right by a rutted country lane, and just across that lane was what remained of the wreckage of the garage Hauptmann had built there. Behind the house, cutting off the lane, were woods, close enough to the house to provide shade, when the leaves returned, anyway.

I parked the Packard in front; Evalyn was with me. She wore a black-and-gray three-piece suit, one piece of which was her top-coat, and a black-and-gray beret. She wore only a few touches of jewelry, at my request—demand, actually, if she were to insist on playing "Thin Man" with me. At least she didn't bring her goddamn dog.

We had stayed, the night before, in separate suites at the Hotel Sterling, where Hoffman had made reservations for us in the section of the hotel known as the Government House; it had once been the governor's mansion, so it was fitting in a way. Fancier digs than necessary, but I wasn't paying.

We had talked into the night, over cocktails in her suite, the death-row confab with Hauptmann weighing heavily on both our minds. If anything romantic or sexual was going to reblossom between us, this was not the time or place or mood. I was curious, however, why Evalyn was still, after four long years, digging into this horrendous fucking case. Hadn't she been burned badly enough by Gaston Means?

"Nate," she said, "I'm sorry I failed to get that child back. I'm sorry I was tricked, I'm sorry I was swindled. But I'll always be glad, in my heart, that there was something that compelled me to try."

"Fine," I said, just a little drunk. "Swell. But that wasn't my question. Why are you still involved?"

She shrugged, and began to ramble in what seemed at first a nonresponsive way. "You know, I had to close down 2020 Massachusetts Avenue—I just couldn't afford such a big place. And for a time I was in an apartment. Can you picture me in an apartment, Nate? Anyway, a while ago, Ned—my husband, remember him?—as our courtroom battles over custody of the children were continuing, took a bad turn. In terms of his health."

"Oh? I'm sorry."

"In terms of his mental health, actually. I'll never divorce Ned—I won't have to. There will be no more struggles over custody—the children are damn near grown, and, well . . . at intervals I get reports from a Maryland hospital concerning a patient there, who has morbid preoccupations and lives in a state of mental exile. Shut off even from himself. If he is addressed by his right name, he grows excited—and swears he is not a McLean."

"I'm sorry, Evalyn."

She smiled it off gaily and it was about as convincing as wax fruit. "At any rate, the court awarded me Friendship, the McLean estate, and that was where I was living when the Hauptmann trial was held. I witnessed it from a distance, with some skepticism, as anyone familiar with the facts of the case well might, and afterward, to fill my rich, idle time, I procured the many-volumed transcript of that trial. If it could be called a trial. To me, it was a disgusting hippodrome."

"And you got interested again."

"I was always interested," she said, with a little laugh. "I think I paid for the right to remain interested, don't you? And I think I have the right to be concerned when someone else is being wronged in this convoluted affair. And the way Mr. Hauptmann is being wronged makes the injustice done me pale in comparison."

"Your concern for Hauptmann is admirable," I granted her. "But the possibility remains that he was, in some way or manner, involved in at least the 'Cemetery John' extortion caper. He was convincing tonight, but many a guilty man is, where his innocence is concerned."

"I'm concerned about more than just Hauptmann's innocence," she said. Her eyes glittered over her cocktail glass. "I have my doubts about that little skeleton they found in the woods."

"Well," I admitted, "after that photo Hoffman showed me, I can see why."

"Nate, thousands upon thousands of people had combed those woods near the very spot the little body was found. Hell, even the brush *underneath* the body was trampled."

"Underneath?"

"Only a few feet away, telephone workmen had put up a pole, laying wires, because of the need for extra communications in those frenzied early days." Her archness was offset by her sincerity. "Those tiny bones, who's-ever they were, must have been placed there, long after the fact."

"Slim's identification of the body *was* pretty hasty," I allowed.

She studied her drink, then made a confession: "Well, there was one other person who made an identification."

That was the first I'd heard of that. "Who in hell?"

"Betty Gow," she said. "The nurse. She viewed the little body, too, and identified it as Charles Lindbergh, Jr."

"Based on what? There was nothing to identify. I saw the photo . . . "

"There was a tiny garment under the bones. Betty Gow claimed to recognize it as a little shirt made by her, the night of the kidnapping, to wrap the child in because he had a cold. She claimed she knew it from the thread, the distinctive blue thread she'd used."

"I see. Still sounds a little thin. But that *is* the most convincing case for those bones being the real child."

"Yes—but couldn't that garment have been planted, as well?"

"I suppose . . . now we're getting a little overmelodramatic, aren't we, Evalyn?"

"Are we? Haven't you always thought someone on the 'inside,' with either the Lindbergh or Morrow family staff, was somehow in on the crime?"

"Yes. So, what? You're saying Betty Gow might have lied, or helped plant that little shirt . . . "

"Not necessarily. The cloth and the thread were provided to Betty Gow, the night of the kidnapping, by the butler's wife—Elsie Whately."

The Hauptmann apartment took up the second floor of the house, a mostly empty five rooms for which Evalyn had been paying, since December, fifty dollars a month to the seventy-year-old widow who lived below.

As I wandered the empty rooms I remembered reading of the new, rather expensive furniture the Hauptmanns owned, which had seemed so suspicious to the cops and prosecutors. A walnut bedroom suite, an ivory crib, a floor-model radio in a nice walnut veneer cabinet—all gone, sold to help pay for the defense effort. Now there was nothing in this apartment but the bare floors, faded wallpaper and our echoing footsteps.

"As many people as have been through here," I said, "I don't know what I expected to find."

Evalyn had been following me like a dutiful puppy through the small living room, the two bedrooms, the kitchen, the bath. "It doesn't seem to me," she said, "that the Hauptmanns were living in the lap of luxury."

"It doesn't even seem that way to me," I said, "although this is about right for a man operating a little contracting business . . . dabbling in the stock market in a minor, amateur way . . . his wife working full-time as a waitress in a bakery. About right. Let's look in those famous closets, shall we?"

In what had been the nursery, I found the closet where the wainscoting had been removed to show the jury the "evidence" of Jafsie's phone number having been written there. Last night I'd told Evalyn what I had heard about the reporter on the *Daily News* named Tim O'Neil who'd reputedly created this evidence for a headline. She'd been suitably outraged, and wondered if we shouldn't "look this fellow up." I said we should.

In the ceiling of what had apparently been a linen closet, off the hall, was the access panel to the attic.

"I'd better make this trip by myself," I advised Evalyn, who had one look inside and agreed. I handed her my suit coat.

To get to the attic hatch, I had to take the shelves down, stack them out in the hall, and scale the shelving cleats like some half-ass mountain-climber.

"Careful!" she said.

"Hauptmann must've needed that one scrap of lumber pretty goddamn bad," I said, breathing hard, plastered to the closet wall like a bug, "to go looking for it up here."

Balancing awkwardly, clutching a cleat with one hand, I pushed the trapdoor-like panel up with the other, then hoisted myself up through the tiny opening—perhaps fifteen inches square. The attic was a dark, musty, dusty inverted V that would make a midget claustrophobic.

I hung my head down the hatch where an eager-eyed Evalyn looked up from the linen closet. "See if the landlady has a flashlight," I said.

"There's one in the car."

"Get it."

I waited, still hanging over the open space—the air was better there—and thought about pudgy Governor Hoffman having to squeeze up through this space, which he had on at least one occasion. That was worth a smile.

Soon she handed me up the flashlight, standing on her toes to do it, and I got a better look at what turned out to be an unfinished attic. The flooring only went down the middle, with the joists, laths and plaster below bared at either side where the roof sloped low.

With the beam of the flashlight, it didn't take long to spot the one floorboard that was half the length of the others—the one from which Hauptmann had supposedly sawed the wood for a rail of the kidnap ladder. It was also easy to spot what made that evidence smell: from the apex of the roof, there were thirteen boards on one side, fourteen on the other. The fourteenth was the odd board out, and not just because it was the half-board: without it, the attic would have been symmetrical, a better, more likely carpenter job. The other boards had seven nails fastening them to the joists; the half-board, twenty-five.

I handed Evalyn down the flash, then lowered myself and dropped, shaking the floor as I landed. I told Evalyn what I'd seen.

"I understand there were something like thirty-five cops up there," she said, with a disgusted smirk, "before anybody 'noticed' that extra, sawed-in-half floorboard."

"One more closet to check," I said, getting back into my suit coat. "I want to see the most famous Hauptmann closet of all: where Fisch's shoebox was stowed."

In the kitchen, the closet's single shelf didn't seem terribly high; this had been a broom closet—the hook where Mrs. Hauptmann had hung her apron was still there. Evalyn, short as she was, could almost reach the shelf, where the Fisch box had been kept, supposedly out of view from Anna Hauptmann.

"I don't get it," I said, looking at this low-flying shelf. "Wilentz made Hauptmann's wife look sick on the stand, because she admitted she kept a Prince Albert tobacco can on the edge of that shelf . . . she kept soap coupons and such in there, and she talked about being barely able to reach it."

"Then Wilentz showed photos and introduced data proving the shelf was lower than Anna claimed," Evalyn said.

It had been a bad moment for Mrs. Hauptmann.

"Why would she lie about something so easily proven? Let's have a closer look . . . "

I removed the single shelf. Then I shined the flashlight on the wall.

"That's funny," I said. "This closet's been painted recently."

"Oh?"

"I don't think the others have." We went back for a second look; and, no, the other closets had well-aged paint jobs, even to the point of chipping and peeling.

I went back to the kitchen closet and ran my hand over that wall like a blind man reading a book in Braille.

"Jesus!" I said. "Give me that flashlight again!"

She did.

"This closet *has* been painted recently—but up here . . . " And I cast the flashlight beam up six inches above the shelf cleats. " . . . there's an area where the paint indents."

"Indents?"

"Yeah. There are layers and layers of paint on these walls, paint on paint on paint. Over the years, when this closet has been repainted, nobody bothered to take the shelf out. Just painted walls and shelf alike."

"Yes. But . . . what . . . ?"

"Well, up here," I said, reaching, running my finger from left to right along the wall the width of the shelf, "the paint is only a coat or two deep. Let me show you."

I lifted her by her tiny waist so she could run her fingertips along there herself. "You're right! Nathan, you're right . . . "

I set her down. "Get your criminologist back in here," I said. "With the right chemicals, he can prove that shelf was moved. I think he can find where those cleats were originally attached, too, and filled in the meantime with putty, and painted over. Originally, that shelf was right where Anna Hauptmann said it was."

"Then she really *couldn't* have seen the shoebox!"

"No she couldn't. The cops lowered the shelves, to make her look like a liar."

Evalyn's look of joy dissolved into a scowl. "Those bastards. Those bastards!"

I shrugged. "Police work," I said.

From the other room, a male voice called, "Yoo hoo! Yoo hoo!"

"In here," Evalyn called.

"You expecting somebody?" I asked.

She nodded. She had a coy little smile; cat that ate the canary.

A tall, skinny bespectacled guy about thirty with pleasant, angular features, wearing a lumpy fedora and a rumpled raincoat under which a blue bow tie peeked, came strolling in. He was blond with a wispy mustache and a smirk.

"You're Mrs. McLean?" he said, grinning, taking off the hat.

"That's right," she said, extending a gloved hand. "Thank you for coming, Mr. O'Neil."

"O'Neil?" I said.

She nodded, smiling at me. "I took the liberty of asking Mr. O'Neil to stop by. Called him this morning from the hotel. I told him we had an exclusive for him on the Hauptmann case."

"You're Tim O'Neil, with the *Daily News*?" I asked.

"That's right," he said, and he extended his hand.

I decked him.

He sat on the kitchen floor, rubbing his jaw, arms and legs pointing every which way, eyes as confused as a drowning kitten's. "What the hell was that for?"

I leaned over him; both my hands were fists. "That was for faking that fucking phone number. In the closet in the other room?"

His face went slack, his eyes filled with fear and something else. What? Remorse?

"Oh Christ," he said. "Who are you?"

"The guy who's going to beat the ever-loving crap out of you, if you don't 'fess up."

On his ass, he scuttled back into a corner between kitchen cabinets and stove, like the world's tallest, skinniest rat. "Listen . . . I don't want any trouble . . . this isn't gonna pay off for anybody . . . "

I went over and grabbed him by his raincoat and hauled him off the floor and started slapping him around; his glasses flew off. Evalyn was watching, doing a nervous little jump every time I slapped him. But she liked it.

"Stop!" he said. "Stop!"

I stopped. I was starting to get embarrassed. The guy wasn't fighting back at all.

"Stop," he said.

He was crying.

"Jesus," I said, softly. I let go of him.

He sat on the floor and cried.

"I didn't hit him that hard," I said to Evalyn.

She also seemed embarrassed. "I don't think you did . . . I think it's something else."

I got down on my haunches and said, "You want to talk, Tim?"

Now all three of us were embarrassed.

"Fuck," he said, wiping tears and snot off his face with big flat hands. Then said to Evalyn, "Excuse the language, ma'am."

I gave him my handkerchief. He wiped off his face, blew his nose. Awkwardly, he started to hand the hanky back to me.

"It's yours now," I said, and helped him to his feet. Evalyn handed him his glasses; they hadn't broken.

"You . . . you're right," he said, slipping on the specs. "You didn't hit me that hard. What's your name, anyway?"

"My name is Heller. I'm a detective from Chicago."

"What are the Chicago cops doing in this, at this late date?"

"I'm private. Working for Governor Hoffman, and Mrs. McLean, here. You did write Jafsie's number on the wainscoting, didn't you?"

He nodded. Sighed heavily. "I got myself a real nice front-page scoop out of it. Got myself a big fat byline. But I never dreamed it would be one of the key goddamn pieces of evidence they used to nail that poor son of a bitch."

"I never met a reporter with a conscience before."

"I never knew I had a conscience, till you started slapping me around."

"So it bothers you."

"More than I even knew, apparently. I'm sorry. Blubbering like a baby like that . . . it's really humiliating . . . "

"Will you come forward?"

"No," he said.

"No!" Evalyn said, dumbfounded. The blood, and the sympathy, drained out of her face. She clutched my arm. "Give him the Chicago lie-detector test, Nate!"

"Huh?" O'Neil said. His eyes were large and scared.

"Easy, Evalyn," I said. "I'm not so young and reckless, anymore."

Besides, my gun was in my suitcase.

I put a firm hand on O'Neil's shoulder; he was taller than me, by perhaps three inches, but I outweighed him twenty-five pounds. "You want to run that by me again?"

"I'm not coming forward. I can't." He held out his open palms like a beggar. "Precisely 'cause it did get into the trial, as evidence. I might go to jail. I could lose my job. I would be in very deep shit."

"You are in very deep shit," I said.

"No," he said. "You can beat on me . . . incidentally, I'm prepared to fight you back, now . . . but it's not going to change things. You'll be the one in jail, for assault. And I'd sue Mrs. McLean out of some of that money she obviously has to burn."

He was right. There really wasn't much I could do.

"But if you're investigating Bruno's case," he said, "trying to cheat the executioner out of his fun, at the last minute . . . I can be of help."

"Oh?"

He nodded vigorously. His face was haggard, dark circles under the eyes. "Check the record. I've dug up any number of stories, since the Jafsie phone-number scam, bolstering Hauptmann's position."

"You mean you've been working to clear him?"

"Not exactly. I'm a reporter, and I do my job . . . but I'm working that angle, yeah." He pointed a thumb at his chest. "I'm the guy who tracked down the employment agency records that showed Hauptmann was at work at the Majestic Apartments on March first, 1932, just like he said he was . . . when the cops conveniently lost the time sheets for that week."

"You are trying to balance the books, aren't you, Tim? What can you give me?"

"How about the real lowdown on Izzy Fisch?" he asked, with a wicked little smile, like a jeweler about to show Evalyn a really big rock.

She and I exchanged significant glances.

"What have you got, Tim?" I asked.

"Plenty. See, I've got a big story on Fisch, in the works. Real in-depth. But none of what I've got is public knowledge yet—for example, I know that the cops have ledger books and letters they confiscated from this apartment, that tend to back up the so-called Fisch story—none of which was used at the trial. I know lab tests back up Hauptmann's claim that the money he had was water-soaked. And I know that Fisch was a confidence man who borrowed money from friends to invest in nonexistent businesses. I can tell you, based upon dozens of instances I've tracked, that Isidor Fisch never once repaid a loan."

"So he was a small-time con artist. But was he a large-scale crook?"

O'Neil shook his head, made a clicking sound in his cheek. "That I don't know. Could he have been in on the kidnapping? Sure. Masterminded it? I dunno. I know this: the rooming house he lived in was right smack in the middle of the Italian mob's stomping grounds."

"Luciano territory?"

"And how." He seemed amused as he asked: "Does a Chicago boy like you know what Luciano's best-paying racket is, since Repeal?"

I nodded. "Dope."

"Give the man a cigar. And here Izzy Fisch is, importing furs and making trips to Europe. Think he might have been importing more than just sealskins? And I was able to connect Fisch to at least one Luciano hoodlum, a guy named Charley DeGrasie, who's dead now, unfortunately. That was when the story started getting a little warm, and I backed off."

I was taking notes, by this time. "Is that all you have on Fisch, then?"

"Not hardly. I talked to a guy named Arthur Trost. He's a paint contractor. He said he knew Fisch since the summer of '31, that he used to run into Fisch at a billiard parlor in Yorkville— German section of Manhattan. Around the time of the Lindbergh kidnapping, Fisch stopped frequenting the place."

"So?"

"So in the summer of '32, a painter pal of Trost's asks him if he wanted to buy some hot money for fifty cents on the dollar from a friend of his. Trost told the guy he'd have to meet the person doing the selling, and got escorted to that very same billiard parlor, where who should be waiting but Isidor Fisch. Trost told his pal that he already knew Fisch and that Fisch already owed him money and that he wouldn't believe Fisch if he was calling for help from the window of a burning building."

"So Trost never actually saw this 'hot money.' "

"No. But it connects Fisch to dealing in hot cash, doesn't it? Considering the timing, very likely Lindbergh cash. I also talked to a guy named Gustave Mancke, who runs an ice-cream parlor in New Rochelle. He and his wife Sophie swear that for an eight-week period in January and February of '32, right up to the Sunday before the kidnapping, Izzy Fisch ate in their shop every Sunday evening."

"That doesn't sound like much of a revelation."

"It does when you consider Mancke claims Fisch would always meet with the same two people."

"Oh? And who did he meet with?"

"Violet Sharpe," he said, "and Ollie Whately."

e had lunch on Italian Harlem's market street—First Avenue—in a modest place called Guido's where we had spaghetti and espresso. From our window seat we could see the crowded sidewalk where housewives bickered with vendors over greens, olives, cheeses, clams, whatever; it was an Italian version of Maxwell Street, a barrel of work gloves here, a bin of bread there, anything you needed, from pomegranates to underwear.

"I always think of Harlem as Negro," Evalyn admitted, as we began dessert, each of us working on a gaudy pastry.

"East Harlem isn't," I said, cutting the dick-shaped sweet with a knife. "Lucky Luciano operates out of this part of town. Lucky and the boys noticed a long time ago there was money to be made in Negro Harlem."

"Money?"

"Sure. Most of the big nightclubs in Harlem have Italian owners, or anyway mob guys like Owney Madden—you've heard of the Cotton Club, Evalyn? And a couple years ago, Luciano made his move on the colored numbers racket, from here."

"This apartment house we're going to," she said, "seems to be mostly Germans."

"Not surprising."

"In an Italian neighborhood?"

"German immigrants can enter on a level the Italians have to work their way up to," I said. "Don't forget, wops are about as dark as white people get."

My remark seemed to disturb her. "Do you mean that, Nate?"

"What do you mean, do I mean that?"

"You don't strike me as a bigoted person."

"Hey, I'm half Jew. I'd be in the same boat, if I hadn't been dealt my mother's physical traits. Don't let's go high-hat on me, Evalyn—most of your servants are colored, while none of the guests at your Washington soirees are . . . unless it's the King of Zanzibar or something."

"Sometimes I don't know when you're kidding."

"That's easy—when it sounds like I'm kidding, I'm not. When it sounds like I'm not kidding, I am." I checked my watch. "I think we've killed enough time—we can visit Mrs. Henkel, now."

We'd called ahead to see Gerta Henkel, friend of both Richard and Anna Hauptmann, and she'd said to come over in the early afternoon; she and her husband Carl lived in Kohl's rooming house at 149 East 127th, where Isidor Fisch had also lived. So had several other good friends of the Hauptmanns, from the clique of German immigrants who made merry at Hunter's Island.

I pulled the Packard into the Warner-Quinlan filling station at the corner of East 127th and Lexington, a large modern station with a service garage and billboards trumpeting itself on either side.

"Do you know what this place is?" I asked Evalyn.

"It's a gas station, Nate. Don't they have these in Chicago?"

"It's *the* gas station: the one where Hauptmann passed the gold certificate that got him caught. And just three doors down from here is Fisch's apartment house."

Her eyes narrowed. "Does that mean anything?"

"I don't know."

I got out of the Packard and, as he was filling the tank, asked the attendant if the manager was here.

"Walter?" the mustached, geeky attendant asked. "Sure. You want I should get him?"

"Please."

Walter Lyle, the filling-station manager, came out rubbing grease off his hands with a rag. He was a somewhat stocky, pleasant-looking guy in his late thirties; he wore a cap and a coin-changer.

"Help you?" he asked with a neutral smile.

"My name's Heller," I said, and I flashed him my badge. "Doing one final follow-up investigation on the Hauptmann case."

He smiled. You could see in his eyes that this was a big deal in his life; he hadn't got tired yet of people asking him about how he helped nab Hauptmann.

"Always glad to help, Officer," he said.

I hadn't said I was a cop, of course, but there was no law saying I had to correct him.

"We understand," I said, "that Hauptmann had some friends in the neighborhood."

"Still does—some of 'em live just down the block."

"Did you know that at the time?"

That seemed to confuse him. "What do you mean?"

"Was Hauptmann a regular customer? Stands to reason he might've stopped in here before, since he had friends just down the street."

"He wasn't a regular customer, no. I might've seen him around."

"Might've?"

He shrugged. "I don't think it was his first time in. I think that blue sedan of his had rolled in here now and then. First time he passed a gold certificate, though."

That in itself was interesting.

"How about this guy Isidor Fisch?"

"That's the 'Fisch story' fella, right? I guess he did live around here."

"Just a few doors down the street."

"Maybe so, but I didn't know him. He was poor as a church mouse, I hear, so stands to reason he wouldn't even *have* a car."

"That's probably right," I said. "Well, thank you."

"Any time, Officer. You didn't want to go over how I come

to notice the gold certificate? We'd been told to be careful of counterfeits, so . . . "

"No, that's okay, Mr. Lyle."

"Oh. Well, fine." He couldn't hide his disappointment. "Good afternoon to you, Officer."

The brownstone down the block was a five-story walk-up; this was a fairly busy thoroughfare, and many of the buildings had a bottom-floor storefront, but not this one. It had obviously been an apartment house at one time, but as the neighborhood had begun to slide got converted to a rooming house, large apartments turned into modest one- and two-room suites.

Gerta Henkel was an apple-cheeked strudel in a cream-colored sweater that showed off her finer points. Around her pale neck she wore some cheap pearls, which she toyed with as she met us at the door. Her eyes were small and dark and wide-set, and her mouth was generous if rather thin-lipped. She smiled frequently. She offered me her hand, at the door of the little flat, and her grasp was warm and soft.

"Thank you for seeing us, Mrs. Henkel."

We stepped inside and she closed the door.

"Mr. Heller," she said, "anything I can do to help Richard, I will."

Her accent touched certain words—"anyt'ing"—in an appealing way.

"This is Evalyn McLean," I said, introducing the two women, who gave each other cold appraisals. They instinctively did not like each other, not uncommon between two women who are attractive in differing ways, but shook hands and smiled in a bad approximation of cordiality.

She led us to a little table near a gauzily curtained window overlooking the street. Her hips were sheathed in a black skirt and she walked with a sway as compelling as the swing of a hypnotist's watch.

"I'll get coffee," she said. "Cream or sugar, anyone?"

"Black is fine," I said, and Evalyn asked for cream.

Evalyn whispered to me, "Do you think Hauptmann . . . you know."

What she meant was, did Hauptmann have an affair with

Gerta, as Prosecutor Wilentz had done his best to imply at the trial.

"If he didn't," I said, "he's nuts."

She made a face and boxed my arm.

Gerta returned with a tray of small brimming coffee cups and some tiny, crunchy sugar cookies.

"I'd like to speak to your husband, too, Mrs. Henkel."

"He be gone till six, at least," she said. "Working a job in the Bronx."

Henkel was a house painter. Seemed like many of Hauptmann's friends were in the construction trades.

"That man Wilentz," Gerta said, nibbling a cookie with tiny white teeth, "tried to make Richard and me look bad. There was nothing bad between us, Mr. Heller. Richard was always a gentleman."

"You met at Hunter's Island?"

"Yes. We all go there for good time."

"But wasn't Mrs. Hauptmann away, when you met Dick?"

"I guess. But Anna and me become good friends. We are real good friends. I spend much time with her. I have spend time with her in Trenton; we stay at a hotel, so she can be near Richard, sometimes."

"Gerta . . . may I call you Gerta?"

"Sure. Can I call you by your first name?"

Evalyn drank her coffee; it had cream in it, but her expression was black.

"Yes, please—call me Nate."

"You look Irish, Nate—but your name is German, isn't it?"

"My people came from Halle."

"I grew up in Leipzig. Went to school there with Fisch. That's who you want to know about, right?"

"Yes. He lived in this building?"

"He had one furnished room—thirteen dollars a week; on this same floor. He moved from here, though, in the spring of '33, to a bigger place, in Yorkville, near the brokerage office where he and Richard would go."

When she said "though," it sounded like "dough."

"Before Fisch moved, Richard would meet him, here, at your place?"

"Yes. This is what give Wilentz ideas about Richard and me." She made a face; what a cutie—I couldn't blame Wilentz for any ideas he might have about her. "Richard would stop and have coffee with me, when he come to pick up Fisch. But we were not alone together. Fisch was here, or Carl, or sometimes my sister."

"Gerta, frankly, it doesn't matter to me either way, about you and Dick."

That made her eyes spark. She smiled. "Really?" she asked, and she nibbled a cookie.

"What kind of fellow," Evalyn said tightly, getting us back on track, "was this Isidor Fisch?"

She shrugged; her breasts under the pale creamy sweater had a life of their own. "He was a liar. A sneaky little shrimp. The only thing he ever told the truth about was he really was sick. He got very run-down. He said his lungs were bad 'cause of years he spent in Frigidaire rooms dressing fur pelts."

"You never liked him?" I asked.

"He got on my nerves. He always get me nervous, pacing up and down on the floor and looking out this window to see if Richard come or not. He would go away with Richard, but sometimes Richard didn't come, and he go away alone. I say, 'Where you go, Izzy, working or what?' He say he go down to the stock market."

"You wouldn't happen to have a picture of him, would you?"

"I do," she said. "A snapshot from Hunter's Island. You can take it. I don't look so good in it, though."

"That's all right," Evalyn said, and smiled sweetly.

Gerta got up and I watched the cheeks of her ass moving like pistons under the black skirt as she made her way across the tiny, tidy living room and Evalyn kicked me in the shins under the table.

"Do you believe her?" Evalyn whispered.

"About the affair?"

"Yes."

"It doesn't matter. If every man who wanted to sleep with Gerta was a kidnapper, no baby in this country would be safe."

Soon Gerta was back, and the picture of Fisch revealed a dark-haired, acned, jug-eared, smirky Jew in his twenties; bow tie and tweed sportcoat. Even in a still photo he looked like a cocky little smart-ass. In the photo, Gerta, cute as a button but not as cute as in real life, sat behind him and leaned forward, her hands on his shoulders.

Evalyn was looking at the picture. "You seem friendly enough with him here."

"He was fun, at first. His English was the best of us all. Had a swell line of bull. But even back in the old country, as teenager, he was in the black market. And here, with his schemes, he took fifteen hundred from my Carl's mother for this pie company that never was, and another almost three thousand from her for invest in furs."

"That's a lot of dough," I said.

"People's life saving," she said bitterly. "And my mother, he get from her four thousand."

It sounded like "t'ousand."

"And he got some from Erica, too," she said, "how much, I don't know."

"Erica?" Evalyn asked.

"My sister," she said. "And all our friends—hundreds dollars here, thousands dollars there. But you know what? We thought he was rich—he always said he was worth thirty thousand, easy. But he had other friends, who thought he was poor! I heard that when he moved out of here, he told these other friends that he was evicted! That he had to sleep wherever he could, in Hooverville and on benches in Grand Central depot. That way he could beg off them."

"What a weasel," I said.

"I tell you how I figure out he is keeping one group of friends away from the other. When Izzy is going down to the steamship, to go to Germany, Erica and me decide to go down and say goodbye, to surprise him. We go aboard and see Izzy talking with four or five men, strangers to us, but you can tell they was friends with him. Izzy saw us and his face went white as sheet; he came over, angry, and said, 'What the hell are you doing here, you girls?' I say, 'The hell with you, Izzy—we just want to surprise you, to say goodbye, you nasty little bastard!' The nerve of him. He apologize, show us to his cabin, but then said he was busy and shooed us away fast as he could."

"He was conning everybody," I said. "Getting money from your circle by playing the big-shot investor, and milking others using the poor-mouth routine."

"It worked," Gerta said, shrugging. "But he was a strange one."

"Strange, how?" Evalyn said.

"Well, I never see him with a woman. When I first meet him, I thought he was kind of . . . cute, in a way. Like a little boy. But, uh . . . he never seemed interested. Most men like me. I don't mean to be bragging, but . . . "

"I believe you," I said.

"And there was this crazy religion of his."

"What, Judaism?"

"No!" She grinned. "Spooks and stuff."

"Spooks and stuff?"

"What do they call it? Spiritualist."

I sat up, knocking the table; coffee spilled. I apologized and said, "Tell me more about this."

She shrugged. "He belonged to this little church. Not a church, really—just a storefront, all cleared out for benches and stuff. They do silly things over there, I hear."

"Like what?"

"What do they call them—séances. Did you know Izzy Fisch knew this girl Violet Sharpe?"

Evalyn and I traded quick looks.

"The maid Violet Sharpe, who killed herself," she continued, "and this older man, who was supposed to be a butler for the Lindberghs, they often come to that church. I think they were members."

"One of the butlers was named Septimus Banks," I said. My nerves were jumping, suddenly.

"I don't think that's the name."

"Another was Oliver Whately."

"That is the name."

Evalyn set her coffee cup down clatteringly.

"This is important, Gerta!" I said. "Haven't you ever told anybody this?"

She shrugged. "Nobody asked." She lowered her head, embarrassed. "I didn't want to get Richard in trouble."

"In trouble?"

"If they knew his friend Fisch knew those Lindbergh people . . . well . . . Carl thought we should say nothing."

"But this helps confirm Hauptmann's claims about Fisch."

She shook her head, sadly. "Nobody believed the 'Fisch story.' How could this help? It could only hurt."

My head was reeling. "Where was this church?"

She drew back the curtain and pointed. "Just across the street."

"Across the street?"

"Izzy always say it was very interesting. They call it the One Hundred Twenty-Seventh Street Spiritualist Church . . . Mr. Heller? Nate?"

I was standing; looking out the window. My heart was racing. "Is it still there?"

"I don't think so. I think they move it . . . "

"Thank you, Gerta, you've been very kind." I nodded to Evalyn, who got the point and got up. "We may be back . . . "

"I'm sure Carl would be glad to talk to you," she said, following along after us. "If you need to talk to me, alone, Nate, I'm here all day by myself, most days . . . 'less I'm helping Anna."

At the door I took Gerta's hand and squeezed it and soon we were down on the sidewalk and Evalyn was saying, "What's the rush? What's going on?"

"I could kick myself," I said. "How could I not make the connection?"

"What connection?"

I got in the trunk of the Packard and opened my suitcase and fumbled for my packet of field notes from '32. I thumbed through the notebook pages quickly, like a jumbled card hand I was trying to make sense of.

"Here," I said, my finger on the line. "The address is 164 East 127th. Damn! How could I not put this together."

"Put what together?"

I got my nine millimeter out of my suitcase, slipped it in my topcoat pocket, shut the trunk back up.

"Come on," I said. I cut diagonally across the street, getting honked at by a cabbie, to whom I displayed my middle finger, as Evalyn hustled along behind me, doing the best she could in her heels.

Then we were standing before a storefront; it was a shoe-repair shop. The number was 164.

"This used to be a spiritualist church," I said, "run by a pair called Martin Marinelli and Sarah Sivella. They were the spiritualists who, a few days after the kidnapping, made some startling 'predictions' about the case."

"Oh my. I think I remember you telling me this . . . "

"They conjured up the name 'Jafsie' before Condon was on the scene, before Condon claimed he'd even thought of the moniker. They predicted a ransom note would be delivered to Colonel Breckinridge's office. They even predicted the body of a baby would be found in the Sourland Mountains."

"Good Lord! And Isidor Fisch was in their congregation? And Violet Sharpe? And Whately?"

I nodded. I put a hand on her shoulder. "We have to find those fakers, Evalyn. Today."

And I got lucky, fast: the guy behind the shoe-repair counter knew where the church had been relocated. It was called the Temple of Divine Power, now.

"Over on 114th," the guy said. "Near the East River."

"That's not far, is it?"

"Hell, no. You could walk it."

We drove.

Chapter 32

The Temple of Divine Power announced itself in white letters against a large front window painted a vivid blue; the meeting hours were "2–6–8–10 P.M., Friday through Sunday." The sign stuck in the window said "Closed," with a phone number for "Personal Consultations" below, as well as the name "Rev. M. J. Marinelli." Three steps led up to a similarly blue, painted-out door labeled in white letters, Entrance. The temple was only half a storefront: the other half was taken up by a small Italian deli.

Behind a couple garbage cans was a walk-down to a basement apartment; I went down the steps and knocked on the door and got no response.

I joined Evalyn on the sidewalk.

"You could try the phone number," she suggested. "You could ask about them at that little food market next door."

"Maybe they're in the church, closed or not," I said, shrugging, and went up and knocked on the narrow Entrance door. Nothing. I could hear something going inside, something that sounded like a motor. I put my ear to the door and there was definitely something going on in there. I tried a second time, knock-ing so hard the glass rattled. Then I could hear the motor stop.

And the door cracked open.

"Yes?" she said.

She was still very pretty, though she had a double chin now; the eyes were just as brown, flecked gold, the face creamy pale, the lips full and sensuous, though untouched by lip rouge at the mo-ment.

"Hi, Sarah," I said.

"Do I know you?"

"Yes. Just a moment." I walked down the steps to Evalyn and said, "See that little café across the street? Get yourself a cup of espresso."

"But Nate—Nathan!"

"I have to handle this one alone."

Evalyn's mouth formed a thin tight line; she wasn't used to being told what to do. But she nodded, and I watched her cross the street, her heels clicking. A cabbie honked and she gave him the finger. A gloved one.

"That's my girl," I said under my breath.

I returned to Sister Sarah Sivella, watching me from the cracked-open door of her storefront temple.

"I remember you," she said, and her smile was very faint. "I remember that night with you."

I grinned at her. "I thought you might. Your husband home?"

"No."

"Good. You want to talk in your apartment downstairs, or in the church?"

Her eyes tensed. "How did you know the downstairs apartment was ours?"

"Well, I could be psychic," I said. "Or just a detective."

She let me in. Pleasantly plump now, she was wearing a simple black frock, the sort of thing Evalyn might wear, if she had only a buck ninety-eight to spend and no jewelry. A Hoover stand-up vacuum cleaner leaned against the wall—that had been the sound I'd heard through the door. The walls were stark, as blue as the painted-out window, up to the chair rail, then whitewashed above. There were half a dozen rows of hard, stiff chairs, facing a pulpit, with a blue curtain behind. It looked more than a little like the death chamber at the New Jersey state prison.

She shut the door; locked it. "I didn't expect to ever see you again."

"Working the same old case," I said, hat in my hands.

Her unplucked eyebrows met in thought. "The Lindbergh kidnapping . . . ?"

"That's right. Let's sit down, shall we?"

Rather tentatively, she did, pulling up one of the chairs. I pulled mine around so I could face her.

"But the man who did that is in jail," she said.

"Is he?"

She moved her head to one side, to avert my gaze. "Actually— in the trance state, Martin says I've said otherwise."

"Oh?"

"Yes. I've said, in a trance, that this German is not the kidnapper. That there were many persons in this plot. Four who did the kidnapping. One of them a woman. One of them dead."

"Is it the woman who's dead?"

She shrugged shyly; her long dark hair bounced on her shoulders. "That's all I know. I only know what Martin tells me. I have no memory of what I say, in that state."

"Well, you could've meant Violet Sharpe."

Her eyes flickered. She said nothing.

"Violet was in your congregation, wasn't she?"

She swallowed.

I reached out and squeezed her arm; not quite hard enough to hurt, but hard enough to make a point. "Wasn't she?"

She nodded.

"Sometimes she came to services," she said. "I'm not sure she was a member."

"Who else?"

"So many people."

I stamped my foot on the floor. The chairs bounced. So did she.

"Who else, Sarah?"

She swallowed again, shook her head. "That funny-looking little man, Fisch. He was a member."

"Don't stop now, Sarah. You're getting hot."

"There was a man named Whately. A butler, I think."

"A butler, you think. Anyone else? Think hard, now."

She shook her head, no. "I don't think so."

"Remember back in that hotel room, in Princeton? You mentioned a name."

"I don't remember what I said in the trance state . . . "

"You said 'Jafsie.' You said you saw the letters J-A-F-S-I-E."

"I remember Martin told me I said that."

"Was Professor John Condon a member of the One Hundred Twenty-Seventh Street church?"

"No . . . no."

"No?"

"But . . . "

"But what, Sarah?"

"But . . . he did attend a few times."

I felt myself trembling; I smiled at her—it must've been a terrible smile. "Tell me about it, Sarah. Tell me about Jafsie. . . . "

A resonant male voice behind me said, "He was only an occasional visitor."

I turned and Martin Marinelli, wearing a black turtleneck and black slacks, looking like a priest who lost his collar if not quite his calling, had entered through the curtain behind the pulpit. His head was as bald as ever, though his eyebrows had grown out and were wild and woolly, not plucked for effect; he still wore a devil beard. He had a small paper bag tucked under one arm.

He walked slowly to us and handed the paper bag to Sarah, who appeared on the verge of tears. "Here are the supplies you requested, my dear."

I could see as she set it on a nearby chair that in the bag were various cleaning products, cleanser, disinfectant, soap flakes.

Marinelli pulled a chair up and made it a threesome. "We're the janitors of this building, Mr. Heller. That's how we keep our rent down."

"You remember my name," I said. "I'm impressed, Reverend."

"I've had to keep an eye on the Lindbergh case," he said, with a little flourish of a gesture. "We've been harassed so many times, it's become a necessity to be well informed."

"I like to be well informed, myself. Tell me more about this star-studded congregation of yours."

"There's nothing to tell. As far as Dr. Condon is concerned, he's a philosophy instructor, with quite an avid interest in spiritualism. I'm sure we're not the only spiritualist church he's visited."

"Condon taught school in Harlem," I said. "Either one of you happen to attend Old Public School Number Thirty-Eight?"

Sarah closed her eyes; she began to rock back and forth slowly.

Marinelli put his hands on his knees; they were powerful-looking hands. "I don't see that our schooling has anything to do with anything, Mr. Heller."

"Then let's change the subject. Tell me about Isidor Fisch, and Violet Sharpe, and Ollie Whately. They were in your congregation, Reverend. Surely you must've got to know them on a personal basis."

"We had many parishioners on One Hundred Twenty-Seventh Street in those years. That was a larger church. People walked in off the street all the time. One night we had a Chinaman!"

"I'm not interested in the Chinaman, Rev. How did Violet and Whately wind up in your church?"

He shrugged. "They found their way to me. I never ask my flock about their pasts, unless they offer it. But one, or both of them, had been interested in spiritualism before coming to this country."

"One of 'em, at least, had been involved in a spiritualist church in England?"

"Yes. I believe it was Whately. I think Violet had lost her parents, and had hoped to contact them, through the spirit world. We helped her do that."

"Did you. You and Sarah and old, what was that Injun's name? Chief Yellow Feather?"

Sarah, eyes shut tight, twitched.

"As for Fisch," Marinelli said, ignoring me, "he lived across the street and down, in a rooming house. He wandered in off the street one night, curious, and became interested in what we do."

"And what is it you do, exactly? I've never been able to tell."

"We are dedicated to the cause of spiritualism, Mr. Heller, whether you believe that or not. We've not gotten wealthy, as you can see."

"You're doing all right. Better than most in these times, I'd say."

"Now that I've answered your questions, Mr. Heller," Marinelli said, folding his arms, "I would appreciate it if you would leave."

"What about Bruno Richard Hauptmann? Was he in your church?"

"No. He never set foot there."

"Still, Rev—I think the cops might be very interested in knowing that, back in '32, your church on One Twenty-Seventh was a veritable hotbed of people associated with the Lindbergh case."

Marinelli shrugged. "They already know," he said.

"What?"

"We were arrested in January 1934, Mr. Heller. On a fortune-telling charge. But we were questioned at length about the Lindbergh case, and we held nothing back. While we were indisposed, our lodgings were ransacked, an address book was stolen, and so on. Typical police behavior."

Sister Sarah was stone quiet, and motionless; eyes shut tight.

"What's with her?" I said.

"You scared her," he said, matter-of-factly. "She withdrew into the trance state."

"Aw, baloney."

"Mr. Heller, my wife is a genuine psychic."

I got the nine millimeter out of my topcoat.

He stood and backed up, knocking over several chairs; she remained still as death.

"Izzy Fisch and Violet Sharpe and Ollie Whately," I said, rising, "have a lot in common, don't they? They're all members of your church—and they're all dead. Maybe we can have a little informal séance, and conjure 'em up."

"What . . . what do you want from me, Heller? What do you want me to do?"

I inched forward, gun in hand. "Spill, you phony bastard. Spill it all, or I'll start spilling you . . . "

He was backing up; backing into the pulpit. "I don't know anything!"

"Ugh," someone said.

I turned and looked at Sarah.

She had begun to speak. "Who seeks Yellow Feather?"

"Aw, fuck," I said, moving toward her. "I'm going to slap her silly . . ."

"No!" he said, moving forward. He touched my arm. "No. Whatever I am, Mr. Heller, Sarah is an innocent. And truly is genuinely psychic . . ."

"I can see a child," she said, her voice a register lower than normal. "He is in a high place. There is a small house, low, with a high barn behind. The child is in the house. On the second floor. There is a bald-headed man, with pouches under his eyes. He is looking down at the child. There is a woman in the house, too. The house is on a hill."

She shuddered, and her eyes popped open. It made me jump.

"I'm sorry," she said, quietly. "Did I fall asleep?"

He went to her, touched her shoulder, gently. "You were in a trance, my dear." He told her what she'd said.

"How can you see the baby," I said, sarcasm hanging on my words like a week's worth of wash, "when you already 'predicted,' accurately, its dead body on the heights over Hopewell?"

"She never said it was the Lindbergh baby's body," Marinelli said, his arm around his wife's shoulder.

"First, she sees a dead baby in the heights, four years ago. And now she sees it alive, only now it's a 'child,' not a baby, and it's in some farmhouse?"

"It may not be the same child," Marinelli said. "We can't always know the meaning of what a medium says in a trance—interpretation is required, Mr. Heller. Will you put your gun away, please?"

He was standing there protecting his wife, who looked small and pitiful and, hell, I'd screwed her once upon a time, so maybe I owed them this one.

"All right," I said. And I put the gun away. "Will you cooperate, if I need you to talk to somebody?"

"Certainly," Marinelli said, summoning his dignity. "Who?"

"Governor Hoffman of New Jersey," I said.

He nodded solemnly.

I went to the door.

"Goodbye, Nate," she said, quietly.

"So long, Sarah," I said, shaking my head, and I went down to the sidewalk and stood there and shook my head some more and sighed. Evalyn, watching from the café across the street, came over and joined me.

"What did you find?"

"I'll tell you all about it," I said, "on the way."

"On the way where?"

"We have one more stop this afternoon. . . ."

The neat, trim two-story white clapboard in the Bronx was unchanged; so was the quiet residential street it was perched along. The lawn was brown, but evergreens hugged the porch.

I told Evalyn to stay in the car; she didn't like it, but I made her understand.

"If there's a witness," I said, "this guy is liable not to say anything."

The attractive dark-haired woman who answered the door did not recognize me at first.

"Yes?" she said, warily, the door only a third of the way open.

"Is Professor Condon in? Tell him an old friend's dropped by."

Her face had tightened. "Detective Heller," she said.

"Hiya, Myra."

The door shut suddenly—not quite a slam.

I glanced back at Evalyn, sitting in the Packard, and smiled and shrugged. She looked at me curiously, wondering if this interview was over before it began.

The door opened again and there he stood, in white shirtsleeves and vest and pocket watch, in all his walrus-mustached glory.

"Long time no see, Professor."

"Detective Heller," Dr. John F. Condon said stiffly. He extended his hand and I shook it; he squeezed to impress me with his strength, as usual. "I hope you've been well."

"I've been okay. You're nice and tan."

"I have just returned from Panama."

"So I hear. You took off, day before Hauptmann's case came up before the Court of Pardons."

He snorted. "That's true. Though it is of no particular significance."

"Isn't it? Didn't the Governor of New Jersey request that you stick around? And help clear up a few discrepancies in your various versions of various events?"

He raised his head. Looked down his nose at me with his vague watery blue eyes. "I had full permission of Attorney General Wilentz to depart on my holiday."

"I'm sure you did." I smiled blandly at him. "You might be wondering why I'm still interested in this case, after all these years."

"Frankly, sir, I am."

"Well, I'm working for Governor Hoffman now."

He backed away, stepping into the entrance hall; I half expected him to hold up a cross, as if I were a vampire.

"Sir," he said, pompously, "during my stay in Panama, I followed all reported developments in the Lindbergh case, and this man Hoffman seems bound and determined to maliciously impugn my character, my motives, my behavior."

"Really," I said.

He took a step forward and shook a fist in the air. "I would like to face this Governor Hoffman! I would like to nail these lies of his. I know he would have a good many men there, stronger than I—but even at my age, I can put up a good fight, Detective Heller! I can still handle myself."

"Come along then. I'll drive you there."

His fist dissolved into loose fingers, which he used to wave me off. "Ah, I said I would *like* to. But my womenfolk wouldn't allow it."

"Then why don't you ask me in, and I'll put the Governor's questions to you, myself."

"Detective Heller, I'm afraid I must decline, though I *am* willing to answer the Governor's questions."

"You are?"

"Certainly. If they're submitted in writing."

"In writing?"

"Yes—and I will of course submit my answers in the same fashion."

"I see. How about answering just a couple of little questions for me, not in writing? For old times' sake?"

He smiled in what I'm sure he imagined was a devilish manner. "Perhaps I'll answer. Go ahead and pose your questions, young man."

"Did you ever meet Isidor Fisch, when you were hanging around that spiritualist church on One Twenty-Seventh Street in Harlem?"

His eyes bugged. He stepped back.

"Or maybe Violet Sharpe, or Ollie Whately? Maybe all four of you sat at the same séance table, one night. By the way, the Marinellis wouldn't happen to have been students of yours, would they?"

The door slammed in my face.

"Yeah, Jafsie," I said, "you can still handle yourself," and joined Evalyn in the car.

Chapter 33

Ghent was a tree-shaded residential section of Norfolk, just off the downtown, its narrow brick streets lined with old two- and three-story brick houses, some shoulder-to-shoulder and hugging the sidewalk, others with shamrock-green lawns moist from sheltering boxwood, magnolia and winter-barren crape myrtle. Piercing Ghent was the Hague, a small horseshoe-shaped body of water where skiffs and pleasure craft were moored. Nothing larger could navigate the pond-like harbor. Presumably it connected to the nearby Elizabeth River, but from the rubbery dock where Evalyn and I stood, you couldn't tell; the funnels and masts of the busy bay were obscured by a bastion of riverfront buildings. The day was cool, the sky overcast, the water, indeed the world, a peaceful but chill gray-blue.

The sign on the central of several white-frame, green-roofed shambling dockside structures said "J. H. Curtis Boat and Engine Corporation." Not a small operation, but not a large one, either—an obvious step down from the owner's previous shipbuilding company, which had had among its many customers the German government. It was in that central building, in a modest, glassed-in office (no secretary, no receptionist) looking out on a big cement work area where several boatmen were sanding down the hull of a small racing craft, that we met with Commodore John H. Curtis.

"Mrs. McLean," Curtis said, standing from a swivel chair at an obsessively neat rolltop desk, grasping the hand she'd extended, "it's a great pleasure to meet you at last."

"Thank you, Commodore," she said. Evalyn wore another black frock, this one trimmed in white and gray, with a white-and-gray pillbox hat; she looked neat enough for a department-store window. "You're looking well."

"I feel well," he said, with a nod of his large head, "all things considered." And he looked pretty good at that: tall, tanned, rather stout; in his light-brown business suit, his brown-and-yellow tie, he could have stood next to Evalyn in that department-store window. Only the lines around his eyes gave away the stress.

"Thank you for seeing us at such short notice," I said, and shook hands with the Commodore. He'd put two wood chairs with cushioned seats out, in anticipation of our arrival, and he gestured to them, and we sat, and so did he.

"We seem to have mutual interests, Mr. Heller," he said, with a friendly but serious smile. Looking at Evalyn, he said, "I feel we have much in common, Mrs. McLean."

"I believe we do, Commodore," she said. "I feel we both suffered a certain public . . . humiliation . . . as a result of our sincere desire to do good in the Lindbergh tragedy."

"I've been fortunate," he said, swaying a bit in the swivel chair, "having my family stand behind me. My wife . . . well, without her, perhaps I would have been lost. But my business is going well, and my personal reputation, here in the Norfolk area, and in the shipping trade in general, remains untarnished."

"I would assume that means, Commodore," I said, "that you'd like to put this mess behind you, and get on with your life."

"I'm getting on with my life quite nicely," he said, sitting forward, his lips tightening, "but I don't intend to allow the indignities done to me to stand unredressed."

"You were accused of being a hoaxer, at first," I said, "but were tried and convicted for obstructing justice—the state arguing that you aided and abetted the kidnap gang."

"Yes," Curtis said, with a mirthless smirk, "by failing to give 'accurate information' about them to the authorities."

"So the State of New Jersey," Evalyn said, eyes narrowing, "acknowledged that you were in fact in touch with the kidnappers."

Curtis nodded. "The language of the court was 'the actual kidnappers of the Lindbergh baby numbering seven or eight, and including a member of the Lindbergh household.' "

Early on, the position of Schwarzkopf and Inspector Welch and others was that Violet Sharpe's suicide was an admission of guilt; by the time of Hauptmann's trial, that stance had been conveniently forgotten.

"It seems to me," Evalyn said, her gloved hands folded in her lap, "that if the Hauptmann conviction was correct, your conviction should be set aside, Mr. Curtis . . . and your record cleared, and the fine you paid refunded."

"And if *your* conviction was correct," I said to Curtis, "then Hauptmann's conviction should be set aside, and he should be a free man again."

"You might think that," Curtis said, with a wry, world-weary smile. "It was the same courtroom, one of the same prosecutors. . . . Did you know that I offered to testify against Hauptmann?"

"I'd heard that," I said. God, was I glad *he* brought it up. "That's one of the things I hoped to ask you about."

The intermittent whine of a power drill in the outer work-area provided an uncomfortable edge to the conversation.

"I told them I thought I could positively identify Hauptmann as the 'John' I dealt with," he said, blandly. "There'd been much speculation that 'Cemetery John' and the rumrunner John I encountered might be one and the same."

"Did you recognize Hauptmann?" I asked. "*Was* he your 'John'?"

"From newspaper pictures and newsreels I'd seen," Curtis said, "he could have been. I told Wilentz and crew that I would testify against Hauptmann in exchange for full exoneration and the return of the thousand-dollar fine. Schwarzkopf thought it was a swell idea, and couldn't have cared less if I was telling the truth or not. But Wilentz was afraid to put me on the stand."

"Why?" Evalyn asked.

"Because my story, the story I'd been telling all along, which *was* true, did not fit the tale *they* were spinning, this fantasy of Hauptmann being a 'lone-wolf' kidnapper."

Curtis's yarn, I remembered, involved a large cast of characters, Sam and Hilda and Nils and Eric and Larsen and assorted rumrunners.

"Would you have testified against Hauptmann?" I asked.

"Yes," Curtis said.

"Even if you didn't really recognize him?" Evalyn asked, dumbfounded.

"Probably," he said. "I'm not proud to admit it, Mrs. McLean. But at the time, it looked as though they had so much evidence against Hauptmann, it looked so convincing reading the papers, he seemed so undoubtedly guilty, I didn't see the harm."

Evalyn fell into a dark silence.

"I was at wit's end in those months," he said. "Several years ago, before my involvement with the Lindbergh case, I suffered a nervous breakdown, having to do with anxiety related to business difficulties. I was very near that point again."

"That's another reason they kept you off the stand," I said bluntly.

"Perhaps. And perhaps they knew there was at least some chance that, face-to-face with Hauptmann in a courtroom, under oath, I might not point the accusing finger at him. I might simply tell the truth. And *my* truth is something the State of New Jersey has never been interested in."

"You're saying that had you ID'ed Hauptmann," I said, "you most likely would've withdrawn that identification, in time."

"Perhaps," he said, nodding. Then he shrugged. "But perhaps not—had my good name been restored, and my thousand dollars, the better part of valor might have been to fade into respectable obscurity. I can only tell you, truthfully, that today, with my full mental faculties at my command, I would not wrongly testify against that man. Or any man. And having studied the case in some detail—and having had a firsthand view of Jersey justice—I've become convinced that poor bastard was railroaded. Pardon my French, Mrs. McLean."

"Let me back up, just a second," I said. "Do I understand you to say that now, today, with your 'full mental faculties' at your command, you claim the story I heard you tell Lindbergh was true? That you *were* in contact with the kidnappers, or at least with an extortion group that had inside information about the kidnapping?"

"I lied about one thing," he said, raising a cautionary finger. "I said I'd seen ransom bills—that I was able to check serial numbers. I never did. I embellished the truth, because I was afraid that otherwise Colonel Lindbergh wouldn't believe me when I said I was in contact with the kidnappers."

That had been the part of Curtis's story that had been the most compelling to Lindbergh.

"He seemed reluctant to get involved," Curtis went on. "You were there, Mr. Heller, you should remember this. I did it for his own good. To get him off the dime."

"Otherwise, your story was true."

"One hundred percent," Curtis said. His eyes were hard and clear; his voice was the same. "I'm not a liar. I'm an honest man."

"You were ready to lie about Hauptmann," Evalyn said. Her eyes were hard, too, in a different way.

"And I lied about the ransom bills," he admitted, and shrugged again, and sighed. Then he smiled, sadly. "But I've been honest with you about both of those things. And I've been honest with you about the mental strain I was under."

"Is that why you confessed?" she asked. "Why you 'admitted' everything you'd said was a hoax, when in fact everything you'd said was true?"

"But *not* everything I'd said was true. I was kept awake for days, dragged here and there by the police, not allowed to get a change of clothes, rarely fed, and yes, under great mental strain. After a while, I admitted that one thing: that I hadn't really seen any ransom money. And that, Mrs. McLean, was when the fun began."

"I'd like to hear about that," I said. "But from the beginning."

Curtis told us how, while on Cape May for a meeting with

"Hilda," his contact with the kidnappers, he'd been informed by phone of the discovery of the body of Charles Augustus Lindbergh, Jr., in a shallow grave in the Sourland Mountains. How he had driven at breakneck speed through a rainstorm and arrived at Hopewell at two P.M.. Here he was questioned, politely, but in a manner that already indicated he was something of a suspect, by Schwarzkopf, Inspector Welch and Frank J. Wilson.

Curtis had suggested they wait for Colonel Lindbergh to arrive, but the interrogators pressed on; he also suggested that if they were going to question him, he ought to have his "memoranda" brought to him—some were in a lockbox in a New York hotel, others were in his bag on the ketch, the *Cachalot*, still more with his secretary in Norfolk. This request was ignored.

He answered the questions to the best of his ability, though he was tired and emotionally wrung-out; and they pressed for auto license numbers, house numbers, phone numbers, none of which he could guarantee the accuracy of without his notes being brought to him.

"When Colonel Lindbergh finally arrived," Curtis said, "he seemed pleased to see me. You can imagine my relief at seeing a familiar, friendly face. He asked me what I made of this . . . meaning the discovery of the child in the midst of negotiations for its return from Hilda and Sam and the rest. I said I couldn't fathom it, and pledged I'd do anything in my power to help. And I suggested if we moved fast, because Hilda and Sam were on land, we could nab them."

"How did Slim respond?" I asked.

"Very positively," Curtis said. "But he went into his library with Schwarzkopf and Wilson and did not come back."

Inspector Welch and various troopers and plainclothes officers, including at times Wilson, questioned him all night, taking a lengthy statement despite his requests that he be allowed to have his notes brought to him for the sake of accuracy. The tone was one of suspicious, insistent interrogation, and Curtis knew he was in deep trouble.

Finally he convinced his captors to take him to Cape May, where he might lead them to the various locations where he'd made contact with the kidnappers. At dawn Inspector Welch and a trooper set out with Curtis in a squad car. Curtis led them to three houses, two of them vacant cottages, one of them occupied by a family named Larsen, the last name of one of the gang. But the Mrs. Larsen who answered the door said she didn't know any "George Olaf Larsen" and Welch let it go at that.

They were back at the Lindbergh house in Hopewell by nine that night. Welch informed all concerned that the trip had been a waste of damn time and that Curtis was a goddamned liar. Another statement, under increasingly hostile conditions, was forced out of Curtis, who continued to request his notes.

After this, Curtis was driven to the Hildebrecht Hotel in Trenton, where he was registered under a false name and remained essentially a prisoner; he slept three hours, and the next day was spent successfully leading two Newark cops to the Scandinavian neighborhood where one of the meetings had taken place. But he couldn't lead them to the exact house; he asked them to come back at night, as that was when he'd been driven there. At the Newark police station, he went over mug photo books and found a shot that might have been Nils. The suspect was in custody at Morrisville on another matter, and Curtis would look at him the next day.

That night they returned to the Scandinavian neighborhood, but Curtis could still not zero in on the specific house, and suggested a house-to-house canvas. At the hotel Curtis was sent to bed at two-thirty A.M. and was woken at seven. His requests to have fresh laundry sent from New York were denied, as were his requests to call his family, though he was allowed to shave.

The next day the house-to-house canvas began, without any success, and the suspect at Morrisville was viewed; but the suspect proved noticeably shorter than Nils, despite a strong resemblance. This day, too, ended around two-thirty A.M., and at seven Curtis was hauled back to Hopewell.

"I wandered all morning around the grounds," he said. "I was given the silent treatment, except for a few troopers who on the sly gave me a sympathetic comment or two. Some of the troopers seemed sore at Lindbergh for wanting to run the investigation himself. They said they should be at 'headquarters,' not in this 'godforsaken place.' I wasn't given anything to eat. Finally a trooper passed the word to me: Schwarzkopf and Welch were planning to arrest me. I asked to talk to Lindbergh. Pretty soon he came out."

Curtis had asked Lindbergh, "What's this all about, my being arrested for 'obstructing justice'?"

"I don't know anything about it," Lindbergh had said. "I do know that a phone number you said you called in Freeport, Long Island, did not check out."

"What number?"

"Five-six-three-oh."

"I said, five-six-*four*-oh. Colonel, I've been asking from the start that I be given the opportunity to consult my notes! I've been up day and night for practically the last ten days, and I can't recall numbers like that—I'm not sure I could if I *were* rested!"

Lindbergh nodded, went into the house, didn't come back.

"I wandered, and waited. Sat on the running board of Colonel Lindbergh's car, feeling pretty goddamn low and dejected. Then something happened that should have been a warning flag, but I didn't recognize it as such: Inspector Welch came by and was nice to me. It was hard to accept, this kindness from so cruel a man, but I grasped it, like a life jacket. He asked if I'd care to play a game of checkers. I said I'd like that. We played and he talked about what a great weight I must have on my mind."

"And you admitted lying about seeing the ransom money," I said.

"Yes," Curtis said, nodded, lips tight across his teeth. "He trotted me inside and had me admit that to the Colonel. I did, and Lindbergh gave me a cold look, a look to kill that I will never forget. He nodded to Welch, who dragged me out of there. I was taken to Schwarzkopf's office, where I made a statement adding this new fact. Then I was taken into the basement of the Lindbergh home, and the beatings began."

They started at ten in the evening, the beatings; ended at four-thirty A.M., when the final, most complete of the several statements he signed, he signed. Then he was left tied up in the dank basement laundry room. He was not yet under arrest, or even formally ac-cused of any wrongdoing.

"The next morning, unshaven, in filthy clothes," he said, lips trembling, "I was dragged into Colonel Lindbergh's library. A court of arraignment was waiting—the justice of the peace was there, so was Breckinridge, Lindbergh, Wilson and Prosecutor Hauck. I was charged with obstructing justice and taken away to jail. I stayed there until the trial. I couldn't afford the bail. My wife came and brought me a change of clothes."

Evalyn believed him. The tears in her eyes said so.

I believed him, too. I knew all about cops beating confessions out of suspects—having been both a cop and a suspect, at various times.

But what was more important, I believed he'd been telling the truth all along: I didn't know who exactly Sam, Hilda, Nils and the rest were . . . nor whether they were in on the kidnapping, or just interloping extortionists.

But I was convinced they existed.

"One thing I don't understand," Evalyn asked earnestly. "Why weren't Admiral Burrage and Reverend Dobson-Peacock accused and brought to trial?"

"Admiral Burrage never had any direct contact with the gang," Curtis said. He had calmed himself, but it was a surface calm, only. "Also, the Admiral's friendship with Colonel Lindbergh protected him. His only public comment, incidentally, has been 'no comment'—and he has never responded to my calls or letters."

"What about Dobson-Peacock?" I asked.

"The Reverend refused to come to New Jersey for questioning," Curtis said, "which was undoubtedly wise. His public stance was that I'd put one over on him—though he did have some contact with the kidnappers."

"I'd like to talk to him."

"I hope you're prepared to travel, Mr. Heller," Curtis said. He smiled but there was nothing happy about it. "Like Colonel Lindbergh, the Reverend resides in England, now."

Evalyn and I exchanged looks of quiet frustration.

"What else can I tell you?" Curtis asked.

"What about the allegations," Evalyn asked, gently, "that all this was a hoax you concocted to sell your story to the newspapers?"

"I did have a deal with the *Herald-Tribune*," he said forthrightly. "But it was contingent upon the recovery of the child. No money exchanged hands."

It was time to take another tack.

"Did you ever hear of Max Greenberg," I asked, "or Max Hassel?"

"Yes," Curtis said, and saw me perk up, and then stopped me: "Only in the papers. I understand, Gaston Means identified them as bootleggers involved in the kidnapping."

"Did you see their pictures in the paper at the time?"

"Yes. And no, I'd never seen them before."

"What about this guy?"

I showed him the picture of Fisch that Gerta Henkel, who was also in the picture, had given me.

"No," he said, shaking his head. "I'm sorry. Who is it?"

"The infamous Isidor Fisch," I said.

"You're in the right place for a fish," Curtis said, with his wry smile. "But not that one."

"Commodore," I said, rising, offering him my hand, "thank you."

"I don't know what I've said that could be helpful," he said regretfully, taking my hand. "The Hauptmann case and mine are apparently unconnected."

"Commodore," Evalyn said, straightening her skirt as she rose, "they're connected in this way: if we're successful in clearing Richard Hauptmann, you may well be vindicated, too."

"I appreciate that," he said heartily. "But if you don't mind, I'm going to continue my own efforts. If it takes the rest of my life, I'm going to clear my name through the courts."

"I'm sure Hauptmann feels the same way," I said. "Only the rest of his life is most likely a couple weeks."

And we went out into the gray-blue world, where skiffs skimmed the water like ducks in a pond, and pointed the nose of the Packard north.

I had somebody to see at a nuthouse.

Chapter 34

"**N**athan Heller," Gaston Means said, sitting up in bed, with his usual puckish smile, though his eyes had no twinkle, just a disturbed, disturbing glaze, and his dimples were lost in the hollows of his cheeks. He'd lost weight and his skin, which bore a yellowish cast from frequent gallstone attacks, had the loose look of oversize clothing. He wore a hospital nightgown, and was under the sheets and horsehair blankets of a bed in the prison ward in the Medical and Surgical Building of St. Elizabeth's, a government mental hospital in Congress Heights, Maryland, near Washington, D.C. The window next to him had both bars and mesh, like the skylight near Hauptmann's death-row cell.

Evalyn and I were standing next to his bed. Evalyn was wearing white, for a change, though the outfit was trimmed in black and her hat was white with black trim, too; she looked like a wealthy nurse.

"I never told you my name, Means," I said.

"Ah, but you made an impression on me, Heller," he said, and some twinkle almost cracked the glaze on the eyes. "Any man who puts a gun barrel in my mouth leaves his imprint on my psyche. Effective piece of psychology—I must compliment you."

"Thanks."

"I made a point to check up on you, yes indeedy. Like me, you've made your mark in the field of private investigation. You have certain acquaintances of influence in the underworld, as do I. You have, to put it mildly, quite a reputation, young man."

"Coming from you," I said, "I guess that's a compliment."

He looked at Evalyn warmly, placing a hand on his heart, as if about to be sworn on the witness stand, where he would of course lie his gallstones off.

"My dear Eleven," he said, reverting to Evalyn's long-ago code number, "you look charming. Are you lovely because you're so rich, or are you rich because you're so lovely? I'll leave that question to the philosophers. At any rate, I want you to know that I harbor no ill feelings toward you."

"You harbor no ill feelings toward *me*?" Evalyn said, eyes wide, her white-gloved hand touching her generous bosom.

"For testifying against me," he said, seemingly astounded that she hadn't known what he meant.

"You wouldn't want to demonstrate your good will," I said, "by telling us where Mrs. McLean's one hundred thousand is, would you?"

He cocked his head and raised a lecturing finger. "That's one hundred and four thousand," he said. "And, no—that's a point on which I'm rather fuzzy. I have a vague memory of stuffing the cash in a piece of pipe and throwing it into the Potomac. But from which pier exactly, I'm afraid it's just not clear."

"Right," I said.

He began to cough; it did not seem feigned—it rattled the steel bed and his yellow face turned purple.

When the coughing subsided, and his color (such as it was) returned, Evalyn asked him, "How ill are you, Means?"

He straightened his bedclothing, summoned his dignity. "These gallstones are a damned nuisance, my dear. That's not why I've come to St. Elizabeth's, however. I'm here for serious psychiatric evaluation. I have had, on occasion, a tendency to fabricate, and to have difficulty differentiating illusion from reality."

"No shit," I said.

"Please, Heller," Means said, flashing me a stern look. "There *is* a lady present." He smiled at Evalyn like Friar Tuck. "All my troubles date to that fateful night of December eighth, 1911, when I fell from the upper berth of a Pullman car and struck my head."

"Your first major insurance scam," I said.

"Fourteen thousand dollars," Means said, with a nostalgic sigh. "And fourteen thousand was *money*, then."

A doctor interrupted us to read Means's charts, and we stood to one side and waited; a not unattractive nurse brought him some pills and a cup of water and he smiled at her and called her "my dear" and harmlessly flirted.

When they'd gone, he said to us, "I'm suffering from high blood pressure of the brain, you see. It's a direct result of that fall from the Pullman berth. It made me develop this fantastic imagination, which has gotten me into so much trouble. I've never profited a dime from any of my bootlegging or blackmail schemes, because I've always returned the money . . . except in your case, Eleven, because I simply can't remember where it is."

"That's not why we're here," I said.

"Oh?" he said. Interested. "And why are you here, Heller?"

"I'm working for Governor Hoffman."

He lit up like a Halloween pumpkin; the dimples in the hollows of the cheeks asserted themselves. "Splendid! I've sent numerous letters to Governor Hoffman. I'm delighted that he's decided to help me in my mission."

Evalyn blinked. "Your 'mission'?"

Means nodded solemnly; he folded his hands prayer-like on what remained of his once formidable belly. "I have decided to dedicate all of my efforts to aid that poor, so unfairly maligned soul, Bruno Hauptmann."

I sat on the edge of his bed. "No kidding. Your sense of justice is offended, is it?"

"It most certainly is. I've written not only to Governor Hoffman but Prosecutor Wilentz and Colonel Lindbergh, in England, and many other of the principals in the case. I'm doing my level best, in the midst of my illnesses, to help secure a stay of execution for Mr. Hauptmann."

"You're quite a guy, Means. Why are you doing this?"

"Because," he said, with a simple shrug, "*I* masterminded the Lindbergh kidnapping."

Neither Evalyn nor I reacted.

That disappointed him; he seemed almost hurt. "Did you understand me? I said, *I* am the man. Hauptmann does not deserve the blame, nor for that matter the credit, for this elaborate crime. A simple ignorant carpenter. Ludicrous. The crime of the century was masterminded by the criminal mind of the century: Gaston Bullock Means!"

"That's not what you told us a few years ago," I reminded him.

He waggled a finger in the air. "Ah, but I was lying then, at least in part. Why do the two of you take this admission of mine so lightly? This is the most important confession ever made in the history of American jurisprudence."

"Means," I said, "I told you I was working for Hoffman. He showed me several of your letters. I know about your claims to have 'masterminded' this thing. So does Evalyn—*that* is why we're here."

"Oh. Then I suppose you're hoping to fill in some of the details."

"You might say that. You claim you built the ladder yourself?"

"Absolutely. In my garage at home at Chevy Chase. Hauptmann would have done a more professional job of it; he's a carpenter, after all. The ladder, by the way, was used only to look in the window and see if the child was in the room, not to bring him out—the child was handed out the front door to operatives of mine by the butler. That's why the ladder was found discarded seventy-some feet away."

"What about Max Greenberg and Max Hassel? I thought *they* were the 'masterminds.'"

"They worked for me. I had my connections with all of those rumrunners and bootleggers. The gang that Curtis came into contact with, they worked for me, too. It was my show from the start."

Evalyn moved nearer the bed. "In one letter to Governor Hoffman, you claimed you'd been hired by relatives of Mrs. Lindbergh, to take the child."

"Ah, yes—because the boy was retarded. And I was aided by Greenberg and Hassel, and that pair on the inside, Violet Sharpe and Ollie Whately."

"Are you saying that's *true*?" Evalyn asked.

"Which part?" he asked innocently.

"Which part *isn't* true?" I asked.

"The part about the retarded baby. It's a rumor I heard once, and liked the sound of."

I wondered if they had an extra bed open in this mental ward.

"Your friends Greenberg and Hassel," I said, "somebody murdered them, you know."

He nodded slowly, gravely. "Life can be so unkind."

"Death, too," I said. "Funny thing: they were murdered shortly after you gave me their names. After you fingered 'em as the real kidnappers."

"Coincidence has a long arm."

"Maybe you do, too, Means. Or people you're allied with."

"Means," Evalyn said harshly, "is that baby still alive?"

His smile was angelic. "Let me first say that the body of the baby found in New Jersey was a 'plant'—not the Lindbergh baby at all."

"Why was that done?" I asked.

"To bring certain things to a halt," he said. "For example, bootlegging activities in the Sourlands hills had been much disrupted. Too many troopers, too much activity, too much company. With the discovery of the child, things could go back to normal. Business as usual."

"Is that baby still alive?" Evalyn repeated.

"My dear," he said, "to my knowledge he is. I took that child to Mexico and left him there, unharmed. As God is my witness."

I got off the edge of the bed, in case lightning struck the fucker.

"Where is the child now?" she asked.

"I have no idea," he said, with an elaborate shrug. "I do know that the boy is in safe hands. As long as he lives, there are powerful people who can never be threatened with a murder charge."

"No one believes you, Means," I said.

"Pardon?"

"About being the mastermind of the Lindbergh kidnapping. You're the wolf who cried little boy."

He laughed silently. "Well put, Heller. Well put. And what do *you* think?"

"I think you may be telling the truth, for once in your life, or at least more truth than usual. Whether you really want to be believed or not, is a question I couldn't begin to answer. What truly goes on in the twisted corridors of your brain is anybody's guess."

He was nodding, smiling his puckish smile.

"If I were Al Capone," I said, and his smile disappeared momentarily, as if the very name gave him pause, "I might choose you as the perfect middleman . . . a man with connections among bootlegging circles, political circles, high society—you're ideal, except of course for being completely untrustworthy."

"Ah," Means said, tickling the air with a forefinger, "but if I were *afraid* of my employer . . . "

"If it were Capone, or an East-Coast equivalent like Luciano or Schultz, you'd play straighter than usual. To guard your fat ass."

"Heller, that's unkind. Language of that sort in front of Mrs. McLean is really uncalled-for."

"You go to hell, sir," she said to him.

He was crestfallen. "I may have wronged you, my dear, but surely such hostility is not called for, between old friends."

"For one hundred grand," I said, "she's earned the right."

"One hundred and four," he reminded me.

I shook my head, smiled. "You really have no shame, do you, Means?"

"These things are beyond my control," he said somberly. "My imagination is a by-product of mental disease. That, my friends, is why I lobbied to be brought to St. E's."

"It doesn't have anything to do," I said, "with avoiding hard time at Leavenworth?"

"It's more pleasant here, I admit," he said brightly. Then he made his face serious: "You see, it's my hope to have a brain operation, so that afterward, when I've been made a fit member of society, I can be paroled."

Gaston Means was pulling his final, biggest con: fooling himself that he would ever get out from behind bars—although the glaze on his eyes suggested his mark might not be buying the scam, either.

"Tell me one thing, Means," I said. "Level with me on just one thing: it's not even important, in the great scheme of events. It's just something I'd like to know."

"Heller—we've been friends for so many years. Would I deny you such a small favor?"

"Back in '32 when Evalyn and I and her maid Inga were camped out at her country place, Far View, did you come back at night, and sneak around, pulling the sheets off beds and walking around in the closed-off upstairs, just generally doing your best to spook us?"

"Ah—Far View," Means said wistfully. "They say it's haunted, you know. Some things go bump in the night, did they?"

"I think you know they did."

He loved this. "So many years later, that brush with the supernatural has stuck with you, has it, Heller? A hard-nosed, clear-eyed realist of a lad like yourself?"

"You're not going to level with me, are you, Means?"

"Heller, you're the kind of man who would make love to a woman with the lights on." He turned apologetically to Evalyn. "Please pardon the near crudity, Eleven." He looked at me again, with an expression both scolding and amused. "Don't you know there are some things in life that are better left a mystery?"

"So long, Means," I sighed.

Evalyn said nothing to him.

"Thank you for stopping by, my friends," he said cheerily. "And Eleven—if it comes to me which pier I tossed your money off of, I will contact you at once."

We left him sitting up in bed with his pixie puss frozen in a silly smile, looking vaguely mournful, like Tweedledum had Tweedledee died.

Friendship, the McLean estate behind a high wall on the outskirts of Washington, D.C., was smaller than the White House. A bit. Her place at 2020 Massachusetts Avenue, which at the time was the largest private residence I'd ever been in, could've been a porch, here.

"It used to be a monastery," she said, as I navigated the driveway through lavishly landscaped grounds. "Can't you just imagine those brown-robed monks, tending all the gardens and bushes? Like dozens of mute obedient gardeners."

"Help like that is hard to find," I said.

It was dusk and overcast and cold, and the huge house—dating to the early nineteenth century, but restored and remodeled into a modern-looking, sprawling, only vaguely colonial structure—loomed before me indistinctly, miragelike. I swung the Packard around by the big French fountain in front and, with her permission, parked it there.

I'd gotten used to being around Evalyn, who for all her melodrama and archness was a pretty down-to-earth gal; we'd even stopped for supper at a diner along the way where she ate with literal and figurative relish a greasy hamburger and greasier french-fried potatoes. But I hadn't forgotten I was keeping company with a dame who ate with heads of state and entertained Washington society at her estate—an estate, I had discovered, complete with private golf course, greenhouse and duck pond.

Tonight was Thursday, my second night at Friendship. The Norfolk trip had taken all day Wednesday, setting out from New York in the morning and meeting with Curtis in the afternoon and driving back to Washington, D.C., in the evening, so we could have our meeting with Means at St. Elizabeth's today. I had my own room at Friendship, and the same was true for the night we spent in New York, at the St. Moritz. Evalyn and I were getting along famously, but not intimately.

We sprawled in overstuffed chairs that were angled toward a fireplace over which a framed oil painting of her husband's father hung and in which a fire lazily crackled, casting an orangish glow over this large sitting room. The room had pale plaster walls, part of the recent remodeling, and new, expensive furnishings, running to dark wood and floral upholstery, and was littered with end tables with lavish lamps and framed family photos; a much more modern feel to it than any room at 2020, despite a vast, decidedly old-fashioned oriental carpet.

Everything we'd learned, at least anything that I thought to be of importance, we'd conveyed to Governor Hoffman by phone. Today we'd gotten news from the governor: Robert Hicks, his criminologist (actually, Evalyn's, as she was paying the bill), had confirmed—through chemical analysis and paint scrapings—my theory about the shelf in the Hauptmanns' kitchen closet.

"You've done well, Nathan," she said, sipping a glass of wine. She was wearing black lounging pajamas and high-heel black slippers.

I was working on a Bacardi cocktail; my second. "We've made some progress, but nothing yet that will carry enough weight to buy Hauptmann another reprieve, let alone a new trial."

She smiled and shook her head in supportive disagreement. "You've connected Fisch to those Harlem spiritualists, and Ollie Whately and Violet Sharpe, too. Not to mention Jafsie."

"It's thin," I said, shaking my head back at her. "Gerta Henkel will be dismissed as Hauptmann's lying kraut girlfriend. Who knows what the Marinellis will say, if they haven't skipped town already. Whately and Sharpe are dead, and Jafsie's dead from the neck up. Talking to Curtis leads me to believe most if not all of his story is true—but there's nothing solid to back it up; and some of what Means told us today tallies with Curtis and other facts at our disposal. But again—what good does that do us? Means is a pathological liar in the loony bin. What we've most clearly found is police tampering with, and creating, evidence—and that's not going to make us popular in New Jersey."

"What's it going to take?"

I laughed and it echoed off the plaster walls. "Maybe what I told the Governor: sitting Lindy's kid down on Hoffman's Statehouse desk."

"You really think that child is alive?"

"I think it's a possibility."

"Then why aren't we searching for it?"

"How exactly would we do that, Evalyn?"

She shook her head, smirked humorlessly. "I don't know. I don't know. Maybe we should ask one of those damn psychics."

I laughed again. "Maybe we should've stopped in on ol' Edgar

Cayce, at Virginia Beach, while we were in his neck of the woods, yesterday."

"Edgar Cayce?"

"Yeah. He's this hick soothsayer who did a 'reading' on the kidnapping, way back in the first week or so of the case."

She was sitting up. "Nate, Edgar Cayce is a very *famous* psychic. I've read a good deal about him. He's no charlatan like the Marinellis."

I gestured with an open hand. "Evalyn, you got to understand that some of these people are well intentioned. I don't think Sister Sarah Sivella Marinelli Indian Princess Shit Feather knows she's a fake. But her husband is, and he feeds her stuff, hypnotizes her maybe, and she winds up thinking she's got a pipeline to the past, future and God almighty."

She seemed to be only half-listening to my diatribe. "You met Cayce?" she asked.

"Yeah, I was there."

"During the reading?"

"Yeah, yeah."

"What happened?"

I shrugged. "He gave his version of where the kid was taken, including a bunch of street names. It was supposed to be in some section of New Haven, Connecticut, only the feds checked up on it and none of those street names, or even that part of town, was there."

Her eyes had narrowed. "Do you have your field notes on the Cayce readings?"

"Sure. They're up in my room, in my bag."

"Can I see them?"

"Sure. I'll bring 'em down tomorrow morning; we'll have a look at 'em over breakfast."

"No, Nate—I mean, now."

"Evalyn, I'm tired, and I'm working on getting drunk. Can't this wait?"

"The clock is ticking for Hauptmann."

"Oh, fuck, spare me the violins. I've about had my fill of this screwball tragedy for one day and night, and maybe for one lifetime. It can fucking wait."

She said nothing for a while. That was fine with me.

Then she said, "You know, people close to me over the years say that I am fey."

"Fey? What does that mean, you like to sleep with girls, now?"

"No, you silly son of a bitch. It means . . . visionary. In the psychic sense."

"Oh. So you believe in this spook stuff, too."

"You asked Means about those supernatural doings at Far View, didn't you? That happened a long time ago, to still be lingering in your mind."

"There was nothing supernatural about any of that. Means was sneaking around in his socks doing a number on us. He all but admitted as much this afternoon."

"That's not the way I took it. Nate, there have been psychic elements in this case from the beginning."

"A big case like Lindbergh attracts screwballs like shit attracts flies."

"How elegantly said." She sat forward, her hands folded in her lap, a demure posture for a woman in black pj's. "In my life I've had premonitions, Nate, that have come to pass. It simply happens to me, from time to time that, without being able to say how exactly, I know that death impends for someone in my circle . . . "

"That's bunk, Evalyn."

"I had that feeling the weekend my son died. I heard the inner voice but I didn't listen, and went off on a trip, and my precious boy died while I was away. . . . Ned and I at Churchill Downs, to watch the running of the Kentucky Derby. For which I never will forgive myself."

She covered her face with a hand.

I went over to her, knelt by her, gave her my handkerchief, patted her knee. "I'm sorry, Evalyn. It hurts. I know it hurts."

"If that child is still alive," she said, and for a moment I thought she meant her own son but she meant instead the Lindbergh boy, "we should try to find him."

"You want those notes? I'll get those notes. Will that make you feel better, baby?"

She nodded.

I went up and got the notes.

When I came down she was standing in the black pool that was the discarded lounging pajamas; she wore nothing but the high-heel black slippers. The orange glow of the fire made her body look like something in a painting. A very sensual painting by an artist who wasn't fey, if you get my drift.

She must've been in her mid-forties by now, but she had the body of a woman ten years younger, slender, smooth, the large breasts drooping a bit but so lovely, and waiting to be lifted.

"Come here, big boy," she said. She held her arms out gently. "Come to mama."

I fucked her on the oriental carpet with my trousers down around my ankles; her stark naked, me half-dressed, there was something very nasty about it, and at the same time sweet. She made a lot of noise. I made some myself.

Then I was a puddle of flesh on her pajamas, half-unconscious, as tired as if I'd run a mile, while she was sitting, nude as a grape, in her overstuffed chair, lighting up a cigarette as she read the Cayce field notes in the firelight.

After a while, I started to put my clothes back on. She looked up from her reading and said, very businesslike, "Don't get dressed. What's the point? Why don't you take the rest of your things off."

"You mean, just sit here naked on the floor . . . "

"The servants have retired to their quarters. We won't be disturbed. Now get your clothes off." She returned to her reading.

I must've slept a little.

Then, having rolled over on my back, I looked up and she was standing over me. The exaggeration of the angle made her figure look more naked than naked, like looking at a living statue representing everything that made a man want a woman; I wanted to worship her and dominate her and be dominated and worshiped all at once. She smiled down at me over enormous breasts, her shape sharply outlined, the fireplace at her back. My dick stood to attention and she sat on me, easing herself down on me, with a subtle, shimmering motion.

This time we made love; fucking was part of it, but this time was far less urgent, far more sweet, and not at all nasty, churning to a slow, gradual, mutual release that lasted forever but not near long enough.

"Should I have used something?" I panted, after a while, as we lay entangled in each other's nakedness.

"I'm not menopausal just yet, Nathan Heller."

"Then maybe I should've used something."

"Nate, if you made a baby tonight, he's a rich little bastard. So don't worry about it."

"I won't," I said, and smiled. "Is that bodyguard, chauffeur, security chief-type job still open?"

Her smile crinkled her chin. "It's not fair to ask me right now."

"If it's still open, I accept."

"Can I get back to you on that?"

"Sure."

I put my pants on and she put her pajamas on and I had another cocktail and she had another glass of wine and sat in my lap in one of the big overstuffed chairs while we drank.

"Those notes," she said.

"Hmmm?" I said.

"Those field notes about Edgar Cayce. I think we should go to New Haven. I think we should look for ourselves. Follow his clues."

"They're not clues, they're ramblings, delusional goddamn bullshit."

"Cayce is not a charlatan. He's the genuine article."

"There's no such thing, baby, and besides, the feds checked it out, and found nothing."

"How much confidence do you have in the 'feds'?"

"Well . . . "

She had a point. Irey had sent a man to infiltrate the Marinelli church, way back when, and that undercover ace had either not come up with the Fisch/Whately/Sharpe/Jafsie connection, or had suppressed it.

"Let's go take a look," she said.

I shook my head, no. "I have to go see Ellis Parker tomorrow. That's a genuine lead. Hoffman says Parker has a real suspect."

"It would only take a day."

"Hauptmann doesn't have very many of those. Besides, I looked at a New Haven map myself, back then. Those streets aren't there. There's no Adams Street, no Scharten Street. The section called, what?"

"Cordova."

"There's no Cordova section in New Haven."

She shrugged, tossed her head. "Maybe some of these street names are inexact. Maybe they're phonetic. Maybe they're phonetic and a bit off, and some interpretation is required."

"What did you say?"

She shrugged. "Maybe some interpretation is required."

What had Marinelli said to me the other day? When I was asking his wife why she'd seen a dead baby on a hillside, in one vision, and then a child on a farm, in another? *We can't always know the meaning of what a medium says in a trance—interpretation is required.*

"I tell you what, Evalyn," I said, stroking her smooth back. "If you want to check out this 'lead'—this stale, improbable lead— you can. You've got more than one car?"

"Certainly," she said, as if everyone did.

"Got someone you can take with you? Some big lug who can share the driving and look out for you? That butler, Garboni, can he handle himself?"

"Why, yes."

I touched her arm. "Then check it out yourself. Take my field notes. It shouldn't take more than a day, as you've said. Give it a try. And we'll meet back here either Friday night or Saturday, whenever we're both done."

She was smiling. I don't remember seeing her happier.

"Thank you, Nathan. What can I ever do to repay you?"

I sipped my Bacardi. "I'm sure you'll think of something."

Chapter 35

Mount Holly, New Jersey, was a sleepy little village at the base of the holly-covered hill from which it took its name. Despite some modern stores, the effect was of a place where time had frozen toward the middle of the previous century; along the broad, tree-lined streets were the simple square two- and three-story brick homes erected by the village's early Quaker residents—solid-wood shutters and wrought-iron fences and rails. On this cheerless, chill March afternoon, the smell of smoke from old-fashioned wood-burning stoves singed the air.

I parked the Packard on Main Street right in front of the old courthouse where Ellis Parker had kept his office for over forty years. The courthouse was a two-story yellow-brick structure with green shutters, white trim and a stately bell tower—wearing the date it was built like a badge: 1796. Moving across a patterned brick sidewalk over a small flat lawn to the front door—a vast oak slab with a colonial lantern nearby and the coat of arms of New Jersey in granite just above it—I felt I'd taken a left turn into another era.

Parker was in the second-floor rear office, in back of a bustling reception area where his deputies and his secretary had desks. The secretary, a dark-haired, bespectacled matronly woman, ushered me into Parker's presence.

The Old Fox, sitting in a swivel chair at a cluttered desk, was in shirtsleeves and suspenders, a food-flecked tie loose around his unbuttoned collar. He was as I remembered him: paunchy, bald, what little remained of his hair white, his mustache and eyebrows salt-and-pepper. His eyes were wide-set and drowsy. He was puffing a corncob pipe and looked like a farmer halfheartedly dressed for church.

The office was as quaint as a Currier and Ives print, only not near as cute: the desk littered with correspondence, reports, case histories and memos; a windowsill precariously balancing numerous telephones and directories; baskets and boxes in corners teeming with books, trial-exhibit photographs and maps; bulletin boards papered with police-department circulars, some boldly inscribed "Captured" and "Convicted" in black grease pencil; and sitting in one corner, on a chair, wearing a hat, a human skeleton.

"The Chicago man," he said, smiling with the natural condescension of the rural for the urban. "Have a seat, young fella."

I pulled up a hardwood chair. "I'm surprised you remembered me," I said, as we shook hands.

He snorted, holding onto the corncob pipe with his other hand; the tobacco smelled like damp leaves burning. "Couldn't forget the feller who ran interference for me—got me in to see Colonel Lindbergh, when that son of a bitch Schwarzkopf was set on keeping me out."

"As I recall," I said, "getting in to see Lindbergh didn't do you much good."

He shook his head, no. "He'd been poisoned against me. Politics. It's all politics." He smiled privately. "But he'll listen to me now."

"It'll have to be by wireless," I said. "He lives in England these days, you know."

"He'll come back for this," Parker said confidently. "It's gonna be a whole new ball game, when this hits the fan."

"What is 'this'?"

He ignored the question. "You said on the phone you're working for the Governor."

I nodded. "You realize, of course, that Governor Hoffman is concerned about this investigation of yours."

"And here I thought I had his blessing."

"You've got his blessing, as I understand it, but he'd like to know what the hell you're up to. Time is running out for Richard Hauptmann."

The smile disappeared from around the corncob pipe. "That poor unfortunate son of a bitch. Sitting in the death house waiting to be executed for a crime he's completely innocent of."

"I think he's innocent myself," I said. "Why do you feel that way?"

"Nathan . . . mind if I call you Nathan? Nathan, you're the kidnapper of this baby, you're the master criminal of this century, you plan the crime of the century and you execute it. If you're such a genius do you take a piece of wood from your own attic to make a ladder and then leave it behind as a clue?"

"Probably not."

"Never. Especially not if you're Hauptmann, who has all kinds of lumber in his garage and his yard. That was contrived evidence, I know that from my friends in the State Police. It's bullshit."

"Well, you're right."

"Let me ask you something, Nathan. If you had the brains to collect this ransom, would you go to a gas station with your own car, your own face, your own license plate, and give the guy a gold note and add insult to injury and tell him you got more like it at home?"

"I guess not." I shifted in the hard chair. "No offense, Ellis— you don't mind if I call you Ellis? Ellis, this is all old news to me. I didn't drive up here from Washington, D.C., to sit around the pickle barrel and chew the fat."

His mouth twitched around the pipe. "Do you know that that little corpse found on that mountainside probably wasn't the Lindbergh baby?"

"I suspect it."

He sat forward and his jaw jutted like the prow of a ship. "Yes, but do you *know* it? I'm not talking about the unlikelihood of them bones going undetected when the woods had been searched by everybody from the New Jersey State Police to the Boy Scouts of America. I'm talking about talking to pathologists about the rate of decomposition. I'm talking about looking up the weather records for that region in those three months."

"Weather records?"

He leaned back, smiling like a fisherman who'd just made a big, easy catch. "Ever build a compost heap, Nathan?"

"I'm a city boy, Ellis. I don't know shit about compost."

He laughed. "In a compost heap, even tiny leaves take more than three months to decompose and you're doin' everything humanly possible to make 'em decompose faster, you're adding manure and such to make it break down as quick as you can. And it still takes months. This body they want us to believe was the Lindbergh baby, it decomposed way too fast to have been out there in that cold, cold weather for three months."

"That's interesting," I admitted, and it was. I was even writing it down. "Is that it?"

The sleepy blue eyes woke up. "You're not impressed, city boy? You want to know what I *know* that you *don't?*"

"Sure."

"Well," he said, and I'll be goddamned if he didn't hook a thumb in his suspenders, "I know who the real kidnapper is."

"Oh, really. Who?" I pointed to the skeleton in the hat in the chair. "Him?"

"No. This is the feller." He was searching in the papers on his desk; finally he withdrew a mug shot and passed it to me.

I looked at the front and side views of a bucket-headed man with inexpertly slicked-back gray hair, dark eyebrows, a lumpy drink-dissipated nose, a fleshy face that looked pasty even in a black-and-white photo. His mouth was a crinkly line, a bow tie bumping a saggy double chin. He could have been fifty, he could have been seventy. His eyes had the dull, sullen look of a man who cared about nothing, except maybe himself. I wouldn't have trusted him for the time.

"His name is Paul H. Wendel," Parker said. "Known him all his life."

That didn't quite seem possible. "How old *is* he?"

"About forty-two, forty-three, I'd say."

Jesus. This guy was decomposing faster than the little Sourlands corpse.

"Knew his father before him," Parker was saying, "knew the boy since he was born. His daddy was a Lutheran minister, and tried to push his son into following in his footsteps. Didn't take."

"Looks like he's been around."

"He practiced pharmacy at one time. But when he was in that business he perpetrated a holdup against himself to collect the insurance money. He was saving up for night classes. Studying law."

"Law?"

Parker nodded, grinned around the corncob pipe. "So before you know it, he become a lawyer. And as a young lawyer, he embezzled clients' funds and was convicted and went to the pokey. Yours truly, as a friend of his old Bible-beating daddy, helped him get a parole. I tried to get him reinstated with the Bar Association but I didn't pull 'er off."

I studied Wendel's battered face. "And you think this guy is the Lindbergh kidnapper?"

"I *know* he is. The man has a brilliant mind—studied medicine for a while, too, you know. Medicine, the law, the ministry, pharmacy—that's Paul Wendel."

"It sounds like you're . . . friends."

"We are, or we were, before he committed this crime. Smartest man I ever met, Paul Wendel, but a failure in so many ways, and bitter about it. He felt that all the things he'd tried to accomplish came to nothing, that nothing good had ever happened to him; that he never got a break."

"Was this self-pity occasional, like when he was in his cups, or . . . "

"It was constant. He'd say, 'The world has always mistreated me, Ellis, but one day I'll do something that will make the world sit up and take notice.' "

"And you think he finally did."

Parker's mouth was tight, but his eyes smiled, as he nodded. "Not long before the kidnapping, Paul was getting himself into trouble writing bad checks. There were warrants out for him in New Jersey. He came to me and asked if I could help, and I said

I would try, but in the meantime he should go away someplace."

"When was this, exactly?"

"Several months before the kidnapping. He began living in New York, in various cheap hotels, but his wife and his daughter and son stayed behind in Trenton—he'd sneak home and visit 'em from time to time, when the coast was clear."

"It wasn't like there was a big manhunt out for him."

"Not at all. He just had warrants on him for this bad paper he passed. Anyway, after the kidnapping, I made a statement to the press and the radio that if the kidnapper would just come forward and talk to me, I would do all in my power to see that he was not punished. All I wanted to do was get that baby back safe."

"Figuring with your reputation, it might just draw the kidnapper out."

"Such was my thinking, yes. Hell, pretty soon I had bags of mail, phone calls from here to hell and back. My secretary would screen these calls. She'd only have me listen in on the more promising ones. And one of these calls was from Wendel—trying to disguise his voice."

"You're sure it was him?"

"Positive. I know Paul Wendel's voice, for Christ's sake; heard it for forty-some years. He calls disguising his voice, and even my secretary recognizes it, so she puts him on the line with me, and he's saying he knows who has the baby, and he'd like to come in and talk to me about it. I pretended not to recognize who it was, and invited him in."

"Did he come?"

"Yup. But he didn't even mention having called. Just announced that he'd had contact with the people who had the Lindbergh baby, and how he wanted to work with me to get that baby back. I told him, why, go ahead; see what you can do. But nothing come of it."

"Sounds like he was just a blowhard. Maybe trying to pressure you into getting those bad-check warrants pulled off his back."

"I would've thought so, too, but I kept remembering something Wendel had said to me, not long before the kidnapping. He was sitting in this office, in that very chair you're sitting in, having coffee . . . oh, do you want some coffee, Nathan?"

"No, that's okay. I'd rather have the rest of the story . . . black."

"Right. Anyway, he said, 'You know, Ellis, I'm getting damned tired of trying to save some money, a five-dollar bill here, a ten-dollar bill there. I want some real money.' So I asked him, 'What do you consider 'real' money, Paul?' And Wendel says, 'I want to make fifty thousand dollars at one time. Fifty thousand, fifty thousand.' He kept going on about it."

"And when you heard about the fifty-thousand-dollar ransom, then you suspected Wendel?"

"When I put it together with his story about having 'friends' who had the baby, you bet I did."

I sighed. "You've been reading your own press clippings, Ellis. That's the thinnest piece of deduction I've heard this side of the radio."

He didn't like that. He shook the pipe at me. "My instincts have never done me wrong, not in over forty years in this game, you young pup."

"Really? Well, I've been a detective since, what, '31? And this is the first time I've been called a 'young pup.' "

"You don't know what you're talking about! And you don't know Paul Wendel! Remember, he thought the world had mistreated him." He hunched his shoulders, gesturing with both hands. "This man is a psychotic, a very brilliant man with a criminal twist to his mind. The world was always against him. So what does he decide to do? Strike at the world's biggest hero. Kidnap the baby of this international hero, this Lucky Lindy. And that way, he could be more famous than Lindy, and yet anonymous at the same time. In his mind, he'd know he was better than Lindbergh; in his mind, he was a bigger hero."

"If he did this, why would he come to you with this cock-and-bull story about 'friends' of his who had the baby? You're a cop, and a famous one. That's inviting hell in a hand basket. . . ."

He threw up his hands. "It's the key, Nathan! Wendel did something that he believes *proves* he is bigger than Lindbergh. But he couldn't be a 'hero,' and not let somebody know! He can't be the man who planned and executed the crime of the century and then remain *silent* about it."

"And he was acquainted with you, the 'barnyard Sherlock Holmes,' a world-famous detective, who could appreciate his accomplishment."

"Now you're getting it."

I shook my head. "No, I'm not. And if this is all you have, I don't think you have much of a suspect at all."

He snorted. "You think that's all I have? When my instincts kick in, that's when I start digging. On this and on any case. So I began investigating my dear old friend. Would you like to hear some of what I discovered?"

"Why not." The day was shot to hell, anyway.

"For openers, in the weeks before the kidnapping, Wendel was frequenting a candy store in Hopewell, for sweets and cigarettes; I have a deposition to that effect from the female proprietor."

"Next you'll tell me Hochmuth and Whited saw him in Hopewell, too."

"Nathan, this woman does not have cataracts, and she does not live in a hillbilly shack. Here's another little fact you may enjoy . . . Wendel's sister lives in back of St. Raymond's Cemetery in the Bronx."

I blinked. "What?"

"His sister." He was grinning, but his eyes were dead serious. "St. Raymond's is where this lying fool Condon paid off the fifty thousand—and Wendel would not have had far to go to hide out afterwards, would he?"

This, too, I wrote down. I was getting interested.

"I'm jumping around a bit, Nathan—hope you can follow me. Now, when Wendel was still a practicing attorney in Trenton, he got one of his clients off on a narcotics rap. You know what that client's name was, Nathan?"

"Why don't you tell me, Ellis?"

"Why, sure, Nathan. It was Isidor Fisch."

I just looked at him; I had about as much to say at that moment as the skeleton.

"With their lawyer-client relationship," Parker said casually, "I figure maybe Wendel turned the fifty thousand in marked ransom bills over to Fisch, who some people say was a 'hot-money' fence."

I was sitting forward. "Ellis, this may be important. You have my apologies for doubting you."

"Well, thank you, young man." He relit the corncob pipe, shook the match out. "Now I'll tell you about Paul Wendel and Al Capone."

He was showing off, but it was working. I felt like I'd been poleaxed.

"Al Capone?" I asked. Because it was clear that he wouldn't continue until I did ask.

He nodded smugly. "Paul Wendel tried to work a confidence game on Al Capone some years ago, around 1929 or '30. I have an affidavit to that effect from a Frank Cristano, who has had some contact with underworld figures, from time to time. To make a long story short, Wendel convinced both Cristano and Capone that he could turn common tar into alcohol for four cents a gallon. At some point, however, the scam unraveled and Capone said if Wendel—who had come to visit Capone at the Lexington Hotel in your fair city—ever darkened his door again he'd get taken for what I believe you Chicago boys refer to as a 'ride.' "

"I don't think that term is unknown on the East Coast, either, Ellis."

"What's really interesting, Nathan, is that Wendel approached Cristano again, in early 1932—with a scheme to get Al Capone out of his income-tax troubles by kidnapping—and then arranging for Capone to be a hero by returning—the Lindbergh baby."

There it was.

I said, "Did this Cristano say he delivered the message?"

"No. He threw Paul Wendel out on his ass. But don't you suppose Wendel found a way to get that message to Capone?"

I nodded. "So maybe you do have a hell of a suspect in Wendel."

"I think so."

"But there isn't much time to develop any of this. You have him under surveillance, I suppose?"

"Why, Nathan," Ellis Parker said innocently, removing the corncob pipe. "I have him under wraps over at the local insane asylum. Care to meet him?"

Chapter 36

Ellis Parker was my passenger as, at his direction, I guided the Packard sixteen peacefully rural miles to the New Lisbon Colony, a state hospital for the insane. I seemed to be making a habit of dropping in at nuthouses; but nothing could have prepared me for the insanity of what I heard along the way.

The Cornfield Sherlock, wearing a bulky brown topcoat and a formless gray fedora, had left his corncob pipe behind. Settling himself in the passenger seat, he began the journey by using a pocketknife to cut the tip off a cigar. He fired up the stogie, and cracked a window; ventilation or not, the smell made me long for the corncob.

"Got an extry, if you want, Nathan," he said, gesturing with the cigar, embers flying. I brushed them from Evalyn's upholstery.

"No thanks. Care to tell me why your suspect is in custody at a madhouse?"

"I didn't say he was in custody. I said we had him under wraps. You could call it a kind of protective custody."

"You don't have enough to arrest him formally, yet?"

"We need a confession," Parker allowed. "Of course, we've got several from him already—just not quite the right one yet."

"He's confessed? More than once?"

"Keep your eye on the road, son. You don't know this country." He blew a formidable smoke ring; it wreathed his head—he smiled, like a partly shaven, not entirely benign Santa Claus. "Early this year, I sent some deputies of mine to New York to keep an eye on Wendel. He was living in the Stanford Hotel at the time. They took a room at the Martinique next door, watched his movements with binoculars and so on. My son Ellis, Jr., was in charge."

"I didn't know your son was in your line of work."

"Well, he is, and I'm damn proud of him. I needed him there to ramrod the group. Those other deputies weren't professional lawmen by any means. They were just . . . contacts of mine."

"Contacts?"

He shrugged. "I've got my network of snitches and such in New Jersey and New York alike."

That probably meant they were gamblers and minor-league hustlers. Nice class of "deputy."

"How did the surveillance pan out?" I asked.

"Not well. By the middle of February, with time running out for Bruno Hauptmann, I figured we should move."

"Move?"

He nodded, eyes narrowed, jaw jutting, cigar clamped in one corner of his mouth. "I got Ellis, Jr., outa there, 'cause Wendel would recognize him, and the other three waited till Wendel was coming out of the hotel, told him they were cops, put a gun in his ribs and drove him to Brooklyn."

I about hit the brakes. "That's kidnapping, Ellis."

"Horseshit, son. Didn't you ever break a rule to crack a case? Didn't you ever bust a window to go in and pick up a clue? Anyway, the fellas took Wendel to a house belonging to one of their fathers; all arranged in advance. They kept him in the basement, blindfolded at first."

"For how long?" I managed.

"Eight days," he said, shrugging.

I didn't know what to say. I could barely keep my eyes focused on the road. Parker just sat puffing his cigar, telling his story, proud of himself.

"I told my deputies, you tell Wendel you're not really cops, what you are is mobsters. Tell him because of what he did—kidnapping the Lindbergh baby, which from inside sources you know that he done—he's made things hot for the 'Boys.' I said, tell him the police know Hauptmann didn't do it and they won't get off the Boys' back till they find the men who did."

"Your deputies," I said softly, "pretended to be gangsters, holding him hostage?"

Parker nodded, smiling. "They used Italian names, and acted tough, threatened to put him in cement and dump him in the river."

"Did they beat him?"

"Hell no! What do you think I am, Nathan? A damn torturer? My deputies let him take baths, fed him, even gave him a cot to sleep on, and a radio so's he could listen to music."

"They tie him up?"

"No, sir. Somebody was guarding him all the time; he was down in the basement, with the windows boarded up. He wasn't going nowhere. Somebody was always listening, waiting for him to break down."

"How were they going to do that, Ellis, without feeding him the goldfish?"

He snorted a laugh. "My deputies wondered the same thing. They said, Ellis, this man is sitting there and he's eating and sleeping, he's listening to music, he bathes every day and he shaves, but he doesn't tell us anything. And I said, don't worry—one day, when you least expect it, this man will break down and tell you the whole story. For one thing, this man is dying to tell the story to somebody, and I figured he would tell them because he took 'em to be criminals and he'd want them to know how he was this master criminal who did this big crime."

"That's one thing," I said. "What's the other?"

"Wendel's a drinking man," Ellis said, with a little shrug. "I had 'em make it clear to Wendel that the only way he could get a drink was by way of giving a full confession."

"Jesus, Ellis," I said, finally betraying my feelings. "A confession a drunk gives in exchange for a drink isn't worth the empty glass. And keeping a guy in a dark cellar for eight days makes the rubber-hose treatment seem like kid gloves."

Parker's smile had disappeared. He looked at me hard. "We don't have time for social niceties in this case, Nathan. The New York cops beat up Hauptmann, didn't they? That bastard Welch third-degreed Violet Sharpe into a bottle of poison. That fella Curtis from Norfolk got the crap kicked out of him. If that's the rules of the game, and we want to play the game, maybe even *win* it, well, by God, those are the rules we'll play by."

I shook my head. "Can't argue with logic like that."

"Anyway, Wendel did break down, on the sixth day," Parker said, defensively. "Bawled like a baby and tells his story from beginning to end."

"What exactly was in his confession?"

"How he made those three interlocking ladders himself with wood he took from a church being constructed in Trenton. Put stockings over his shoes and a laundry bag around his neck, and gloves on his hands. When he went up the ladder, he broke a rung, big fella that he was, and knew he couldn't come back down with the baby around his neck like he planned. The baby was fast asleep in its crib and he rubbed paregoric on the baby's lips to keep it sleeping. Then he put it in the laundry bag, sneaked downstairs and out the front door."

"No inside help? What about Violet Sharpe, or Whately the butler?"

"Didn't mention 'em. I think the Sharpe girl was involved, myself, but so far he hasn't said so. Anyway, he took the child to his house in Trenton where his wife and two children helped care for the kid. But he says a week later, the kid fell out of its crib and fractured its skull. So he took the baby back and buried it in the woods just a few miles from its home."

"That's it? That's the confession?"

"Well, it's far more detailed, of course."

"It's bullshit, Ellis!"

"Eyes on the road, son."

"Eyes on the road, my ass. Wendel's done everything he can to conform to the state's ridiculous lone-wolf theory—which the state never believed in, in the first place. And what about your own theory that that kid in the woods wasn't Baby Lindbergh?"

"I know," Parker admitted, "I know. That's why we're working to get a better confession."

"Oh, Jesus. Ellis, you've outsmarted yourself. Let's assume, for the sake of argument, Wendel really is guilty. Really did mastermind the kidnapping, and either sold Capone on the idea, or was put up to it, by Capone. Wendel had to think your deputies were mobsters looking for a fall guy to make a phony confession! A fall guy willing to go along with the scam, to keep himself out of cement overshoes."

Parker was looking out the window at passing farmland. "Wendel's father was German, you know."

"Oh, really. That's pretty goddamn incriminating. So was my father. Where was I, March first, 1932?"

"He says in his confession, he wrote the ransom note trying to sound like an illiterate or a foreigner. So of course, with his German heritage, the notes ended up sounding German. Those symbols he signed the notes with, by the by, were off the cover of a law book."

We were approaching the rolling grounds of the insane asylum. I was ready to check in.

We pulled up to one of several free-standing bungalows, away from the main institutional buildings. A chill wind whistled through skeletal trees. Lonely figures in sweaters and slacks walked the grounds aimlessly; male nurses in parkas were keeping an eye on the mental children. We walked up a gentle slope.

"Ellis, how long have you been keeping Wendel here?"

He paused to relight his cigar. "Near three weeks. He's here of his own free will. He signed a paper to that effect."

"Right. How did he end up here, Ellis?"

He began to walk again; it was just cold enough for the smoke of his breath to mingle with that of the stogie. "Well . . . after he wrote his confession, the first one, that is, my deputies asked if there was somebody he could trust, somebody he could send the confession to. And of course Wendel chose me."

"You knew him well enough to know he'd do that?"

"I predicted his psychology every step of the way. Then my

men waited a couple of days and dropped him in Mount Holly and he came up to my house and rang the bell. He told me about the mobsters who'd held him and I told him we'd better hide him out for a while. I suggested New Lisbon as a good, safe place. Like I said, he's here of his own free will."

"Well, perhaps I'm mistaken," I said, pointing to the uniformed guard in front of the small frame bungalow, "but isn't that an armed deputy?"

"Sure is," Parker said. "Wendel's been under armed guard since the first night. You see, I broke it to him early on, that after I read the confession the 'mobsters' got out of him, I believed he *had* committed the crime."

"But that as his friend, you'd help him as best you could."

"That's the God's honest truth," he said, with no irony, and no sign of recognizing my sarcasm. "Shall we go in and meet him?"

I touched Parker's arm. "I'm just along as an observer. You can say I'm from Governor Hoffman's office, but if you mention my name, I'll put your cigar out where the sun don't shine."

He smiled at me, but the smile disappeared when he saw I wasn't kidding.

At the bungalow, the armed deputy grinned at us, revealing a space between his teeth; he was an apple-cheeked bumpkin.

"Well, Nate Heller," he said.

"Pardon me?"

The deputy thrust out one hand, jerking the thumb of the other to his chest. "Willis Dixon! Remember me? I used to be on the Hopewell Police Department, such as it was."

"Well, Willis," I said, recognizing him finally, shaking his hand, "it's good to see you."

"Remember, I said I'd applied to work at Mount Holly with Chief Parker." He pointed at the badge on his chest. "Finally made the grade."

"I guess you did."

Parker said, "Let me go in and prepare Paul for company."

Dixon unlocked the door and Parker went in.

The deputy beamed, shaking his head. "Is the old boy something, or what?"

"He's something."

"Do you believe after all these years, we're still workin' the Lindbergh case? And finally cracked it, by God."

"Think you got the real kidnapper, here, do you?"

"Sure. Ellis Parker is the greatest detective alive. It's an honor serving him."

"How's Wendel being treated?"

"Fine. He's a guest . . . except for being held under lock and key."

Small detail.

Parker stuck his head out the door. "Come on in, Nathan."

I went to him and plucked the cigar out of his mouth. I held it up. "My name stays out here, Ellis. Remember?"

He scowled, but he nodded, and I tossed the cigar away and followed him in.

Paul Wendel was a big, gray, woeful man in a baggy brown suit and no tie. His eyes were dead. His nose was a lumpy, vein-shot thing that would have given W. C. Fields a start. He was sitting on a couch in the small, sparsely furnished parlor; the walls were painted a pale institutional green. There was a bedroom and a bath; no kitchen.

"This is the officer I was telling you about, Paul," Parker said, pointing a thumb at me.

"Ellis says the Governor will treat me right," Wendel said to me. His voice was a baritone, lawyer-rich but soggy with self-pity.

"I'm sure he will," I said.

Parker sat next to Wendel on the couch; Wendel looked at him with the mournful eyes of a basset hound.

"You know, Paul," the grizzled chief of detectives said, "you could make a lot of money off a confession. You just write a full and frank statement—without them shadings of truth you did for those mobsters' benefit—and say you were out of your mind at the time, but that now, having regained your proper senses, you realize you did a terrible thing, and you want to make a clean breast of it."

"Temporary insanity as a defense," Wendel said, thinking about it.

"You could make a million dollars off the true story of what happened. You and your family could be on easy street for the rest of your life. And you'd be famous."

"A kidnapping charge I could abide," Wendel said. "But not murder."

Parker placed a hand on Wendel's shoulder. "Paul, I know what you've been through. I'm going to try to protect your family, do everything I can in my power, through friends and contacts, to see that your wife and son and daughter are not involved . . . even though they're conspirators in the case."

"They are? Why?"

" 'Cause they helped you tend the baby."

"I need law books. I need to brush up."

"Well, all right, Paul. We'll get you some. But you know time is running short. You don't want the life of this fellow Hauptmann on your conscience."

Wendel was looking at me. He was a big, sad man with eyes that stuck to you like gum on your shoe.

"What's your name?" he asked me.

"That's not important," I said.

The eyes widened; then narrowed. "You're from Chicago."

The accent.

He turned to Parker. Agitated. "He's from Chicago!"

I moved closer. "What is it about Chicago that makes you nervous, Mr. Wendel? Al Capone isn't in Chicago, anymore."

Wendel raised a palm, as if bestowing a blessing—or saying stop. "I want him to leave, Ellis."

"Of course, Frank Nitti is still there," I said. "And Paul Ricca."

"I want him to leave!"

Parker, confused by this, got up, and escorted me out.

Wendel had never risen off that couch.

In the cool air, Parker said, "You got him riled up. Those names spooked him. Nitti's a Capone boy, ain't he?"

"That's right. Ellis, I'm going to drive you back now. Go get in the car."

"Who in hell are you ordering around?"

"You. Get in the goddamn car." He trundled off, muttering.

I turned to Deputy Dixon, who was taking this in with wide, confused eyes. "I was never here."

"Pardon?"

"You didn't see me today, Willis. Understood?"

"Sure, Nate." He didn't really understand, but he knew I meant it.

In the Packard, without turning the engine over, I whirled to Parker. "You blew this one, Ellis. You blew this one big."

"Did I? I'll have a confession out of Paul H. Wendel that'll hold water, before you can say Jack Robinson."

"You don't have shit. You ever hear of something called the Lindbergh law? You have put your foot in a great big federal cowpie, Ellis. You've kidnapped that son of a bitch; you took him across a state line, you hick bastard."

"I did nothing of the kind."

"Your cronies did. Your 'deputies.' The pity of it is, I think that psycho back there maybe did have some role in the crime. But you'll never prove it now."

"I'll prove it."

"Ellis, I'm not reporting to Governor Hoffman on this."

"You're not?"

"No. You tell him what you want, when you want. I dropped by the office, but I didn't see Wendel. You didn't even tell me you had him 'under wraps.' "

"What in hell are you up to?"

"I'm up to having no part of this. If Hoffman wants to play your crazy game, that's up to him. I have no interest in being your accomplice or co-conspirator or any such thing. You mention my name, and I'll make a career out of testifying against you. Goddamn you! I've had your 'Jersey justice' up to here. You and Schwarzkopf and Wilentz and all the rest . . . torture and abduction and fabrication . . ."

He scowled; it was as nasty a look as I ever got, and I've gotten my share. "Then go back to Chicago, why don't you? You goddamn pantywaist."

"That's not a bad idea," I said. "At least there, we stop at rubber hoses. Get out."

We were at the courthouse in Mount Holly, where the rampant Americana now made me a little sick.

He climbed out and then bent down and peeked in and said, "You'll be singing a different tune, 'fore long. You'll be telling your grandchildren you knew Ellis Parker."

"Maybe I will," I said. "And you probably were a hell of a detective, before it went to your head. But unless you're even cagier than I think you are, old man, you'll likely die in jail."

He was pondering that as I pulled away.

Chapter 37

For an estate like Friendship, the study was almost cozy; lots of books, a fireplace, prints and paintings of race horses. A dark, masculine room that hadn't been used much, or at all, since Evalyn's husband moved out. I sat at a mahogany desk about the size of the Packard and used the phone. It was a long-distance call, but I figured Evalyn could afford it.

I couldn't get Frank Nitti right away, of course. The number I had on a small slip of paper in my billfold was that of Louis Campagna, the cold-eyed, putty-faced Capone enforcer who since his mentor's incarceration had become Nitti's right-hand man. Actually, I had to go through somebody who answered that number, gave me another number, which got me to Campagna, who had me give him the number I was at, and finally Nitti called me, five minutes later.

"So what do you have, Nate?"

"Not a lot," I said. I felt uneasy. I always felt uneasy talking to Nitti. "I just thought I should touch base."

"I know you, Nate. You wouldn't call unless you thought you had something."

"Well, Frank," I said, feeling awkward calling him that, "I been nosing around, talking to people, and it's pretty clear this Hauptmann character is a patsy. For one thing, the lawyer the Hearst people provided him was a guy named Reilly, who . . ."

"Yeah, yeah, the Bull of Brooklyn, Frankie Yale's old mouthpiece. 'Death House' Reilly. That I know."

"Well, it smells, wouldn't you say? And none other than Capone's old lawyer Sam Leibowitz also offered his services to Hauptmann; telling the world his client was guilty seemed to be his idea of fair representation . . ."

"Sure, sure. All this I know. Nate, tell me something I *don't* know."

Getting off to a swell start: Nitti aggravated with me already.

"Well," I went on, "the late Isidor Fisch was clearly some kind of small-time hustler—smuggling furs, probably smuggling dope, too, for Luciano, working out of East Harlem, which is Luciano's turf, after all. Also a petty con man and maybe a hot-money fence. Hauptmann was his pal, maybe even his accomplice in fur and dope smuggling—*maybe*—but not in the kidnapping or extortion or anything."

"So Fisch was just a fence who bought some marked bills?"

"No, that's not my reading of it at all. I think Fisch plays a bigger role in this than that. Fisch seems involved in the extortion itself and maybe the kidnapping. He and two of the Lindbergh servants, including the dame who supposedly killed herself, belonged to a spiritualist church right across the street from Fisch's apartment house."

There was a pause.

Then Nitti said: "I can't see Al getting Luciano or Madden or Costello or any of the East-Coast guys involved in this. They're too smart. Dutch Schultz, maybe. If this little Fisch is the only connection to the people we do business with . . ."

"No. There's also a guy named Wendel."

"Wendel?"

"He's a disbarred lawyer. A half-nuts con man who tried to scam Capone a few years back."

"*Paul* Wendel?"

Nitti knowing the name made my skin crawl.

"That's him. There's a story I haven't confirmed yet that Wendel approached Capone with the kidnap plan. At the moment, some hick cops have got Wendel under lock-and-key and armed guard, out in the boonies, squeezing worthless confessions out of him like popping pimples."

There was urgency in his voice; whether this news made him happy, angry, worried, or what, I could not read. "Is this going to come back to Al? Or the Waiter?"

"Ricca's name has not come up," I said. "Wendel, and the inimitable Gaston Means, who I also talked to, are bad witnesses. They are both such fucking liars and con men that if they do tell the truth, no one will be able to tell. Both of 'em are being held in the nuthouse, by the way. Well, two different nuthouses."

"Their testimony would be worthless?"

"Unless somebody checked out their stories, and came up with better witnesses. And time is goddamn short for that; Hauptmann sits down in a couple weeks, you know. How well do you know Gaston Means?"

"Know of him, is all."

"It occurs to me that enlisting the likes of Wendel and Means, unreliable as they are, would be a stroke of genius on somebody's part—whether Capone or Ricca."

"How the hell do you figure that?"

"Well, even lunatics like Wendel and Means know enough not to cross Capone, or Ricca. Means likes his skin too much, and Wendel had an instructive close call with Capone back around '30. Yet in their way, these guys are savvy crooks, with connections in the underworld and elsewhere. They also both got more balls than sense. So they could get the job done. But suppose the kidnapping goes awry? Capone and Ricca had to know this thing was risky at best, that it might just blow up in everybody's face."

"I wouldn't trust screwballs like Wendel or Means with the garbage."

"Ah, but Frank, that's the beauty part. Even if Means or Wendel decide to talk, were dumb enough to finger Capone and

Ricca—who would believe them? With their records, with their individual eccentricities, they make the perfect fall guys."

There was a pause; I let him think. Then he said: "So what's going to happen?"

"I'm working to try to clear Hauptmann. That's what Governor Hoffman's paying me to do. I'm finding a lot out, but so far I don't see any of it doing any good."

"You don't see this coming back to Chicago. You don't see this landing in the Outfit's lap."

"No. Not yet, anyway." The hell of it was, I didn't know whether Nitti wanted it to, or not.

"Okay," Nitti said. "Okay. Appreciate you checkin' in, Nate. You're a good boy."

The phone clicked dead.

I hung up.

"Who were you talking to, Nate?"

I turned in the chair and saw Evalyn standing in the doorway of the study. How long she'd been there, I didn't know. She looked a trifle confused. She was wearing flowing wide-legged black slacks and a black cashmere sweater with pearls; and looked sporty and stylish, but a tad frazzled. It had been a long day for her, too.

I stood, smiled, approached her; put my hands on her tiny waist. "Contact of mine in Chicago," I said. "Bouncing a few ideas back and forth."

"Oh," she said, vaguely troubled. Then that look transformed itself into a girlish smile. "Nate, I have exciting news. The New Haven trip was a success!"

"Huh?" I'd damn near forgotten that was what she'd been up to today: trying to follow the "lead" of the long-ago Edgar Cayce reading. This would be rich.

"You're going to be proud of me. I don't even want to freshen up. Let's go in the other room and talk."

Once again that fireplace was aglow, in a room otherwise dim, and she led me before it, where she curled up catlike on the oriental carpet to bask in the warmth of the fire. It painted her a lush orange. I stood over her and suggested I get us some drinks from the nearby liquor cart; she agreed, requesting champagne ("To celebrate"), studying the fire, smiling enigmatically, looking at once as sophisticated as a *Vogue* cover girl and as naive as a Girl Scout wishing she had a wienie to roast.

She sipped her wine and, sitting Indian-style next to her, I sipped my Bacardi.

She said, "Was your day eventful?"

I had already decided not to tell her about Wendel's captivity; it could only get her in trouble. I gave her a brief rundown of what Parker had told me about his suspect, and left it at that.

"Do you think this Wendel fellow might be the kidnapper, or at least involved in the kidnapping somehow?"

"It's possible. But Parker's pursuing that angle. We have to look elsewhere. Now, Evalyn, I know you're dying to tell me what you've discovered. And I," I lied, "am dying to hear all about it."

She sat up, striking a more serious posture. "In your notes, Nate, you wrote that Edgar Cayce spoke of a house in a 'mill section' on the east side of New Haven. In the region of 'Cordova,' he said."

"Only there is no Cordova."

She smiled; her eyes sparkled like the champagne in her glass. "But there *is* a *Dover* section. Some interpretation is required, re-member? A man in a trance pronounces things indistinctly; he gathers information from the haze, after all."

"I guess," I said, somewhat impressed by the Cordova/Dover notion, but not bowled over.

"Garboni and I," she said, "were able to locate a densely built-up mill section in East New Haven. We stopped at a filling station there, inquiring about an area called 'Cordova,' and were informed that just across the Quinnipiac River from New Haven there was a *Dover* section."

"Okay," I said.

"Then I asked if he knew of an Adams Street. That was the street that Cayce said led to Scharten Street."

"Right." This was truly idiotic. I was embarrassed to be having this conversation. I sipped my Bacardi. Maybe I'd get laid, later, if I could keep a straight face through all this horse-doodle.

She was as serious as the portrait of her husband's daddy over the fireplace. "The gas-station man didn't know of an Adams Street, so I asked him if he knew of a street that might sound *similar* to 'Adams.' He suggested Chatham Street."

Well, that was pretty close.

"We went to Chatham Street, Garboni and I, and we followed Cayce's directions. The child, according to Cayce in his trance, was supposed to have been taken first to a two-story shingled house, then moved to another house nearby—a brown house—that was two-tenths of a mile from the end of 'Adams' Street.'"

"Right. I remember, more or less."

She grinned. "The house number Cayce gave was Seventy-Three. And do you know what we found at Seventy-Three Chatham Street? A two-story shingled house."

"No kidding." Those must be scarcer than hens' teeth.

"Next we turned right from a point two-tenths of a mile from the waterfront end of Chatham, and found a brown store building."

"What was the name of the street?"

"Not Scharten," she admitted. "Maltby."

"Evalyn, that's not even close, phonetically or backwards or sideways."

"I know. Maybe it *used* to be Scharten or something closer. Anyway, the brown building was there: an apartment over a neighborhood grocery store. We went into the store, but the manager wasn't there, so we kept asking around the neighborhood, if anybody knew who'd been the tenant in the apartment over that store, back in 1932. We were referred to a local gossip, in a candy store, a few blocks away."

All in all, this was sounding like a trip I was glad I didn't make.

"We went into the candy store and it was indeed run by a very talkative old woman. We asked her if she'd ever heard any rumors about the Lindbergh baby being in the area."

"Christ, that was subtle, Evalyn."

She frowned defensively. "Well, she had! And Nate, I hadn't even mentioned the apartment over the grocery store to her. But out of the blue, she said there was a rumor that, for a short time, a couple was caring for the Lindbergh baby, in that very apartment! That there was a house-to-house search of the neighborhood, in the early weeks or maybe even days after the kidnapping, and the couple took off. The house search made a big impression on her, and everybody in the neighborhood. She called it, 'King Herod time.' "

"Why?"

Evalyn shrugged, smiled. "Seems the police were taking the diapers off every baby around, to check the sex."

I tried to express my skepticism gently. "You know, Evalyn, I remember hearing about a New Haven search, because some of the construction workers who built Lindbergh's house were from there, and were early suspects—so that could naturally give rise to a rumor like that. It doesn't mean . . ."

"Nate, there's something else. There was a name in Cayce's notes. An Italian name, remember? The man who Cayce said was the leader of the kidnap gang."

"Yes . . ."

"That name was Maglio, right? It must have been important—you underlined it in your notes, three times."

"Yeah, uh, right." Now I was getting an uncomfortable tingling.

"Well, we asked the old lady at the candy store, and a couple of other people as well, if they knew who owned or rented or lived in that shingled two-story house at Seventy-Three Chatham in '32."

"Yes? And?"

"Well, there were two apartments. The man living in the top apartment was named Maglio. Maglio, Nate! Can *that* be a coincidence?"

My mouth was dry. I sipped the Bacardi. It didn't help.

Paul Ricca, the Waiter, also known as Paul DeLucia, had frequently used the name Paul Maglio, particularly out east.

Of course, Evalyn didn't even know who Paul Ricca was, and I wasn't about to tell her. Nor was I about to call Frank Nitti back and say a soothsayer, four years ago, fingered the Waiter.

"How did I do?" she asked.

"You did well. That's potentially interesting."

"Where do we go from here?"

"I'm not sure. I've got to find the right person to approach with this."

"Someone needs to go to New Haven and really dig in, really investigate, right? Will it be us?"

"I think we need a bigger gun," I said.

"I think your gun is big enough, Nate," she said, and she was smiling in a whole other way now, putting her hand on me, crawling on top of me. We made love before the fireplace again, and she seemed to enjoy herself, but I was goddamn distracted.

I shared a bed with her that night, in a sumptuous bedroom, on silk sheets, and she slept contentedly, smiling through the night, while I sat up wide-eyed, untouched by sleep, putting the pieces together.

Chapter 38

The Treasury Building was on Pennsylvania Avenue and Fifteenth Street. It wasn't a bad neighborhood; the White House was across the street. The many-pillared granite-and-sandstone structure loomed imposingly on this cold, rain-spitting Monday morning, an illusion of a perfect government, an American Athens. If the dollar were as sound as the Treasury Building looked, maybe I wouldn't have to sleep in my office.

I went in the Fifteenth Street entrance, where amidst the bustle of bureaucrats I soon found the central office corridor, and the room number I was seeking. At the far end of a large, busy bullpen, Frank J. Wilson sat in a glassed-in office, burrowed in at a work-cluttered desk.

There was no secretary. I knocked and Wilson looked up and smiled indifferently and waved me in. He was sitting sideways, working at a typewriter on a stand. Like the army of accountants in the large room beyond, he worked in his suit and tie; the tie wasn't even loosened.

Frank Wilson had changed only marginally since 1932—he

wore wire-rim glasses, now, not black-rims, and his face was flesh-ier, his thinning hair grayer. I'd seen Wilson on several occasions since the early phase of the Lindbergh case. Just last year we'd bumped into each other in Louisiana. We'd grown guardedly friendly; warily respectful.

"Thanks for seeing me, Frank," I said. I hung my raincoat and hat next to his on a coat tree.

"Nice to see you again, Heller," he said. He hadn't stopped typing yet. "Be with you in a moment."

I found a chair.

The small office had several filing cabinets; on the wall behind him were framed photos of himself and various dignitaries, includ-ing President Roosevelt, Secretary of the Treasury Morgenthau and Charles Lindbergh.

"Sorry," he said, with a tight smile, as he turned and sat facing me at the desk; huge piles of manila case folders were on either side of the central blotter. "I'm hip deep in procedural recommen-dations."

"Oh really," I said, not terribly interested.

"There's been a big influx of counterfeiting," he said, "and Secretary Morgenthau has asked me to recommend methods of bringing it under control."

"Isn't that the job of the Secret Service?"

"Well, yes, but the Secretary has asked me, as a favor, to do a survey of the investigative and administrative procedures of the Service." He said this casually, but I knew he was bragging.

"That's why your office isn't in the wing with the Intelligence Unit, anymore."

"Right. Temporary quarters, these. You see, Moran is going to retire soon, so some changes are going to be made, obviously. I'm just doing a little advance work."

William H. Moran was the longtime head of the Secret Service; this was Wilson's way of telling me he was being groomed for the job.

"Well, gee, Frank, it sounds like things are going well for you, busy as you are."

"Yes. Not too busy to see you, of course. You say you have new information about the Lindbergh case?" He smiled doubtfully.

"At this late date, Heller? If it was anybody but you, I'd have dismissed it as a crank call."

"I didn't know who else to turn to—you and Irey are the only real possibilities, and Irey's up so high in the government now, I don't know if I could get to him."

His brow was knit, the eyes behind the wire-frames were tight. "Nate, I know you well enough to know you're not in this out of altruism. No offense, but surely there's a client in the woodpile."

"There is. I'm working for Governor Harold Hoffman."

He bristled. Shifting in his chair, his mouth a thin line, he said, "I'm disappointed to hear that, Nate. Hoffman is a publicity hound; he's exploiting the Lindbergh case, using it as a political football."

"Frank, no offense to you, either—but that's bullshit. I don't see how being on Hauptmann's side would be politically advantageous to anybody."

"Hoffman's got his eye on the Republican nomination for Vice President," Wilson said, squinting. "If he could embarrass the Democrats in his state, if he could crack the Lindbergh case, well . . ."

"If he could crack the Lindbergh case," I said, "I'd think you'd approve."

"Damn it, Heller, the case *was* cracked!"

"Then I may be wasting my time, here, Frank, not to mention yours. Perhaps you don't care to hear about what I've uncovered. . . ."

He grimaced, impatient—whether with me or himself, I can't say. Then he smiled politely and said, "Nonsense. If you've come up with something new, I want to know about it."

"I thought so. After all, you were never a big proponent of the 'lone wolf' theory."

"No. But I *am* of the theory that Hauptmann'll spill his guts before he goes to the chair. Only, as long as bleeding hearts like Hoffman keep the case open, and keep his false hopes up, Bruno's not about to finger his accomplices."

"Well, maybe we can find those 'accomplices' without his help. But Frank—my opinion is, Hauptmann's a minor figure in the case at best, and probably a flat-out patsy."

Wilson sighed. He shook his head wearily. "Out of respect to you, Nate, I'll hear you out."

"All right. Now in some instances, I can't tell you how I've been made privy to information. You'll have to view at least some of what I'm going to tell you the way you'd view a tip from a good informant."

He accepted that with a nod.

"What I'd like to present is my scenario for how the kidnapping and the extortion may have happened. This isn't the only way it could have played. There are several variant ways you could interpret the things I've learned; but I think I've put the puzzle together. I spent the weekend going over old field notes, working it out."

He had to smile. "Nate Heller devotes his weekend to solving the case that has mystified the world for over four years. That was damn white of you."

I grinned. "Okay—I deserve that. Anyway, my explanation, or theory if you will, is a hell of a lot more likely than the one Wilentz got Hauptmann convicted on."

Wilson nodded again. "One thing I'll grant you—it always bothered me that Wilentz in his opening statement to the jury said he was going to prove the child died dropping to the ground, fracturing its skull, when the ladder rung broke. Then in his closing argument, Wilentz stated flatly that Hauptmann bludgeoned the boy in his crib, with the chisel. Wilentz is lucky that blunder didn't get the conviction overturned."

"Especially," I said, "since neither version of the child's death is supported by any evidence. No impression of the child's body in the soft ground below, from falling; and no blood or other matter splattered in the crib, from a bludgeoning."

Wilson was nodding again, which made me feel better.

I began by telling him about Paul Wendel. He had never heard of Wendel, and wrote the name down on a notepad. I, of course, didn't mention that Wendel was in Ellis Parker's illegal custody—just that Parker was investigating Wendel.

"Paul Wendel concocts this plan to kidnap the baby," I said, "and sells Capone on it. It's too dangerous and loony a plan for

Capone to share with Frank Nitti, who is comparatively conservative in such matters; and it's unlikely something this wild would interest Luciano, Madden or any of the others."

"Dutch Schultz might have been that crazy," Wilson said.

I had to restrain myself from telling him that Nitti had said the same thing.

"But that's a case in point," I said. "Not so long ago, Schultz had his own crazy idea—kill Tom Dewey. And we both know how that wound up."

When Dutch Schultz wanted to hit Dewey the star prosecutor, it was vetoed by Luciano, Meyer Lansky and the boys; when Schultz bridled, he got lead poisoning in a Newark restaurant.

"Now I'm not sure whether Capone or Wendel approaches them," I said, "but Max Hassel and Max Greenberg are recruited to engineer the snatch. Why would they go along with such a thing? Probably because they, and possibly their boss Waxey Gordon, want to curry Capone's favor. A beer war seems to be abrewing, shall we say, and the more powerful elements on the East Coast—Luciano, Schultz and so on—are in a position to crush the Hassel and Greenberg operation. It doesn't hurt them to do a favor for Capone, and make some money at the same time. Besides, Hassel and Greenberg won't get their hands dirty—they can dispatch some of their minor bootlegger, rumrunner minions to take the risks and provide the insulation."

Wilson was listening intently.

"Let me interrupt myself to ask you a question, Frank—who was Capone's most frequent contact on the East Coast in '32?"

"Well, Frankie Yale was dead by this point," Wilson said, thoughtfully. "Our intelligence back then indicated that the guy doing the Outfit's courier work, and the general Capone contact man with East-Coast mobsters, was Ricca. Paul Ricca—the Waiter."

"Right on the money, Mr. Wilson," I said, with a smile. "Ricca is unfailingly loyal to Capone. If Capone wanted to launch something that Frank Nitti and Jake Guzik and the rest of the Outfit hierarchy would reject—and after debacles like the Jake Lingle murder and the St. Valentine's Day Massacre, these business-oriented types are hardly likely to embrace kidnapping the goddamn Lindbergh baby—who would Capone go to? Who was ruthless enough, and loyal enough?"

"Ricca, of course," Wilson said. Nodding. Going along with me for the ride.

I drove on. "I think Ricca may have enlisted Gaston Means to be the intermediary between the underworld and the upperworld. Con man, ex-government agent, Means was clever and connected with everybody from bootleggers to congressmen to high society."

"Why the hell would Capone resort to unreliable rabble like this Wendel character and, of all people, Gaston Means?"

I gave him the same explanation I'd given Nitti: they were smart, savvy crooks, who were probably smart enough not to cross Capone, and who would make perfect fall guys. They could call out Capone's name in court and everybody would just laugh.

"Means didn't contact Evalyn McLean at first, you know," I said. "He contacted Colonel M. Robert Guggenheim, and a prominent judge—this was in the earliest days of the case. He seems likely to have been truly attempting to become the intermediary, at the bidding of Capone. He's a hell of a lot more likely go-between than Jafsie Condon!"

Wilson smiled.

"Now as for the kidnapping itself, disbarred lawyer Wendel— as I mentioned—has a client named Isidor Fisch. Fisch is a con man, fence and probable dope-smuggler . . ."

"Nate, pardon me, but we checked Fisch a hundred different ways. He was a harmless Jewish boy suffering from tuberculosis."

"Frank, maybe you should've checked one hundred and one ways." It was time to get tough. "I know you had a man in that spiritualist church of Marinelli's . . ."

"One of the best undercover agents in the Unit. Pat O'Rourke."

"I know O'Rourke, and he is a good man. But this time he didn't do a good job. Are you aware that Fisch lived across the street from that spiritualist church?"

"Certainly," he said, and shrugged dismissively.

That surprised me. "You did? Didn't you find that significant?"

"Not particularly," he said. "Fisch didn't even meet Hauptmann until two years after the kidnapping. Just one of the many coincidental red herrings we were always running into on the case."

I hardly knew how to respond to that brilliant piece of deductive thinking.

"Frank, you're operating from the premise that Hauptmann is guilty," I said, trying to maintain control, and stay reasonable. "Assuming that Hauptmann may *not* be guilty, then his not having met Fisch until two years after the crime speaks only of Hauptmann's *innocence*."

He made a small dismissive wave. "Well, for the sake of argument . . . but I can't accept your characterizing Pat O'Rourke's undercover work as anything but exceptional."

"Oh, really? Then did you know Isidor Fisch was a *member* of that spiritualist church?"

His face remained impassive, but his eyes flickered.

"So was Oliver Whately. So was Violet Sharpe."

He sat forward. "Are you certain?"

"I have witnesses who say so. And if you send some of these famous Washington G-men or T-men into the field checking, I think you'll come up with a lot more witnesses. Can I continue my scenario?"

He nodded; his expression was grave.

"Paul Wendel uses his client Fisch to arrange for Violet and Ollie to help, in various ways. I think Violet's a dupe, actually, providing inside information possibly through a boyfriend, while Ollie is, on the other hand, an active participant in the scheme. He is, in fact, the prime inside accomplice. The night of the kidnapping, he probably handed the baby either down the ladder or out the front door to one of Hassel and Greenberg's cronies. There's a possibility these bootleggers have a connection to the servants that can be traced, even at this late date, because I understand deliveries of beer and booze were made to Whately and others."

Wilson wore a faint humorless smirk. "I suppose Whately's role explains why the dog didn't bark."

"Oh, yes and then some—you see, Whately looked after Wahgoosh. He in fact brought the dog into the household, raised it, trained it. There's no way around it, Frank, it has to be said . . ."

"Oh, Heller, please don't."

I shrugged and smiled. "The butler did it."

"You had to say it."

"I was born to say it. Frank, the child was spirited away by these bootleggers, Hassel and Greenberg's boys, and possibly along for the ride was a Capone representative."

"Surely not Ricca."

"No. But I have a hunch this is where Bob Conroy was positioned; he'd been on the outs with Capone, and maybe was willing to do almost anything to get back into the boss's good graces . . . setting himself up, unwittingly of course, to be Capone's fall guy."

"Conroy is the guy that Capone was offering up, all right," Wilson admitted. "Go on."

"The first note, planted in the nursery, was written by Wendel; his background, incidentally, is German, although he's apparently at least second-generation. The note was not really for ransom purposes, but merely to lead Lindbergh and the authorities into thinking the kidnapping was for real."

"So that Capone could ride in on his white horse," Wilson said, playing along, "and give us the kidnapper—Conroy—and the kid back."

"And get his freedom. Right. Meanwhile, this weasel Fisch tries to interlope; he knows nobody's really going after any ransom, so decides it's his for the asking. He sends a second note, patterning it on the original."

Wilson's expression was openly skeptical. "How would he have access to that?"

"About three different ways, Frank. He may have been there when Wendel wrote the first note, and sneaked out a copy or an earlier draft. He may have gotten it through underworld circles—Rosner and Spitale were circulating a copy, remember? Or a tracing could have come from Violet Sharpe or Whately—the note was just stuck in Slim's desk drawer, where the servants had easy access. Remember?"

Glumly, he nodded.

"Now, it's also possible Wendel and Fisch were in league, in this interloping extortion effort. Since Wendel once tried to scam Capone, maybe Wendel was working for nothing, to even the slate with Snorkey. So Wendel, wanting some dough to show for his trouble, might have gone in with Fisch on the extortion scheme. Hard to say. At any rate, about this time, you and Irey come along and convince Lindbergh that Capone is bluffing, and Slim says, either way, he's not going to deal with slime like Scarface Al— even if it means his little boy's life. So soon it's clear that Lindbergh won't play—that the kidnapping has been for nothing. Capone cuts his losses, and fades."

"Where is the child?"

"I'll get to that. But I'll say this much, at this point: the kid is not dead. In fact, he still isn't."

Wilson's eyes clouded. I was losing him.

"Never mind that, right now. Stick with me."

Reluctantly, Wilson nodded.

"Now that Capone is out of the picture, the way is clear for Fisch to go full throttle into his negotiations. He sends more notes. The spiritualist group, with Marinelli probably in on the game but his wife probably not, manipulates this old fool they know, Professor John Condon, into offering himself up as intermediary."

"And how do they know Condon?"

"Why, Frank—didn't Pat O'Rourke mention that? Jafsie attended that spiritualist church, too!"

His mouth dropped open, just a bit. He swallowed and scribbled something on his notepad.

I shrugged. "I don't think Jafsie is a bad enough person, or smart enough person either, to be part of this extortion scheme. But he was a visible, easily manipulated blowhard—I think he may have been Marinelli and Sivella's grade-school teacher, in Harlem—and a prime candidate to funnel information to Lindbergh, and to funnel cash back through to them. The Marinellis even gave that hotel-room séance I attended at Princeton to help prime the pump, mentioning Jafsie by name and nudging Breckinridge about a note he'd receive soon; and maybe to get some play in the press for the veracity of Sister Sarah's psychic abilities. That was a stupid risk, and the mistake that should have cracked this thing wide open. But it didn't."

"You're saying this spiritualist church group, led by Fisch, got the cemetery money. And that they never had the child?"

"Exactly."

"What about the sleeping suit that was delivered to Jafsie?"

"That could have happened a couple ways. Jafsie slept in the nursery, the night he came to Lindbergh with the note from the 'kidnappers.' I caught him red-handed going through a chest. He took any number of things to use to identify the child—some of these were toys he asked for . . . maybe you remember the safety pins he took and showed to 'Cemetery John' and asked him to identify?"

Wilson nodded.

"Well, he may have taken the sleeping suit at that time, as a souvenir, or for ID purposes. But I think it's more likely that Violet Sharpe provided the sleeping suit."

"Violet Sharpe?"

"Yes. The child had a sizeable, unspecified number of the sleepers that were exactly the same. A good many of them were kept in the *other* nursery, at the Morrow estate at Englewood— where Violet lived and worked. Everybody wondered why the sleeper seemed freshly laundered, and why it took two days for the 'kidnappers' to provide Jafsie this proof."

"Well, the answer is obvious," Wilson said, almost testily. "They had to go back to the woods where they'd buried the child, to remove the sleeper."

"Do you *really* think that's likely? Besides, these are extortionists, not kidnappers—they don't have the kid, they never did have the kid. Didn't you wonder why they didn't have better proof than a fucking sleeping suit? Why not a photo, or a phone call from the tot—he could talk a little, you know."

"If he was dead, he couldn't talk."

"If he was alive, and they didn't have him, he couldn't talk, either, not for them, anyway. But one of their inside contacts, either Violet at Englewood or Ollie at Hopewell, could take another sleeper from a drawer in either nursery—and *of course* the sleeper would seem freshly laundered. It hadn't been worn since it was last washed!"

Wilson was thinking. I knew I'd made a dent. I let him think for a bit.

Then I pressed on. "Now the actual kidnappers, the bootleggers who worked for Hassel and Greenberg, they also know that Capone has picked up his cards and gone home. They, too, figure that there's extortion dough for the asking. So they contact this respectable fella in Norfolk, who has some vague connections to the Lindberghs through society, a shipbuilder they know 'cause he's repaired boats for guys in their line of work."

"John Curtis?" Wilson said, dumbfounded. "*That* hoaxer?"

"He wasn't a hoaxer, Frank. He was telling the truth. So pretty soon Curtis is contacting Lindbergh, and now we have two extortion groups who are active—both with inside information about the kidnapping, and neither of whom at this point possesses the baby."

"Heller, isn't this getting a little Byzantine?"

"This case has been Byzantine since the day I showed up in March of 1932. If you'd care to point out any one part of this case that has ever made rational sense, I'll slip on my raincoat and go home. Right now."

"Go on. Go on."

"Let me touch on Gaston Means. He also has been told, by Ricca probably or maybe Hassel and Greenberg, that Capone is cutting his losses; Means has been told to stop trying to contact Lindbergh through the likes of Guggenheim and others. So what does Means do? He begins using *his* inside information, not to swindle Lindbergh, but over to one side, where Capone is unlikely to notice or care . . . he focuses on a soft-hearted, deep-pocketed society matron, Mrs. Evalyn Walsh McLean."

Wilson made a note.

I went on. "Now the payoff in the cemetery takes place, and the kid isn't returned, and all of a sudden it's all over the papers; so Capone obviously now knows that somebody is interloping. Capone also knows from the papers that Lindbergh and Jafsie are trying to get back in touch with the 'kidnappers,' and are obviously willing to pay more money, and this thing Capone has put in motion just seems to have no end, to be completely out of fucking control. Capone and Ricca don't necessarily know for sure that these extortionists are anybody who was really in on the kidnapping—it could be somebody from the outside entirely. Whatever the case, Capone decides to bring this farce to a halt. He has a baby planted in the woods not far from the Lindbergh estate . . ."

"Hold it, Heller! That baby was identified by its father, for God's sake."

"That baby was a pile of decomposed bones that couldn't even be identified as to sex; the family pediatrician said he couldn't ID that kid as the Little Eaglet if you paid him ten million bucks! Those woods were trampled over and over again by search parties and telephone linemen, and in any case, that corpse was decomposed way beyond what it should've, in that period of time, with weather that cold."

"There was an identifying garment . . ."

"Yes, a few scraps of cloth with blue thread. It was the blue thread that Betty Gow recognized, because she'd made this makeshift garment the night of the kidnapping, with thread provided by Elsie Whately—the butler's wife. I'm sure Capone could have reached out through his various intermediaries and procured that simple spool of thread from his accomplices among the Lindbergh servants. Or, the little shirt itself may have been within Capone's grasp."

"The garment was planted, you're saying."

"Like the little body was planted. It was an act of closure, on Capone and Ricca's part. To shut down the extortion schemes. To put an end to this goddamn case."

Wilson was thinking. "Capone was in Atlanta at this point."

"Right. And optimistic about getting out via traditional avenues, such as his lawyers and bribery, not outlandish schemes like the ill-fated Lindbergh snatch. And Ricca's on the outside, cleaning house. Ricca uses the beer war between Waxey Gordon and the New York mob as a convenient front for bumping off Hassel and Greenberg and maybe a few others involved in the conspiracy; Bob Conroy and his wife get iced about this time, too."

"No," Wilson said flatly. "Conroy and his wife, that was a double suicide."

"My ass! And why in fucking hell didn't you ever tell me you finally tracked Conroy down? I must've called you about Conroy half a dozen times."

Rather meekly, he said, "You were off the case, at that point. Never occurred to me, frankly. If you're right about all this rampant assassination, why was Gaston Means allowed to stay among the living?"

"Why kill Means? Nobody believes anything he says, anyway. Besides, I was closing in on Hassel and Greenberg, right before they got hit. I found out about them by beating their names out of Means . . . but before I could follow up, they got theirs in the 'beer war.' "

"You think Means sold them out to Ricca."

"I sure do. That allowed Means to go to court, and lay everything on Hassel and Greenberg, who were nice and dead and blameable. Meanwhile, Violet Sharpe starts coming unhinged after the little corpse in the woods turns up; however she's been involved, to whatever extent—and she has two unexplained g's in her bank account, remember—she certainly never counted on the baby getting killed, and of course she has no way of knowing that the baby they found wasn't the real Lindy, Jr."

"So she takes poison," Wilson said.

"Or she's murdered. No one actually saw her take poison. She was ill, taking medicine for her nerves; maybe she was poisoned by Whately."

"He didn't work at the Englewood estate."

"He was there frequently. They were a close-knit 'family' of servants, those two estates. At any rate, she was another loose end tied off. Whately's death strikes me as similarly suspicious. I think looking into that—seeing why a guy who was healthy all his life suddenly dies of an ulcer—would be a nice use of the taxpayers' money. Was there an autopsy?"

"I don't know," he admitted.

"Even if it was natural causes, what stress exactly caused this bleeding ulcer? Kind of makes you wonder, doesn't it? And wasn't Fisch's death convenient? Speaking of whom, I'm not precisely sure how Fisch and Wendel intersect. Wendel may or may not have been involved in the cemetery extortion; I do know that Wendel's sister lived in back of St. Raymond's."

"What?"

"You heard me. Jot that down, too. At any rate, Fisch wound

up with at least part of the money, and either his illness or worry about Capone or Ricca or even the cops catching up with him sent him scurrying off to Germany, leaving some cash stashed with his buddy Hauptmann."

"So you see Hauptmann as a dupe in this," Wilson said, with a mocking smile.

"The only thing he may be guilty of is being in on Fisch's dope smuggling, using furs as a partial front. But I doubt even that." I cracked my knuckles. "Anyway, that's what I think happened. As for Charles Lindbergh, Jr., he's salted away somewhere. I have a good idea where he was kept immediately after the kidnapping—in New Haven, Connecticut. Where he is now, I haven't a clue. But Capone and Ricca aren't about to bump him off—there's no statute of limitations on murder."

Wilson raised an eyebrow, smiled tightly and put down his pencil. "Nate, this is an interesting theory, and you've mentioned some things that I admit I didn't know—but you completely ignore and overlook the overwhelming evidence gathered against Bruno Hauptmann."

I laughed. "Christ, Frank, I shouldn't dignify that with a response. I've never seen such shameless tampering with, and concoction of, evidence . . . or so many lying witnesses from Condon to Whited and Hochmuth and even Slim Lindbergh himself."

"You're calling Charles Lindbergh a liar?"

"Yes. I think he was prompted into lying by police who assured him that they had the right man. Did you ever give Slim that reassurance, Frank?"

Wilson said nothing.

"I'm not suggesting there was any great police conspiracy to frame Hauptmann, or even that the Outfit sought to frame him. Hauptmann dropped himself into the fall-guy slot by being Fisch's friend and business partner. And then forces somewhat independently rallied to 'help' him fit that role. You know how sloppy cops like Schwarzkopf and Welch think, Frank—they center on their suspect, led there by minimal but fairly convincing evidence, and then they proceed to fudge this, lie about that, suppress one thing, fake the other. Witnesses are made to feel with absolute certainty that they are testifying against a guilty man—the cops have assured them thus. So, to do the 'right' thing so that society can have retribution, and/or for the brief moment center stage in the public eye, or, hell, just to share in reward money, an otherwise honest witness tells a little lie. Distorts a piece of evidence just slightly. What harm is a little embroidery, after all, in so large and official a cloth? So a cop fudges ladder evidence, and a teller at a movie theater makes a bogus eyewitness ID, and a prosecutor withholds letters and ledgers that back up Hauptmann's 'Fisch story,' and on, and on, and on."

He was frowning. "You're casting doubt on the reputations of a lot of fine public officials, and good citizens."

"No, I'm not. Because there is no 'doubt' about this. Hauptmann was framed; he was a German carpenter who fit the psychological profile and the miniscule evidence on hand. He was perfect. Now, I do think the Outfit may have helped from the sidelines. 'Death House' Reilly and Sam Leibowitz, for example, who volunteered their legal services, both had strong Capone ties. So do a lot of New Jersey and New York City cops, whether you like to hear me say it or not."

"You're also casting doubt," he said stiffly, "on the work the IRS Intelligence Unit performed. Jesus, Heller, we're the people who put Capone away. You can't dream that the Outfit's influence extends to . . ."

"No. That's why I came to you. One of the reasons, anyway. You have the manpower and the skills to follow up my leads and my scenario. You can do it in a short period of time, which if we want to keep Hauptmann's ass from getting scorched is a must. And here's the really sweet part, Frank—you can get Capone again, big-time."

He raised his chin; his eyes sharpened.

"You nailed him once, but only temporarily. He'll be out in a few years. Imagine if you could pin a murder and kidnapping rap on him. Imagine pinning the *Lindbergh* kidnapping on him. You'd be more famous than J. Edgar Hoover."

"Fame means little to me, Heller."

Maybe so, but he sure was doing his best to climb the bureaucratic ladder.

"How about the simple satisfaction of finally solving this goddamn case?" I said.

"Heller, this case *is* solved."

"Frank, after all I've laid out in front of you, how can you . . ."

"Look," he said edgily, "most of these people you're talking about are dead. Fisch, Hassel, Greenberg, Violet Sharpe, Ollie Whately . . ."

"Whately's wife Elsie is in Great Britain; she had to be at least peripherally involved. Get her!"

"Heller, she's dead, too."

"What? What . . . what were the circumstances?"

"I don't know exactly." He shrugged. "Natural causes, I understand."

"Jesus! Find out! All these deaths are a little goddamn convenient, don't you think?"

He was shaking his head slowly, no. "If there is anything left to solve here, short of Hauptmann fingering his confederates at the last minute, there's little chance at this point of clearing it up. Too many dead. The rest are fringe characters like Means, Wendel, Jafsie, the Marinellis. Dead ends. Red herrings."

I leaned forward, put my hands on his desk. "You're one of the few people on earth, Frank, who can pick up the phone, reopen this investigation and save Hauptmann's life."

He shrugged. "I don't want to save Hauptmann's life. Even if your 'scenario' is correct, and it strikes me as extremely farfetched and fanciful, I still see Hauptmann as a major figure—Fisch's accomplice. There's no doubt in my mind, Heller: Hauptmann is guilty, one hundred percent. He had a previous record in Germany and is, without a doubt, as cold, hard and vicious a criminal as I have ever run into."

I just looked at him.

"Let me read you something," he said, and he reached behind him and plucked the picture of Lindbergh off the wall. With a sad, proud smile, he read: " 'To Frank J. Wilson—if it had not been for you fellows being in on the case, Hauptmann would not have gone to trial and your organization deserves the full credit for his apprehension.' "

I stood. "Well, jeez, Frank—I'd hate like hell to fuck up your inscribed photo with the truth."

He gave me a sharp look; he put the photo back on the wall, hastily, and it swung crookedly on its nail, unnoticed by him. "Heller, I gave you a fair hearing. Now if you'll excuse me, I've got real work to do."

I leaned on his desk. "Let me just ask you something. Just one thing. You were on the Bob Conroy case, weren't you? You and Lt. Finn from Manhattan. Did you see the crime scene? This 'double suicide'?"

He nodded.

"Well, come on, Frank—what did your nose tell you? I don't know anything about the case, but that 'suicide' *had* to smell. It had to be Capone and Ricca tyin' up loose ends."

"You want to look at the file?" he asked. And he started riffling through a stack of manila folders. "You can look at the damn file."

"What's it doing on your desk?"

"It's a counterfeiting-related case. I told you, that's the area I'm working in right now."

"Why is it counterfeiting-related?"

"They were living in poverty, Conroy and his wife . . ."

"Lying low, it sounds like."

He shrugged that off. "Well, they'd come up with a new scheme, it appears, 'cause they had a neat little printing press in their flop, and plates that turned out embarrassingly good counterfeit money."

"That doesn't sound like somebody getting ready to commit suicide."

"Who knows why people kill themselves? Here. Here it is. Sit down and look at it, if you like, but I got to get back to business."

I started flipping through the file, and came to a mug-shot photo of a woman, an attractive, hard-looking pockmarked brunette. I froze.

"Heller? Nate? What's wrong with you? You look like you saw a ghost."

"No, uh, it's nothing," I said, and I sat and I quietly read the file and then I set it on Wilson's desk, and thanked him for his time.

"You look funny," he said. "Don't you feel good?"

"See you, Frank," I said, and went out.

I leaned against the wall in the hall, government workers moving briskly by. Had I seen a ghost? In a way.

The better half of the Conroy double suicide, Bob's wife, Bernice, was someone I'd seen before. Someone I'd briefly known. She'd been a blonde, then. It had been years ago—a little over four years, but the memory of her was vivid.

I'd seen her in Chicago, in LaSalle Street Station, where she stepped down off the Twentieth Century Limited.

With a baby in her arms.

Chapter 39

The brick terra-cotta six-flat on Sheridan looked just the same; it might have been yesterday I stood before it, not four years. Even the day was the same: gray, cold, the air flecked with icy snow. I stood on the sidewalk, studying the six-flat like a clue I couldn't decipher.

Only I had deciphered it.

This was Tuesday, late Tuesday morning—almost twenty-four hours to the minute from when I saw Bernice Conroy's mug-shot picture in Frank Wilson's office in Washington. I had taken the train in the afternoon, got into Chicago in the middle of the night, slept like a baby in my Murphy bed in my office, till about an hour ago.

On the train, I hadn't slept a wink. I lay in my Pullman upper with my eyes wide open and staring, slowly piecing *this* together, instantly piecing *that* together, until I knew. I knew exactly what had happened.

Evalyn, I told nothing. I said only that I had a long-shot lead, from something I'd seen in Wilson's office, and that it required me going back to Chicago to follow up. She'd wanted to come, but I said no. She tried to argue, but I wasn't having any.

This was for me to do.

"I'll be back as soon as I can," I told her.

"What do I do till then?"

"Same as Hauptmann," I said, touching her face. "Wait, and pray."

Interpretation was required: that's what Marinelli had said. Not long ago I thought psychics were the bunk; and I still thought most of them, Marinelli included, were scam artists. The "fortune" in "fortune-teller" was the money those sons of bitches plucked off their marks.

But a few of these screwballs were sincere—Edgar Cayce a prime example. Even in '32 I'd sensed that he at least *thought* he was for real; he, and his nice little wife and quiet little life, had impressed me, back then, though I hadn't wanted to admit it to myself.

Now, as I stood before the brick building on Sheridan Road, I knew he'd somehow tapped into something very real. But interpretation was required: he'd gotten so much right—the mill section of New Haven; the two-story shingled house on "Adams" (Chatham) Street, numbered 73; the name of the man who lived in that house, Paul Maglio, a.k.a. Paul Ricca; the brown building two-tenths of a mile from the end of Chatham, where neighborhood rumor had it Little Lindy had been baby-sat . . .

But the child was on Scharten Street, Cayce had said. And that brown building was on Maltby.

Interpretation: Scharten. Sounds like Scharten, sounds like Scharten . . .

Sheridan?

Only that baby had never been in the six-flat on Sheridan. I'd followed Bernice Rogers, a.k.a. Bernice Conroy, a twenty-month-old baby bundled in her arms, from LaSalle Street Station to this apartment building. And that baby had turned out to belong to Hymie Goldberg.

You remember—it was in all the papers.

That was the sweetest irony of all: I was picked to be the police liaison from Chicago because I'd cracked the Hymie Goldberg kidnapping. It had impressed Lindbergh himself, got me immediately into the inner circle with Breckinridge and assorted colonels and underworld types.

But had I really cracked the Goldberg kidnapping? No charges had been pressed against Bernice Rogers, after all—Hymie Goldberg, upon return of his kid, had claimed Bernice had been acting as his Jafsie. The Goldberg kidnapping may have been a sham, a front, all along.

What I most certainly *had* done, that fourth day of March in 1932, when I got suspicious of a hard-looking blonde and an innocent-looking baby in a Chicago train station, was royally botch the Lindbergh case.

Funny, I remembered how I'd speculated that cracking the crime of the century would send my career skyrocketing. But I was a green kid, and what did I know? Certainly not what I was doing.

That great old detective, though, my Chief of Detectives, "Old Shoes" Schoemaker, had been right on the money. We knew at the time that Bernice Rogers had adopted a boy, of a specific age, from an Evanston agency. Old Shoes had theorized that she had then gone east with the kid and set up housekeeping in some quiet neighborhood and let herself, and her charge, be seen—but not too close up. Then after the kidnapping, Charles Lindbergh, Jr., was substituted for the adoption-agency kid, who was disposed of, somehow.

I now knew that the "quiet neighborhood" out east had been in New Haven, "in the region of" Dover, in an apartment over a grocery store in a brown building on Maltby Street. At the behest of "Paul Maglio," whose shingled two-story on Chatham had briefly been used as a safe house. That adopted kid had probably been smothered or whatever, and buried in the basement on Chatham or something—possibly winding up, months later, in a shallow grave in the Sourland Mountains.

Only Paul Ricca hadn't counted on the feds pouring into New Haven in the days immediately following the snatch, looking for suspects and babies; Ricca had no way of knowing that the construction workers on Lindbergh's estate had largely come from New Haven, and had become immediate suspects.

So the plan was hastily changed, and Ricca had sent Bernice

Rogers and her hot little package (its hair dyed black) back to Chicago, where somebody other than Bernice would take charge of the child, who would be sent deep into hiding and safekeeping.

And that was how, and where, plainclothes officer Nathan Heller of the pickpocket detail screwed up.

On the train last night, not long before it pulled into (of all places) LaSalle Street Station, the truth had come to me—only four years and several days too late.

A switch had been pulled.

Bernice Rogers had hustled her pretty ass off that train and into the train station and directly in the ladies' room. She'd been in there less than two minutes. Not time enough to change a diaper; not time enough to take a decent pee.

But plenty of time to trade babies with another surrogate mother, waiting for her in that can.

Bernice Rogers Conroy had turned Charles Lindbergh, Jr., over to an awaiting accomplice, who had given her in return the son of a Jewish bootlegger named Goldberg.

Substituting not only another child, but another *kidnapped* child, would make it possible for all of Bernice's elaborate precautions—adopting another kid, going east, shuttling home—to be written off as having been done in relation to the *Goldberg* kidnapping. Which probably wasn't a kidnapping at all, of course.

What this boiled down to was, young detective Heller fucked up, major league. I should have followed that bitch into the bathroom. Grabbed her, and the kid. But I was too fucking shy—I didn't want to wound the sensibilities of any ladies going potty.

I was the potty one. Fuck! The grief I could have saved myself, Lindbergh, Hauptmann, the world, if I'd just had the balls to go in a goddamn ladies' room!

On such trivialities does history hinge—not to mention my sanity.

Well, that was a long time ago, and now I was back in Chicago, back on Sheridan, back in front of the apartment building I'd tracked Bernice Rogers to, once upon a time. I was older, wiser, and Bernice Rogers presumably was, too—though you'd have to add "dead" to her list.

The building janitor had a small basement apartment, shot

through with pipes and scattered with dreary secondhand furniture, stacks of sleazy magazines, and pointless knickknacks. There were several pinup calendars taped to the painted cement wall, none of them the current year. The guy was a scavenger, and a pack rat. For my purposes, that was good.

"Sure I remember Mrs. Rogers," he rasped. He was younger than thirty and older than time, a stooped lunger with four days of stubble, a sweated-out gray T-shirt and baggy blue pants with suspenders. He had a chipmunk overbite yellow as piss, no chin and eyes that were as clear and blue as a summer sky.

"She sure had a good build," I said, and grinned.

"She sure did! She got in trouble, though." He narrowed his inexplicably beautiful blue eyes and leaned forward, to get confidential; his breath smelled of Sen-Sen. "There was a shooting upstairs, back in '32. She was involved in a kidnapping, I heard. But she got off."

"Did she stick around after that?"

"A while, is all. A month, maybe. Then one night, all of a sudden, no notice or nothing, she lit out. Took her clothes, but she left the furniture. It wasn't a furnished flat, neither."

I imagined some of that furniture was in this very room. "Did she leave anything else behind, besides furniture? Personal effects? Like letters, for example?"

He coughed for a while; I waited. Then he said, "No, sir. But I remember, a week or so after she left, a letter did come for her. She didn't leave no forwarding address. Sometimes people do that, you know. Move on without no forwarding address."

"What do you do with their mail, then? Return it to the post office?"

He shook his head, no. "I keep it in a box. In case they should ever come for it."

"I'd like to see that letter."

"Mister, no offense, but that badge you showed me—it was a private badge, wasn't it?"

"Right. Would you like to see some more identification?"

And I showed him a five-dollar bill.

"That's very official-looking," he said, taking it, grinning wolfishly, sticking it into a deep pocket. "You stay here."

He opened a door and I caught a glimpse of the basement laundry room and storage bins for each apartment. The door stood open, but I couldn't see him. I could hear him, rustling in there, ratlike.

He soon returned, baring his yellow overbite. He was holding a cigar box in one hand, like a church usher with a collection plate. In the other hand was a letter, which had been opened, but then so had several dozen more in the cigar box.

I reached for the letter.

He pulled it back; his mouth was tight and pouty. "I want more 'identification.' I could get in trouble with the landlord for this kind of thing."

"I already gave you five bucks, pal." I grinned at him again, but it wasn't at all friendly. "And your landlord isn't going to give you the kind of trouble *I'm* going to give you, if you don't hand that fucker over."

"No," he said, shaking his head, coughing some more. "I mean it. I'm taking a big risk, even talking to somebody like you. Mr. Ricca has strict rules."

That stopped me.

"Mr. Ricca? That's the landlord's name?"

"Owns the building," he said with a somber nod. "And I hear he's connected."

I'd heard that, too.

I gave him another five dollars.

I didn't look at the letter until I was sitting in my car. My hands were trembling as I fished out the single page; I'm not ashamed to say so.

It was from a woman named Madge. No last name, but the envelope had a return address: M. Belliance, Three Oaks, Michigan, a rural route.

Cayce had mentioned a woman named "Belliance" as guarding the child. Son of a bitch, I was a believer. I couldn't keep my goddamn hand from shaking, but I managed to read the letter.

Dear B.,
    The boy is doing fine. He is over his cold. He and Carl are getting along famously. Carl will be a good daddy. No more

boats and worry for us. This farm life is going to be a real nice change.

It's sweet of you to ask about the boy. He is not hard to love. I can see how you got attached to him so quick.

If you know what's best, you ought to tear this up. The picture too, but I couldn't not send one.

Madge

And there was a photo. A snapshot.

Cayce had been right again, in a roundabout way. I had found the child on "Scharten Street." At least, this picture of a child.

A child perhaps twenty-one months old, a beautiful toddler in a little playsuit with suspenders over a T-shirt; he had light curly hair and a dimpled chin, and stood between, with his either hand held by, a thin-faced man in a cap and bib overalls, and an apple-cheeked woman in a calico print housedress; behind them seemed to be a farmhouse. The man and woman were smiling, the little boy was frowning, though he might have been squinting in the sun.

He was Charles Lindbergh, Jr.

And I was on my way to Three Oaks, Michigan.

Chapter 40

I caught Lake Shore Drive and headed to the South Side, cutting through the industrial southeastern side of the city, till the steel mills of Chicago gave way to those of Gary, Indiana. Soon the sooty scent of free enterprise was replaced by the clear, fresh air of the country, and I guided my sporty '32 Auburn along the shore road that curved around Lake Michigan, and before long sand dunes were rising around me like a mirage of the desert. I drove quickly, but I didn't speed, pressing forward with the single-mindedness of a hungry animal. The village of New Buffalo, in southwestern Michigan, in the heart of a summer-camp and resort area, was known as the gateway to that state. It was in that village that I stopped at a hardware store and bought a hunting knife, a coil of rope and a wide roll of electrical tape. They also sold ammunition, but I'd brought some from home.

It wasn't far to Three Oaks, another quaint village, where a gas-station attendant gave me directions to the Belliance farm. I turned right at the traffic light on North Elm Street and at a junction with a macadam road turned left; I passed Warren Woods, a vast acreage of virgin beech and maple, a state bird and game sanctuary. I made a left and a right, on gravel roads, passing through an area of orchards alternating with empty fields, and there it was.

Basking in afternoon sunshine, bucolic as a feed-store lithograph, the Belliance farm rested on a gentle slope, even some green amidst the grass—whether that was because spring was coming, or the lake was relatively close, I was too citified to know. The farmhouse was a small, white, two-story clapboard, with a large red barn behind and to one side. Sarah Sivella had seen such a place, last week, in that trance she'd fallen into at the Temple of Divine Power. I swung into the drive; it was gravel, but the earth that fell to ditches on either side had a reddish cast. Edgar Cayce had said there was "red dirt on the pavement" near the house where the child was kept. I was beginning to wonder if I should trade my nine millimeter in on a crystal ball.

For now, however, I'd stick to the nine millimeter, which I'd already slipped into the pocket of my raincoat. The wide roll of electrical tape was in the other pocket. And I had looped the coil of rope around my belt, and the hunting knife, in a leather sheath, was stuck through my belt as well; neither would show under the bulky, lined raincoat.

I was ready to call on the Belliance family.

Chickens scurrying noisily out of my way, I pulled the Auburn up around the side of the house, where the gravel near a fenced-in area was already accommodating a pickup truck, a late-model Chevy and a green, new-looking tractor. In addition to the recently painted, bright red barn, several other structures huddled, including a toolshed and a windmill.

The sun slid under a cloud and reminded me how cold it still was; but there was no snow on the frozen ground. I walked to the front porch and knocked. There was a swing; the breeze was making it sway, some.

A woman answered—the woman I'd seen in the photograph inserted in the letter to Bernice Rogers Conroy; she was in her early forties, wearing a crisp pink-and-white checked housedress with a white apron, on which she was drying her hands. She was dark blonde, apple-cheeked, and had blue eyes almost as lovely as the janitor's back in the Sheridan six-flat.

"Can I help you, young man?" Her smile was pleasant, her tone sincere.

"Excuse me for bothering, but I'm having some car trouble. Is your husband home?"

"Why, yes. He's out back. I can get him . . . ?"

"Would you please? I'm sorry to be such a bother."

"Step in, step in."

I did. She went away, still wiping her hands on the apron; I heard the back door open. I slipped my hand in my raincoat pocket, gripped the nine millimeter. I put my back to the wall just inside the door, so that I could see the front door as well as where she'd gone into the kitchen. A stairway rose before me. The house was simple and wellkept, wood floors, floral wallpaper. The furnishings were not expensive, but they were relatively new; there was a spinet piano in the living room. In the midst of the depression, these people had been set up out here on the farm with nice, new things.

A scarecrow of a man in coveralls came in through the kitchen, his wife following dutifully behind him; he was wiping grease from his hands with a rag. In his mid-forties, he was bald with pouches under his eyes—like Sarah Sivella had said. His somewhat weathered face was that of the man I'd seen in the photo.

He extended his freshly cleaned hand and smiled. "I'm Carl Belliance. I understand you've got a little problem."

"No," I said, and I showed him the nine millimeter. "You've got the problem."

His face tightened and I thought he was going to jump me but I caught his eyes and shook my head, no. He sighed, got off the balls of his feet, and went limp, arms dangling, head lowered. He backed up a pace. His wife had raised a hand to her mouth.

"What do you want, mister?" he said. "We got no money in the house."

"Can it. I'm here for the boy."

They glanced at each other; she seemed near tears. He shook his head, as if to say, *It's no use.*

"I figured it would catch up with us someday," Belliance said softly.

"Why? Who do you figure I am?"

He smiled with one side of his face and it wasn't really a smile. "Does it matter? You're either a cop, or you're not a cop. And if you're not a cop, somebody's decided to take everything away from us." His mouth tightened into something bitter. "We've done what we were told. We never made a peep. But I suppose it was hoping for too much just to live our damn lives in peace."

"Who *are* you, Carl?"

His eyes twitched. "I'm nobody. I'm just a farmer."

"Well, if you don't want to tell me, I'll tell you. You used to be a rumrunner for the Outfit. Repeal was on the way and you'd be out of work, soon. But you were a good man. Trustworthy. So somebody big—somebody named Capone maybe, or maybe somebody named Ricca—asked if you wanted to go straight. Go into farming. Drop out of that life."

He looked at me blankly, but there was respect in his eyes. "You're pretty good, mister. *Are* you a cop?"

"Of sorts. Let me guess something else, while I'm at it. You two are a childless couple. You've been married for maybe twenty years, maybe twenty-five, but there was never an offspring. You wanted a family. With your background, adoption was tricky. But then, finally, like a miracle—somebody gave you a son."

He took a small step back and slipped his arm around his wife's shoulder; she pressed close to him, weeping quietly. "That's right," he said. "And we love our son, mister. And he loves us."

"That's just swell. You do know who the boy is?"

"Yes, we do. He's Carl Belliance, Jr."

"You got the 'junior' right, anyway."

Madge Belliance, lip trembling, said, "We've never said that . . . never said that name. Never spoken it."

I raised an eyebrow, the gun still trained carefully on them. "Charles Lindbergh, Jr., you mean? Where is he?"

"He's at school," she said. She was trying to summon some defiance, but it wasn't playing.

"When does he get home?"

"You're not going to hurt him . . ." she wondered, gripping her husband's shirt; he patted her.

"Hell no, lady. I'm giving him back to his real parents. When does he get home?"

"It's a long walk," she said. She licked her lips. "In half an hour, maybe. We never did anything wrong, mister."

"Ever hear of a guy named Hauptmann?"

"Yes," Belliance said, and he raised his chin. "We hear he was a goddamn extortionist and is getting what he deserves."

"Oh, is that what they told you? That's a good one. You got a hired hand?"

"Not now," he said. "Some of the year I do."

I glanced quickly around the place. "You seem to be faring pretty well, here, despite hard times. What are you raising on this farm, besides a stolen kid? Berries? Corn? Never mind—I don't really care. Here."

With my left hand, I extended the roll of electrical tape toward Madge Belliance. She took it, with reluctance and confusion.

"Use some of that to tie your husband's wrists behind his back. Do it now."

"But . . ."

"*Now,* I said. Let's get this done before Junior gets home, and that'll lessen the chance anything bad does happen."

She exchanged glances with her husband; he looked at her gravely, and nodded, and she sighed heavily and nodded back. He turned his back to her, put his wrists behind him and she bound him with the tape.

When she was done, she held the tape out to me. I took it and told her to turn around and put her wrists behind her. With the nine millimeter held in the crotch of my left arm, I quickly wound the black tape around her wrists. Then I nudged her forward. I told them to turn and face me again, and they did.

"Let's go to the cellar," I said.

They led me there; the double storm-cellar doors were along the side of the house where I was parked. They went down the half-flight of wooden steps ahead of me. The basement was hard-packed dirt. It had that same reddish cast.

"Sit against that wall," I said. "I don't want to have to knock anybody out."

They sat. Keeping back from them, the gun tucked under my arm, I used the hunting knife to cut the rope. I bound both their ankles, and added a length of rope to the wrists of each. Then I had them sit back to back against a support beam and tied them together, around the chest and waist, the beam between them. Nobody said anything through any of this.

Her apron I cut into strips with the knife and gagged them that way; that was kinder than using the electrical tape, which had been my original plan. When you're pulling a kidnapping, you have to be flexible.

I stood before them. "I don't want you to make a sound," I said. "Don't alert that boy you're down here."

Belliance's eyes were hard; his wife's were soft.

"You behave yourselves," I said, "and maybe I won't turn you in. All I want is to put that boy back with his rightful parents. Understood?"

They just looked at me.

"Understood?" I repeated.

The father nodded curtly; then, hesitantly, his wife nodded, too, several times.

I put my gun in my shoulder holster, not in my raincoat pocket, and left them in the cellar with the dirt and some rakes and a wall of jarred preserves.

Then I climbed from the cellar to the cool fresh air and walked around and sat on the front-porch swing and waited for Charles Lindbergh, Jr., to come home from school.

It wasn't a long wait. Less than fifteen minutes.

From my vantage point on the porch of the hillside farmhouse, I could see down on the gravel road where half a dozen kids of various ages were walking, kicking up a little dust as they did. He was the youngest—what would he be, now? Six? Almost six. This was either his first or second year of school.

He came up the gravel lane all alone, a tiny figure in a brown coat and gray slacks; his hat—it made something catch in my throat to see it—was an aviation-style helmet with decorative goggles that the kids had been wearing the last couple years. He had mittens. No schoolbooks—too young for that yet, I guessed. He walked up the lane like a little soldier. A little man. And the closer he got, the more that face was Slim's.

He hesitated when he saw me, then he moved confidently toward the porch and said, "Who are you, mister?"

I got up off the swing. I smiled. "I'm a friend of your parents. Come on up here, Carl."

He thought about that. The dimpled chin, the baby face, were so familiar. Was he hesitating, because somewhere in his memory he remembered getting pulled here and there by strange people?

"Where are Mom and Dad?"

"They had to go away, suddenly. They asked me to pick you up after school, and take you to them."

The little eyes narrowed. "I'm supposed to go with you?"

"That's right. I'm going to take you to your folks, real soon."

"Well. Okay. But I'm hungry."

"Let's see if we can find you something in the kitchen," I said.

A pie was cooling on the kitchen table. Other food was still in various stages of preparation; some chicken Madge had been about to roll in breading sat naked on the counter. Peeled potatoes were in the sink. But the little boy didn't put it together.

"Can I have a piece pie?" he asked. He was taking off his coat and hat and putting them neatly on a chair; his mittens were already off.

"Sure," I said. "Then later we'll stop for a hamburger on the way to see your folks, okay?"

"Okay."

So I cut him a "piece pie." Dutch apple. I had a big slice myself; I'd worked up an appetite. Delicious.

I gave him a napkin and he wiped off his cute little Lindy mug and said, "I have to go to the bathroom."

"Okay," I said.

I followed him upstairs. He asked me to undo his pants and I did. But he went in by himself and did what he had to. I stood by the closed door and listened as he flushed the toilet and ran the water and washed his hands.

He was drying them on his pants as he came out.

"Let's go in your room," I said, bending to button the pants back up, "and get some of your things, and then we'll go. If you have some special toys you want to take with you, pick 'em out. We can't take everything."

"Why do you keep your raincoat on in the house?"

"Because we're going, real soon. Now, let's get your things."

He was picking some toys out of a chest by the window, while from a dresser I was getting a few of his clothes, which I was in the process of stuffing in a pillowcase, when I heard something outside. Something like gravel stirring. I went to the window.

A car was pulling in, next to mine. It was a black Ford, brand shiny new. Two men got quickly out.

"Jesus," I said.

"What's wrong, mister?"

"We're going to play a game, Carl," I said, bending down again, taking him by his little shoulders and looking him straight in his dark-blue eyes. "It's like hide-and-go-seek. I want you to hide under your bed, and I don't want you to say a word or make a sound, okay? Until you hear me say, olly olly oxen free."

"Okay."

He scurried under the bed.

"Quiet as a mouse, now," I said, and got my gun in my hand.

The two men I'd seen were old friends. I hadn't seen them in a very long time. The last time had been four years ago in a suite at the Carteret Hotel in Elizabeth, New Jersey. When they'd been shooting Max Greenberg and Max Hassel to shit.

I stood just around the corner from the top of the stairs as I heard the front door open.

"Where is everybody?" A high-pitched whiny voice.

"I'll check the house." A gravelly baritone.

They were whispering, but I could hear them.

"What should I do?"

"Like the boss said—nobody breathing."

"Jesus, a little kid, Phil?"

"Yes. Check around outside. Do Heller, the farmer and his wife and the kid and any chickens and cows that get in your fuckin' way."

While this was going on, I got on my belly and snake-crawled to the edge of the stairs and soon I could see them down there: Phil was the flat-faced guy with oriental eyes, wearing a black coat and a gray hat and gray gloves with a great big .45 auto in one mitt; and Jimmy (I remembered his name from our first encounter) was the pug-nosed, bright-eyed, round-faced guy, who I'd winged last time, and who wore a gray tweedy-looking topcoat, and he too had a .45 in one gloved hand. No silencers. Who was going to hear it out here?

Jimmy was opening the door to go out when I opened fire on the fuckers. I got Jimmy in the side of the head and it shook him, made him jump like he was startled, only he was more than startled, because the inside of Jimmy's head made it outside before the rest of him did, and he flopped sideways on the porch, on his brains, wedging the door open with his dead body.

Phil caught one in the arm, but unfortunately not the arm of his shooting hand, and he was returning fire, and .45 slugs chewed up the world around me, wall and banister and stairs and then he was gone, not out the door, where Jimmy's body blocked the way, but into the house somewhere.

I didn't see any other way to play it: I started down the stairs two and three at a time, the nine millimeter pointed off to my left, where Phil had gone, and I was looking at an empty living room when the son of a bitch popped up from behind a chair and fired off one well-placed round, clipping me in the side, sending me tumbling headfirst, clattering my way to the bottom in a jumbled mess of arms and legs, all tangled in my raincoat. I was stunned by the fall more than the gunshot, having hit my head five or six times on the way down; but I didn't feel pain in my side yet, just wetness, and still on the floor, I fired back at where Phil had been, but he was gone and all I managed to do was put a bullet into the upright piano. It made a little musical ouch.

I wasn't the only one bleeding: Phil had left a trail, and I followed it. I stumbled through the house, through a sitting room, into the kitchen, where a doorway led, goddammit, to the upstairs. Carefully, hugging the narrow walls of the stairwell, I made my way up the back stairs, and was following the bloody trail when I heard the child yelp.

I ran to his room; now it hurt.

Phil had pulled the boy out from under the bed, obviously, and was clutching the boy to him; the blond-haired baby-faced child looked at me with wide beseeching eyes as Phil hugged the boy to him like a shield and pointed that .45 at me.

I was weak, and I could feel myself slipping, but I steadied the nine millimeter at him and said, "Phil—there's something you should know."

Phil, whose face was whiter than the peeled potatoes in the sink downstairs, said, "What, asshole?"

I shot him between the eyes.

"A shot in the head," I said, "kills all reflex action."

Phil didn't hear me, of course. He'd gone where Jimmy went. The little boy dropped himself to the floor, landing nimbly on his toes, as the dead Phil teetered on feet waiting for signals they'd never receive. Then Phil's corpse decided to land on its face, rather than its ass, and the furniture in the room shook.

"Nice shot, huh, kid?" I said.

"Mister—you don't look so good."

"I know . . ."

"Mister, I'm afraid."

"Son . . . your parents . . . they're downstairs . . . in the cellar. They're tied up . . ."

Concern gripped his face. "Are Mommy and Daddy hurt?"

"They're fine, just . . . you go down there, go out the back way . . . untie 'em. Bring your daddy . . . bring your daddy up here."

He was thinking that over.

I fell to my knees. "Do . . . do that, son, please . . . do it . . . now."

"Okay, mister," he said.

And then I flopped on my face.

Vaguely I remember Carl Belliance turning me over, gently, then hovering over me like a homely angel.

I whispered, "They came to . . . came to kill . . . you . . . too."

"What?" he said.

The boy was with him; the boy was hugging Carl's arm. I could hear him saying: "Daddy, Daddy, Daddy. . . ."

I said, "Don't call Ricca . . . don't call the Waiter. . . ."

"What?"

Daddy . . . Daddy . . . Daddy . . .

"You'll die, too, if you do . . . he sent them . . . Ricca sent them . . . call number . . . in my wall . . ."

"Your wall?"

Daddy . . . Daddy . . . Daddy . . .

"Wallet. In my . . . wall . . . call Nitti. . . ."

I saw my father's face. I saw my mother's face. I went to sleep.

Chapter 41

I woke up.

My mouth felt thick with the taste of sleep, and with something else, something bitter. Medication?

I was on my back in a bed. Hospital bed. I felt weak.

"Ah, you're awake," a woman said. "Good. Let me crank you up."

The grinding sound signaled my being raised to a sitting position. I was in a private room. I had an IV in my arm. I could feel, or sense, the bandage on my side. Out the window, it was day.

"Where . . . ?"

The nurse was an attractive brunette with lipstick as bright as a cigarette girl's, but her nose was too big. Italian.

She smiled and it was white and nice and I forgave her her honker. "You're in Jefferson Park Hospital," she said.

"How . . . how'd I get here?"

"Private ambulance, I believe." She checked my pulse, then brushed hair off my forehead. She gently pulled back the sheets; for a second I thought she was going to blow me, but I was only getting my dressing checked. Just my luck. I drifted away then.

When I woke up again, a small dark man with slicked-back, graying, perfectly barbered hair was sitting in a chair next to my bed, hands folded in his lap, patiently. He was wearing a tailored gray suit and a black-and-gray-and-white knit tie; he might have been attending a wedding, or a funeral.

"Hello, Frank," I said, having to work to make my eyes focus on him.

"Nate," Nitti said neutrally, and he smiled. It was a restrained smile.

Out the window, it was night.

"How'd I get here? Don't tell me an ambulance."

"That's not important."

I started to remember. "Belliance! He called you . . ."

"Somebody called. Who is not important."

"Thank God. If he'd called Ricca . . . what about those torpedoes I shot?"

Nitti glanced around behind him, making sure the door was shut. He scooted his chair closer to the bed.

"You insist on talking about this," he said, a little bit weary, a little bit irritated.

"What about those guys I shot?"

"Fish food."

I swallowed thickly. Sleep taste. Medicine taste. The IV was still in my arm, I noticed. "Who were they, Frank?"

"Out-of-state talent. Free-lancers. People the Waiter uses . . . used . . . time to time."

"How'd they find me?"

"How should I know."

That janitor at the Sheridan six-flat? Maybe he called Ricca.

"I think," Nitti said quietly, "that Paul might've been having them watched."

"The Belliances?"

He nodded. "He knew you was sniffing around. But I don't think he was having you tailed. He knew you was under my protection, wouldn't go against me unless he had no other choice. Besides, he knew the only way you could spring Hauptmann was if you found the kid. So he must've had the farmer and his wife staked out, in case you found the kid." He shrugged. "You found the kid."

"They were gonna rub out the whole fuckin' family, Frank."

He frowned, shook his head. "That's terrible. That's a bad thing. You stopped a bad thing, Nate. I admire that."

I couldn't hear any irony in the words. "You do?"

He touched his chest with both hands. "I'm a father. I got a son. You don't kill fuckin' kids. Paul oughta know that; he's got a boy."

"So does Capone."

Nitti shook his head. "Some people got no morality. These are churchgoing people, too, Nate. Hard to picture."

"Frank!" I tried to sit up.

"Here," he said, and he rose and cranked the bed up, some; then he sat calmly back down.

I was not calm. "What have you done with the boy?"

"The boy?"

"Don't do this to me, Frank. I don't feel good."

"He's safe. He's with his family."

"He's back with Slim . . . ?"

"Slim?"

"Lindbergh!"

Nitti laughed, shortly. "Hell, no. He's with his family."

"The Belliances, you mean."

"That's not their name, now."

"Where are they?"

"That's something you can't know, Nate. Something you can't ever know."

"Frank . . . I can't let Hauptmann fry. He's a fucking patsy, and I can stop it, now, all I gotta do is sit that kid on the Governor's desk, and . . ."

"Don't get yourself worked up. You'll start bleeding or something."

"I got to get out of here, I got to stop them, if I don't . . ."

"Hauptmann's dead."

"Exactly!"

"No. I mean: Hauptmann's dead."

"What? He's . . . what?"

"Executed couple nights ago," Nitti said, matter-of-factly. "By the State of New Jersey."

"What the fuck day is this?"

"Monday."

"What *date?*"

"April six."

"Jesus. Jesus."

"You were hurt bad, Nate. We brought you back here, but you lost a lot of blood."

"Fuck! You want me to believe I was in a coma or something? Bullshit, Frank. You kept me doped up! You kept me out of commission, out of the game."

"This is a hospital, Nate. Don't say foolish things."

"Hell. You run this fucking place."

He shrugged. "What's the difference? You're alive, and Hauptmann isn't. I'd suggest you go along about your business."

"They . . . must've given him a few days' reprieve. He was supposed to go at the end of March."

Nitti was nodding. "Yeah. Right at the last minute, that hick detective Ellis Parker had Wendel arrested for confessing; it even went before a grand jury. They had to give Hauptmann a temporary stay."

"What the hell happened?"

"Wilentz and Wendel got together and repudiated the confession. Wendel told tales of getting the shit beat out of him in basements and so on. Ellis Parker and a bunch of his boys are under arrest, now."

"Can't say I'm surprised. Goddamn!"

"Easy, now. Take it easy."

"What about the Lindbergh kid?"

"They found that baby dead a long time ago."

I tried to sit up but couldn't. "You expect me to keep quiet about . . ."

"Yes."

Rage and frustration bubbled in me; if I hadn't been so goddamn weak, so fucking tired, I might have screamed or even grabbed the little bastard. But all I could manage was, "Or I'm fish food, Frank?"

He stood; he patted my arm, like a father soothing an infant. "Be a good boy, Nate. You think I let Hauptmann die? I didn't let him die. Your pal Lindbergh did. You think that phony son of a bitch deserves his son? The only thing I'd like about that kid turning up is the embarrassment that phony flyboy would suffer. Any time anybody suggests to him his son might still be alive, he bites their goddamn head off. That boy is with a family who loves him. He'll have a good home, a good upbringing, out of the public eye. What's wrong with that?"

I couldn't think of anything to say. The image of the little boy clinging to Carl Belliance, saying "Daddy, Daddy, Daddy," popped into my brain. The little boy loved the father he had, the father he knew. Would it be such a wonderful thing to yank him away from that? Hadn't once been enough?

But the thought passed as quickly as it came. "That's a bunch of bullshit, Frank, and you damn well know it."

"You go looking for that boy, Nate, and you probably are going to have a dead kid on your conscience."

"Why . . . what . . . ?"

His lip curled ever so slightly; it was almost a sneer. "You think Paul and Al are gonna let this come out? You saw what the Waiter was gonna do; you were part of what he was gonna do. You go public, or you go looking, you'd be giving the Belliances a death sentence, and probably the boy, too. You want that on your conscience, Nate? You go ahead. You go look for 'em. I won't be able to protect them, then. Or you."

I thought about that. Finally I said, "What about you and Ricca?"

His smile was faint but it was there. "Now I *have* something, now I *know* something, something I can use, where Paul and Al are concerned. Now I'm not so worried about Al getting out, or Paul moving up."

"Ricca could go looking for the Belliances and the boy . . ."

"Not without crossing me. Paul's not ready to openly defy me just yet. And by the time he ever does, this will be ancient history."

I shook my head, smiled mirthlessly. "You would never have let this come back on the Outfit, would you, Frank?"

"Never," he admitted.

Hauptmann wasn't the only patsy in this case.

Now I was worried. "Maybe you're right that Ricca won't go after the Belliances and their 'son.' But he sent those fuckers to kill me, too, Frank. What's going to keep him from doing that again?"

He patted my arm. "Me, Nate. And you. Our respective reputations. I told Paul you were took care of. You been paid off. He's heard about you, about the Lingle case; he knows you're . . . discreet."

I laughed harshly; it made my side hurt. "He figures I'm for sale. Maybe I am, at that. So what's this worth to you, Frank? How much am I gonna get for keeping quiet about the 'crime of the century'? It ought to be worth a lot."

"Oh, it is. And I think you're gonna like what you get."

"What do you mean?"

"You get to wake up tomorrow, Nate."

"Oh." I tasted my tongue again. "Well. That is fair."

"I'm even throwin' in picking up your hospital bill."

I was shaking my head. "Frank, there are people who are going to want explanations from me. Governor Hoffman, for one. . . ."

He gestured with an open palm. "You came to Chicago to follow up a lead. You got shot up by some nasty fellows who didn't like you. You wound up in the hospital. But the lead didn't pan out. End of story."

"I got no choice in this at all, do I, Frank?"

"Nate, every man has free will. Every man can choose his destiny. This is America. In America, a man can do whatever he thinks is right."

I might've cracked wise, but he believed that shit; he was an immigrant who made good.

"Well," I said. "That family loves that little boy. And he loves them. And you're telling me, they're protected, they're off somewhere raising that little boy, living a nice quiet life?"

"Yes."

"Well. I guess I can live with that."

"My point exactly," Nitti said, and patted my arm and went out.

A few days later I was back in my office, trying to pick up the pieces of my life, my health and my business. I was calling a list of my regular credit-check customers on the phone when the damn thing rang under my hand and scared the hell out of me.

"A-1 Detective Agency," I said. "Nathan Heller speaking."

"Nate," a voice said. A familiar, throaty female voice, conveyed in that one word a world of disappointment.

"Evalyn," I said.

"What happened to you?"

"I was going to call tonight," I lied. I did intend to call her, but I wasn't near ready. Governor Hoffman I intended to write, refunding the balance of my retainer minus the days I'd worked and my somewhat padded expenses.

"What happened, Nate?"

"I just got out of the hospital. I was following up a lead, and stepped on the wrong toes. I got shot in the side, actually."

"I see," she said.

It was an odd reaction: I thought when she heard I'd been shot, I might buy myself some sympathy. For Evalyn Walsh McLean, her response was uncharacteristically cold.

"By the time I woke up," I said, "it was too late. Hauptmann was already dead. The cause was already a lost one. I'm sorry, Evalyn."

"You disappoint me, Nathan."

Now I was feeling tired; just plain tired. "Why is that, Evalyn?"

"You're not the only private detective in the world, you know."

"What's that supposed to mean, exactly, Evalyn?"

"I was worried about you." Now I could hear emotion in her voice. "I hired someone to look for you, to see if you were all right, to see if you were in trouble. . . ."

Oh shit.

"Well, that was sweet, Evalyn, but . . ."

"Sweet! The first thing the operative discovered was that you'd made a phone call from my house to a number in Chicago. The number was that of a business, a 'cigar stand,' owned by a certain

Mr. Campagna, who is a Chicago mobster, as you well know."

"Evalyn."

The husky voice sounded strangely brittle, now. "You lied to me. You were reporting back to them, weren't you?"

"This isn't anything you should pursue, Evalyn. It could be dangerous for you, if you did."

"Are you threatening me, now?"

"No! Hell, no . . . I just don't want you to get yourself in trouble."

"You were in the hospital, all right. And I know it was a gunshot wound, and I was concerned, I am concerned, and maybe there's a good explanation, maybe you can make me feel good about you again, but can you answer one thing?"

I sighed. "What's that, Evalyn?"

"Why were you in a hospital where the chief of surgery is the in-law of some top gangster?"

"Your private detective found this out, did he."

"Yes, he did."

"Evalyn, those 'gangsters' run Chicago. It's just a coincidence. Don't make it something it's not."

"Do they run you?"

"Sometimes, yes. When they want to. And when I want to keep breathing, I sometimes accommodate them."

"Bruno Richard Hauptmann is dead."

"So I hear. What exactly can I do about that at this juncture?"

"Nothing. Nothing."

"Evalyn. Evalyn, are you crying?"

"Fuck you, Heller! Fuck you, Heller."

Most women get around to saying that to me, eventually. Even the toney ones.

"I'm sorry, Evalyn. I'm sorry I'm not what you'd like me to be."

"You still could be. I know you're a good man, underneath it all."

"Oh, really? Does that mean the chauffeur's position is still open?"

"Now you're being cruel," she said, and I'd hurt her. I'd meant to, but I was sorry.

I told her so.

The earnestness of her voice would've broken my heart, if I'd let it. "Nate, that little boy is out there somewhere . . . I just know he is. If we can find him, we can clear Richard Hauptmann's name."

"A posthumous pardon will leave him just as dead as he is now. Maybe history will clear the poor bastard; but I'm not going to. Besides, I'm not so convinced that kid is alive."

"I'm going to keep looking, Nate. I'll never stop."

"Yes, you will, Evalyn. You'll find some new cause. There's always another cause to support, just like there's always another diamond to buy."

"You are cruel."

"Sometimes. But not foolish. Goodbye, Evalyn."

And I hung up.

I just sat there for a while, and then I slammed my fist on the desk, and the phone jumped, and I split a fucking stitch. It hurt like hell. I unbuttoned my shirt and there was blood on the bandage. I'd have to go back to the hospital for a little out-patient number. God, it hurt. I started to cry.

I cried like a baby for several minutes.

I told myself it was the wound. But there are all kinds of those.

EPILOGUE

1936–1990

Chapter 42

I never saw Evalyn again.

She continued investigating the case, and wrote a series of articles about her experiences for *Liberty* magazine in 1938; but eventually her obsession subsided. Her husband died in an insane asylum in 1941. In 1946, Evalyn's daughter—who shared her mother's first name—took an overdose of sleeping pills and never woke up; Evalyn was heartbroken and died, technically of pneumonia, the next year. Sad as that sounds, there was a typically madcap aspect to Evalyn's last hours: her bedside was surrounded with as many famous friends and relatives as one of her star-studded dinner parties.

Many of the people in the case I never saw again. My uneasy "friendship" with Frank Nitti, on the other hand, continued no matter what I did to try to stop it, until he stopped it himself, with his suicide-under-suspicious-circumstances in 1943.

He and Ricca and Campagna and a few others had just been indicted in the Hollywood movie-union extortion case; the general belief was that Nitti couldn't face going back to prison. In fact, the recent death of his beloved wife Anna had depressed Nitti, and finally allowed the forceful Ricca to make his move. It was a peaceful overthrow, the force of Ricca's personality compared to that of the faltering Nitti bringing the Boys over to the Waiter's side.

Nitti's suicide was an act of defiance toward Ricca, whose reign as Chicago crime lord began with a prison sentence.

The ruthless Waiter, as Nitti predicted, eventually did learn a lesson about fathers and sons. His own son became a drug addict and Ricca, during his rule, banned the Outfit from narcotics trafficking. Ricca became inclined toward concentrating on victimless crimes, like gambling. He spent his declining years using legal tactics to avoid deportation, and died in his sleep in 1972 at the age of 74.

Capone, of course, never did make his comeback; syphilis caught up with him, and after his stay in Alcatraz, he died a near-vegetable in 1947.

Some of the minor crooks, like Rosner, Spitale and Bitz, I never had contact with again; no idea what became of them. Some of the cops I ran into now and then, of course.

Eliot Ness fought syphilis in a different way from Capone—he was the government's top vice cop during World War II. But Eliot's glory days faded in the postwar years, after he lost a mayoral bid in Cleveland, where he'd once been so successful as Director of Public Safety. He died an unsuccessful businessman in 1957, right before his autobiography *The Untouchables* made him posthumously a legend.

Elmer Irey became the coordinator of the Treasury Department's law-enforcement agencies, not only the Intelligence Unit but the Secret Service and agents of the Alcohol Tax Unit, Customs, Narcotics Unit and Coast Guard Intelligence. His integrity was unquestioned, and he attacked various investigations regardless of their political implications; because he'd put away Missouri's political boss Tom Pendergast, he retired in 1946 rather than tangle with the incoming Truman administration. He died a little over a year later.

Frank J. Wilson did become the head of the Secret Service, later in 1936, and remained such till 1947. His major accomplishment in that office was cracking down on counterfeiters. After retiring he became security consultant for the Atomic Energy Commission. He died in 1970 at age 83.

Schwarzkopf was fired by Governor Hoffman in June of 1936. The ex-floorwalker rebounded in an unexpected way: Phillips H. Lord, the radio producer, hired Schwarzkopf at the same rate as his old state-police salary to be an "official police announcer" on Lord's famous show *Gangbusters*. During the same period, Schwarzkopf became a trucking executive in New Jersey; good research for a guy working on *Gangbusters,* I'd say. Like a number of Lindbergh cronies, Schwarzkopf served in unspecified ways overseas during World War II, in Italy and Germany—possibly in the OSS. Anyway, he became, of all things, the chief of police of Iran for five postwar years; doing more OSS/CIA-type stuff? Who knows.

Ultimately, Schwarzkopf wound up back in New Jersey, heading a newly created law-enforcement agency investigating financial irregularities in state government. Schwarzkopf's first major investigation was into the Unemployment Compensation Committee, and he soon discovered that the committee's director had been embezzling. The director's name? Former Governor Harold Hoffman.

Hoffman, it seemed, had been embezzling for years, starting with a bank he'd been president of in South Amboy long before he became governor. He'd lost his reelection bid in '37, tried again in '40 and '46, losing both times, the Wendel case coming back to haunt him. During World War II, he managed to join the ranks of the many Lindbergh-case colonels, serving in the Army Transport Command.

Harold Hoffman was a dedicated public servant in many respects, and he threw his career away on Bruno Richard Hauptmann, either because he was gambling on the fame he'd win if he managed to clear the guy; or because he sincerely felt Hauptmann was innocent. He liked wine, women and song, too well apparently, and died in a hotel room in 1954 while under investigation by the man who brought him down—Colonel Norman Schwarzkopf.

Schwarzkopf died in 1958 of a stomach ailment.

The Wendel case also brought Ellis Parker down, of course. He and his "deputies" all went to jail. The new "Lindbergh kidnapping law" got 'em. Both father and son went to the federal prison at Lewisburg, Pennsylvania. Parker never changed his tune about Wendel's guilt, and the Cornfield Sherlock's supporters were lobbying for a presidential pardon when he died in the prison hospital of a brain tumor in 1940. I hear his son died a few years ago.

Wendel himself had a burst of fame: for one national magazine, he went into a photo studio with actors and posed melodramatic reenactments of the tortures he claimed to have endured. He published a book about his captivity and became something of a celebrity, even a hero. Then he faded into obscurity and I don't know what the hell became of him.

Gaston Means, in a prison hospital in 1938 after a heart attack, found FBI agents at his bedside, sent by J. Edgar Hoover to inquire once again about Evalyn's money. Means smiled his puckish smile at them, winked and passed away.

John H. Curtis tried for years to have his conviction overturned, but was turned down by the New Jersey Supreme Court. He remained in the boat-building and marine business and was quietly successful. In 1957 he supervised the construction of three replicas of colonial-period British warships that sailed at a major Norfolk festival. He died in 1962, a respected citizen of his community.

Another prominent Norfolk citizen, Admiral Burrage, never again spoke publicly of the Lindbergh case; he died in 1954. Reverend Dobson-Peacock died in England in 1959.

The Bull of Brooklyn, a.k.a. "Death House" Reilly, alias Edward J. Reilly, only occasionally appeared in court after the Hauptmann trial. He alternated between living at home with his mother and being institutionalized at the King's Park state mental hospital, his drinking and three failed marriages taking their toll. He died of a blood clot on the brain, at King's Park, on Christmas Day, 1946.

David T. Wilentz fared much better. While the run for the governorship that was rumored during the Hauptmann case never materialized—he was a Jew, after all—Wilentz became a major political boss among the New Jersey Demos. He continued with his law practice, but his real job was that of power broker. By 1950 he was influencing national politics, including the selection of Democratic vice-presidential and presidential candidates. There were those who said Wilentz had mob ties, and in his later days he was representing Atlantic City casinos. He died July 7, 1988—at 93.

Wilentz's star witness, John F. Condon, who like Wendel enjoyed notoriety by writing magazine articles and a self-promoting book, died of pneumonia at age 84 with his wife Myra and daughter Myra both at his bedside—exactly ten years from the day that Hauptmann went to trial.

Some of the others, I lost track of. I don't know what happened to Gerta Henkel and her husband. Nor do I know what became of Martin Marinelli and his wife Sister Sarah Sivella. Edgar Cayce went on to great fame, of course; in Virginia Beach, in January 1946, on his deathbed, he predicted he was about to be healed.

Colonel Henry Breckinridge remained friendly with Lindbergh, and continued on as his lawyer. Having run for the U.S. Senate in 1934, and lost, Breckinridge took a shot at the presidency in 1936; he was an anti-New Deal Democrat. I guess you know how he fared. After that, he devoted himself primarily to his law practice. He died in 1960 at age 73.

Slim Lindbergh went on to have something in common with Dick Hauptmann: both of them suffered due to anti-German sentiment. Lindbergh, while living in England, was invited by Major Truman Smith, military attaché at the American Embassy in Berlin, to inspect the German air forces, with the blessing of General Goering, head of the Luftwaffe. Here began Lindbergh's ill-fated association with Germany—he at one point accepted a Service Cross from Goering—which resulted in his isolationist stance concerning the war in Europe. He was branded pro-Nazi by the press and public who had so recently idolized him; after America's entry into the war, he flew as a test pilot and on combat missions—but the Nazi-sympathizer image stuck. Perhaps this wasn't all bad— he finally could have the anonymity and privacy he'd craved. He continued his research on matters aeronautic and otherwise, including inventing an early artificial heart. He and Anne raised four more children. In 1974, he died on the island of Maui, where he had lived, and where he is buried.

Some of the others are, as I write this, still alive. Several of the cops and reporters. Betty Gow, still in England. Anne Lindbergh, whose literary skill has won her fame of her own. Anna Hauptmann, who after quietly raising her son in obscurity, reentered the public eye in the 1970s, fighting in the press and in the courts to clear her husband's name.

Over the years a number of men came forward claiming to be, or expressing the suspicion that they might be, Charles Lindbergh, Jr. One of these was an advertising executive from Michigan who, starting four or five years ago, contacted me several times for information about the case.

His name was Harlan C. Jensen—the "C" stood for Carl—and he was always quiet and respectful in our several phone conversations; he seemed not at all a crank, but I wasn't terribly cooperative. I did hear him out on a couple occasions.

He had been raised in Escabana, Michigan, by Bill and Sara Jensen. When he was a young boy, he was told (by an uncle) that his mother and father were not his natural parents; naturally, he wondered about this, and as a young teenager confronted his father, who said only that "you're legitimate." Before he went to Korea, for combat in 1952, his mother's cousin had confided in him that "family rumor" had it that he was Charles Lindbergh, Jr.

Several years later, on his honeymoon, Harlan and his wife had been in a boatyard in Wickford, Rhode Island, where they were enjoying the nautical scenery while they waited to catch the ferry to Cape Cod. An elderly woman approached, with a redheaded woman in her twenties, and introduced herself as Mrs. Kurtzel. She said to Jensen, "You were with us as a baby—I helped care for you. This is my daughter—she was like your sister." Jensen had been understandably taken aback, but then the woman said, "May I feel the dent in your head?" Shocked that a stranger knew about this defect, which he'd been told was from a slip of the forceps during delivery, he allowed her to touch the back of his head.

"You are the Lindbergh baby," she said. "I helped care for you."

At this point, the ferry arrived, and Jensen and his bride left, covering their confusion and fear with nervous laughter.

He began to read about the Lindbergh case, but rejected the notion that Bill and Sara Jensen were not his real parents. He never talked to them about the "family rumor," but on their respective deathbeds, each parent had tried to tell him something. His mother had become ill while he was in Korea and had lapsed into a coma before he could get home to be at her side; his father, suffering a stroke in 1967, struggled to give his son some message, but could not make himself understood.

Years later, in a medical exam for recurring headaches, Jensen was shown X-rays and told by a doctor that his skull had been severely fractured in his early childhood. Also, the doctor asked why he'd had so much plastic surgery as a child—Jensen said that he wasn't aware that he had. But the doctor demonstrated on the X-rays that reconstructive surgery had taken place beneath his eyes and on his chin, possibly removing a cleft.

He had begun, then, in earnest, making a search for his identity his spare-time obsession. Unlike the others who claimed to be Charles Lindbergh, Jr., Jensen had disclaimed any rights to the Lindbergh estate, putting that in writing in a letter to the probate judge on Maui.

There was more, but I wouldn't let him tell me. I told him I was retired from the detective business, that the Lindbergh case was something I didn't think about anymore, and had no interest in discussing with anybody. He called, I think, three times, telling me a little more of his story each time.

About a year ago, I was sitting in my little condo in Coral Springs; my wife—my second wife, but who's counting—was out, playing bridge with some of the other old girls who live in this same complex we do. Occasionally I fish, but most days I either read or write or watch TV. That afternoon I was watching a videocassette of an old Hitchcock movie. Well, hell—I guess all Hitchcock movies are old, at this point. Like me.

Anyway, I answered the door and found a slender man in his mid-fifties standing there, looking shy and a little embarrassed. He wore a yellow sweater over a light blue Banlon shirt; his slacks were white and so were his rubber-soled shoes—he looked like somebody on vacation.

Which he was, as it turned out.

"I'm sorry to drop by unannounced," he said. For a man in

his fifties, he had a youthful face; not that it wasn't lined—but the nose, the eyes, the mouth, were boyish. "My wife and I are visiting her mom down here and . . . look, I'm Harlan Jensen."

"Oh. Oh yeah."

"I know you don't want to see me, but we were in the area, and I knew you lived around here, and . . ."

"Come in, Mr. Jensen."

"Thank you. Nice place you got here."

"Thanks. Let's sit here at the kitchen table."

He sat and talked and told me his story; he had a lot of facts and rumors and suppositions to share. He was obviously quietly tortured by this quest of his.

"I found the daughter of the woman who approached me in the boatyard on my honeymoon," he said. "The mother is dead, but the girl, the redhead, is alive and well. Her name is Mary."

"How'd you find her?"

"Did you know that Edgar Cayce, the famous psychic, did a reading on the case?"

"No. Really."

"Well, my wife and I followed his directions, and by doing a little interpretation, you know—phonetic sounds instead of literal readings—we found this building in New Haven, on Maltby Street, where I think I may have been kept."

"Yeah?"

"I got the name of the tenant that had lived there in 1932, and it was a Margaret Kurtzel, and through the mother's sister, managed to track the daughter down. She was in Middletown, Connecticut. She still is."

"Really."

He sighed. "She didn't know much. Just that her mother was a nurse, back then, working for private individuals, not hospitals or anything. And that all her life, her mother had proclaimed Hauptmann's innocence. She didn't know if, in fact, her mother had cared for the Lindbergh child."

"I see."

"You know, I've been trying for years to get this thing settled. It's driving me nuts. I used the Freedom of Information Act, to try to get the baby's fingerprints, but they're missing."

"Hunh. There were plenty of 'em around, once."

"Somebody at some point got rid of them. I've tried to approach Mrs. Lindbergh, but it's no use. There are DNA tests, you know, that . . ."

"She and her husband decided many years ago that their boy was dead."

He shook his head, wearily.

"What do you want from me, Mr. Jensen? I haven't been a detective for a long time."

"I just want to know what you know," he said.

Shit. How could I tell this guy that if I'd just had the balls to go in the goddamn ladies' room at LaSalle Street Station, back in '32, his whole life might have been different? Whether he was Charles Lindbergh, Jr., or not, that was true.

He was looking at me carefully. "You know, I have a memory of a man who helped me. It may not be a memory—it doesn't seem quite real."

"Oh yeah?"

"Something a kid might *think* he remembered. It sounds silly. I seem to remember a gunfight in my bedroom. A man told me . . . a man told me to hide under my bed and not come out until he said, 'Olly olly oxen free.' "

I felt my eyes getting damp.

He grinned at me; it was Slim's grin. "Are you that man, Mr. Heller? Did you save my little ass?"

I didn't say anything. I got up, went to the Mr. Coffee and got myself a cup. I asked him if he wanted any and he said sure—black.

"Let's go in the living room," I said, handing him his coffee, "and get comfy. It's a long story."

I OWE THEM ONE

Despite its extensive basis in history, this is a work of fiction, and a few liberties have been taken with the facts, though as few as possible—and any blame for historical inaccuracies is my own, reflecting, I hope, the limitations of my conflicting source material.

For the most part, events occur in this novel when they occurred in reality (an exception is the slaying of Max Hassel and Max Greenberg, which was shifted in time somewhat). Most of the characters in this novel are real and appear with their true names, and the occasional fictional characters have real-life counterparts (notably, Tim O'Neil and Harlan Jensen). The characters Martin Marinelli and Sister Sarah Sivella are composites, primarily suggested by one real-life husband-and-wife psychic team; however, the tryst between Heller and Sivella has no basis whatever in history. Inspector Welch is a composite character. Heller's role as police liaison was suggested by the real-life roles of Chicago's Pat Roche and Lt. William Cusack, both of whom went to Hopewell; and Governor Harold Hoffman (and Evalyn McLean) did hire a number of private investigators to work on the Hauptmann case.

Bob Conroy and his wife indeed died in a "double suicide," after Conroy had been pointed out to the authorities as the probable kidnapper by the incarcerated Capone; but my speculation about the real role of the Conroys in the kidnapping is just that: speculation. The false alarm on Sheridan Road in the first chapter, however, is loosely based on fact.

Several hardworking people helped me research this book.

George Hagenauer, whose many contributions include developing an extensive time chart of events, spent hours in libraries gathering book and newspaper references, and on the phone discussing with me the ins and outs of this complicated and very strange case. He also went to Virginia Beach to do Edgar Cayce research, and toured the Indonesian Embassy (the former home of Evalyn McLean at 2020 Massachusetts Avenue) in Washington, D.C. George is a valued collaborator on the Heller "memoirs" and I appreciate his contribution as much as his friendship.

Lynn Myers, one of the nicest people I know, dug in and did research rivaling George's. Against considerable odds, he rounded up the voluminous and invaluable *Liberty* magazine material that became the backbone of this novel. The interest of *Liberty* publisher, Bernarr MacFadden, in the Lindbergh case resulted in book-length multipart stories by Governor Harold Hoffman, John Condon, Paul Wendel, Evalyn Walsh McLean, Lt. James J. Finn and Lloyd Fisher, as well as individual articles by Edward J. Reilly, Fulton Oursler and Lou Wedemar. One of these articles, "Before the Body Was Found She Said the Lindbergh Baby Was Murdered," by Frederick L. Collins, was the best source of information on the involvement of psychics (other than Cayce) in the case. All in all, the *Liberty* articles constitute over a thousand pages of coverage on the Lindbergh case. Lynn also dug out numerous individual articles on the case, as well as background on Hassel and Greenberg, Edgar Cayce and John Hughes Curtis. A big tip of the fedora to this methodical, obsessive researcher.

Mike Gold, a Chicago history buff with an eye for detail, provided a vivid impromptu telephone tour through LaSalle Street Station. Dominick Abel, my agent, provided some tough, valuable advice midway that helped shape this novel. My keen-eyed editor Coleen O'Shea deserves special thanks for her longtime interest in, and support of, Nate Heller and his coauthor; thanks also to editors Charles Michener (who, among much else, helped come up with a title) and Marjorie Braman.

Other tips of the fedora for support along the way go to my old high-school pal Jim Hoffmann (who provided a videotape of the 1976 TV docudrama, "The Lindbergh Kidnapping Case"); Janiece Mull for Norfolk background material; Bob Randisi for New York reference material; loyal Heller fan William C. Wilson for assorted background details; and booksellers Patterson Smith and Ed Ebeling, for digging up rare vintage books, magazines and newspapers covering the case.

Mickey Spillane provided information about Elizabeth, New Jersey, and put me in contact with his friend Walter Milos, who did extensive research and legwork on the Elizabeth Carteret Hotel. Thank you, gentlemen.

While all were useful, none of the books contemporary to the Lindbergh case proved entirely reliable: *Jafsie Tells All!* (1936), by Dr. John F. Condon, is predictably pompous and often at odds with Condon's courtroom testimony; *The Hand of Hauptmann* (1937), by J. Vreeland Haring, is a biased account by one of the prosecution's many handwriting experts, although one who never testified; *The Great Lindbergh Hullabaloo* (1932), by Laura Vitray, is an odd exercise in unintentional whimsy by a former Hearst reporter who apparently felt the kidnapping was a hoax; and *The Lindbergh Crime* (1935), by Sidney Whipple, is a United Press reporter's proprosecution account. Whipple, though occasionally wildly inaccurate, does present the most detailed contemporary book-length account; and his later *The Trial of Bruno Hauptmann* (1937) presents a valuable edited version of the court transcript.

The latter-day nonfiction accounts are also a mixed bag; each has its merits, but each also has its limitations.

The most coherent, straightforward and readable narrative is the admirably researched *The Lindbergh Case* (1987) by Jim Fisher; unfortunately, ex-FBI agent Fisher is almost laughably pro-law enforcement, and in interviews has referred to the New Jersey State Police as mounting an "inspired" investigation. Also, Fisher tends to either omit any pro-Hauptmann evidence or relegate it to a footnote.

The most literate Lindbergh account is *The Airman and the Carpenter* (1985), by celebrated British crime historian Ludovic Kennedy; but Kennedy's logical, convincing defense of Hauptmann has a rather narrow focus—John H. Curtis and Paul Wendel are barely mentioned, and Gaston Means and Evalyn McLean appear not at all.

The groundbreaking *Scapegoat* (1976) by *New York Post* reporter Anthony Scaduto was an especially important resource for this novel; but Scaduto concentrates on the Ellis Parker/Paul Wendel aspect of the case, with Curtis getting rather short shrift and Gaston Means (and Mrs. McLean) absent but for one brief mention. On the other hand, his coverage of Isidor Fisch is extensive and impressive. Scaduto jumps around considerably; readers looking for a nonfiction balance probably need to read Fisher and Kennedy and Scaduto.

The first major account of the case was George Waller's best-seller *Kidnap* (1961), a readable if conventional and occasionally inaccurate pro-prosecution depiction. Annoyingly, the nearly 600-page nonfiction novel does not have an index.

An extremely important source was journalist Theon Wright's *In Search of the Lindbergh Baby* (1981), which is the only one of these books that pulls in all the disparate elements of this convoluted case, and attempts to make sense of them. Like *Scapegoat*, however, Wright's book is scattershot, and is best appreciated by readers already familiar with the basic facts.

My candidate for the best nonfiction look at the Lindbergh case is "Everybody Wanted in the Act," a lengthy article by crime reporter Alan Hynd, published in *True* (March 1949); it has been reprinted several times in various anthologies, including *Violence in the Night* (1955) and *A Treasury of* True (1956). Hynd covered the case for *True Detective Mysteries* and was the coauthor of Evalyn Walsh McLean's *Liberty* magazine serial, "Why I Am Still Investigating the Lindbergh Case" (1938). His cynical reporter's-eye view—neither pro-prosecution nor pro-Hauptmann—is refreshing; he was also one of the first to voice doubt about the identity of the small corpse found in the woods of the Sourland Mountains. My account of the ghostly doings at Far View derives from this article, and from Hynd's coauthored piece with Mrs. McLean.

The portrait of Evalyn Walsh McLean herein is drawn from the *Liberty* magazine serial mentioned above, and Mrs. McLean's autobiography *Father Struck It Rich* (1936, cowritten with Boyden Sparkes). Also helpful was *Blue Mystery: The Story of the Hope Diamond* (1976), by Susanne Steinem Patch. The romance between Evalyn and Nate Heller is, of course, fictional, and I know of no parallel to it in Mrs. McLean's life.

The portrait of Charles and Anne Lindbergh was drawn largely from their own writings: *We* (1927), *The Spirit of St. Louis* (1953), and *Autobiography of Values* (1977) by Charles; and *Hour of Gold, Hour of Lead* (1973) by Anne. Also beneficial were *Lindbergh: A Biography* (1976), Leonard Mosley; and *The Last Hero: Charles A. Lindbergh* (1968), Walter S. Ross.

Helpful in depicting Ellis Parker were *The Cunning Mulatto and Other Cases of Ellis Parker, American Detective* (1935), Fletcher Pratt, and a 1938 *Liberty* magazine series, "Whatever Happened to Ellis Parker?" by Fred Allhoff. Helpful in depicting Gaston Means was *Spectacular Rogue: Gaston B. Means* (1963), by Edwin P. Hoyt, and "Gaston Means, King of Swindlers," a three-part serial in *Startling Detective Adventures* (1933) by Judson Wyatt.

Frank J. Wilson is the subject of two books, both of which were useful in determining the role of the federal government in the Lindbergh case: *Special Agent: A Quarter Century with the Treasury Department and the Secret Service* (1956) by Wilson himself with Beth Day, and *The Man Who Got Capone* (1976), by Frank Spiering. Similarly useful were *The Tax Dodgers* (1948), a memoir by Elmer L. Irey with William J. Slocum; *Secret File* (1969) by Hank Messick, a thorough study of the IRS Intelligence Division with Messick's usual unsubstantiated, gratuitous smearing of Eliot Ness; *Treasury Agent—The Inside Story* (1958) by Andrew Tully, which explores the Capone, Lindbergh and Waxey Gordon cases; and *Where My Shadow Falls* (1949), a memoir by FBI man Leon Turrou, who calls into doubt the reliability of Jafsie Condon as an eyewitness.

The portrayal of Edgar Cayce is based on material in *Edgar Cayce—Mystery Man of Miracles* (1956) by Joseph Millard; also consulted were *My Life with Edgar Cayce* (1970), David E. Kahn as told to Will Oursler, *The Psychic Detectives* (1984), Colin Wilson, and *A Prophet in His Own Country—The Story of the Young Edgar Cayce* (1974),

Jess Stearn. Cayce's involvement in the Lindbergh case is drawn from the aforementioned Theon Wright book and *The Outer Limits of Edgar Cayce's Power* (1971), by Edgar Evans Cayce and Hugh Lynn Cayce, as well as photocopies of transcripts of his actual psychic "readings" and related correspondence. (Although I report only one, Cayce did several readings on the Lindbergh case.)

The story of the fictional character Harlan Jensen's search for his identity is patterned upon that of Harold Olson, as reported in Wright and Scaduto, including Mr. Olson's latter-day tracing of the route Edgar Cayce described.

Hundreds of newspaper articles (from the *Tribune, Daily News, Herald-American* and other Chicago papers, as well as *The New York Times* and *The Virginia Pilot and the Ledger Star*) served as source material for *Stolen Away*. A number of "true detective" magazines of the day proved helpful, including *Daring Detective, Startling Detective Adventures* and *True Detective Mysteries*. Among magazine articles that proved useful were "Did They *Really* Solve the Lindbergh Case?" by Craig Thompson, *Saturday Evening Post,* March 8, 1952; "The Baby is Found . . . Dead!" by Allan Keller, *American History Illustrated,* May 1975; "The Story of the Century" by David Davidson, *American Heritage,* February 1976; and "Did the Evidence Fit the Crime?" by Tom Zito, *Life,* March 1982.

I am also indebted to the anonymous authors of the Federal Writers Project guides on the states of Connecticut, Illinois, New Jersey, New York, Michigan and Virginia, as well as the massive volume on Washington, D.C.; all of these appeared in the late 1930s and early 1940s.

A number of books dealing with organized crime were helpful: *The Don* (1977), William Brashler; *Captive City* (1969), Ovid Demaris; *Capone: The Life and World of Al Capone* (1971), John Kobler; *Roemer: Man Against the Mob* (1989), William F. Roemer, Jr.; *The Mobs and the Mafia* (1972), Hank Messick and Burt Goldblatt; *The Legacy of Al Capone* (1975), George Murray; *Barbarians in Our Midst* (1952), Virgil W. Peterson; *Encyclopedia of American Crime* (1982), Carl Sifakis; *The Mafia Encyclopedia* (1987), Carl Sifakis; *Syndicate City* (1954), Alson J. Smith; and *Murder, Inc.* (1951), Burton B. Turkus and Sid Feder.

A few other books deserve singling out: *Ransom Kidnapping in*

America, 1874–1974 (1978), Ernest Kahlar Alix; *Facts, Frauds, and Phantasms* (1972), Georgess McHargue; *Twelve Against Crime* (1950), Edward D. Radin; *Courtroom* (1950), Quentin Reynolds; and *The Snatch Racket* (1932), Edward Dean Sullivan.

And fedora tips to: Abdullah Balbed and the information staff of the Indonesian Embassy; Bosler Free Library, the Boyd F. Spahr Library, Dickinson College (especially Sue Norman and Steve Rehrer), and the Cumberland County Historical Society, all of Carlisle, Pennsylvania; Barbara Gill of the Historical Society of Berks County, Reading, Pennsylvania; the *New Jersey Journal*, Elizabeth, New Jersey; Elizabeth, New Jersey, Public Library; the Union County Historical Society, Elizabeth, New Jersey; the Reading, Pennsylvania, Public Library; and the Ezra Lehman Memorial Library, Shippensburg University, Shippensburg, Pennsylvania.

When all the debts have been paid, or at least acknowledged, one remains: this book could not have been written without the love, help and support of my wife, Barbara Collins. And without trying at all, my son Nathan—who was six years old when this book was written—provided poignant inspiration.

MAX ALLAN COLLINS is the author of some thirty novels in the suspense field. He has also written the internationally syndicated comic strip "Dick Tracy" since its creator, the late Chester Gould, retired in 1977.

His acclaimed historical novel *True Dectective*, introducing Chicago P.I. Nate Heller, won the Private Eye Writers of America Shamus award for best novel of 1983; its sequels *True Crime* (1984), *The Million-Dollar Wound* (1986), and *Neon Mirage* (1988) were Shamus-nominated in their respective years, as well. *Dying in the Post-War World*, a collection of Heller short stories, is forthcoming.

In addition, Collins has three contemporary suspense series—Nolan, Quarry and Mallory (a thief, hitman and mystery writer respectively); and has written several historical thrillers about real-life "untouchable" Eliot Ness. He is also the author of the bestselling novel *Dick Tracy*, based on the Warren Beatty film; his recent follow-up novel, *Dick Tracy Goes to War* (Bantam, 1991), is the first of a projected Tracy trilogy.

With artist Terry Beatty, he is creator of the comic book features "Ms. Tree" and "Wild Dog," and has scripted the "Batman" comic book and newspaper strip. He has co-authored critical studies on Mickey Spillane (with James Traylor) and TV detectives (with John Javna). A rock musician since the mid-1960s, he is still performing and recording.

Collins lives in Muscatine, Iowa, with his wife Barbara, who writes the "Crimestoppers Textbook" Sunday feature in "Dick Tracy," and their eight-year-old son, Nathan.